LENA'S SECRET WAR

ALSO BY FRED G. BAKER

FICTION
The Black Freighter
Life, Death, and Espionage

ZONA: The Forbidden Land
Einstein's Raven

The Detective Sanchez/Father Montero Mysteries:
An Imperfect Crime
Desert Sanctuary
Desert Underworld

The Modern Pirate Series:

Seizing the Tiger	*Prowling Tiger*
Restless Tiger	*Raging Tiger*
Hong Kong Takedown	*The Good Deed/Chen*

NON-FICTION
Growing Up Wisconsin:
The Life and Times of Con James Baker

The Ancestors of Con James Baker of
Des Moines, Iowa, and Chicago, Illinois,
Volumes 1–3

The Descendants of John Baker (ca. 1640–1704) of
Hartford, Connecticut, Through Thirteen Generations,
Volumes 1–2

Light from a Thousand Campfires,
with Hannah Pavlik

Lena's Secret War

A Spy Thriller

Fred G. Baker

Other Voices Press
Golden, Colorado

Published by Other Voices Press, Golden, Colorado
ISBN 978-1-949336-31-3 paperback 2nd edition
ISBN 978-1-949336-22-1 paperback
ISBN 978-1-949336-23-8 eBook

Cover Design by Nick Zelinger, NZ Graphics.com
All Rights Reserved by Fred G. Baker.

Printed in the United States.

Acknowledgments

I would like to thank the following people for their aid and support in the writing and production of this book: Dr. Hannah Pavlik for her support and encouragement, my beta readers who provided helpful comments and idea, Donna Zimmerman for word processing and interior design; and Nick Zelinger for cover design.

Prologue

Europe
September 1971

In the fall of 1971, the world was in the depths of the Cold War. The United States and its allies were deadlocked in a long battle against the Soviet and Chinese Blocs for influence in the world. Europe hadn't yet recovered from the audacity of the Soviet invasion of Czechoslovakia in 1968.

The Cold War was the most active period in world history for espionage. The clandestine war was most intense between the Americans and the British on one side and the Soviets and the East Germans on the other. The information sought was not only about military plans, weapons, and spy agencies but also included fundamental economic, industrial, and social data that revealed the basic strength and determination of a nation. Sometimes something as simple as a poor crop report in Russia could suggest an upcoming food shortage, which indicated how well the bureaucracy was performing and therefore whether the sector manager was a rising political star or a failure within the closed society of the Soviet Union.

Much of the intelligence-gathering efforts in Europe were channeled across or around the Iron Curtain, the border between Western Europe and the Eastern Bloc of the Soviet satellite states. Several nonaligned nations in Europe, such as Sweden and Finland, were viewed by Moscow as nonthreatening. They became countries to which Soviet citizens could travel for conferences or vacation, a just reward for loyal servants of the government. Travel opportunities also provided a crossroads for the trading of information and recruiting of agents.

Such was the setting in northern Europe during the autumn of 1971. It was an important time in history, and there were great unseen forces at work. Espionage was in the air, and soon several unsuspecting people would be intimately involved in a new phase of the Cold War.

PART 1
Dark Waters

Chapter 1

Uppsala, Sweden
Monday, October 4, 1971

Eric Barrenger rode his bicycle through the park, admiring the majestic maple trees now endowed with colorful autumn leaves. The trees flourished and surrounded the massive Gothic structure of the Uppsala Cathedral, with its twin spires nearly four hundred feet tall rising into the pale-blue northern sky. Students on bicycles, along with many on foot, surrounded him as they made their way to or from classes on this busy morning. It was a very pleasant milieu now that he had begun to settle into his new life.

"Hej!" said a young woman from his university department as she passed by, calling out the friendly Swedish greeting.

He responded, *"Hej, hej!"* Eric couldn't quite believe he was really here in Sweden, learning and speaking the language and taking classes. But he was, and it felt good.

He directed his new blue Crescent bicycle along the path to the stately pale-yellow paleontology museum on campus. That was where he had a cubicle and a mailbox to receive department memos and notices of campus events. He locked his bike on the rack by the building's main entry and walked up the stairs to the front door.

"*Hej,* Eric," said Carlos, one of the students in the department. "Are you coming to the ISA meeting? It should be a wild election." The ISA was the International Student Association, an organization that represented all foreign students on campus.

"I'll try to be there, Carlos. Who are you voting for?"

"For Tika, of course. He will be a *buen presidente*, and he knows how to party." With that, Carlos hurried out of the office.

Eric checked his mailbox and stuffed the papers he found there into his backpack. Then he exited the building and turned his bike toward home. He rode through the crisp air along the street that would take him to the small student town of Flogsta.

Eric had arrived in Uppsala in mid-September, just as the leaves were beginning to turn. It was a beautiful time of year in that old and scenic city, with its rural surroundings and magnificent aged buildings. Uppsala was a college town and had been so for generations. There was a small commercial area surrounded by the university, along with picturesque neighborhoods. The cathedral dominated the skyline with its grand bell towers and spires. The narrow streets lent themselves to bicycle travel, and there was a good bus system. The only thing in short supply was housing. Eric had finally found a place to live in the dormitory complex being constructed in the small enclave of Flogsta, two miles west of the university campus, and had soon settled into residency. From there, he could ride his bike into town rather than take the bus.

The route to Flogsta joined an old country road that passed through rolling farmland typical of southern Sweden. Birch and pine trees lined the street and bordered the fields. Some of the leaves were gone now, but many still clung to their branches, serving as colorful reminders of a pleasant autumn.

Flogsta was comprised of nearly twenty dormitory buildings, each eight stories tall with residents grouped along two corridors. One corridor was located to the north, with the other to the south of the central elevator. Each corridor consisted of twelve rooms, six per side, served by a common area and kitchen. Eric parked his bike and rode the elevator to his fifth-floor room.

As he entered the corridor, music blasted down the hall—the latest rock tune by Björn and Benny, the hot new Swedish band that was so popular all over campus. Eric liked the song but thought the band needed a catchier name to make it on the tough music scene. The music came from the kitchen where one of the students, Ulla, was cooking dinner.

He walked down to his room, where he planned to study. Ulla called out to him as he unlocked the door.

"Eric, are you going to the ISA meeting?"

Ulla lived two doors down the hall from him, a second-year student from Sweden who was a biology major. She was a cheerful and pretty blonde who studied hard during the week and partied harder on the weekends. She was friendly and knew everyone on the corridor. "Your friend Sabrina stopped by to be sure you were coming."

"I guess so. Everyone is talking about it." He smiled at her, and she turned back toward the corridor's kitchen.

He entered the room and took stock of his simple abode. It was large enough to accommodate a single bed, which was pushed into one corner, and a study desk placed against the opposite wall near the wide picture window. A small bathroom was off the main living space, and a coffee table and chairs completed the furniture set. The architects assumed that students would eat at the kitchen where a large dining table and chairs were provided. He sat at the desk intending to study, but he couldn't help thinking of his situation.

Eric had recently finished his bachelor's degree in the field of geology at the University of Minnesota in Minneapolis. He had won a small scholarship that allowed him to enroll in the paleontology program at Uppsala University, with the intent of getting a master's degree in the field. He had signed up for three classes but was soon overwhelmed by the need to read required texts in Swedish, English, German, French, and Spanish. He opted to defer one course until he could get settled, learn basic Swedish, and brush up on the additional languages.

In the meantime, he met with other students in the program and attended lectures to familiarize himself with the way the university worked here in the new country. The Swedish approach to graduate programs was different from in the States because they did not require students to attend classes nearly as often, relying instead on comprehensive examinations. Although this gave him a flexible schedule, it also increased the pressure to perform well on exams.

Fortunately, this schedule left him with a good deal of time to learn Swedish, read books, and meet people. There were many immigrants in his Swedish classes, typically refugees who came from Africa, Asia, and

Europe, especially from the Baltic states. The housing area in Flogsta was also teeming with Swedish and international students. Many of his new friends came from distant lands. Because he was a good listener, Eric heard of the problems and repression that seemed to be so widespread in the world.

Perhaps he fell asleep for a few moments, but he suddenly felt nauseated and saw himself on a fishing boat at night on a foggy sea. *The boat rocked back and forth on choppy water as he lay uncomfortably on a pile of wet fishing nets. He had just enough time to look over the stern of the boat to see the dimly lit face of a woman who stared back at him like a ghost.*

Then the dream came to an end, and he caught his head as it sagged to the tabletop. He awoke, unsure of what had happened.

"Oh yeah. The dream again," he muttered.

He walked to the bathroom to throw cold water on his face in an attempt to reinvigorate his mind. After a few splashes, he felt more alert and stared at his visage in the mirror. It wasn't his best look. Tired brown eyes peered back at him, and his shock of brown hair was rumpled and rather long after being at school for a few weeks. His face was wide, with prominent cheekbones that he inherited from his German grandmother and tanned skin from hiking all summer. His nose was nondescript, and he had a broad smile that a few girlfriends had said was his best feature. *Well,* he thought, *I guess I'll be all right here in the land of the midnight sun.*

Eric left the bathroom to answer a knock on his door. When he opened it, a young Indian man smiled at him.

"Tika said to see you about whisky. I am Ashok from his building." He spoke perfect English with a distinctive Indian accent. "I met you at a party at his place last week."

Eric smiled, then said, "Oh yeah. I remember you. You're studying economics, aren't you?"

"Yes," he said, then grinned. "When I'm not partying." They both laughed, and Ashok looked cautiously up and down the corridor to be sure no one was listening.

"I need a bottle of Dewar's whisky, if you can get it for me." He hesitated. "Should I pay you now?" He reached in his pants pocket and withdrew a handful of Swedish paper money. "I have kronor or dollars."

"The price will be three hundred kronor. If you can pay me now, that would be great. I am a little short of cash at the moment."

"When will you have the bottle?" Ashok seemed excited. He handed over three hundred kronor in hundred-krona notes.

"I plan to make a trip to Finland this weekend. Is that soon enough?" Eric asked as he pocketed the money. "I can have your whisky on Monday." It worried him that he would have to travel to Finland again so soon.

"Oh yes. That would be very good." He nodded, said "*Hejdå*," and walked away toward the elevator.

Eric shuffled back to his desk, sat down, and looked out the window as a few snowflakes began to fall. It was strange the way things had worked out for him, with the smuggling of alcohol and cigarettes having become his main source of income.

It was this economic opportunity that had invited Eric to use his status as a foreign resident to import cigarettes and liquor into Sweden for sale to his new friends. His visa let him travel freely in and out of the country and allowed him to bring in substantially more alcohol and tobacco than a Swede was allowed. He had calculated that if he sneaked in twice his legal amount of liquor and tobacco, and still discounted the price of the goods for his clients by 20 percent below the government price, he could make more than a US$300 profit for each trip out of the country. Three hundred dollars was very good money for the time spent, so he had begun a shady import business. He felt compelled to make the smuggling trips to supplement his extremely tight budget.

***

Perhaps it was the turmoil of the move or the challenges of learning new languages and how to fare in a different culture all at once, but Eric found himself having trouble sleeping on some of those cold autumn nights. As a result, he would often stay up late with his newfound friends, drinking and talking. On this particular evening, when he finally fell asleep, he continued the unusual dream from earlier in the day that would recur again and again for several nights during the autumn.

He was engulfed in a pea-soup fog that shrouded the sea and the wharf. He was already down on the deck of the fishing boat with the captain, but the woman had lagged behind to ensure their escape. As he watched from the deck, Eric realized that she had lingered too long for her own safety. A guard had just emerged from the fog and approached her, cutting off any escape under the cover of darkness and the mist. The guard shouted an order to her in Russian and began to level his rifle at her. She responded, but he clearly didn't like the words he had heard. The woman backed away from the guard, moving farther down the length of the rough planking, until she reached the end of the pier.

Before he knew what he was doing, Eric had climbed back up on the pier with an oar in hand and quietly approached the guard from behind. As the guard shouted a final order at the woman to halt and then pulled back the bolt on his rifle, Eric made a wild swing with the oar at the guard's head. The blade of the oar sailed a bit on the air, resulting in only a glancing blow to the back of the guard's head. But it was enough. He went down.

Suddenly Eric was pushed off his feet and into the boat, still holding the oar in his hand. The captain had seen him leave the craft and had roughly thrown him back on board. In a harsh but muted voice, the captain shouted, "Ve mus' go!" The first mate released the last mooring line. The woman looked down sadly from the pier and said, "Go!" With that, the fishing boat slipped away into the fogbank.

As they gradually lost sight of the little fishing harbor,
Eric saw headlights appear and soldiers rush onto the
pier. Gunshots flashed in the night, and there was much
shouting. The woman who had lingered too long on the
end of the pier suddenly fell sideways and rolled off the
edge of the wooden planks into the sea. Then the fog swept
the whole scene away as they sailed.

Eric awoke from the dream. Climbing carefully out of bed, he shuffled
to the window. He stood there to let the nightmare dissipate before
trying to sleep again. Snowflakes drifted through the branches of the
pine trees outside. A late-autumn storm had crept up on Flogsta during
the night, an ominous precursor to the bitter winter snows that lay
ahead.

He wondered why the dream had come to him. Why did it seem so
real, and why did he seem to know the woman on the pier? Who was she?
Someone from his past? He couldn't explain it but knew he had dreamed
before about events that sometimes came true.

He wondered if this one would turn out to be just a dream or if it
somehow foreshadowed a future reality.

Chapter 2

Leningrad, Russia
Monday, October 4, 1971

The trees of the Admiralty Embankment were fully enflamed in wild crimson and orange colors as autumn enveloped the northern realm. The Neva River sparkled an unusual hue of blue, accented by the reflected sunset and the late-evening indigo depths of the arctic sky. People had come out to enjoy nature's colorful display when they realized that it would be one of the last clear evenings of the season. Many had noticed what a wonderful day it had been and had made extra time to appreciate it after their work was finished. A few had prepared a picnic for dinner and came down along the river to the Summer Garden or the Admiralty Square to sit and take advantage of the event.

That was what Lena Kristoff and Nadya Michaijlovich had done when they saw the glory of the evening. They had left their office at the university where they worked and taken a bus downtown to the grounds of the Admiralty building, where the large park of open grass and trees lent them a fabulous view. They had brought along a couple of bottles of beer, plus bread and cheese for their dinner. Without enough time to return home to get a proper blanket to put on the grass, they had borrowed a tablecloth from the lunchroom at work to use instead. Now they sat on the lawn, sipped beer, and had a simple repast in the orange rays of fading summer. It was early October, and they knew the low clouds of fall would sweep away the warmth and color of such a fine day, as winter snow would soon arrive. They enjoyed the present and pushed their thoughts of all else aside.

"*Èto takoj zamečatel'nyj den', ne tak li?* This is such a wonderful day, isn't it?" Nadya said cheerfully. "Lena, I'm glad you thought of this escape from the office, or we might have toiled away the day without even knowing how glorious it truly is." Nadya spoke in Russian.

"I was just lucky to walk over to the cafeteria at the right time to see the sky," Lena replied in the same language. "But I'm glad we came down here. Look at all the people who have come out to enjoy it. All of Leningrad must be here!"

They looked around the park at the multitude of people sitting on the grass or walking on the pathways of the park and riverfront. From their location they could look across the water at the cathedral of the Peter and Paul Fortress, with its impossibly tall golden steeple that rose high above the river. The Admiralty building, with its nearly as impressive spire, bounded their view along the embankment on their right side. The magnificent bronze statue of Peter the Great atop a rearing stallion dominated the front of the park as he gazed out on the famous Neva River, looking to the north toward Peter's ancient nemesis, Sweden. Alexander Pushkin's renowned epic poem, "The Bronze Horseman," memorialized the statue and what it meant for generations of fellow Russians.

The two young women finished their beers and stretched out across their makeshift picnic blanket on the ground. They talked as they stared up at the nearly cloudless sky overhead. On a day like today, they seemed to have no real cares, and so the conversation was lighthearted. But beneath it all, they had their concerns, and it wasn't long before they would have to return to the reality of their everyday lives.

"I'm going to apply for the new position as secretary of the modeling group," Nadya announced. "You weren't going to apply for it too, were you?"

"No. I'm happy working with the data, and in any case, the director told me that he had a new project in mind for me soon." Lena paused. "I will wait to see what he means. He is good to work with and looks out for my interests." She glanced sideways at her friend. "So I am content."

Lena propped up her head on her shoulder bag to better view the riverbank and watch the people walk along the quay in their best clothes. For a few of them, this was like a Sunday promenade, many with their families in tow and some perhaps with a sweetheart on their arm. She imagined a few of their stories as they passed and commented on them to Nadya.

Before long, Lena dozed off and Nadya was very quiet, so perhaps she napped too. As she lay on her back on the lawn, Lena dreamed that she was floating on water. It was pleasant in the sunshine as she glided along just at the surface of the water, with gentle wavelets occasionally splashing across her face. Perhaps she was on the Neva River or drifting on the clear blue Baltic Sea. But then it seemed that the water became cooler, and she began to sink below the surface. She looked up and the bright sky was gone, replaced by an increasing darkness as she passed deeper into the water. She opened her eyes under the water, looking up to see a night sky, and she was suddenly freezing. She tried to call out for help, but there was no sound.

"Lena, wake up! You are dreaming. How can you fall asleep on such a beautiful day?" Nadya shook Lena by the arm to rouse her from her whimpering state. "What were you dreaming? I hope a man was somehow involved."

Lena awoke to her longtime friend's voice with a start. "Oh, Nadya!" she said nervously. "It was awful. I was floating on the water and then I began to sink and grow cold. And it was dark."

A cloud had blocked the sun for a couple of minutes but had now moved away. They were flooded with warm sunlight again. Lena settled down as she took in the pleasant park camaraderie.

"You were just napping, Lena. A cloud crossed the sun, and you got a chill. That is all." Nadya stood up, shading her eyes with one hand as if a mariner at sea, searching the horizon. "But where is that crazy sister of yours? She was supposed to meet us here an hour ago."

As Nadya said this, a thin, purple-haired teenager dressed in a black T-shirt and purple skirt appeared on the stonework base of the Horseman statue and waved at Nadya. The girl dropped down to the ground and gleefully raced among the other picnicking parties as she came to meet them. "Hey, Nadie! Hey, Lena! Have you been waiting long?"

Lena looked up at the purple vision who was her sixteen-year-old sister, Katya. There would be no napping now. Katya was an active girl who was beginning to look like a woman faster than her youthful personality could adjust to the change. Fortunately, she wore mostly loose clothing so that her curves were partially hidden from the many amorous young men she knew who were beginning to notice the change too. Today her clear and pretty face was adorned with bright-red lipstick and an unusual kind of sparkling violet rouge that made her look older and more provocative than usual. Many people around them no doubt imagined she was more irritating than she should be.

"You didn't wear that makeup at the store, did you?" Lena scolded. "I thought they had a strict policy on dress there."

"No. I put it on after I left work. How do you like my new look?" Katya vamped around a bit, striking what she thought were effective poses to show off her new facial decorations. She plopped down on the tablecloth and wriggled between Lena and Nadya. Without fanfare, she hiked up her skirt to expose her nearly white thighs to the sun and lay down to take in its rays.

"Isn't it a wonderful day?"

The girls all lay there with their legs partially exposed in the late-day sun and talked about the day's events. They had all known each other since their early school days, Lena and Nadya sharing the same grade and many adventures since that time. They had always been good friends and confided all the various ups and downs of their lives together. Katya was several years younger than them but had always been included in their adventures. They were happy and viewed each other as family, as they had little real family alive in these heady days of young adulthood. Only Katya had a boyfriend at the moment while the other two were in between lovers. They still searched for someone to share their lives with.

Low clouds moved in on the horizon and intercepted the warmth of the sun. They picked up their things and decided that they would go home to eat a more substantial meal than their simple picnic had provided. Nadya would come over for dinner with Lena and Katya, as she often did. They walked to the bus stop in front of the Admiralty to catch a bus that would go up the broad boulevard of Nevskiy Prospekt before changing to the bus that went to their neighborhood. They would stop at the local market to see what they could buy for dinner, perhaps spaghetti with a cheap wine, if there was any available on the shelf. They could continue celebrating the fine day and talk late into the night before preparing for work the next morning.

***

Lena had a frantic day on Tuesday. Her office at the economics department was in complete chaos now that the new economic data set had arrived from the Steel Manufacturing Sector Committee. The information filled several cardboard boxes with printed reports and binders of raw computer printouts. She looked around her at the results of her new request for the "real" data. This committee had tried to pull the same trick as many other departments had by giving her so much raw and uncorrelated data that she wouldn't be able to find out what they had been doing. Who knew what levels of malfeasance, corruption, incompetence, and sheer neglect were being hidden by these people?

She had seen this type of aggressive noncompliance before. She had to prepare a case for her director to present to the Economic Planning Bureau in order to get the committee to cooperate with the modeling project. As with other committees, she would make the case that the committee staff were incapable of keeping their own records. Her director would suggest that the function should be transferred to the university and taken away from that particular department. The mere threat of such action usually resulted in the proper cooperation and correct documentation that should have been provided in the first place. Such rivalries between agencies in the Soviet government were not only common but also were the source of much of the mismanagement and political infighting that defined the miserable organization.

She had to first catalog the entire collection of documents she had received, and luckily, she had a student assistant assigned to her who she could burden with the unpleasant task. Such was the risk of interning in the economics field, where vast amounts of often useless information had to be reviewed before the few nuggets of truth could be discovered. She decided to assign the work to Helga, the new and enthusiastic girl, and to try to find her another poor soul to help with the thankless misery.

And Lena had something else she needed to do. She had to collect economic information that would be interesting for her other employer—the man she worked for surreptitiously—who paid her in cash. She needed to find something useful, and it wouldn't come from this pile of jumbled dross before her. *No,* she thought, *I must find something of political value to earn my clandestine income. Something new to keep my contact happy and generous. What could it be?*

Lena shifted down the hallway to see if Nadya was ready to eat lunch. They had planned to go to a small café near the campus, but with the rain, it would be easier to eat at the cafeteria nearby. She found Nadya in the computer tape control room, where she was preparing to write files onto a large open-reel magnetic tape. When ready, they ran through the rain and across the little plaza to the cafeteria. Neither had thought to bring an umbrella today. They each had a bowl of lentil soup and an apple, the only fruit they could easily afford at this time of year. They sat at a table near the windows where they could talk quietly.

Nadya asked her in a familiar Russian tone, "What's the matter? You seem very down today."

Lena looked up from her soup. "It's Katie," she muttered grimly in the same style of the language. "We had an argument this morning about her continuing in school. You know she was supposed to begin university next year, but she wants to take a year off before classes. She wants to work, make some money, and have fun." Lena put down her spoon and covered her face for a moment to hide the tears that were building there.

Nadya laughed, then said, "She is just young, that's all."

"Fun, fun, fun. It's all she can think of now. She has the new boyfriend, and they spend all their time having fun. Sex, sex, sex. That's all they do!" Lena looked up at Nadya sheepishly. "I'm sounding like an old babushka now, am I not? An old woman? Like her mother, perhaps?" She smiled and wiped her eyes with the napkin.

Nadya sipped soup from her spoon, then smiled in support of her friend.

"I want her to be happy—in the long term—not just for now." She looked at Nadya. "You know, she called me that too. An old prude. *Me!* Can you imagine?" They both laughed at the image the word brought up.

"The Lena I know isn't a prude," Nadya said while suppressing a smile. "This I know for a fact."

"She told me I'm not her mother and I cannot tell her what to do with her life. But what else is new? She says it to me all the time when we disagree." She smiled at Nadya.

"You have been too long without a man in your bed," Nadya whispered as Lena reacted to her statement. "Don't smile at me, you foolish girl! You know what I mean, and I need a man too. It's true for us both. *Da?*"

Lena chuckled at this idea.

Nadya laughed and tried to be sympathetic at the same time. "Look, you are her sister, and you have a right to be concerned. You don't want her to make mistakes that will affect her future. I'm sure she understands this inside. But she is young—oh so very young compared to us at her age. And she has found this man, Misha. He seems like a good fellow. And he likes you very much too." She paused to take a bite out of her apple. "You need to talk to him and let him know you are concerned for your little sister. Maybe he can help you with Katie."

Lena smiled thinly at the advice.

Nadya reached across the table and touched Lena's hand. "Don't be so upset. You have done a good job with her. She's very lucky to have you as her sister."

"What we really need is a good man for each of us." A sparkle came into Lena's eyes as she smiled in a conspiratorial manner. "Let's make a pact to do something about it. Let's go out tonight to the Northern Lights. We can invite Katie and Misha and show them that we can be crazy sometimes too. I will ask Misha how he really feels about my sister when he is drunk and suspects nothing." Lena grinned wickedly. "And we will search for some good-looking male company too. What do you say? Should we let down our hair?"

The two friends went back to work in much better moods than when they began lunch. They had a plan and something to look forward to. Maybe their luck was looking up and they would find a tall, dark stranger to spice up their monotonous lives.

Chapter 3

Uppsala, Sweden
Tuesday, October 5, 1971

When Eric arrived in Sweden, he quickly learned about the country's system of government and how it differed from the world he had grown up in. Sweden had a well-run social welfare form of government that was still a vast experiment in socialism. Health care was free for all, and a university education was also free for the limited number of people who qualified for admission. Taxes on income were as high as 85 percent. Gasoline was running around five dollars a gallon, almost ten times what it cost in the States, mostly due to high taxes. But the biggest complaint he heard from students he met was regarding alcohol and tobacco. They could only buy real beer, tobacco, wine, and liquor from the state-controlled liquor store, the Systembolaget, which had a monopoly. The store had limited hours of operation, quotas on the number of bottles or cigarettes each person could buy, and extremely high prices, again mainly due to taxes. The cost of most wine and liquor was several times what it was in nearby Finland and Denmark.

There were reasons why the government controlled the price and obtainment of alcohol, and it had to do with the climate and the Scandinavian psyche. Sweden was located very far up in the northern hemisphere, with most of the country falling above latitude 55° north. The city of Uppsala lay at nearly latitude 60° north, which was as far north as Anchorage, Alaska. That meant winter nights could be up to twenty-two hours long, and the winters seemed eternal. Many Scandinavians were subject to depression as a result of such long winters and the lack of sufficient sunshine each day.

He had heard from his friends that, left to their own devices, many Swedes would drink themselves into oblivion as their only way to cope with this depression. They told him that suicide rates were elevated in the winter and spring here, as they were in many high-latitude countries. But the control of alcohol really cut into the party life of students.

Eric's life took on a sort of inconsistent routine during the late autumn in Uppsala with studying and making liquor runs, as he called them. He had friends in the dormitory building who he met for coffee or dinner to discuss politics or their studies. He spent hours with foreign students and learned that a little humor overcame misunderstandings of language and culture. He wasn't like the American stereotype they had read about because he was a quiet, thoughtful person rather than the brash, loud cowboy trumpeted in European media. Many of his customers became friends and invited him to their parties. There were few Americans in his social circle largely because he had encountered few Americans at the university.

Eric hung out a good deal with a contingent of Indian students who studied hard and partied harder. A few of them, including Tika Kumar and his sister, Leela, were also his customers. They would often get together for dinners and parties to celebrate whatever was worth commemorating on a given day.

***

Eric came to dinner at 6:00 p.m., ready to take Leela up on her offer of fine Indian fare. He also hoped to run into a young woman named Sabrina there.

Sabrina Santiago was a second-year student from Catalonia in Spain. Her parents were leaders of the independence movement for Catalonia, a Spanish province that had long sought to be free of Spanish rule. She studied archeology and had become quite friendly with Eric recently. She had a room on the same corridor as Tika and Leela. Sabrina often partied with the Indian contingent of the international community.

There were nearly thirty people there, as word had spread among friends on the corridor and other Indian students. Swedish rock music flooded the corridor—a sign that Leela had chosen the tunes. Tika and his sister were very popular in the ISA, where Tika was an influential player. They came from an important Hindu family from Kashmir and apparently had an unending stipend from their family back home. Tika was one of Eric's regular customers for whisky, especially White Horse and Black and White Scotch. Eric noted that much of his last supply run was consumed in one night.

As soon as he entered, Leela took him by the hand and placed him in a chair next to Tika. She gave him a plateful of Indian delicacies—fiery samosas, tasty chicken tikka masala, and goat curry. Then she rushed off to serve other friends as they arrived for dinner. Tika was surrounded by friends, and others sat at small tables in the student lounge across the hallway. Everyone drank beer and conversed avidly.

After an hour, a second wave of friends arrived for a party of Indian finger food and drinks of all sorts, most of it brought by the happy guests. Eric met another of his customers who was also in the ISA, Omar Kadish. Omar was a Kurdish refugee who was studying economics. He and his friends had a passion for Kurdish tea, Marlboro cigarettes, and politics.

"Omar, how are you?" Eric called out. "I see you found the best party on campus." He walked over to Omar, who was surrounded by four other students and his bodyguard, Abdullah. Omar needed a bodyguard because of his family's status in his home country of Kurdish Iraq, otherwise known as Kurdistan to his people.

"Good evening, Eric." Omar shook hands with Eric and introduced him to the others who stood in the small circle around him. "We were just talking about the ISA election that is to be held tomorrow night. I assume you will vote for your friend Tika."

"Yes. I think Tika will be a good president, don't you?"

"I haven't declared support for any candidate as of this time. I still have time to make up my mind." He nodded to the rest of the group. "My friends think Tika is a good choice."

Eric smiled at Omar and understood that he did not want to reveal his support for anyone running for office. He was very politically astute, due to his experience in his homeland.

"We'll see who wins tomorrow," Eric said as his eyes swept the room for Sabrina. "But didn't you say you were going home for a visit soon?"

Omar had previously told Eric all about his situation and the plight of the Kurds in the world. He was from Iraq originally, but his mother was a Persian Kurd from Iran. Omar was descended from a notable family in Iraq who were now persecuted for their role in the Kurdish freedom movement. His father was in prison in Baghdad. Omar's grandfather had died a freedom fighter and was a Kurdish national hero.

"Yes, I will leave in several days, but there are arrangements to be made." Omar looked at Abdullah and grinned. "Abdullah won't let me tell even my friends what day we will travel. He is worried that someone will assassinate me at any time." He chuckled, and Eric noticed that Abdullah wasn't comfortable discussing his charge's security.

Omar had a price on his head and was laying low in Sweden until he could return home to fight for his people. On nights when he was really wound up, he would pull out his grandfather's sword and swear he would cut off the heads of his enemies. At that point his friends would kindly disarm him and take him away to settle down. He was the most passionate man Eric had ever met, and he was a good friend.

"Well, it's good to see you again." Eric excused himself, refilled his Scotch glass, and mingled with the other partygoers. He felt a sense of melancholy at that point of the evening because the image of the woman drowning in his dream suddenly formed like a shadow in the back of his mind. He tried to shake off the vision and walked over to look out the kitchen window until the unanticipated feelings of loss dissipated.

After several minutes and another drink, he felt better and talked to many people while relaxing on the sofa in the common sitting room of Tika's corridor. He ended up entertaining two young Indian women from Delhi who spoke singsong English and who were a lot of fun. One of them was very drunk and sat on his lap while she told him how much she liked Sweden. When her sister tried to occupy the same space, Eric was rescued by Leela.

"Eric," she said, "I think you must come and talk to Tika." She raised her eyebrows and gave him a disappointed look. "If you can pull yourself away from these young girls." The girl on his lap made a face at Leela but allowed Eric to lift her off his body. Leela took Eric's hand and led him down the corridor toward Tika's room.

Eric found Tika immersed in conversation with three other Indian students in his room. When Eric entered, the others ducked out, partly to give Tika and Eric some privacy and partly to refill their glasses.

"Eric, my friend, tomorrow night is the most important night of my life," Tika said loudly. "It is the night of elections for the president of the International Student Association, and I am running for this office."

"Yes, I know. I will be there to vote for you. I think you will win."

"Ah. I know you will. But I have my concerns. My opponent, Amad Hussain, has a strong backing among the Arab students, and he expects them to vote as a block for him."

"But nearly everyone I have talked to is in your camp."

"Yes, and yet I had not expected the vote among the Arab students to come down along religious lines."

Eric was startled by this news. "Religious lines? What do you mean?"

"I have heard rumors that Amad is telling the Iraqis and other Arab students that Allah requires them to vote for their fellow Muslim." Tika raised his hands in front of him in a questioning motion. "I don't know if it is true or if it will affect how the others vote, but I'm worried."

"I just talked to Omar tonight, and the friends he has with him seem like they will vote for you."

"That is the favor I must ask of you, Eric. Can you talk to Omar for me and see where he stands? Better yet, can you ask him to talk to me tonight?" Tika looked concerned. "It would be a big help to me."

"No problem, Tika. He's here. I'll ask him if he'll come back here and talk to you directly."

Eric walked down the corridor and located Omar standing in the kitchen by the buffet table that Sabrina and a friend were busy restocking. He caught Omar's eye and signaled him to step over to the hallway.

"My friend Tika has heard some rumors that Amad may be asking all Muslims to vote for him on religious grounds," Eric whispered in

Omar's ear, with Abdullah very close by. "Have you heard anything about this?"

"Yes, I have." Omar took Eric's elbow and led him farther along the corridor for privacy. "As you know, I have a good deal of influence among the Iraqis. They support me because they know that I am a devout Muslim. I pride myself on this support." He paused as if trying to find the right words for the occasion. "Eric, I personally do not like Amad because he is a bad Muslim and his people oppressed my people, the Kurds. I have tried to be neutral in the elections so far, but I believe that Allah should not be invoked in this way for personal gain."

"I understand. It is a surprise to me too," Eric whispered. "In any case, Tika would like to talk to you, if you care to discuss the election."

Omar nodded. Eric led him down the hall to Tika's dorm room, where the two of them could talk privately. Abdullah took up a position outside the door. Tika, who was deep in discussions with his advisers, thanked Eric and then invited Omar to step inside. Eric stood outside with Abdullah to avoid any interruptions. Sabrina came along and kept Eric company.

All went well, and after twenty minutes, Omar emerged and thanked Eric for his help. He then gathered his entourage and said his goodbyes to Leela and Tika, thanking them for the party in a very public way. Then he signaled to his bodyguard, and they all left the corridor as a group.

Eric arranged to get a ride to the ISA meeting the next night and left the party too, returning to his empty room. He stayed up talking to a few of the other corridor neighbors before turning in for the night. As he crawled into bed, he reflected on the impending showdown at the ISA meeting. With so much bad blood between Amad and Omar, it foretold trouble to come.

Chapter 4

Eric was in the habit of breakfasting at a small café on the main village square, called the Stora Torget, meaning Great Square. In reality, it was a rather medium-size, uncrowded plaza where most of the bus routes coincided. It was located close to the Fyrisån River and not far from both the university campus and the cathedral. There he could have good Swedish coffee and pastry while reading the newspaper, something he liked to do when he could make the time once or twice a week.

He took the city bus to the café the morning after Tika's party. As he sat there reading the *International Herald Tribune*, a man walked over to his table and asked if the second chair was taken. This often happened because the shop was small and sometimes there weren't enough tables to seat all the customers. Eric invited him to sit down and share the space.

"My name is Mike Turner. I've seen you in here a few times before this," he said, offering his hand. "I noticed you read the *Tribune* most days you're here."

He was an American who spoke in passable Swedish to order his coffee, but he talked to Eric in English, perhaps observing that Eric was reading an English-language newspaper. He was a lean, tallish man in his late thirties with dark hair and earnest gray eyes. He seemed friendly, if a little tense, and was dressed in a woolen tweed jacket and wool slacks. Eric had seen him in the café a few times recently. Eric assumed that the man was probably just looking for someone to have a conversation with.

"I'm Eric," he replied. "It's the easiest way for me to catch up on world news."

Turner sat down across from Eric while holding his coffee cup and saucer. "I usually don't have a lot of time to read in the morning. Too many meetings to get through."

"I've seen you around a few times. Are you a businessman?"

"I'm in the information business," Turner said, then smiled. "I sell books and magazines, that sort of thing. I travel a lot."

"Oh, sounds interesting. Have you been in Sweden long?"

"I'm based out of Copenhagen mostly but have extra work up here for a few weeks." Turner sipped his coffee and then asked, "How about you? Are you a student or faculty here?"

"Just a grad student in paleontology. I've only been here a few weeks," Eric answered. "I really like the school. Friendly people and a great university."

"That's what I hear, an excellent school. Lots of people come here from all over the world. I was surprised to learn that many people from the Middle East come here to study." Turner waved his hand to indicate a pair of Arab men at another table. "You know—even though it's really cold compared to where they are from. It must be tough for them to adapt."

"Yeah, I know a few Arab students who say it was hard to get used to wearing so many clothes in winter. That's a real shift if your home is Iraq or Egypt."

Turner changed the subject. "Say, how come you're studying here and not in the States? You're not here because of the war, are you? One of those conscientious objectors?" He seemed very interested. "I heard that some Americans came here to avoid the draft."

Eric was taken aback by the question. "I guess there may be a few here, but I haven't met any of them." He looked at Turner, who seemed to be ready to ask another question. "That's not why I'm here, but what do you care?"

Turner seemed to understand that he had been too personal. "Oh, I'm sorry. I didn't mean anything by that question. I was just interested, that's all."

"Yeah, OK. No problem." Eric looked at his watch and then started to fold up his newspaper to leave the coffee shop. "Well, I have to take care of something on campus. It was nice meeting you, Mr. Turner."

He stood up to leave, and Turner rose also. "Say, Eric, are you going anywhere close to the administration building? I have to see someone there in a little while, and I haven't been there before. Maybe you could show me where it is."

"Sure, I'm going there myself." Eric shrugged on his jacket.

They left the café, walked west toward the river, and then crossed the bridge to Drottninggatan, the street that went uphill toward the main university building where most administrative functions were performed. As they started their ascent, Turner said that he was very proud of his country and asked where Eric stood on the Vietnam War and whether he supported the US government in general.

"You know, Turner, I try not to think about all the things my government is doing around the world. What difference is it to you anyway?" Eric didn't want to get into a political discussion with a stranger. Besides, it wasn't any of Turner's business.

They walked up the long grade of the hill leading to the university building. As they huffed along for a few minutes, they were silent until Turner spoke again.

"I just wondered how you feel about your country, that's all. You know, are you a patriot and happy to be an American?"

This seemed pretty odd to Eric—for someone he had just met to be asking these sorts of questions. It wasn't normal conversation. Maybe Turner was one of those guys who promoted America every chance he got. That usually made foreigners nervous—a real turnoff. Anyway, Eric didn't care for it.

"Say, what are you after, Turner?" He glanced sideways at Turner. "That seems like a strange thing to ask someone you've just met." Eric stopped in the middle of the student foot traffic that flowed up and down the sidewalk. He looked at Turner to see how he would respond.

At first, Turner seemed apologetic. "Look, I'm sorry. I guess that was pretty direct. I didn't mean to offend you in any way. I just wondered where you stand on America." He paused and looked at the ground a moment, seemingly choosing his next words carefully. "You know, a lot of people overseas are against American involvement in foreign affairs."

Eric asked, "So?"

"I just wondered if you were one of them. That's all. Just trying to be friendly and see where you stood." He raised his head to look Eric in the eye. It seemed like he was trying to decide what to say next.

"Look," Eric blurted out, exasperated that the conversation had come to politics. "I'm not sure we should be involved in Vietnam, if that's what you mean. But I'm not a conscientious objector, and I generally support my country. Well, except for some of the weird foreign policy we have going on now."

"OK, fair enough." Turner smiled. "I guess that answers that question." He looked around and then reached out and took Eric by the elbow. "Step over here for a minute out of the way, will you?"

Eric shrugged off Turner's hand but followed him a few paces out of the heavy foot traffic. Many students had suddenly appeared after a class ended.

"Listen, Eric," he said. "I was just checking you out to see where you stand on the US government. I wanted to talk to you about something important. Something you could help with." He raised his eyebrows, and his expression turned even more serious than it had been before.

Eric stepped back from Turner and into the snow at the side of the walkway. "What the hell?" This was getting strange.

"Don't worry, Eric. It's not something weird." Turner smiled and chuckled. "We're not after you or anything like that. It's just that you know someone we would like to meet. And we need someone to act as a go-between to set up an introduction." He raised his open hand in a show of being forthright.

Eric didn't understand what he meant. "What are you talking about?"

Turner lowered his voice to just above a whisper as a pair of students walked by engrossed in conversation. "We want you to introduce us to a friend of yours. We want to talk to him, and he's hard to meet under current conditions."

"What do you mean? Who?" Eric was surprised. No one had ever asked him to perform an introduction—at least not since high school when a friend wanted him to act as a go-between with a girl he was afraid to ask out on a date.

Turner said, "His name is Omar Kadish."

Eric was completely shocked at this revelation and was immediately concerned for the welfare of his friend. "What the hell do you mean? He lives just off campus. You could call him up if you want to talk."

"It's not that easy. He may be suspicious of us if we try to contact him directly."

"Wait a minute. Who are these people you represent?"

"I can't really say directly."

"Who in the hell are you then?"

"I shouldn't tell you this, but you'll need to know anyway. I'm with naval intelligence and have been attached to a NATO task force stationed in Denmark." He pulled out an ID card from his wallet and passed it to Eric. "We're collecting certain types of information about people of interest. Most of what I do is routine communications surveillance and analysis. But I was told to contact you to ask a favor. We know you're friendly with Omar and can talk to him freely. We need you to make an introduction for us."

"Why don't you just contact him yourself and leave me out of it?" Eric passed the card back to Turner, but he still didn't get it. *What was going on? Why involve me?*

"It's a little complicated," Turner said. "You see, the people I represent cannot talk to him directly, at least not initially, because he may not want to talk to us at all. We just need you to tell him that we would like a meeting to discuss our mutual interests. You would be doing your government and Kadish a favor."

"But again, I don't get it." Eric was getting irritated by this cat and mouse routine. "If you know who he is and he knows your people, why not just talk to him directly?"

"Well, there's a problem. We have had disagreements with some of his countrymen before. He may not trust us." Turner was getting a little defensive now and tried to explain his role. "Look, it's not like we're going to cause him any trouble or anything, but we can help him and his people if we can meet and work something out to our mutual benefit. We just need to know if he's open to getting together."

Eric wondered if he was becoming paranoid. *What was Turner talking about?* He eyed Turner suspiciously, trying to figure out who he worked for. *Who were his people? What did he mean by "your government"? And why involve me in the first place?*

"Look, Turner. I don't know who you are, but this is crazy," Eric said, trying to reason with the man. "I've only just met you, and you want me to introduce you to my friend when I don't know anything about you. Why should I trust you at all?" He stared at Turner's face for a reaction. "I don't want to get involved in this, OK? Just leave me alone."

He turned to walk away, but curiosity got the better of him. He turned back. "Who are these people you keep speaking of? Are they NATO people?"

Turner hesitated. "No, they're not NATO people. They are an agency that collects intelligence in overseas countries. I can't tell you the name of the agency, but you have certainly heard of them."

"Oh my God!" Eric whispered excitedly. He practically jumped at the news and its implications. He knew of only one agency that traveled the world and operated clandestinely. "You mean the fucking CIA?" He couldn't believe it. Turner was some sort of spy. He didn't want to talk to any spy.

"Now wait a minute," Turner said.

"I'm just going to walk away from here. Leave me alone." With that, Eric turned onto Trädgårdsgatan and trudged up the hill in the direction of the main university building. Turner jogged after him, catching up and walking quickly alongside him as he talked.

"Eric, stop! It's not what you think," he puffed. "We need to talk to your friend, and we will do it with your assistance or without it. If you do, it will happen sooner, and he needs that. He isn't safe here, but we can help him, if he'll let us." He stopped as Eric staggered on up the hill and said in a deadpan voice, "Besides, it's not like you have a real choice here anyway."

Eric stopped walking and looked back at Turner, who had a stern expression on his face. "What do you mean by that?"

"You don't want to be deported, do you, Mr. Barrenger?"

The last thing he said caught Eric's attention. *I didn't mention my last name when I met Turner in the café. How'd he know it?* He wheeled on Turner and walked back to him, stopping a few inches from his face.

"What do you mean by that?" Eric asked in a low growl.

"Look, I don't want to be the heavy here, but we know of your little smuggling operation. We don't care about it, but the Swedish authorities might. If you don't play ball with us, we may have to take measures to alert those authorities." He stared at Eric matter-of-factly. "They're our allies, after all," Turner said and took a step backward.

Eric just stood there and stared at him, his mind racing a mile a minute.

Turner shrugged his shoulders, holding his arms up in an open gesture. "I'm going to let you think about this for a while. Then I'll contact you again."

As Eric watched silently, Turner walked back down the hill into the brisk autumn morning.

***

Eric had to stop and think about the encounter. He walked over to the paleontology museum and sat in his cubicle to sort out what he had just heard.

He knew right away that he did not want any part of Turner and his people—not with everything he had read in the newspapers about the CIA. He was concerned for Omar and had no idea what these people wanted from him. He assumed it had to do with the Kurdish resistance movement in which Omar was a leader. Maybe the CIA was planning to assassinate him. There were rumors that the US government supported the new de facto ruler in Iraq, Saddam Hussein, a savage dictator and a megalomaniac. According to the *Herald Tribune*, Hussein was out to eliminate the Kurds in northern Iraq. Maybe this meeting with Omar was related to that. He didn't know, but he wondered if his friendship would get Omar killed.

The other big thing on Eric's mind was the threat Turner had made that he would turn him in for his liquor and cigarette runs. It might not be just an idle threat. If the Swedes found out he was involved in such activities, he could be forced to leave the country. Or even worse, Eric could be convicted of a crime and have to do jail time. He had never thought he would get caught for something so innocuous, but now it was a possibility.

He was also nervous about who Turner really was and what kind of situation he would get into if he helped him out with an introduction. What would it do to Omar?

He got through the rest of the day by carrying on as normal, keeping an eye out for Turner in case he suddenly showed up again. After going to the administration office, he attended a lecture for his paleontology class at the Gustavianum, the university museum where most of Eric's lectures were held. Then he biked back to Flogsta and his room to study and reflect on the day, his head full of questions.

***

Later that evening, Eric was still thinking about his encounter with Turner when someone pounded on his door. He opened it to find Amir, dressed in a heavy coat and hat, looking very excited.

"Come, Eric!" he shouted. "We have to go, or we will miss the election." Amir took him by the arm to pull him out of the room.

Eric realized that he had been so overwhelmed by the Turner incident that he had forgotten about the ISA meeting.

"Let me get my jacket, Amir. Stop pulling." He stepped back inside and looked at the desk clock as he picked up his coat.

They dashed downstairs and piled into an old 1957 Volvo sedan crammed with Indian students. They drove away at high speed to the meeting as a light snow began to fall.

Chapter 5

The party at Tika's corridor went on until midnight. Eric circulated to talk to several people about Tika's success in the election to become president of the ISA. He had defeated Amad, his only competitor for the post, who became unusually angry about the loss. He accused Tika of somehow rigging the election and a brawl had ensued. Eric and Tika had both suffered bruises in the altercation that took place. They had recovered after some first aid administered by Leela and a few glasses of Scotch.

When the party began to slow down, Eric sought out Omar for conversation. He asked him when he would return to his homeland for a visit.

"It is so tranquil here in Uppsala," Omar said lightly. "It causes me to miss my lively homeland. There is never a dull moment in Kurdistan."

Eric decided that this was a good time to talk to him of the encounter with Mike Turner and his interest in speaking to Omar. Omar listened carefully while Eric told him what had happened. He appeared very thoughtful as he responded.

"So you are the one I was told about. I did not expect it to be you, but I can see now that you were a good choice to make an introduction."

"You knew they wanted to talk to you?"

"Yes, Eric," he said in a hushed voice. "I received a message before I left Mosul that your government had reconsidered its decision to support that madman Saddam Hussein and was seeking a balance to his excesses. I was told that your clandestine agency would find a way to contact me about possible mutual interests. When that did not happen at home, I expected contact here in Uppsala." He smiled at Eric. "You were just lucky to be in the right place at the right time to help me with this matter. I thank you, my friend." He reached out and shook Eric's hand.

"Listen, Omar. I don't know anything about this guy Turner. He showed me an official-looking ID from US Naval Intelligence, but it could be a forgery. He could be anyone." The last thing Eric wanted was for Omar to think he could vouch for the man.

"It is OK, Eric. This is the way these things are done in my country. If you want to meet someone important, you find someone who can introduce you. This gives the person you want to see time to check you out and not be surprised when you do meet. I will have to investigate this man, Mike Turner, or whatever his real name is."

"What do we do now? I don't know how to contact him except possibly at the café." Eric was unclear how this process was supposed to work.

"Maybe you could go to the café tomorrow and see if you encounter Turner. If you do, you can say that I am open to a meeting." Omar put a hand on Eric's shoulder as he spoke softly. "One of my people can shadow you while you are at the café and talking to Turner, just to be safe. He can also take a photo of him for our use."

Eric wasn't sure that he should get involved but felt that he owed it to Omar to help in any way. "OK, I can do that. Who will you send to cover me?"

"I will send Abdullah." He turned to indicate his bodyguard. "You will not see him, even though you know what he looks like. He is very good at this game." Omar looked at his watch. "Shall we say be at the café at ten a.m.?"

"OK, I'll be there."

"Very well," Omar said, then waved for his entourage to gather around. "I have much to do before the meeting, so I will leave now." He shook Eric's hand with both of his. "Thank you for your help, Eric."

As people began to depart, Eric decided that he should go home and get some sleep too. Sabrina saw him pick up his coat and asked him to linger until the others had gone. Soon only Tika, Leela, Sabrina, and the rest of their usual group of friends remained. Tika and a few close friends held an earnest discussion of the ISA politics in the kitchen.

Sabrina sidled over to Eric and said in a quiet, coy voice, "Come with me, Eric. We can finally talk alone." She gave him a sly smile, then led him out of the kitchen and back to her dorm room. He wondered what this was all about.

She was acting more flirtatious tonight than usual. She was very mature for her twenty years, and she had seen many things in that time. She was a dark beauty with brown eyes, a small yet well-defined nose, and a wide smile, which came to her easily among friends. She wasn't tall, but she was slender, with a graceful figure. As she led him down the hallway, she showed off her best moves and ran her fingers through her long black hair.

Once in her room, she pulled out a bottle of Eric's favorite blended Scotch, Johnnie Walker Black Label. "I hid this from the others," she said. "Now we can talk about that crazy fight we all were part of tonight. The election wasn't at all what I expected."

She poured them each two fingers of Scotch and added a few ice cubes to both drinks. Eric sat in a small Turkish chair while she reclined on her bed. She talked of the night's events and what Amad would do next to get back at the Indians and the Kurds, especially Omar.

"You know that Amad will be very angry," Sabrina said in her soft-spoken English. "He will seek revenge on us all somehow." She grinned. "We will have to be on our toes for a countermove. Maybe he will try to interfere with you in some way." She looked anxious. "You must be prepared."

By one o'clock, Eric was feeling very tired and told Sabrina that he should go home. But she wouldn't have it. She had been drinking freely and was feeling romantic now. In her bare feet, she walked over to where Eric was sitting and sat down on his lap. Her warmth and perfume were subtle as she set his drink aside and pulled his arms around her.

Then she brought her face close to his and purred in a husky voice, "You have very gentle brown eyes, you know. And you are a handsome man, even if you are not Catalonian." She ran her hand through his brown hair and kissed his mouth gently. Sabrina giggled and did it again, this time pleased as he returned the favor with a deep kiss that seemed to increase her longing. Eric let his hands roam across her body as they became more and more involved.

Then she pulled away a few inches and whispered, "You know, I must be very careful, for I believe I could definitely fall in love with you."

She kissed him and stood up. "It is very quiet out there. Maybe everyone has gone to bed by now. Can you go and see if this is true?" She gave him a mischievous look.

Eric rose and looked out the door of her room to find that the others had turned in for the night. He padded down the hall to be sure no one had fallen asleep in the kitchen. He came back to her room to report that everyone had gone to bed. When he reentered the room, he found Sabrina undressed and under the covers.

"Come over here," she said. "You can't go home alone with a bump on your head. You could pass out and then what would happen? Besides, it is much more cozy right here next to me." She pulled the covers down just low enough to expose her bare, firm breasts, her slender waist, and her intentions.

Chapter 6

The next morning, Eric arrived at the café on the Stora Torget right at ten o'clock. He ordered his usual coffee and mandeltårta, a creamy Swedish almond pastry, and found a seat near the window so that he could be easily seen from outside. He read the paper slowly and finished his breakfast while looking around for Turner. He didn't show up, so Eric left the café right at noon. He stopped outside and was met by Omar's guard, Abdullah, who left to report on Turner's absence.

Eric decided that he would check in with his professor at the museum, and he headed up the sidewalk that led to the department.

It had snowed a few inches overnight, and the trees were white with warm, sticky flakes on every branch. It was beautiful in the midday light on this crisp, calm day. As he reached the museum, someone called his name. It was Turner, coming up the hill behind him. He walked up to Eric huffing and puffing as Eric waited on the sidewalk.

"I just missed you at the café," Turner said quietly as he caught his breath. "I spotted the guard and wasn't sure whether he was protecting you or following you, so I didn't go in." He paused. "Then I saw you talk to the guy." He raised his eyebrows. "One of Omar's men?"

"Yeah. Omar wanted someone to be there in case you showed up."

"Sounds like SOP—you know, standard operating procedure."

"I talked to Omar last night. He said he was expecting someone to contact him." Eric watched Turner for any response. He played it deadpan. "He said he'd meet you, but it would have to be under his conditions."

"Sounds normal." Turner reached in his pocket and pulled out a small envelope, which he handed to Eric.

"What's this?"

"Give it to Omar personally, and don't worry. It's not a bomb or anything like that."

Eric examined the envelope and surmised that it housed papers only, not anything dangerous.

"It contains my credentials, some information Omar would want to see before a meeting, and my contact information."

"OK, I'll get it to him." Eric turned to go.

Turner took him by the elbow. "Don't worry about last night. I made sure, through channels, that the university police made no record of you or your friends at the little ISA skirmish you were involved in."

Eric looked at him and wondered how long he had been followed. "What do you mean?"

"Look," Turner said, then smiled. "It's the least I could do for you after you've done me a favor."

Eric stopped and considered this news. "Thanks—I guess."

"Say, when are you making another smuggling run?"

"Soon. Why?"

"Well, if you're interested and you're going to Helsinki soon—say, this weekend—you could do me another favor."

"What kind of favor, Turner?"

"I need to have a package delivered there. Discreetly, if you know what I mean."

"How did you know I was going to Helsinki?"

"Just a guess. It follows your pattern, that's all. You visit Helsinki every third trip."

Eric was shocked. This wasn't good. It meant that Turner had been observing Eric for some time, and worse, Eric was getting predictable in his travel. That was bad news for a smuggler.

"Why me?" Eric asked. "Why would I?"

"I can pay you, and you're going anyway, right? What's one more thing to do if you get some extra cash?"

Eric didn't respond right away. Maybe this was some form of entrapment.

"Look," Turner grinned. "I know it's sudden, but think about it, OK? I can match whatever you make on your liquor run. It's extra cash. I'm sure you can use it."

Eric wondered what he was getting into. "OK, Turner, I'll think about it."

"And call me Mike. We're going to be working together." He handed Eric a business card that listed him as proprietor of a small shipping business. He said goodbye and headed back down the hill the way he had come.

Eric walked past the paleontology museum and went to the bus stop where the Flogsta bus passed. As he stood there waiting, a familiar-looking Saab sedan pulled up to the curb, and the passenger door opened. He saw that Abdullah was driving. He motioned Eric over and offered him a ride to Flogsta. Eric got in and told him that he needed to see Omar right away.

"This man saw me at the café, so I disappeared after talking to you. Then I returned to watch you talk to him." Abdullah seemed satisfied with the meeting. "I watched you from the trees over there." He pointed to the large spruces by the paleontology museum.

"Thanks for keeping an eye on me."

Abdullah flashed his teeth for a moment as he drove to Flogsta.

They went directly to Omar's building and had coffee while Omar finished a telephone call in the common room. Then they went to Omar's room to meet. Eric immediately handed him the package.

"He said it was his credentials for you to check out."

Omar gave the package to one of his friends, who went out into the hallway to open it. He returned shortly and handed the contents to Omar.

After examining the papers, Omar said, "It is as he said, his credentials and contact information. We will set up a meeting soon. I will keep you out of it so that you don't have to be involved further. But just to set your mind at ease, I had him investigated by people who owe me a favor." Omar grinned at Eric and then sipped his coffee. "He is as he appears. He works for the US Naval Attaché's office in Copenhagen as a NATO observer, whatever that means. We think he is also harvesting information for another agency, your NSA. Do you know what that is? It is one of your country's counterespionage agencies. No doubt he is also fronting for your CIA as a go-between."

Eric was surprised that Omar had found out so much regarding Turner in so little time. His contacts were apparently very well informed. But Eric was relieved to learn that Turner was really a US government employee and not someone else posing as an American agent.

"Don't worry, Eric." Omar walked Eric to the door with an arm draped around his shoulder in friendship. "I will take it from here. It could be a good thing for my countrymen."

Eric left Omar's place and went back to his own room to contemplate the situation. Turner's offer now looked like a potentially good thing. Maybe Eric could carry a package for him and make nearly twice the money as usual on this next run.

Eric called over to Sabrina's building and learned that she would be back later in the afternoon. He decided that he would ask her opinion of the arrangement with Turner. But mostly he just wanted to see her again.

He worked through what had happened as he biked to the university campus. Ultimately, he decided that he needed to be alone to think things out, and so he was in no mood to talk to Sabrina tonight. He called and said that something had come up and he wouldn't be able to see her.

She seemed surprised and disappointed. "You are not the type of man who does the one night stayover, are you?" He told her that something had happened and that he was in a bad mood. And no, he intended to be a many night stayover kind of guy. She was appeased but still disappointed.

Eric ate dinner at a cafeteria near the campus and then had a few beers at a local tavern. Upon further reflection, he decided that he wouldn't bother Sabrina with the decision involving the work for Turner. He would keep it secret. He spent the rest of the night planning his upcoming trip to Helsinki. Then he called Turner's telephone number and left a message as instructed.

He would have to see if this was an opportunity or a risky proposition. He would find out in a few more days.

Chapter 7

Eric took the Silja Line ferry on Saturday from Stockholm to Helsinki. It was his fourth trip since he had agreed to work for Turner. He boarded at 4:00 p.m. at Stockholm's harbor, and he planned to arrive in Helsinki the next afternoon at 2:00 p.m. At this time of year, it meant that he could arrive and have just enough time to do his business before it got dark due to the shortness of the winter days.

All went well on the voyage as the ferry stopped close to midnight on the little island of Åland off the coast of Sweden in the Gulf of Bothnia. There was no time to get off the boat, but Eric thought that someday it would be nice to explore the island. He had seen it in daylight only once, but it looked interesting.

The ship set sail again and continued on to Helsinki. After dinner, he found a sleeper chair and managed to fall asleep in short order.

The next day, while the ship was in international waters, Eric went to the duty-free shop and purchased his limit of alcohol and cigarettes. He bought two bottles of Dewar's Scotch, two bottles of French Bordeaux, and two cartons of Marlboro unfiltered cigarettes, the Kurdish favorite. He packed them away in his bags with his other possessions. He finished the book he was reading, *Atlas Shrugged*, and struck up a conversation with an English couple who were also traveling to Helsinki. They were on holiday and were interested in Eric's description of life in Uppsala. They arrived in Helsinki on schedule, and saying goodbye, Eric passed through immigration with no problems.

Normally he checked his duffel bag at the ferry station and wandered around Helsinki taking photos and seeing the sights until it was time to catch the return ferry in the afternoon. On this trip, he checked the bag and set out to find the location he had been given by Turner for the package delivery. He had the parcel in his backpack and wanted to deliver it on time. The delivery made him nervous, maybe a little paranoid, and he wanted to get it over with.

Eric took a bus into the downtown area, traveling along Mannerheimintie, or Mannerheim Avenue, which was the main thoroughfare through the city. The street was named after Carl Gustaf Emil Mannerheim, the great military hero of the Finnish Civil War and Second World War. He was also elected president of Finland in 1944. A giant statue of him on horseback dominated Mannerheim Avenue.

He got off the bus when he could first see the monument. Walking to the small park close to the statue, Eric sat on one of the granite benches. The package was in a small shopping bag marked with the Stockmann Department Store logo. He was wearing a red jacket and blue stocking cap as planned. He waited for contact and, for the first time in this business, his palms began to sweat.

It was cold on the bench, and Eric had to get up once to stretch and to warm up a little. At 3:00 p.m., a woman wearing a long blue coat came into the park and sat on a nearby bench, smoking a cigarette. After the prescribed number of minutes, she got up and sauntered over.

She smiled wanly and asked Eric, "*Ursëkta me. Vad är klockan?* What time is it?"

He replied, "*Halv två.* One thirty." This was obviously not the correct time.

"*Jag måste ta en buss.* I have to catch my bus."

He stood up and abandoned the package next to the bench as she sat down. As he walked away, he looked back and saw the woman heading in the opposite direction with the shopping bag in her hand. He walked the length of Mannerheim Avenue and stopped for a late lunch at a small restaurant. Eric returned to the ferry terminal in time to catch the ship back to Stockholm.

The rest of the trip was uneventful. He purchased his limit of liquor and tobacco in international waters again on the return voyage, buying two bottles of Johnnie Walker Black Label for Sabrina as well as more wine and cigarettes. He reached Stockholm the next afternoon. Eric passed through customs and immigration without a hitch and caught a train back to Uppsala, arriving in time to meet Sabrina for dinner at a small pizza shop.

They spent the night together at her place, and he told her how uneventful his trip had been. They drank Black Label on ice.

***

Mid-December arrived, and life in Uppsala went on as usual. Eric studied for an upcoming paleontology exam and passed it reasonably well, in spite of not fully understanding a portion of the literature he had to read. He received help with translation of the Danish textbook by one of the other students who seemed genuinely concerned that he just didn't comprehend the importance of the early Cenozoic history of the Jutland peninsula. He found the class to be difficult because of all the material they had to read and digest. He toyed with the idea of opting out of the following semester of the class until his language skills improved.

The weather had turned extremely cold, and there were very short days now that winter had set in. The sun barely crept above the horizon for midwinter, providing only pale whitish light at midday. Every day, Eric would ride his bike to the campus in the dark and ride back home in the night. The lack of light each day began to affect everybody's attitudes. It was one of the worst parts of living in Sweden—dealing with the prolonged gloom of the Scandinavian winter. In addition to the darkness, there were regular snowstorms that were preceded by blasts of arctic wind that cut through his clothes like an icy knife.

During this time Eric made only one quick trip to Turku, Finland, by boat, just to stock up on supplies for the coming holidays. Somehow crossing the Gulf of Finland on the rough and frigid sea held no magic for him any longer.

He also learned the fate of Amad, who had been suspended from the university for his role in the ISA riot, as the school called the election night folly. Two of Amad's associates had also been suspended, and one had spent a few weeks in jail for assaulting a police officer. Swedish law allowed for much leniency in cases involving foreign students, who were guests in the country, but striking a police officer was considered a serious crime.

The Swedes celebrated two official holidays in December. The first was Saint Lucia's Day, which was the feast day of Saint Lucia, a Sicilian saint who was honored by the Swedes for her purity and life. The second was Christmas, which most families celebrated on Christmas Eve. They also marked the passing of the winter solstice, the shortest day of the year and when the days began to grow longer. This was an unofficial event that students observed with another bout of drinking parties.

Eric attended Saint Lucia's Day at the home of his department's head professor, Dr. Svensen. He had all the staff from the office, as well as the students and their families, over for a gala celebration in which his oldest daughter, per an old tradition, led a small procession of children through the house in honor of Saint Lucia. His daughter was dressed in a white robe with a red sash and wore a garland on her head made of fresh flowers with five lighted candles in it. This was a big success, and many photos were taken of the procession. A huge feast ensued, and everyone had a good time. The traditional dish of malodorous lutfisk was the center of the smorgasbord dinner. Svensen announced that the department had received a new grant, and he introduced two new researchers who were joining the staff next year.

This meant that Eric had a lot of free time to spend over the holidays, and he decided to make a trip to Cologne in West Germany to visit an old friend he knew from Minneapolis. It was a pleasant break from the long winter nights, but alas, it lasted only seven days, and he returned to Uppsala after the New Year.

The full force of winter descended on Sweden just as he returned to Flogsta. The long and miserable days of the arctic north weighed on Eric's spirits.

Chapter 8

Leningrad, Russia
December 1971

Lena had only one chance to take the written materials. She knew the meeting was about the reorganization of the Economic Planning Bureau and the new projects that would be upcoming during the New Year. The itinerary and the summary of those projects would be of great interest to the shadowy people she had been working for part-time.

The problem was that the documents were likely to be numbered and tracked, so it would be difficult to borrow a copy for a few minutes and photocopy it on the department copy machine while the meeting was in session. She also knew that anything truly confidential or classified would probably be collected at the end of the meeting except for a few copies that would be locked in briefcases as the attendees left the room. The remaining copies that were collected would be placed in the burn bag for destruction either immediately or at the end of the day with other classified papers.

She knew of the documents because her friend Nadya had mentioned it to her the night before. She had said that important people from the Economic Planning Bureau were to come into their offices for a far-ranging meeting to discuss future plans for the organization. Apparently, a major shake-up of leadership was about to occur, and secret plans were being conceived.

Nadya had been asked to make fourteen copies of the memo containing the main planning document. And she had been instructed to number the copies and provide them to the director of the economics department for his safekeeping until the meeting began. Another assistant had been present to watch her make the copies and to verify the numbering of each one. She had visually scanned the contents of the papers as she handled the documents. They contained the names of several high-ranking members of the economics department, as well as the director of the bureau itself, along with their positions that were to be filled by new people from other divisions of the government.

Nadya recognized several names from department gossip about corruption in the bureau as well. It would be interesting to know what they were going to talk about at this meeting. Perhaps they would discuss people who were to be removed and made to disappear, as sometimes happened in her country.

Lena and Nadya talked of it vicariously last evening and had come up with several interesting interpretations of the importance of the meeting.

"They must be having the gathering in our conference room so that the people who will be removed will not know what will happen," Lena said. "They need to meet in a place where few people will notice the particular individuals involved and so they chose our sleepy little department. Heaven knows that we never do anything political or controversial over here. Or maybe there will be a big putsch going on within the department." Lena was intrigued by the possibilities. "How exciting it would be!"

"Lena, don't be too enthusiastic about such a thing. It is always the little people who suffer when there is a sudden shake-up of the bureaucracy. Maybe we will lose our jobs. Don't wish for something you don't know."

Nadya refilled their glasses with vodka and offered a toast. "Here is to our glorious leaders. May they finally realize how much work we do for them and suddenly decide to pay us more for all the hours we provide." Lena, Nadya, and Katya all raised their glasses and cheerfully downed the peppermint vodka in thanksgiving.

Katya made a face as if she had tasted something bitter. "Where did you get this odd vodka, Nadya? It seems to taste worse with every glass." She smirked at her friend. "Did you make it at your apartment in the bathtub? If so, you should have cleaned the tub before the endeavor!"

"Endeavor?" Lena said loudly. "My sister used the word *endeavor* in a sentence? What could be happening to us? Can we hear clearly any longer? Or is this just a very bad and excellent drink in our hands?"

Lena poked her sister in the arm as she spoke. "No. But seriously, there must be something important happening at the meeting tomorrow."

Katya giggled but then tried to be helpful. "You should see what you can learn in the morning." She looked over the table at Nadya and raised one eyebrow in question. Nadya looked at Katya and then back at Lena and shook her head. They discussed the meeting late into the night.

***

Before the meeting, the director of the economics department made an announcement that all nonessential personnel should evacuate the second floor of the building where the conference room was located. He simply said that important dignitaries would be visiting the department and that they would need a certain amount of privacy for their meeting. Those persons with offices on that floor should take their work with them if possible and relocate to the library or cafeteria for the afternoon when the meeting would be in progress. If it was not possible, then those people affected could leave early. Many of the staff decided that, given a choice, they couldn't work effectively in any place other than their offices on the second floor. They vanished for the afternoon, along with several others who didn't have offices there.

The problem with this approach to limiting access became apparent at lunchtime when the director was informed that the first-floor ladies' restroom had been out of service for two days and, therefore, women in the building would need to use the facilities on the second floor. This created a stir because security people who were to accompany many of the guests for the meeting did not want anyone to suddenly pop up unannounced on the second floor during the meeting. It was decided to block out the glass doors of the conference room with paper and tape so that any busybody workers couldn't see who was present. They would only allow the troublesome females access to the toilets if accompanied by one of the security people.

Guests began to arrive for the meeting shortly before 1:00 p.m., and there was a commotion because some people did not want to be seen going from the car to the conference room. They were cloaked by security guards holding extra umbrellas around their heads and were ushered up the back staircase, which was also quarantined. In any case, the meeting got underway shortly after the appointed time.

Both Nadya and Lena held jobs that required them to be present in the building either because other people needed to talk to them or, in Nadya's case, because she had been assigned by the director to help with the meeting. At the last minute, he had insisted that she be available outside the meeting room in case he needed more copies made or something typed up for the meeting. She therefore stood dutifully beside the door. The director came out several times to give her urgent assignments.

He also had her shuttling back and forth to the cafeteria with one of the security guards to get coffee, tea, and snacks for the guests who had eaten all the cakes and blini that had been prepared for the hungry bureaucrats. When the food arrived, the meeting paused while she and Lena, who had been recruited to help with the refreshments, entered the room with the goods to replenish the buffet.

Lena had a good look at some of the men in the meeting and recognized a few of them from photos she had seen. She also saw the documents Nadya had prepared on the table, one copy resting before each person. While the food was distributed, everyone stood to stretch and move into line to obtain drinks and snacks.

That was when the guard who had been helping them managed to knock over one of the tea samovars, flooding one end of the conference table. People jumped up to avoid being inundated with the hot beverage, and general confusion reigned.

"You oaf!" shouted one of the participants as tea engulfed the end of the table and dribbled down the leg of his trousers.

"I'm sorry, sir," the guard said as he tried to block the tea from sweeping toward other officials.

The director was beside himself that such an incident should occur and that bureau members should be annoyed. His face turned bright red as he apologized profusely to the important men. Fortunately, the ruffled egos settled down when the man with wet trousers realized that he wasn't the only one with tea stains on his pants.

The spill led to a break from the meeting so that several of the attendees could move out into the hallway until the crisis with the tea was corrected. Nadya saved the director some embarrassment by mopping up the spilled tea with cloth towels and placing them into a trash can, along with napkins and anything else that was soaked with liquid.

Inadvertently, several copies of the meeting documents had become wet and unusable. While the director calmed the officials' nerves and looked stressed, Nadya volunteered to make extra copies of the papers as quickly as possible. She rushed to comply as a few of the guests began to complain loudly about the delay. The director gave her his only copy of the document, number thirteen, an unfortunate number to use in making copies.

Nadya and Lena ran downstairs with the document and took over the copy room. The two of them had to unstaple the original document and begin feeding the single pages into the copy machine one by one. Surprisingly, no security man came along to supervise the copying operation.

They had to collate the copies that came out of the machine by hand as rapidly as they could. Lena saw her opportunity to secretly make an extra copy for herself, and she added an extra page to the printing. At first Nadya didn't notice the subterfuge, but when she did, she got angry with her friend.

"Lena, *chto ty delayesh'? chert voz'mi!* What the hell are you doing?" she whispered, cursing in Russian. "You must stop, or we will surely be caught. Are you mad?"

"Be quiet and help me, Nadya. It will be OK." She gave her friend a pleading stare.

"But what if you are caught? We are caught?"

"Then we will both have a visit to the Siberian forest on a long vacation," Lena said, making light of the theft. Nadya's face was locked in a grimace.

But Lena was determined and made her copy, hiding it in the extra paper tray of the machine while they collated the remaining copies. Just as they had the copies spread out all across the little room, the temporary assistant came in to observe their operation. He snarled at them that they should have waited for him.

Lena glared at him. "So we should wait and tell my boss we must stand around while you took your sweet time to stroll down the hallway?"

"Who are you to tell me what to do?" Nadya demanded. "Here are the copies. You can help us collate them. Then you can put your numbers on them, and we can hope no one important is angry that we took so long."

They finished the task and stapled pages together as the assistant numbered them in a specific sequence. He took them upstairs while Lena and Nadya went to the cafeteria and ordered more tea for the conference room. When they came upstairs, Lena was excused, and Nadya and the guard carried in the fresh tea and a few other baked treats. The meeting began again, and Nadya went back to the hallway to stand by for further disasters.

At the end of the meeting, the guests left the building much as they had arrived, but a few of them didn't look as happy as they had earlier in the day. Some were joyful and that probably meant their futures had brightened as other fortunes had diminished. By 6:00 p.m., the building was back to normal and nearly everyone had gone home.

The director seemed not only relieved but also thankful that the day's events had gone as well as they had. It turned out that he had rather excellent news from the meeting, and he went to his office to contemplate his luck over a few shots of vodka from a bottle he kept in his desk drawer for both good and bad occasions. When Nadya and

Lena stopped by his door to see if he needed anything else done, he coaxed them in for a celebratory drink with him.

"We've have some good news today, ladies! And I wanted to thank both of you for your help with the meeting. It was very nearly a disaster." He poured them each a measure of vodka and toasted the day's success.

The three raised their glasses and said, *"Na Zdorovie!"* Each sipped vodka and smiled weakly.

"You cannot imagine how angry a few of those men can be when they have to wait on anything or anyone. The extra cakes and blini you arranged were very well received, Nadya. One of the older gentlemen asked if he could hire you away from my office. Can you imagine?" He chuckled. "But I think he had only nefarious plans for you if I had agreed." Then he suddenly became embarrassed for his comment. "I am sorry for that. It was not sensitive . . ."

He paused and looked askance at Nadya. She nodded to show that she held no hard feelings.

"But I have good news!" he continued. "We have permission to plan for a new department building to house the modeling and data efforts. I will see to it that you each will have a new office in the building. That is how important today was to us in our department."

Their spirits soared.

***

Lena and Nadya rode the bus to Lena's apartment to see if Katya wanted to have dinner with them. On the way home, Nadya asked, "Lena, where is the document?"

Lena lifted her sweater to show that she had it tucked in the waist of her skirt. "Thank you for your help today, Nadya."

She was relieved that it had worked out on the spur of the moment as it had. It could have led to catastrophe. Her face was pale as the reality of what she had done set into her thoughts.

"I have to tell you more of why I did this thing later, I know. But it will all make sense when I do." She searched Nadya's face to see if she was angry. "But let us not worry. We will go to the Northern Lights tonight, and I will treat you to a very fine dinner to celebrate our new offices that we will have someday."

"But I am angry with you." Nadya gave Lena a hard look. "You could have gotten us arrested. It is a crime you have committed."

Lena reached over and took Nadya's hand. "But you will not stay angry with me when I tell you what I am up to. And the vodka will make this all seem far away." She smiled at her friend and tried to get her to smile back.

Finally, Nadya burst out in quiet laughter. "You are such an optimist! And who knows how long it will be before we see any kind of building at all?" She squeezed Lena's hand. "But I am always ready to party if my friend is happy." They rode on and collected Katya and the ever-present Misha for a happy evening among friends.

***

Two weeks after the big meeting, Lena and another woman from the office named Veroushka were to travel with several other department personnel to an economics conference in Helsinki. Lena was very excited and could hardly wait to leave on the trip. She was going as the director's assistant and had much work to do to prepare the materials he would use for a lecture he was giving about several programs under his authority at the economics department. They worked late into the evening for several days to prepare for the trip, but Lena didn't mind the extra hours of drudgery. She would get to travel to a foreign country—Finland—to help the director at the conference.

Veroushka was a very young girl who had only begun to work at the department two years before. She was allowed to travel to Helsinki often because the professor she worked for was spending a semester abroad collaborating with two Finnish economists in that city.

Veroushka had helped Lena once or twice to do things against protocol for a few extra rubles. It seemed that most people in Russia had some scheme to raise a little extra cash to help supplement the meager pay they earned. Lena had recruited her to deliver a package to an unknown person in Helsinki. Lena took a big risk getting the girl involved, but she wouldn't be able to make the delivery herself due to a scheduling glitch. She hoped it would work out as planned.

In any case, the trip would be something new for Lena. She promised her sister and Nadya that she would take photographs and would bring them back something uniquely Finnish. The only problem was that the trip would happen in the dead of winter—in January. There would be no suntanning on the Baltic Sea on this journey.

Chapter 9

Helsinki, Finland
Sunday, January 16, 1972

The New Year brought very cold weather to Uppsala and, indeed, to all of Scandinavia. Travel was treacherous on the roads, especially at night, and even the trains were delayed on a few rare occasions. Airports were closed for hours due to inclement wind and weather. But in spite of this, the sea ferries to Finland ran on their regular schedules, save for a few delays due to frozen harbors and extreme storm events. It was under these conditions that Eric contemplated his next trip to Helsinki.

He had received a message from Mike Turner that he needed Eric to make a trip to that city to deliver not one but three packages. It seemed there would be an international economics conference in Helsinki the third week of January, and several people of interest would be in attendance. The conference began on a Monday, and Eric was to make the transfers at various times, as the schedule would allow. He would make deliveries much as he had in the past, via blind dead drops or casual swaps in public places with the usual cutouts. The trip appealed to Eric because Turner would pay him five times the usual fee, which made it worth his while crossing the angry and storm-tossed Baltic.

Eric and Turner had agreed to a regular business arrangement. Eric would clandestinely deliver packages to persons and addresses in Finland, usually in Helsinki, under specific conditions, and Turner would pay him handsomely for the service. In addition, Turner said that he would handle any problems that Eric might encounter while conducting his smuggling operation—within reason. It was a quid pro quo arrangement. It had required Eric to take a couple of days of training on how to perform clandestine drops and other practical techniques that he would need for his delivery runs. He was now a professional courier for his shadowy employer.

Eric arrived in Helsinki on Sunday morning and checked into the Vikken Hotel near the city center. He unpacked his bag and arranged his few clothes in the closet. While in the hotel room, he opened up the package that Turner had given him. Inside were three other parcels of equal size, all wrapped in brown paper and tied with white cotton string. Each had a letter of the alphabet written on it: T, R, and A. Eric selected the one marked *T* and hid the other two under the center of the mattress on the bed. With that, he set out with the *T* package in his backpack to have lunch and make the first drop.

He walked close to eight city blocks to the district post office. Across the street was a small coffee shop that served as a drop marker. He walked by the doorway and noted the black mark on the outside light fixture. He casually went inside and purchased a cup of coffee to take away. Then he left the shop and walked to a bus stop two blocks farther and waited for the bus that ran along Kasarmikatu Street toward the harbor. When it came, he boarded and took a seat in the rear, where he could watch people come and go from each stop.

He got off the bus after three stops and walked casually around the neighborhood to be sure that no one was following him—as casually as he could in the middle of a winter snowstorm, that is. Although he didn't think that anyone would be interested in his activities, he still adhered to the routine protocol to ensure that he had no unwanted company. He directed his steps toward the corner of Tehtaankatu and Neitsytpolku Streets, which rose above the south harbor. The small park there was his destination, even though he didn't enter it directly. Instead, he walked down Tehtaankatu past the park and went around the block. As he came back to the park from the opposite side, he scanned the area for people or unusual activity. Seeing none, he walked to the park bench by the small stone wall and sat down on the snowy seat to read a paperback novel and finish his coffee. After reading *And Not to Yield* by James Ramsey Ullman for fifteen minutes, Eric began to freeze to death. He got up to leave.

He walked over to the trash can that was built into the wall and deposited his empty coffee cup. At the same time, he secretly moved aside a loose stone on a recessed shelf in the wall, retrieved an envelope wrapped in plastic, and set down his brown paper package marked with

T. He reset the stone that blocked the view of the shelf. He placed the envelope in his coat's inner pocket and walked away, just managing to catch a bus that returned up Kasarmikatu toward his hotel. He had a Scotch at the hotel bar to warm up and to celebrate another seamless recovery and delivery.

The next evening, Eric dressed for dinner, wearing a tweed sport coat with a blue striped tie, and ate at one of the finer hotels downtown where several conference attendees were staying. He had a nice early dinner and then lingered in the small booth after he finished his meal, savoring a glass of Bordeaux. At eight o'clock, a man wearing a heavy brown coat and a brown felt hat with a green feather in it came into the restaurant. As he inquired whether a table was available, Eric stood up and walked to the cashier to pay his bill. The man was shown to a table in the middle of the room, but seeing that a booth had just opened up, he directed the hostess to let him sit in there, where Eric had been. Package R that Eric had left there was set into the narrow space at the rear of the booth's seat.

Eric had to wait until Wednesday evening to make the last of his three deliveries. He arrived at the Palace Linna Hotel at 7:15 p.m. as planned. This one would be a little more difficult because he was to pass his package to someone at the hotel where many of the Russian economists were staying. The timing of the pass was optimized to avoid the possibility of running into the Russians. Most of them were expected to be attending a special session about Russia's unique economic ties to the Arab world.

He had a drink at the bar and observed his fellow patrons while he made a point of studying a train schedule. He talked to the bartender a little, asking him in Swedish for directions to the railroad station and basically killing time. He was supposed to sit at the bar and wait for a woman in a red coat and black gloves to approach. She would have a small Stockmann shopping bag with her, one identical to Eric's, and they would make a classic pass trade. By 7:40 p.m., he began to worry. There was no sign of the woman or the bag, and the agreed-upon time was now long past. He waited a little longer, paid his tab, and walked out of the bar.

As he passed through the doorway from the bar, he bumped into a young woman who was in a great hurry—or, rather, she bumped into him. They collided with enough force to send her backward, and she teetered for balance, falling against Eric and holding on for support. He reached out and held her so that she could right herself.

"Ursëkta me," he said, excusing himself in Swedish. "I didn't see you coming."

"Izvinite," she responded in Russian, looking surprised.

When he let go of her, she straightened up. He realized that the woman was wearing a red coat and black gloves. She was holding a small Stockmann shopping bag.

She looked down and stared at his Stockmann bag. Her eyes opened in surprise. She teetered forward again as if unbalanced and, facing him, drew near.

She whispered urgently in Swedish, "Room four fifteen. Five minutes, please."

She backed away and excused herself profusely in very bad Swedish, tinged with a clear Russian accent. Then she simply walked away to the elevator and stepped through the open doors. A bellman had noticed the accident and asked Eric if he was all right. Eric looked up and saw that the elevator had stopped on the fourth floor. He told the bellman that he was fine and left the hotel by the front door. He still had his Stockmann's bag with him.

Eric walked down the street to the subway station and went down the stairs. At the bottom was a telephone bank, and he pretended to make a phone call. After confirming that he hadn't been followed, he removed his package from the Stockmann's bag, put it in the inside pocket of his coat, and disposed of the bag in a nearby trash can. He crossed the station and emerged again at street level across from where he had entered. He walked across the street, continued around to the side of the hotel, and entered the side doorway. He went left down the hall to the stairwell and climbed up to the fourth floor.

Eric cracked open the stairwell door and looked down the hall. No one was present in the paneled corridor. After a minute of listening for any movement, he pushed open the door and walked softly along the carpeted floor. He walked to the elevator and saw that room 415 was just past it. As he cautiously approached the room, the door opened and the young woman who had bumped into him pulled him inside.

Once in the room, his instincts told Eric that this might be some sort of trap. He quickly scanned the space to be sure that no one else was present and that there were no surprises waiting. All he saw was a typical, if somewhat rundown, hotel suite, composed of a small sitting room and a bedroom door that was ajar, giving a view of the carefully made bed inside. The woman closed the door quietly and turned to look at him.

She was tall and slender, with a pretty, pale face surrounded by long blonde hair. She was younger than Eric first thought when they bumped into each other downstairs, perhaps in her midtwenties. Her eyes were a shade of blue and had a sad look about them.

He was about to speak when she held her finger to her lips to silence him. A knock came on the door. "Lena! Lena?"

The woman silently took Eric's hand and led him to the bedroom closet, where she motioned for him to hide. He watched as she quickly took off her dress and put on a bathrobe, all the while responding in Russian that she was coming. She gave Eric a quick glare because he had watched her undress and motioned for him to close the closet door. Then she went into the sitting room and pulled the bedroom door shut. She responded in Russian through the hallway door, telling whoever was there that she was feeling better but was tired and would go to bed early. At least that was all Eric could gather with his limited understanding of the language. After a moment, she opened the door just far enough to talk to the inquirer, and after a couple of minutes, she said good night and closed the door.

The woman returned to the bedroom and opened the closet. "Did you hear what he said?" she asked in her style of Swedish. Eric walked out and said in English, "All I got was your name—Lena. I don't really speak Russian."

"Oh good!" She looked relieved. "You speak English, and I do not have to guess how to speak Swedish, which I do not know except for a few words." She spoke English fairly well. "You shouldn't have heard that. You should not know my name!"

She seemed very upset, her face turning a shade of pink as she spoke. She went to the foot of the bed and sat down. "I should not have broken protocol," she said mournfully. "I should not have tried to contact you directly. It is just that I didn't know what to do. Veroushka was not able to meet you for the exchange of packages and I panicked." She looked up at Eric meekly. Her eyes signaled a sense of fear and worry.

"*O Bozhe! YA skazal yeye imya.* Oh God! I said her name."

He just stood there and said nothing, not knowing what to do next.

"I must get my information out to the West. It is not much, but it might be important." She looked at Eric, eyes wild with fear.

"Oh my God! I don't even know who you are." She switched from English to Russian. "Maybe you are KGB! Maybe you took Veroushka! What have I done?" She leaped to her feet and backed away toward the bathroom door.

Eric suddenly realized that she was shouting at him and becoming hysterical. He tried to calm her.

"Be quiet," he whispered. "Someone will hear and think there is something wrong. Don't be afraid of me. I am just a courier."

She covered her mouth, as if to hold in the words. Her expression showed confusion and fear. She came back to the edge of the bed and sat down, holding her face in her hands.

"Yes," she said. "You are just the courier. How could you know? Oh, I have ruined everything! I should not have involved you. I should not have interfered with the protocol."

"Look," Eric said. "I don't know what happened or who you are. Are you the woman who I was supposed to connect with in the bar?"

"Oh no. No. No. That was Veroushka." She looked up at him from the bed. "She was to meet you. She called me to say she could not go. She thought someone was following her. How do you say—onto her. She told me what to do, but she did not have the bag. So I had to go to Stockmann store to get shopping bag and then I came too late." She wrung her hands as she stared at Eric. "I am so worrying of her. What could have happened?"

She began to cry, deep quiet sobs paired with a flood of tears, all while sitting at the foot of the bed.

Eric got a few tissues from the bathroom and brought them to her. "Listen. Nothing is your fault. If you had been five minutes earlier or if I had waited five minutes longer, everything would still have worked out. I don't know what happened to your friend Veroushka. Maybe she is OK and just got scared. Maybe she will be all right."

Lena continued to cry but a little less violently. Eric sat down beside her and put an arm around her. She resisted him at first but then slumped onto his shoulder.

"It will be OK," he said. "You'll see. She might have been mistaken and there was no one after her."

They sat that way for a few moments while Lena calmed down and the crying stopped. "You think she might be OK? Maybe she made mistake?" She looked up, her eyes swollen with tears. "Oh, I hope it is so. I should not have involved my friend in these affairs. I could not bear it if she is hurt." She broke into tears again, but it lasted for only a few seconds.

"We have to make this work out," Eric said carefully so as not to upset the woman. "Complete the transfer."

She sat up and removed his arm from her shoulder. Taking a deep breath, she forced herself to carry on with the mission. "We must focus now. We must make it work. Do you have the package for me?"

"Yes."

"You were to give it to the woman wearing red coat and black gloves with the Stockmann bag just like yours, yes?" She looked sideways at Eric and tried to act professional. She stood up to face him. "And you are the man wearing a heavy brown coat with an oxford scarf with black shoes and with the Stockmann bag just like mine. *Da?* So we are who we say we are. Or we must trust that we are the people we say we are. *Da?* And you have something for me."

Eric reached into his inner coat pocket and pulled out the package marked *A*. He hesitated and looked Lena in the eyes. *She must be telling the truth,* he thought. *She's terrified.* He could see the tears just on the edge of flow and knew that he could trust her. She also looked at him a long time and, finally, she seemed to relax a little. She smiled thinly and exhaled.

He realized that they had both been holding their breaths, hoping that they weren't making a fatal mistake. He handed her the brown paper-wrapped package.

"Do you know what this is?" she mumbled and looked at Eric in a knowing way. "It is the new key." She turned her back on him and unwrapped the package. "Yes," she said. "It is here." She hid the package contents from Eric and put it in the deep pocket of her robe. "I suppose that you already know how it works, but it is best if you do not know what it is." She went to the bed, reached under the mattress, and pulled out a small manila envelope.

"Now I have something for you." She handed it to him reluctantly. "You must hide it very well and guard it with your life."

Eric took the sealed envelope and placed it in his inner coat pocket. It felt like papers. He knew that he couldn't look at them, but he wondered what was so important that it made Lena afraid. He hadn't expected to receive a parcel to smuggle out with him, only something that one would buy at Stockmann—a pair of gloves or a scarf that would justify carrying the bag. He was a little confused. He stood up to leave.

"No, you cannot leave just like this. I must help you so no one sees. Wait here."

Lena went to the bedroom and took off her robe. She tossed it on the edge of the bed and disappeared into the bathroom to freshen up. As she closed the door, the robe slid off the edge of the bed and onto the floor. As it landed, something fell out of the pocket—the contents of the package that Eric had brought to her.

It was a paperback published by Penguin Books, *The Wealth of Nations* by Adam Smith. He reached for it and opened it. It was just a book. He placed it back in her robe pocket and set the robe where it had been on the bed.

Lena came out of the bathroom looking much happier than a short time before. She smiled sheepishly as she tiptoed past Eric to get to her clothes. She glanced at him as she dressed. He wondered if he was missing something here.

"I will make sure no one is outside," she said matter-of-factly. "We have a keeper, what you call a chaperone. He is guarding us and also making sure we not try to stay in Helsinki. He is a nice old man, but he must do his job. I will distract him while you go."

She went to the door, and he followed. They listened very carefully but heard nothing. She opened the door a crack.

The old keeper was sitting in a chair in the hallway, apparently dozing off after eating his dinner. Lena closed the door and turned to Eric. "I trust you with my life. I hope you will be OK too. Follow when I leave with old Vlad." With that, she stood on her tiptoes and kissed Eric firmly on the lips. Hers were warm and moist. Eric was bowled over.

"And pray for me!" she said.

She opened the door and called out to the old man. He awoke with a start but smiled immediately when he saw who had called and spoke to her in familiar Russian tones. "Lena, my child. Are you feeling better?"

"Da." She replied in her native tongue, closing the door and walking unsteadily toward him. "I think I need some fresh air and something to eat. But I feel a little dizzy. Can you walk down to the restaurant with me, Vova? I do not feel so good on my feet."

"Of course, my dear," he said in a grandfatherly Russian manner. "I will be only too happy to help my little Lena." They waited for the elevator and boarded when it came. Within seconds, the door swept closed and they were gone, leaving the hallway vacant and the coast clear.

Eric stepped out into the hallway and closed the door to room 415 carefully behind him. He walked directly to the stairwell, descended the stairs, and left the building. Out on the street, he mingled with the crowd on the sidewalk and went to a bar to make sure that his exit was clean.

He couldn't stop thinking about the remarkable woman he had just met and kissed. He thought of their encounter all the way back to Uppsala the next day. As he remembered their meeting at the hotel, he was surprised at how similar Lena looked to the woman in his dreams. How could that be?

Chapter 10

Uppsala, Sweden
Friday, January 21, 1972

After returning to Uppsala on Thursday night, Eric arranged to talk with Turner as soon as possible on Friday. They met for brunch at a small restaurant near the cathedral. Turner was surprised that Eric had been so urgent in his request for a meeting. They ordered coffee and pastries and sat at a small side table where they had a little more privacy.

"You were to follow the standard procedure at all times," Turner said loudly. Then he lowered his voice to avoid attracting undue attention. "Both of you risked losing your cover by following your dumbass instincts. The rules are there for a reason. You both could have endangered other people by your actions!"

"Look, I see that now," Eric said earnestly. "But I did what seemed reasonable." He paused to look around the café to be sure that he wasn't overheard. "I should have walked away, but she didn't give me a choice."

"You're damn right you should have walked away," Turner said. "And she shouldn't have come to substitute for her friend." He looked stern but uncertain as to what to do next. "Look, she's not one of my operatives, but I'll inquire through channels to see if there was any danger to Lena or this other woman, Veroushka." He had an exasperated expression on his face. "Hell, I shouldn't even know their names—not their real names."

Turner sipped his coffee, then stared into his cup for a full minute before speaking again. Eric just sat and anticipated more reprimands.

"What surprises me, Eric, is that you actually met Lena in person and now you know her real name." He appraised Eric for a moment. "Operationally, this is very bad. She shouldn't have told you her name. She should have used her code name, VERNA. She's not new at this, and she knows tradecraft. She should have followed protocol, damn it."

"She didn't tell me her name. The chaperone called out to her to see if she was OK. He is the one who called her Lena," Eric said. "She was only trying to save the transfer. And she was very concerned to send something back to you. She sent her own packet."

"What?" Turner was again surprised. "Do you have it with you?"

"Yes, right here." Eric tapped his coat pocket.

Turner stared at him without saying anything. Eric could tell that he was thinking of what to do about the package. He wrote an address down on a napkin.

"Meet me at this address in half an hour. We can talk there. Be careful that you aren't followed." Then he stood up and spoke in a louder voice. "It was very nice to see you again. We will have to discuss French wines next time." He stood up, threw a fifty-krona bill on the table, and left the restaurant.

Eric finished his coffee and pastry at a leisurely pace, paid the bill, and walked out onto the street. In half an hour, he was at an old apartment building and rang the bell to 3B. The door buzzed open, and he went up to the apartment where Turner was waiting. The first thing Turner did was ask if Eric had destroyed the napkin. He responded affirmatively.

"We can talk here. It is a safe house that we can use for meetings." He waved Eric to an overstuffed chair. "No bugs or nosy neighbors. Now, let me see the packet." He extended a hand for the package and Eric complied.

Turner put on a pair of latex gloves and opened the manila envelope. Inside were several carefully folded pages of letter-size paper. He looked at them one by one. Then he sat down at a small wooden table to go over them again in more detail. After several minutes, he looked up at Eric, who had watched the inspection quietly.

"What you have here are several pages of a high-level, internal memo from inside the Economic Planning Bureau of the Soviet government. I cannot show it to you, but I can tell you that it is very important. The memo names the members of the inner economic council. It lays out proposed changes to a new economic plan that appear to be far reaching. I will have to get this back to my office for analysis right away." He held the pages up to the lamp and examined the paper carefully. Then he reinserted them into the envelope, which he now placed in his own coat pocket.

"She said it was important. That I should protect it with my life."

Turner stared at Eric and nodded his head.

Eric asked, "What now?"

"Now there are many questions that we must try to answer. It is clear why VERNA jumped protocol. She wanted to get this information into the right hands. If she couldn't get rid of it, she would have had to destroy it immediately."

Turner stopped speaking and closed his eyes. "But how did she obtain the memo?" He opened his eyes again and stood up to stare out the window while he worked out what this meant. "She works for the Economic Planning Bureau, the EPB, but she isn't supposed to be privy to this level of meeting. This is a copy of a numbered original memo. It should have been collected at the end of any meeting and burned or shredded."

"So it's important," Eric said.

"Yeah," he replied and turned to Eric while he thought. "Will it be missed? Is it possible that her situation has changed and that she has higher access now? Is this information a plant? Has she been compromised?" He looked up from his musings.

Eric shrugged his shoulders. "Will they know it's missing?" Eric asked. "She didn't seem worried about that. Just that Veroushka might have been found out somehow."

"Then there's you." Turner fixed Eric with a menacing stare. "You were not ever to meet VERNA. You are just a courier, not an agent. You don't have the training for contact with agents or for more than just delivery operations."

Eric didn't know what to say. "Hey, it wasn't my idea."

"You took a great risk in trusting this woman. What if she was a Soviet agent? What if it had been a trap? What if this is an elaborate ruse? Only one person knows what VERNA—or Lena—looks like. That is, until now." Turner held up a hand to silence Eric's response. "She is a valuable asset who could be in danger because of this incident." He paced back and forth in front of the window.

"Well, I'm sorry, but she made the decision to carry out the mission. She's the one who took the risk to get the documents," Eric said hotly. "Seems to me she did great work to get this information to you. She took the risk."

Turner stopped in his tracks. "Yes, but she's a trained agent. And she did good work here. I agree." He paused. "I just hope her cover isn't blown." Then he looked at his watch. "I just have time to make the one fifteen train to Stockholm."

His face changed to a more tranquil expression. "Anyway, you made it back alive with the documents. Good work on that part of it."

"And I did the other deliveries and pickups."

"Yeah, there's that too." Turner reached in his pocket and handed Eric an envelope. "Here is your payment." Then the stern look again. "Don't tell anyone about this affair. Do you understand? *No one.* I will be in touch soon."

Turner left the building ten minutes ahead of Eric, and he watched his back for any tails. Eric left and walked in the opposite direction, again checking for unwanted company. He rushed to his bank and deposited the cash in a safe-deposit box right away so that he wouldn't have to carry it around with him. Uppsala was very safe, but still, the idea of carrying over US$2,000 in cash with him made him nervous. He took a bus back to Flogsta.

***

Eric's life at home was becoming complicated, as he spent many nights with Sabrina. She wanted him to move in with her permanently, whatever that meant. He was in no hurry to change the way things were. He wanted to let time work things out.

Things were more or less normal for the first part of the year. The demands of Eric's classes eased up a bit, and he was able to make more time for his studies, since he didn't need to do as many liquor runs to raise cash. There were parties every weekend, and Leela and Tika outdid themselves with one party in late February.

That same month, Eric learned that Omar was going to make another trip home to Mosul to see his mother and to meet with local leaders. Eric talked to him about the risk involved, but his Kurdish friend told him that he wasn't concerned.

"Allah will do what he will do," Omar said. "I must go and meet those who need to know how I can help my people. I must thank you again for your part in this."

"I didn't do anything."

Omar had a positive expression on his face. "My people now have hope that the great United States may not work against us. In fact, your country may now actually support my people's claim for autonomy within Iraq." He beamed from ear to ear. "It would be so great for my people to be free!"

Eric thought, *Omar is a wonderful optimist.* Eric wasn't so sure of the direction of his country. He wouldn't want to rely on the US keeping its word right now, with all the political dissent at home. He tried to explain to Omar that American politicians weren't the most reliable people in the world, but Omar's enthusiasm would not be deterred.

Turner and Eric had two meetings in as many days in which they discussed their work arrangement and what Turner called a new opportunity for Eric. At one such meeting at a rented office in Stockholm, he told Eric that he had also followed up on the trip to Helsinki.

"I found out that Veroushka and Lena are fine. No covers blown. Veroushka had just panicked. Lena's handler didn't find any reason to believe that her cover had been compromised."

"That's a relief," Eric said. It meant that the mysterious Lena was also safe.

They went over all the details of the Helsinki meeting again and again to be sure that they hadn't missed something. He had Eric verify the identity of the woman he had met with via a file photo that his agency had of Lena. After a thorough investigation, Turner had decided that his own network had not been compromised. It meant they could pick up where they had left off.

"Eric, up until now you have been carrying documents and books that form the basis of the communications system that was used by my agents and those of another network. They have mostly been blind drops to keep everyone's identity safe."

"Why did I take Lena a college textbook?"

"You aren't supposed to look in the packages, Eric. For Christ's sake." Turner gave him one of his *pay attention* looks. "Different agents use somewhat different coding systems for messages. In VERNA's case we use a variation of the classic book cipher. She was given a very specific Penguin Books printing of Adam Smith's *The Wealth of Nations*. It's one of the classic economic texts that nearly every economist like her would be likely to have on her bookshelf, even in Russia. Because VERNA works as an economist, it would be natural for her to have Smith in her library. Her book had a limited press run of only two thousand copies. Most of the books had been destroyed by a fire, but a few survived, and that reduces the chance anyone would have exactly the same pagination as the unusual copy."

"But how does it work with just books?" Eric asked.

"Here, I'll show you," Turner said. "You start with a message in plain text and then you go through the key to find those words wherever they occur in the key." Turner pulled out a copy of Smith's book. "For instance, the word *situation* occurs in the book, the key, on page thirty-five and on line twenty-nine, as the third word in the line. This could be encoded as 35 29 03. So a message would be represented by a long string of sets of three numbers. Without the exact same book, it wouldn't be possible to interpret the message. Even with modern computational techniques, it is difficult to translate because most code-breaking strategies rely on the relative frequency of letters in a given language. Obviously, for the system to work, both the sender and the recipient of a message would need to have the exact same book to use as a key in the coding and decoding of the message."

Eric took the book and paged through it. "So this is the basis of the code Lena uses?"

"Right, and there can be an additional encryption that is used to scramble the numbers again so that it's not clear what type of encoding has been done. This involves the use of a substitution cipher as a second step. There have been many variations on these codes and ciphers that have been used at different times in history. This one is reliable, relatively safe from detection, and simple to use.

"I also learned that Lena—sorry, now you have me doing it—VERNA has indeed changed her position within the EPB. She is on temporary assignment to the Committee on Restructuring. That's a working group that was mentioned in the memo she sent us in Helsinki."

"So that's the Economic Planning Bureau?"

"Yeah," Turner clarified. "And the committee is in charge of restructuring certain industries within the Soviet Union. Apparently the old structure wasn't creating the desired results, and people and whole industrial plants were being redeployed or replaced due to poor performance."

"That sounds like a big deal. Heads must have rolled for such an extensive shake-up to occur," Eric commented.

"Right. It's important because it signaled that the underlying economy of the USSR is crumbling, and along with it, we may see a replacement of many of the old hands that still control much of the economic power in the Kremlin."

"So Lena got ahold of some really useful info then."

"Yes," Turner continued, "and what worries me is the news that the Russians are also working on a computer model of the entire Soviet economy that could help them improve the performance of whole industries. That could be a problem for the West because it could strengthen their economy."

"But we keep hoping that their economy will fail and lead to a change of government," Eric said. "To some people who are more friendly to the West."

"I think you are starting to get the way we think around here." Turner grinned at his courier.

"If the Soviet economy fails, they will have no money for weapons and expansionism, and the population will become unhappy." Eric put it together. "Unhappy people lead to unrest and pressure on the government to change. That is good for Europe and America."

"OK, so the upshot of all this is that you will continue to make deliveries, but now we want you to do it under an assumed name, Eric Larson. We kept your first name the same to make it easier for you to fit into the new role." Turner smiled at Eric. "It will be safer in the long run. If they ever get onto you, at least your name and family will be isolated from any retaliation." He looked doubtful. "At least that's the thinking."

"So I'll get a secret identity? Like an agent?"

"Yes, but you won't be a full-fledged agent, just a courier as before. It's just a precaution." Turner stressed that he wouldn't receive agent training. "You'll now travel on a new US passport with a Swedish resident visa. As Eric Larson, your cover is that you are a new book sales representative for a small dealer in collectible history and economics books. You're an American expatriate who left the US because of political differences with the current administration and because your grandfather's roots are in Sweden. That's why you decided to try living in Uppsala. You are based in Stockholm, where a small bookshop is being used as a cover. You, as Larson, will make two or three trips to Helsinki and Leningrad over the next few weeks to establish a pattern of travel and bona fides as a book representative."

"I'm not sure I can do that. I don't know that much about the book business." Eric wasn't sure this was a good idea.

Turner handed him a passport with his likeness inside next to his new name. "We placed several travel visas in there to make it look used.

They document your travels in Scandinavia and the Germanys. You'll have to extend the record into Finland and the USSR yourself with a few warm-up trips over the next several weeks."

"I'm not so sure, Mike. I need to learn a lot to make this work." Eric was cautious. "What's in it for me?"

"Oh, don't you worry about that. The pay is substantial."

"Can I get someone to tell me what I'm supposed to do? Some training?"

"Already planned," Turner said, then grinned. "Look, Eric. I think you will be a natural bookdealer since you already have an interest in history and know some basic economics. And you'll mostly be doing what you have been doing but now with a few stops at bookstores. You'll have a cover story and the documentation to verify why you are there. The cover also allows you to carry printed material back and forth across the border to Russia. It's a piece of cake."

"I'll give it a try, Mike. Then we'll see how it goes. OK?"

He stepped out into the frigid air, and his breath turned to an icy cloud as he hustled toward the central station to catch the train to return to Uppsala. He thought about his conversation with Turner while he walked. Maybe this could be a good thing. What could possibly go wrong?

Chapter 11

Helsinki, Finland, and Leningrad, Russia
Tuesday, March 14, 1972

Eric Larson made two outings to Helsinki to visit bookdealers who specialized in history texts. He had studied with a bookseller in Stockholm to learn what he needed concerning the books he carried and what he should know about books in general as a new book representative. Eric found it easy to play this role. His fledgling ability in Swedish allowed him to carry on a conversation reasonably well if people spoke slowly. It also allowed him to cover his weaknesses because people thought it was his language skills that accounted for any misstatements he made. With a few dealers, he could even speak English if they preferred.

On Tuesday, Eric made his first trip to Leningrad by train from Helsinki. The train left the Central railway station in Helsinki at 5:20 p.m. and rumbled northeast to Lahti before heading east to Kouvola and finally reaching the border crossing at Vainikkala. The route was through forested land the entire way except for the areas near towns. All Eric could make out from the train's window in the darkness were trees, trees, and more trees—conifers, birch, and occasional larches. Otherwise, he could see the lighted stations when they stopped for passengers.

He had time on the train to learn about the city's history. Leningrad was originally called Saint Petersburg because it was founded by Tsar Peter I of Russia, "Peter the Great," in 1703. It was the capital of the Russian Empire from that time until the Russian Revolution in 1917. It was called Petrograd for several years before being renamed for Comrade Lenin in 1924. While the political power in Russia had migrated largely to Moscow, much of the economic and cultural activity and trade with Western Europe passed through Leningrad.

The Russian border crossing took a great deal of time due to the need to go through passport control and to inspect all cargo on the train. Fortunately, the passengers didn't have to disembark for this process, as they often did when there was political tension between Finland and the Soviets. They crossed at night, so the lost time was made up in sleeping through the whole affair. At dawn, they crossed the embayment at the small Russian city of Vyborg, where they had a half-hour delay while a freight train cleared the tracks in front of them. Their train continued south to Leningrad.

They finally reached the Finlyandsky railway station in Leningrad, which was built in 1870 to handle transport to the north and west of the city. It was the station where Vladimir Lenin arrived from Helsinki in disguise on April 3, 1917, to begin the events leading to the October Revolution in Russia. Eric disembarked after close to seventeen hours of travel from Helsinki.

He cleared the police checkpoint and collected his trunkful of books. He then walked outside to get a government-approved taxi. No doubt the driver would report his movements and the hotel where he would be staying.

The Finlyandsky railway station was located on the north side of the Neva River, and Eric's hotel was in the old central part of town. He took the taxi across the river on the Liteyny Bridge to the south bank of the Neva and continued up Nevskiy Prospekt, where he got out at the somewhat rundown Nevskiy Hotel. It was a good location for him because it was near the subway and several bus stops, which would constitute his main means of transportation around the city. Nevskiy Prospekt was one of the major avenues running directly into the heart of the city.

The hotel was in a large, ancient building that was operated by the state tourism agency, Intourist. Eric checked in at the desk after a very long wait. A room had indeed been reserved for him, and he was told it was one of the "good" rooms, in that most things in it worked.

He trudged up to the room on the third floor and found out why this was true. There was barely anything present in the space to operate. It had an old metal frame bed, two chairs, a table, a dresser, a nightstand, a lamp, and a small closet. Eric had requested a room with a private bath, so he was sent there with linens and a bath curtain that surrounded the bathtub. He unpacked a few things and decided to place some items in the hotel safe downstairs. Then he left his large book trunk in the room, secure with the knowledge of its unique design.

In many ways Leningrad wasn't very different from Helsinki or Stockholm in its layout except that it had several navigable canals and the Neva River, all of which flowed through its center. Because of its canals, the city was often called the Venice of the North, although the canals froze over in the winter. The architecture was similar to other northern cities in Scandinavia, with comparable commercial buildings and street plans. However, the content of the stores and the infrastructure of the city were very different.

Several stores had empty shelves due to periodic shortages of many commodities and supplies. Communications were strained to the point of being nonexistent at times because the telephones often didn't work well, if at all. There were many cars on the street in the daytime but almost none at night except for taxis and public transport.

After dark, much of the city shut down as vendors and other citizens went home to their apartments in the vast urban and suburban panel houses or project-like apartment buildings that the government had constructed as their housing sector. The buildings had little color and often had no new paint on their walls due to supply shortages and lack of pride on the part of the residents.

The people of Leningrad were rather gloomy in their outlook and demeanor. This wasn't entirely different from Scandinavia in the winter, due to the extended darkness and its effects on human psychology. But it seemed much more pronounced here, as if things were never going to get better and summer would never come.

Eric was in town for only three days. He made the rounds of bookdealers he had been assigned and left samples of books at the ones who were to receive them. He also collected a few books that he was to ferry back to Stockholm as samples or to fill special orders. Each day he would eat breakfast at the hotel, where the meal was included in the price of the room. He had lunch either with a dealer who he visited or on his own in the central part of town. In the evening, he had cocktails at the hotel bar and dinner at the little restaurant next door. The food was fairly good and very inexpensive, even at the absurd exchange rate that the Russians gave for rubles to Swedish kronor.

On his final night in Leningrad, he was having drinks at the Nevskiy Bar in the hotel, standing at the counter sipping a local beer. He couldn't remember the full name of the beer, but he recalled that it was nicknamed Peter's pivo by most Russians and that it was a pretty good amber-colored lager. The bartender told him that it was made by a company run by a Dutchman who had come to Leningrad in the 1960s. He had established a brewery that was accepted by the local officials because it wasn't big enough to compete with the government-authorized counterparts. And besides, they liked the beer too.

As he sipped the brew, a young man with spiked black hair pushed up next to him at the bar and ordered vodka for his table. Without looking at Eric he said in English, "A friend wants to see you."

"*Ursëkta me?*" Eric responded first in Swedish and then in his limited Russian. "*Chto ty skazal?* What did you say?"

The man's drinks arrived before he could answer the question. He motioned toward a small table at the rear of the bar, and Eric turned to where he pointed.

A young woman was sitting at the back of the room with two other people—friends by the looks of it, as they all downed their shots of vodka in a toast. On seeing Eric gaze her way, the woman smiled and then hid her face beneath her broad-brimmed fur hat.

He recognized her at once as Lena.

He hurried to pay his tab with a fifty-ruble note, surreptitiously observing other people in the tavern to see if he was being watched. In the meantime, Lena and her friends had gotten up and sauntered toward the exit. She caught Eric's eye as she trailed behind and walked out the door, indicating that he was to follow. He saw her turn to the right on the sidewalk. After a minute, he left the bar.

He stepped out onto the street, buttoning up his coat against the cold arctic wind and putting on his newly purchased fur hat and mittens. He looked both ways on the empty street. Lena was nowhere in sight. A little concerned that he had lost her, he started to walk down the sidewalk to the right. There were few people on the street at this time, and it was just beginning to spit some snowflakes as the wind gusted from the west.

Eric walked briskly to the corner. Around to the right, he saw Lena standing by the open rear door of a battered black sedan. She motioned him over.

"It is so nice to see you again!" she called out as he approached. She gave him a big hug. "I hoped to find you here tonight. I wanted to take you to my favorite place and have you meet some of my comrades. I told them we made good friends when I was in Helsinki several weeks ago."

Without saying more, she bent down and slid into the back seat of the car. "Come on," she beckoned from inside.

He ducked down to look into the vehicle and appraise its occupants to be sure there were no burly policemen inside. The driver was a young girl with a punk haircut, a heavy parka, and a very short skirt. When Eric got in, the car lurched forward and sputtered down the street. Another woman was squeezed into the back seat on the other side of Lena. She was about the same height as Lena, as far as he could see, but the heavy makeup and bulky coat made it difficult to tell much more about her. The young man with spiked black hair and dressed all in black leather sat in the front seat of the car. He was the one who had spoken to Eric in the bar. He was slugging down vodka from a half-liter bottle and carrying on a raucous conversation with the young driver, his apparent girlfriend.

Speaking English, Lena introduced her friends. "This is Nadya here next to me. She is an old friend from my gymnasium days. She has known me forever. That is Mikhail in front. We call him Misha and you can too. He is madly in love with my sister, Katinka. She is the wild girl who is driving. She is much too young for him, but she is also crazy in love. I do not know why."

"*Dobriy Vecher.* Good evening," Eric mumbled in Russian.

This brought a laugh from the man and a hello from Nadya.

Lena leaned in to speak to him now. "I found out you were in my city—*ne sprashivay*—don't ask how—so I came to find you. My handler said a new courier was coming from Sweden, an American. I knew it must be you. He said you would be at this hotel, which has one of my drop sites. It was not easy, but I had to thank you for helping me when we met last. I feel like I know you very well already." Her blue eyes sparkled, but her voice was a little slurred, no doubt from the vodka she had been drinking already.

"*Privet!* My friends, this is the man I told you I met," she blurted out in pleasant if unsteady conversation. "Did I not tell you, Katie? I had just the best luck and ran into him today on the street and now we will show him fun times in our city. OK? *Da?*"

Eric wondered why she had just lied about meeting him on the street. Why misrepresent how she knew he was in town?

Then she spoke in Russian with her friends for a minute, as if working out where they should go for the night.

"You see," she said, laughing and grabbing his left arm, "we will take good care of you. We will go to my favorite bar for drinks and then maybe to a secret club. We have to find out where a party will be."

"If we can." Nadya laughed.

Lena leaned back in the seat next to him. "Relax and enjoy!"

Eric pulled her over close to him so that he could whisper in her ear. "What are you doing? This is against protocol! Why did you want to see me? Is something wrong?" He smelled vodka on her breath as her face nearly bumped into his. "What's going on?"

She mumbled a few words in Russian to him and began to snuggle into his shoulder. She kissed him on the neck and went to sleep.

"She has been talking about you all evening," said Nadya in English. "She seems to like you, and I can see why. But do not worry. She is a little drunk and has been celebrating since she left work." She poked Lena in the arm. "Today is her birthday, you know, and she always gets crazy on her birthday."

"We go now to Severnoye Siyaniye, or the Northern Lights. It is favorite nightspot. We have many friends we meet there," Misha called from the front seat in broken English. "Lena said you are good guy, but she not say much about you. She likes you, so is OK with me."

They drove for some time on the nearly vacant streets. Eric realized that it was unusual for these young people to have a personal car and to be driving around the city at night. There was a city curfew later that they would have to be careful not to break. He realized also that it was very unusual for Lena to contact him in this way and to risk blowing her cover. The more he thought about it, the more he believed she might be a security risk.

After approximately ten minutes, Katya slowed the car and carefully pulled into a dark alley. She squeezed to the side of the narrow passage and parked. It was enough to worry Eric.

"We are here!" Lena cried, becoming wide awake again.

They all stumbled out of the car on the side not crammed against a brick wall and went down the alley. At a metal door, Misha stopped and knocked. A small slide opened over a four-by-four-inch peephole like the ones in the old speakeasies in Chicago.

"*Privet*, Anatoly!" was all Misha said. The eye that appeared looked them over and closed the slide. The door opened and led into a hallway. Anatoly was apparently a serious bodybuilder by the looks of him, short, dark, and very intense—the perfect bouncer. Loud music flooded their ears, coming from farther down the hallway that opened up to a barroom. As they entered, a few people turned to see who had arrived and some of them greeted his companions.

They were in an old tavern with an ancient, carved wooden bar that ran the length of the room. They slid into a booth at the side of the bar, Lena in first, then Eric, and finally Nadya on one side. Misha and Katya sat on the other side, already necking. Katya looked like she was barely sixteen years old, and Eric guessed that Misha was in his early twenties. Katya had thin hair that was cut short and dyed pink. She was a pretty girl but was wearing lots of makeup to look more severe and exotic.

Misha was a well-built man with average features, black hair, and dark stubble on his cheeks, as if he had forgotten to shave that morning. He had shadowy, observant eyes, a small nose, and a roundish face. Eric had the impression that Misha could hold his own in a bar fight. He looked like he hadn't had an easy life, but he laughed freely and was clearly enthralled by the young woman who was pressed against his side.

The bartender came over with a bottle of vodka and five glasses and set them down. "Lena, you should look after your sister better than this," he said sternly in Russian. "She is too young to get on with this Misha fellow, and you know better." He glanced at Misha, and Katya swatted him on the arm with her hand as she grinned wildly at him.

"I know, Andre, I know," Lena answered. "Soon I will tell her what he is really like if she has not found out for herself."

The barman went away, and Misha filled the five glasses to the rims. "S'dniom rozhdeniya!"—happy birthday—he said and lifted his glass to Lena. They began to sing the Russian version of "Happy Birthday to You." Several people from the tavern joined in and came over after it finished, congratulating Lena. Eric wondered how many years she was celebrating.

The five of them talked after that in a mixture of Russian and English and had two or three additional drinks. Eric sipped his vodka slowly, since he was a lightweight by Russian standards.

He learned that Lena's sister was on the university track at gymnasium and would likely enter university next fall. She wasn't sure which school she would attend. He just hoped that, at the rate she was drinking, she would have a few brain cells left for education. Misha was an auto mechanic who hadn't done well in school but who was very gifted with machines. Nadya was a longtime friend who Lena partied with and trusted with her secrets.

They had a good time during the night, settling into a comfortable conversation, with Lena, Nadya, and Eric speaking in English. Lena's friends tried to teach Eric some Russian phrases, but he couldn't seem to pronounce anything properly, to the amusement of Misha especially, who was involved in heavy petting with Katya.

Just before midnight, the bartender, Andre, told them that they must leave in order to beat the curfew. After one more shot for the road, they drove very carefully back to Nevskiy Prospekt to drop off Eric.

Lena and Eric made plans to see each other on his next trip to Leningrad in a few weeks. She gave him the telephone number of Misha's repair shop to memorize. He would call when he arrived, and Misha would relay the message to Lena through her sister because Lena had no phone. Eric and Lena would meet at the Ploshchad Vosstaniya, the plaza near the Moskovsky railway station on Nevskiy Prospekt at 6:00 p.m. She told him it was very safe for them to meet that way.

Lena gave him a warm kiss good night and so did her drunken sister. They left him a block from his hotel so that the car wouldn't be seen by the hotel security guard.

Eric said good night and stood on the sidewalk, watching the black sedan slowly disappear down the street. He was moderately drunk but also elated to have seen Lena again. Part of him wondered whether their meeting was a good idea from a security point of view. He walked quickly to his hotel and entered just before midnight, receiving a glare from the doorman, who undoubtedly disliked foreigners. Eric didn't care. He had a lot on his mind, especially the lovely Lena.

***

The next morning, Eric packed his bags, checked out of the hotel, and made his way to the Finlyandsky railway station to catch the train back to Helsinki. The train left on time at noon, and the return trip to Finland was uneventful. He flew from Helsinki to Stockholm. He was glad to be able to avoid the ferry on these longer trips.

He dropped off the trunk at the bookshop and rode the train to Uppsala, where he deposited a comprehensive report that he had composed on the long train ride, detailing his various contacts with booksellers.

He didn't mention seeing Lena in his report.

The following day, Eric met Turner to complete his debriefing from the Russian trip. He described his appointments with booksellers and the books he had brought back from Leningrad. He also went over the more clandestine drop that he had made. It was a new dead drop to be used by a fresh contact that the CIA had recruited. Because Eric was the first to test the site, there was some concern about how it had gone. Eric was chosen to make the delivery, since Leningrad was now within his normal route.

Eric finally confessed to meeting Lena on the trip. Turner was concerned that Lena had contacted Eric in Leningrad but said that it may be useful to meet with her directly on occasion. Again he told Eric that he must stick to established protocols and to be extremely careful when "in country." He explained that there was little the agency could do for him if he was arrested by police or, worse, by any security personnel.

Eric thought, *Great! Now he tells me.*

Chapter 12

Leningrad, Russia
April 1972

Eric made another trip to Leningrad in early April as planned. It was more or less a repeat of his previous trip: flying to Helsinki, attending several meetings, and then taking the train into Russia. He checked into the Nevskiy Hotel again and ventured out to conduct business with bookdealers.

In the afternoon of the first day, he called Misha to inform him that he was in town and that he wanted to get together with Lena. Misha said he would let her know.

Eric finished his meetings for the day and returned to the hotel to freshen up. He had just enough time to catch a bus headed for the Moskovsky railway station on Nevskiy Prospekt, the planned rendezvous point.

He arrived right at 6:00 p.m. and had to hurry across the street to the plaza called Ploshchad Vosstaniya. It was one of those cold winter nights in Leningrad, with a steady breeze that cut through his coat and flesh to the bone. He had purchased a Russian newspaper, *Izvestia*, in the hotel lobby but hadn't thought of the fact that it would be dark when he arrived. Instead, he used the paper to cover the seat of a bench on one side of the plaza and sat on it despite the limited insulation it provided. Eric waited for nearly fifteen minutes before he noticed a woman on the far side of the plaza in a long wool coat that hung clear to the ground. It looked like she could be Lena, so he got up and nonchalantly walked to that side of the plaza. She crossed the street to a newsstand and waited for him to overtake her as she browsed the rack of government-approved magazines. He approached the stand and scanned her to make sure who it was. He was rewarded with a quick smile. Then she nodded down the street and walked away. He followed in a minute or two after checking for any curious people in the thinning pedestrian traffic.

He found her in the doorway of a building halfway down the block. She reached for Eric's coat and then pulled him in beside her. They kissed cordially.

"Eric, it is so good to see you again!" she gushed, her cheeks bright red from the cold. "We are going to have so much nice time tonight. Come, let's go to the Northern Lights!"

They took a public bus down Nevskiy Prospekt for several blocks and walked the rest of the way in the freezing weather. They were in great need of a hot toddy by the time they reached the tavern with its blacked-out windows and sturdy steel door. They found a booth, and Andre came over with a bottle of vodka and two glasses.

"*Dobriy Vecher!*" he said. "Good evening, on such a cold and windy night."

Eric responded pleasantly, and Andre gave him the once-over, glancing at Lena as if he were her big brother and protector. They each ordered a bowl of steaming corned beef stew for dinner.

Eric and Lena caught up on news and what they had each been doing since they had last met. "Eric, I was so hungover the next day after my birthday. I could hardly believe we had met that night." She smiled sheepishly. "But it was fun, was it not?"

"It was a big surprise, but yes, it was fun."

"You know, the next morning I was late for work, and my boss lectured me about such behavior on a workday." She thought it was very funny and laughed at it again and again as she told Eric what her boss's face looked like as he tried to make his point. "But he likes me and told me that he would cover for me because it was my birthday, after all."

She told him that important things were happening at her office at the EPB. They were compiling all the economic information from the entire country as well as many of the most important trading partners in the Soviet sphere of influence.

"For the first time, we are entering it all onto a mainframe computer in order to summarize the data but also so we can model it to increase productivity." Lena was deadly serious. "I do not know the details of the model, but Nadya is secretary to the chairman of the computer services group. She has heard much about how it will work."

"Really?" Eric said as he stared into her blue eyes. "That sounds like a massive undertaking." He was surprised at this revelation of a project that was supposedly secret. "Is Nadya a programmer then?"

"No, but I am an economist and will be in charge of getting the data sets ready for the program. I can program straightforward projects but not something this complex."

After a few more drinks, Lena told him all about the modeling project. They were making a model of how the economy worked. With it they could experiment on how to change the mixture of industries and trade to improve the country's performance.

"Most of the data has been entered, and the model is working—but the modelers cannot explain why it does not reproduce all the known results." She leaned close to him to whisper, "I myself have seen a portion of the model code, but I have not had time to study it."

"Why is the modeling being done here and not in Moscow?" Eric asked. "Surely it is an important state secret."

"It is being done here in Leningrad because this is where the great Leningrad Technical Institute, the university, is located. We have the fastest and most modern computer in the Soviet Union, except, of course, for the computers managed by the military." She corrected herself with a frown. "Loyal communist professors from the faculty of applied mathematics are the creative brains designing the model while bureaucrats from the EPB are assembling the data." She smiled prettily. "I and my workers."

"But why are you making a computer model of the economy?"

Lena sat up straight and explained that the model had begun as an academic project at the university. As its value as a planning and management tool for the economy became clear to the government, the model was viewed as a new secret weapon in the Cold War with the West. She grinned. "It is now made a classified project of great national security value. And I am a part of it."

"I'm impressed," Eric said seriously.

She grabbed his arm. "Isn't it exciting?"

By this time Lena's sister, Katya, had arrived with Misha, and they changed topics to the more fun things in their lives. The two lovebirds had already eaten, so Eric and Lena simply had a drink and talked freely with them about their day.

After a while, Misha insisted that they should go to a special party. He had found out that there was a Rurik party at a warehouse in the Vyborgskaya sector of town, and they could make it over there if they drove across the "old bridge," whatever that meant. Rurik was an ancient Viking who had helped settle the land called Rus, the ancestral homeland of Russia. He was rumored to have loved wild pagan festivals.

They said goodbye to the barman and then loaded into Misha's car. Misha drove Eric to his hotel. It was only nine o'clock, but they told him that he should make an appearance so that if they got back late after curfew, he wouldn't get into trouble.

Eric thought the party sounded like fun but it might be risky. When he brought this up with Lena, she laughed and said, "The risk is what adds the adventure, yes?"

Eric walked into the lobby and asked for his key and checked for messages. Then he made a big deal of saying good night and took the elevator upstairs. There he picked up a few things he might need and went down the back stairway and out the backdoor. There wasn't a doorman posted there or any real foot traffic except for staff coming and going for work.

Misha's car was parked a hundred yards away down the alley. Eric walked quickly to join his new friends and clambered into the back seat, where Katya passed him a liquor bottle.

"How do you people know all these tricks for skirting the curfew and the authorities?" Eric asked. "You seem to have a plan for everything."

Katya explained, "We live in this country and so we must know how to survive everything. It is not just to avoid curfew, you know." She said loudly with glee, "We have to know who to talk to if we want to buy the right auto parts, or certain foods, or to rent an apartment." She laughed as she leaned over the back of the front seat to talk. "It is the way our system works here—or doesn't work. Here the system fails many ways, so you learn to . . . how do you say it? To compensate."

Misha added, "Comrades who will take a little money to let you get on the list for an apartment quicker, or to get on the list at all."

Katya added, "Even the police—or maybe no surprise—especially the police can be persuaded to look the wrong way sometimes."

"Yes," Misha added. "Once Katie and I were out . . . too late, and a police stopped us to see what we doing. I asked him if he could not report us. I say we were out only little bit past curfew—we are three hours late!" They both laughed crazily.

"He said when he was young man, it happened once to him . . . he missed a bus. He said maybe he forget he seen us, letting us know he was able to be convinced that this was right thing to do. I offer him a little money and he pretend to be offend, but he put the rubles in pocket." Misha laughed.

"Really?" Eric couldn't believe it.

"I offered to help him fix his car sometime, if he needed, and he said this would be a great act of friendship. He let us go, and in week he came with son's car that needs a repair that is hard find parts for. So I helped him and he is my friend now. When I have parking problems or need a permit something, he helps. It is how it is here, one hand wash the other, as you say. *Da?*"

They all laughed at the irony of how things worked and did not work.

Lena chimed in, "The party we are going to will not be raided by the police because the organizers have gotten a form of police permission to have it."

Misha explained, "Probably few bottles of whisky find their way to the policeman's car tonight, and he be very happy. So is with many things. There are work-arounds many everyday living situations here."

"But the really poor people who have nothing to trade," Lena said, "they are the ones destined to stand in line for everything they need—toilet paper or beef or apartments."

Misha drove north across an old bridge and into an industrial area. There were many factories there, some busy even at night, and a few that looked like they were out of business. He seemed to know exactly where he was going and made several turns before coming to an open metal gate into a large work yard. A man at the gate motioned for the car to stop and then came over. Misha said the correct password and was waved through to the far side of the yard. There they could see many cars parked, some brand new and many dilapidated. They could already hear very loud music bursting forth from a large metal building ahead.

Katya began to dance as soon as she got out of the car and screamed with delight. They were all a bit buzzed and ready to burn up the dance floor. Lena took Eric's hand and led him to the warehouse door.

Inside, the music was deafening as a heavy metal rock band raged on in a long, dramatic piece that was dominated by lead guitar riffs that would have made Led Zeppelin proud. The music was so loud that it was impossible to talk or to do anything but dance and drink.

Lena and Eric danced until the band took a break. They went outside to talk as a second band prepared to rock the stage. They had time to chat a little before the music began again, this time with the Russian version of psychedelic rock.

They went back inside for a while to dance, but the music was so forceful that they had to retreat outside once more. Later, when that band went on break, they found Misha and Katya staggering around, drinking vodka and dancing to the music still ringing in their heads.

Eric asked Lena, "Can Misha drive after all this booze? And it looks like Katie is too drunk for her own good."

Lena puzzled at the word *booze*, then smiled. "Maybe you are right. It is time to leave. My sister is also acting very oddly. I hope she didn't take any pills." She tried to get the vodka bottle away from Misha and finally succeeded.

Eric had been drinking only beer that night and was glad of it. Lena had been watching her intake, so she was pleasantly drunk but not incapacitated. Katya had now fallen down and was retching something green from her stomach. Misha kneeled next to her to hold her hair up out of the mess. It turned out that they weren't the only ones getting sick, as dozens of people were vomiting all around them.

Lena said with a concerned look, "Something is wrong. Katinka does not usually get so drunk."

Misha saw Lena's face and said, "Someone at party was selling 'poor man's LSD,' and Katie tried it."

"It was just one little pill," Katya muttered between retches.

Lena decided to leave right away. "Who knows what she has taken? It could be something new or a bad formula. We have to go home now to take care of little Katie."

Katya didn't want to go and shouted some nasty things at her overly controlling sister. It translated roughly as "Fuck you, bitch!"

Misha and Eric manhandled her into the back seat of the car. Lena disentangled the vehicle from the parking lot and drove out of the factory yard, with Eric riding shotgun. The two lovebirds were slumped down in the back seat. Katya at first felt nauseous, but she soon became very rowdy and overheated. She stripped off her sweater and bra and hung out the window, making cries of wild joy. After a few moments of this, Misha hauled her inside, and they settled into serious necking and finally sex.

"Oh God," Lena muttered. "Not with the sex again. It is all they do."

Eric chuckled at the passionate commotion in the back seat. He began to sing his version of one of the songs the final band had played and was joined by Lena, who couldn't carry the tune. They both laughed at their poor rendition.

Lena drove on like a trooper in spite of the back seat activities. At first, she got lost navigating out of the industrial area, but with Misha's help, she found the way back to the bridge and familiar streets.

Lena drove directly to the apartment where she and Katya lived, even though her sister now spent much of her time at Misha's place. Katya had passed out completely by this time, and Misha and Eric carried her up the three flights of stairs. For such a small body, she seemed to get heavier with each floor they ascended. Lena and Misha changed her out of her now badly soiled clothes and into flannel pajamas. Misha climbed into bed beside her and passed out.

Lena and Eric sat in the living room on her pullout sofa. "I had to let her have my bedroom because she had Misha over so many times that I could not use the living room when they were here having sex day and night. Thank God she is on the pill or the apartment would be even more crowded!"

She fell silent for a moment but then began to laugh. "That girl is going to use herself up too fast if she is not careful." She was deep in thought when Eric put an arm around her. "She is so crazy all the time. But I love her completely." She snuggled against him.

Lena and Eric sat and talked for a while about the wild party. She had no idea who the bands were. Then she sat up straight and said, "Eric, it is too late to go back to the hotel. You will have to spend the night here." She gave him a sly smile. "If you want to, of course."

He leaned over and kissed her. She nestled into him with passion, and soon they were pulling off each other's clothes.

"Wait, wait," she said. "Let us make the bed before we get too hot and sexy."

They pulled out the bed, and she brought out pillows. She turned out the lights except for a night-light and vanished into the bathroom for a while. Eric waited, and soon she came out sporting a short flannel nightshirt with bows on the low-cut neckline, looking mischievous.

Eric took his turn in the small bath. When he returned to the living room, she was in bed, and he slid in beside her wearing nothing.

"So that is what you think will happen? Are you so sure of your luck?" She giggled.

As he reached for her, he found that she had already taken off her nightgown. She was very warm and ready beneath the covers.

She apparently believed she would be lucky too, he thought.

***

Katya was sick with a major headache and the sweats for all of the next day after the Rurik party. They still didn't know what drug she had taken, but she said it brought on frightening dreams and even hallucinations. She swore that she wouldn't try a drug from an unknown source again, but Lena was convinced that she would do it again, as she had many times in the past.

"She is too young to have her mind scrambled like an egg," Lena worried. "She is all that I have left of my family, and I do not want her to hurt herself in this way." She sighed. "I have talked to Misha, and he promised he would try to keep her from drinking so much and partying all the time." Her face became serious. "He loves her, but he is just too young to know much better himself."

Eric ventured out each day to carry out his duties with booksellers and to do some pickups and drops at secret sites. Luckily, his work was uneventful and he spent the remains of each day with Lena. It was an enjoyable routine.

Lena and Eric had time to get to know each other well over those few days. She was a gentle and thoughtful person who worried a lot about her family and friends. When alone, she was more serious than when out drinking with her friends. She was concerned about her sister's future and what her own future would be in this crazy country of theirs. They spent time in bed making love, keeping warm, and drinking beer while listening to emotional Russian ballads on Lena's tape player. Eric decided that he would bring her new musical cassettes on his next visit.

On their last night together, she said, "What will we do? We have no future like this. No one can plan on anything, even for a few weeks ahead." She looked morose. "The government controls everything, and they do such a bad job. One year we have no cars, so the next year we have cars but no refrigerators. How can people live like this? Jobs, no jobs. Food, no food. The only thing that we have plenty of is vodka, and that is killing us too." She looked at Eric to see if he understood, a frown on her face, her blue eyes sad.

"Who can have children in a life like this? What would be their future?" she murmured. "If you love your child, would you bring him or her into such a world?"

Eric told her that life in America was different in many ways. Sure, Americans had problems too, but they always had basic food and necessities. They had their poor people also, but based on what Lena told him, the American poor had it much better than the poor in Russia. At least most of the rural poor in America had a piece of land where they could grow food and live. In Russia, nobody really owned the land except the government and a few Communist Party members who had special privileges.

"Now I have to tell you how I got started helping Americans obtain information," Lena said, scanning his face for a reaction.

"I wondered how that happened."

"You see, both of our parents passed away suddenly some years ago. We went to live with our aunt here in Leningrad. I was serious student and made good grades, especially in mathematics." She grinned at the memory. "Katie is smart but hated school, but she was much younger than me and eventually buckled down to study when she got over our parents' death." She looked sad. "It is still hard for her—and me too."

"I'm sorry to hear about your parents," Eric said sympathetically. "That must have been difficult for you both."

"I was allowed to study at Leningrad Technical Institute here in Leningrad and was told to focus with economics and planning because the state needed more economic scientists in its bureaus. I learned a lot at university concerning how other economies worked. I began to doubt the Soviet form of government and especially the Russian style of economic planning."

"So you studied capitalism too?"

Lena stared at Eric to see if he understood. "Yes, but our teachers all said it was only about rich people controlling peasants. They did not really know much about it, I think." She muttered sadly, "Even then our country was failing. Change was needed. So I studied hard and hoped to make a difference one day."

"I can't imagine what it was like growing up here," Eric said quietly.

"I took a job in Moscow, and my sister stayed with our aunt. But I did not like the city. It was too impersonal, and I had no friends or family there. It was difficult for me." She sighed deeply. "Then four years ago, my boss was chosen to work on the special economics project in Leningrad. He and many in his office moved here, and I willingly came along."

They sat on the sofa drinking Peter's pivo.

"I got this apartment, and Katie moved in with me. She was happy to get away from our overly controlling aunt, who would not let her 'go out to party at all,' she claimed." Lena smiled at the memory. "Our aunt was ready to let the teenage hellion go, with her blessing. Katie got a job and settled down a lot since she moved in with me three and half years ago." She looked morose. "We still have our moments and fights."

Lena continued in a soft voice about how she had begun to work for the Americans two years before. A friend had introduced her to a visiting American scholar at the university. He had been an economist, and they had become friends, apparently very good friends, because she blushed when she spoke of him.

"He asked me about my job and was extremely interested. I was excited to talk because most people think that economics is very boring. I felt satisfied that my work was so interesting to a foreigner of his stature." She paused and lowered her head. "He coaxed me into showing him a portion of the data I worked with."

"Oh, that sounds odd," Eric whispered. He spoke softly because he felt that she was making some sort of confession to him—a secret she had kept to herself for many years. She appeared to be on the verge of tears. She looked at Eric for understanding.

"He then convinced me that the only way Russia would improve conditions and that the economy would get better was to have pressure from the outside world. He said he could help me make my government change its oppressive ways." She cried openly on Eric's shoulder.

"And you were lovers?" Eric rubbed her back as she sobbed.

"Yes, it is true," she muttered. "I thought he loved me."

"And then?"

"He told me I should let him take part of the information back to the States to show to interested people there. I was doubtful but agreed to let him have a portion of the data." She continued to cry. "I never saw him again."

Then she stiffened up on the sofa. "Eric, it was terrible."

He said nothing but squeezed her closer to him.

"Soon, another man came to see me and told me he knew that I had given away state secrets. That I could get into trouble if I did not continue to give him information." She turned her head to look at Eric to see how he was reacting. "He was the one who trained me in tradecraft and kept the communications going."

"So he recruited you after they set you up in a honey trap," Eric whispered.

"It is so."

Lena dropped her head. "I was very disappointed at first, but now I believe that the Russian government is too corrupt to change from the inside. The country needs a complete turnover to a Western-style economy and democracy if it is to ever move forward."

She was silent for some time, and Eric didn't know what to say after she had bared her soul to him like this.

"I continued to work with the Americans for political reasons and because we needed the money they paid me—for Katinka and me to survive in this crazy place."

"And so now here we are." He rubbed her back gently.

She leaned in to kiss him. "Then you came along, and I am in love again."

Chapter 13

Eric returned to Uppsala after his trip and realized that conditions had changed since the darkest days of winter. He had to focus on schoolwork again while at the same time processing all that had happened between Lena and him. And then there was his relationship with Sabrina. He didn't know if he could balance his emotions between the two women in his life now that he was making regular trips to Leningrad. His love for Lena was growing, but he didn't know if they could maintain a relationship and, at the same time, carry out their risky espionage existence. Where would this all lead?

Eric attended classes when in town but had fallen behind in his reading and research. He was preparing an important project paper for a paleontology class that made up the majority of his grade. It wasn't going well. An exam was coming up in a few weeks for another class, and he needed to focus on the research required to pass it. The semester would end in early May—in three short weeks—and many students were in the same boat, studying their brains out to make up for all the parties during the year. Eric opted to take his exam right away and get it over with.

He thought it went well at first. Then he thought, *Maybe I'm kidding myself.*

The professor told him, "You have little to worry about in this class. You will just pass, which is not so good, of course. But Professor Johansen is more difficult. You must write a strong paper to please him."

This meant that he was finished attending classes for the semester, a welcome relief. Only the project paper remained. He settled down and forced himself to put in the long hours needed to produce the research paper. He had to let nearly all friendships lapse during those weeks in order to come up with sufficient time to read all the sources he needed to devise the paper.

Sabrina wasn't happy with this lack of attention, and she relentlessly called him to spend quality time with her. The demands to study and maintain their relationship were daunting. He felt as if he were failing in all his endeavors.

The weather was hinting that summer would soon arrive, and the days were now much longer. This made it difficult to study when Eric longed to be outside in the much-anticipated sunshine. He had to buckle down but felt he was losing out as spring surged across the northland.

This was the time of year when some students became "jumpers," especially during the final week of the semester and during exams. Jumpers were those unlucky students who found that they couldn't bear any more of the cold, dark weather, school, and loneliness that they had endured throughout the winter months. Something about the change of the season, the challenge of exams, and the end of the semester caused them to go over the edge—literally. A few reached the end of their ropes and would end it all by jumping off the roof of their dormitory or from some other tall building. Swedes other than students could also find life too much at this time of year. It was a hazard of life in the far north.

There was one fellow in Eric's dormitory named Orla who Eric had been keeping an eye on. He exhibited all the telltale signs of a jumper. He had been a geography student who was forced to study law by his family's tradition. He was having a hell of a time with the law courses. He had taken to drinking up all his spare money and borrowing from everyone who would listen to him or buy him a drink. The students on Eric's corridor collectively felt sorry for him because he had been a happy guy before he changed majors. He also owed money to many of the residents, and so it was in their economic interest to keep him in the here and now.

Eric caught him one night when he went up on the roof to look at the stars and thought he was going to take a dive. Ulla, Håkan, and Eric teamed up to talk him down from such a desperate end.

"Are you crazy?" Orla chuckled loudly, beer in hand. "I find it hilarious that you all thought I would jump."

"Well, you were acting so morose," Eric said. "We thought maybe you had decided to do something crazy."

"Like jump?" he said mischievously. "Law is no fun for me, but I am not going to dive off this roof. I can tell you that."

They all laughed and had a few beers while enjoying the stars overhead. Orla survived the year, later hooked up with Ulla, and eventually became a successful attorney in Stockholm.

Eric's relationship with Sabrina was still going well. He spent many nights with her, and they had meals together when he wasn't studying. But she had an agenda.

"You could come home with me to see my family's orange groves when the semester is over," she said one evening after dinner. "You would like my family's estate in Catalonia. We could ride horses and have the whole summer to ourselves."

She made other not-so-subtle hints that they should live together in the fall as well. Maybe they could rent an apartment? She was very sweet.

Eric wasn't sure that things would work out for him to spend a second year in Uppsala. The funding agency that provided his grant money had strict grade requirements, and he was just in the margin of that standard. Therefore, he didn't promise Sabrina anything that he couldn't follow through on. They were both having a lot of fun, and that was good enough for him. She was disappointed that he wouldn't commit to the Catalonia trip, but he smoothed it over with a maybe.

The good news was that Eric's bank account was gaining a substantial balance. He now only made trips in which he did work for Turner, and at the same time, he brought back as much liquor and cigarettes as he could get away with. His trunk was never searched by customs, so the risk of discovery was very low.

All of Sweden celebrated Walpurgis Eve on April 30 that year, the beginning of the real spring season. On that day, all the students held grand festivities and outdoor parties. Eric's dorm reveled in an all-day party with several of the other dorms at Flogsta. They drank and sang and built huge bonfires to light up the evening sky. It was fitting in Eric's mind that Walpurgis began as a pagan holiday to ward off evil spirits before the planting season. The next day was the traditional Labor Day or May Day celebrated on May 1. These were really big days for jumpers.

Leela, Tika, Sabrina, and Eric made a party of it at Flogsta, where the students had set a goal of creating the largest bonfire of all time. Wood was removed from a storage area, and even a few fallen trees were pulled out of the woods to make a woodpile standing close to fifteen feet high. When the magic hour arrived, someone from the second floor of their building splashed the base of the pyre with gasoline to get things started. He had apparently had more beer than was safe for a fire starter. He got too close and had his shirt burning in no time. His friends pulled him away and doused him with beer to put out the flames.

The fire was magnificent, and it raged ever higher into the night sky. After a half hour, someone noticed that one of the adjacent trees had caught fire and that the building next to it was getting scorched as well. Before long, the fire department arrived and hosed the whole inferno down to smoldering ashes. The students ran in all directions, and no one was charged with arson. Many of Tika's friends wound up seeking refuge at his place and continued to welcome in the new season.

Spring was an exciting harbinger of wonderful things to come. If only it were to be true.

Chapter 14

Eric made his next journey to the east in the early days of May, planning to stay for a week. His agenda was to conduct business as usual: meeting with new book customers, make clandestine drops and pickups, and conduct a few client meetings. His days were largely committed to his clandestine work. His evenings, however, after the secret activities, were reserved to meet surreptitiously with Lena and her clan.

Lena and he went to dinner the first night at a nice little Hungarian restaurant that she wanted to try. They had a wonderful goulash accompanied by Bull's Blood wine. They enjoyed the cuisine and went to a small café for coffee afterward. She came up to Eric's hotel room later, and they crawled into bed for quick lovemaking and to keep warm. They lay in bed afterward and talked while snuggling under the covers. She was very excited about something she had wanted to tell him all evening but had saved until now.

"Now we must whisper because maybe your room has recording devices. You know, what you call a bug, yes?" She pulled her face very close to him, and after looking all around, she continued in a whisper.

"I have a chance to do something very different soon," she said. "I am in charge of backing up the database several times each week, and Nadya does the same for the computer model now. When I begin my backup, I sign out a magnetic tape from the vault and make the copy. I do this late in the afternoon, so sometimes I cannot check the tape back in the same night because the vault has to be closed at certain time. It is on a time lock."

"Do you do this every night?" he asked. "What happens if you're late with a copy?"

"When that happens, I call the night supervisor from the next room, and he places the tape in a late deposit box made for this occasion." She stopped to listen to someone walking down the hallway. "He writes down the tape ID and gives me a receipt, which I then paste in my logbook for the record. But what would happen if I make my copy on another tape that I do not have to turn in?" She smiled at Eric.

"You can make a copy that easily?"

"*Da.* I would have an extra copy of all the data. Is this not a great idea—even cool, as you say in America? I did not think of it. Nadya did. She is very clever. She wants to try the same thing when she makes the backup of the computer model files. She thinks we could get both sets of files on one tape if we use one of the larger reels." She stopped speaking and looked at Eric for his reaction. "Do you think we should do it? You could take the tape with you out of the country next week when you go."

"Wait," Eric said, surprised at this suggestion. "Why would Nadya help with this? Does she work for us too?"

Lena pulled her face away in surprise. "No, she is not a spy." She slid closer to him under the covers to whisper again. "She does this to help me. That is all. She knows what I do, and I help her with money sometimes." She looked as if she wasn't sure he would understand. "It is difficult for a woman living alone. So I help her. She helps me."

"What if you get caught? What will you write on the tape that you deposit?" he asked. "You have to write something, or it will be a blank tape and someone will notice," he said. He tried to think of everything that could go wrong. "They must count all the tapes and keep track of them, don't they?"

"But they never look at the backup tape unless there is a computer crash, you see. Only a crash once in one or two months now. So it is rare that anyone looks at the backup tapes. And Nadya already has an extra big tape." She was excited and raised her voice briefly. "It happened by accident that an extra new tape came into her office. It was misplaced and never recorded in the logbooks. So no one knows it exists," she said with enthusiasm.

Eric couldn't believe this was happening.

"Nadya formatted it today when she was doing other tape management tasks, so no one paid attention," Lena went on. "She wants to make the copy of the model tomorrow. Many people are out of the office this week for the May Day holiday. They have gone to the countryside to be with their families." She gave Eric a conspiratorial glance, eyes wide and alert.

"I don't know," he said, concern showing on his face. "It sounds awfully risky to me. Suppose someone notices there is no copy?" Eric wasn't sure this was a good idea. "It's a clever plan, but we need to think of contingencies."

"Contingencies?"

"Things to do if something goes wrong."

"No, it would be very simple," Lena whispered. "Sometimes the machine doesn't work right and we get a bad copy or no copy at all. Usually, we notice this right away, but sometimes not. In such a case, we use the copy from the day before." Her eyes sparkled. "I don't think it will be a problem."

"What about a mistake?" Eric asked. "Let me think." He lay on his back with one arm around her as she hugged him, her breasts pressed against him. "Won't there be a record if you make a copy? Isn't there a log of tape writes and reads in the computer memory? Maybe you would leave a trace of what you did somehow?"

"No," she said confidently. "It works like this. Put the tape on the tape drive and tell the computer to write the files to the tape on tape drive three, for instance. The computer does not know which tape is on drive three, and it writes to whatever tape is on that drive. There is no trace of what tape is used. During the day when the usual operator is working, you have to tell the computer which tape number goes on which drive so that the operator knows which tape she should load on the machine. Because I do it myself at night, I don't have to write the information in the command." She raised up on one elbow to better see Eric's expression. "The only thing I have to do is go back in memory and delete the response that the computer has finished writing. This is how the computer tells the operator that it is finished with the writing job. So I clean up the response and there is no trace." She raised one eyebrow and ran a finger along his chest. "You see. Very clever."

"And how do you get the tape out of the building when you are done?"

"That is the easy part!" A gleeful look danced across her eyes. "I can drop it out the window into the bushes behind the building. There is a window we keep open to cool off the office. The computer generates much heat, and we are always suffering from it. So we loosened one window in the back where we have the coffee room. Everyone knows about it and uses it. Some people even smoke out the window on very cold days. I can go around and pick up the tape on the way to get my bus." She was very animated. "It is so exciting! We will be like real spies doing this."

Eric didn't share her enthusiasm. It sounded dangerous. He couldn't deny the simplicity of their plan, but it sounded too easy. *What if they got caught?* They would be arrested and interrogated. It could get rough and turn ugly very quickly. And how would he get the tape out of the country? His trunk anticipated that small items would be stowed in its secret compartment. He decided he had better talk to Turner to see what he wanted to do. It was his network that would take the risk, after all.

"Aren't you proud of me? And Nadya? She is an instigator, is she not?" Lena threw her body on top of Eric and purred. "Now we need to make up for all those days that you have been gone. Let us make love." He couldn't resist her charms.

***

The next morning, Lena departed very early via the back stairs, leaving Eric to sleep in. He got dressed and went downstairs for breakfast. As he sipped coffee and waited for his eggs to arrive, he thought of the plan Lena and Nadya had concocted. It was good because it was simple, with very few people involved. He would talk to Turner about it when he got back to Stockholm and then they would decide what to do. His breakfast arrived, and he got on with the day.

Eric had to make one dead drop that day and then see three bookdealers. He completed the drop at the exchange site in the morning. He also found an item to pick up, as expected. He had little time before lunch, and since he was near the Palace Embankment where so many of the museums and gardens were located, he sought out a café where he could have a quick meal. He walked to the Hermitage, one of the greatest art museums in the world. The gardens around the museum looked rather fabulous as the first trees leafed out and the flowers began to bloom. It was a very pleasant day for a walk, and he regretted that he had to rush to his various client meetings. Perhaps he could come here again on the weekend with Lena. She would enjoy that. They could have a picnic on the embankment of the Neva River.

His work finished, Eric returned to the hotel and took a nap to make up for the previous night's activities. He slept longer than planned and was late in arriving at the Northern Lights, where he was to meet Lena and her sister.

The tavern was especially smoky that night, as everyone there was a heavy smoker of unfiltered cigarettes, mostly Turkish. As he entered, he heard Katya's hysterical laughter inside. She and Lena were already there and had a bottle of Italian prosecco open on the table.

"We are celebrating!" Katya cried. "Come join us, Eric."

Eric took off his coat, but before he could sit down, Katya jumped up and gave him a long, wet kiss on the lips. "Kiss me, you fool! I got a promotion. Wahoo!" She had finally gotten the advancement she deserved at the store where she worked. "I am now the senior clerk in charge of merchandise. You will bow to me, you dog!" She pantomimed her role as a goddess as Eric performed a mock bow acknowledging her new stature.

Lena pulled Katya back down into the booth. "You foolish girl. You have already mixed the vodka and champagne and are drunk so early. What will I do with you?" She glanced at Eric with an exasperated look. "She started to party at work already. They might fire her tomorrow if she keeps this up."

Lena was also very excited to talk about something else. She pulled him close to whisper, "I have something important to tell you later." She winked with her right eye and grinned devilishly.

They stayed at the Northern Lights for the evening, and Misha came to join them. He calmed Katya down, and she became more subdued. They ate sausages and potatoes for dinner, followed by a few more drinks. At the last minute, Misha and Katya decided to drop off Lena and Eric at her place and continue to another friend's home for a visit. Lena and he walked up the three flights of stairs holding hands. She was very animated now, bursting with glee.

As soon as they got inside the apartment, she threw herself into his arms and kissed him. She laughed, then said, "I did it! I made the copy. It was so exciting! It was easy, and no one saw me." Her cheeks were red from drink and enthusiasm.

"What are you talking about?" he asked, dumbfounded, holding her at arm's length so that he could see her face. "You didn't copy the database already, did you? Are you crazy? What were you thinking?" His voice was full of concern as he looked into her eyes seeking an explanation. "You don't have a backup plan. What if you get caught?" Eric was flabbergasted.

Lena was surprised that he wasn't excited. "That is why I was celebrating too. I have done it. I wanted to tell you sooner, but I was afraid to talk in the Northern Lights." She was adamant, smiling with her eyes sparkling. "Aren't you excited?" She blurted out, "This is a big thing!"

"But, Lena, I thought we were going to check through channels first to see how to do it," he admonished her, even though he didn't intend to be negative. "It was a huge risk, and what if you got caught? Everyone will be suspected if they find out. You, me, Nadya." His mind was reeling with the possibilities.

Lena was confused by Eric's reaction. She pushed back from him. "I thought you would be pleased." Her face shifted from excitement to disappointment in an instant. "I thought I was doing something very brave and helpful. If we can get the model out to the West, then they can understand what our economy is going through now and maybe help make our government change."

"That is good, but you surprised me," he said.

She brightened up again. "But we did arrange this, Nadya and me. It was a good idea. And it worked. So you see, we did have a plan." Her face became slack, like she was disappointed. "Why are you angry with me?"

"Lena, I'm not angry, just worried. What you did was courageous and bold." He was sure that he had burst her bubble and felt a tinge of remorse. He reached out and pulled her to him for a hug as he spoke. "I'm sure the model and all the data will be extremely useful to our economists." He kissed her before continuing. "But you caught me off guard. I don't know how I will hide the tape to get it out of the country. That's all."

She seemed reassured and kissed his cheek as a grin formed on her lips. She smiled at him mischievously. "Now listen. Let me tell you how it happened." She gleefully detailed the steps that they followed to complete the copying escapade.

"It sounds complicated," he said.

"I put the new tape with the copy in my desk in its canister, unlabeled and unmarked, like it was a new empty tape. Nadya wanted to make her copy of the model on the same tape too, but I told her it would take too long and look suspicious if we took so much time. So that is it. Pretty clever, yes?"

"Yes. Very clever," Eric said as he pulled her down beside him on the bed. They made love in the bedroom for a change.

"It is my bedroom, after all." Lena smiled.

Lena brought them glasses of water and stood in her flannel negligée by the window to smoke a cigarette. "I tried to stop smoking, you know. I cannot stop completely but do much less than before. Cigarettes cost too much anyway, and the good ones are hard to find.

You are lucky that you do not smoke." She gave him a sidelong glance. "It is better for health."

When she finished, she crawled back in bed and warmed up next to him. Then she smiled and said, "Tomorrow is Nadya's turn. She can make the copy of the model on the tape, and I will bring it home to you. It will be Friday night, and everyone will want to leave early. There will not be many people around to watch us."

They talked about where they could hide the tape until Eric left Leningrad. They decided that they couldn't stash it at her apartment or at the hotel. He said he would have to find a place the next day.

"So you see, Eric," Lena said, "I love Mother Russia, but I do not love my government." She gave him a wan smile and rested her head on his shoulder. "And I am good at my job. You do not take me seriously sometimes, but I am a good agent. I timed this data capture for when you were here. It was my plan. You are the key to getting the data out of the country, you see. I have needed you to accomplish my goal. And I love you too. But I must achieve my project too, my dear."

They fell asleep in each other's arms and enjoyed the sleep of innocents.

Chapter 15

Leningrad, Russia
Friday, May 5, 1972

At first Eric thought of leaving the tape at Imperial Books, the store owned by one of his customers who had let him store the trunk there before. This would be very easy but could jeopardize the owner if something went wrong.

He also considered using one of the dead drops that he knew of in Leningrad. The problem with them was that they were designed to hide small objects such as letters and wouldn't be big enough for a magnetic tape canister approximately twelve inches in diameter and nearly one inch thick. His next option was to create his own dead drop somewhere in the city, but he didn't have time to establish such a site.

Eric decided to play it safe, since it was Friday, and he planned to spend the weekend at Lena's apartment. He arranged to move his trunk over to a storage facility near the Moskovsky railway station for the weekend. This left a few personal things in the hotel room; nothing compromising. He made sure that there were no notes of his travel arrangements or the people he had met. The only irreplaceable item was his passport, which the hotel held in safekeeping, the usual procedure for all hotel guests.

After the day was finished, he went to the Northern Lights for a beer and waited for Lena to arrive. He sat at the long bar and talked to Andre for nearly half an hour. Andre was generally the strong, silent type, but he knew several very funny stories that even made sense in his limited English and Eric's limited Russian. He had worked in a local steel plant until it was closed down many years ago. He felt lucky to get this bartending job after that hard work. Now he was able to work indoors, a godsend at his advancing years.

Lena, Nadya, Katya, and Misha arrived after 6:00 p.m., and they all took a booth. Eric had one shot of vodka with them for the traditional toast to the weekend, then went back to drinking beer while they stayed with the national drink. Lena asked Misha if she could borrow his car for a little while to run an errand, and he said yes but to be very careful. Then she told Eric they should go for a ride, and they left the others at the bar.

When they were in the car, Lena whispered, "We did it. Nadya made her copy on the tape." Her eyes sparkled. Eric was at a loss for words.

"It went very well. I hid it in the desk until we were ready to leave." She started the car and let it warm up a few seconds before pulling out onto the street. The aging black Lada complained when she engaged the clutch. "Nadya made small talk with the supervisor in the other room while I taped up the can so that it would be waterproof. I sneaked into the coffee room and checked out the window. Seeing no one, I dropped the tape into the bushes. Nadya and I went out through the front security station, where they searched our bags as usual, and we said good night. Then I went around to the bushes while Nadya stood guard, and I got the tape."

"But you could have been—" Eric began.

With a gleam in her eye, Lena interrupted him by pulling out a large flat can containing the tape. "Here it is!"

He gulped as she handed him the container.

"And," she continued before Eric could respond, "I have the perfect place to hide it. Near my aunt's house."

She drove down toward the Palace Embankment area and across the Troitsky Bridge over the Neva River to the Petrogradsky district. She continued north out of the touristy part of the city and into established neighborhoods of apartments and small row houses. They turned down a narrow side street into an older part of the town where several homes, many now converted to apartment houses, had small backyards. She pulled up to the curb near one corner and parked the car.

"We will leave the car here so that the neighbors will not see us. My aunt lived just around the corner, and that is where Katie and I stayed for many years. When we were children, we played around all these buildings with our friends. We had a special hideout under one home that we used as a clubhouse. I think we can hide the tape there for a while. There are very few children on this street now, and it should be safe." Lena exited the car and was careful not to slam the door.

"Follow me." She motioned for him to come along.

They walked around the corner, and she went directly to the side of a small wooden structure. The lights were on in the closest room, and they could hear a radio playing inside. Lena bent down next to a rose arbor and pulled it to one side. It moved enough to create a small opening. She took out a miniature flashlight, and without a word, squeezed behind the arbor and disappeared.

All Eric could then see was her hand motioning for him to follow. He found that the opening was very tight, and he had to push the arbor open wider. He bumped into Lena's bottom as he came in. They were under the floor joists of the building in a little crawl space. The house beams lay on top of large flat rocks that had been positioned to support the corners and central beams of the house. Lena pulled the tape can out of her shoulder bag and slid it out of sight on the large rock in one corner. "This used to seem like such a large room to me when I was a child. It has gotten smaller, or I have gotten much bigger since then," she whispered, then grinned.

They climbed out from under the house and pushed the arbor back in place. Luckily, no one was outside at this time of the evening. They made their way back to the car in the dark and drove off.

"What do you think of my hiding place? Only Katie knows of it now—and you of course." She flashed him a conspiratorial grin.

On the way back to the Northern Lights, Eric asked, "Have you told Katie or Misha about this?"

"No," she said. "I do not want Katie involved in any of this. Only Nadya knows anything concerning my work for the West. I trust Nadya. I have known her all my life, and she believes in the same things I do." She sounded melancholy. "Nadya helps me sometimes to get information. It is a great risk."

"And Veroushka?"

"I am sorry I involved her." She looked very sad. "I deeply regret it. Veroushka decided to do no more after the Helsinki incident."

"You need nerves of steel for this job," Eric said.

She went on. "Katie knows how I feel about the need for government change. And she knows I am doing something on the side, in addition to my regular job, to make extra money, but that is all she knows. I do not want her to be hurt in any way by what I do."

"How about me? What do they know about me?" Eric asked.

"Katie thinks you are only my lover who I met in Helsinki. That is enough for her to know." She laughed. "She thinks it is romantic. Her world is filled with fun and love right now." She focused on driving for a few moments. "Misha knows only what she knows. Nadya knows that I love you, but she suspects there may be more to the story. Nadya is one tough girl. I trust her with everything, but I will not put her in such a situation where it would lead her into trouble. Do you know what I mean?"

"Yeah. I get it."

"I did not say it well, but that is it. I trust her, and she trusts me." She stopped the car at an intersection before merging onto a wider road. She glanced at Eric. "We share our secrets regarding love and pain and everything, but I did not tell her what you do, only that you are a bookseller and that we met in Helsinki. She doesn't know that we are spies." She parked and kissed him lightly before they left the car. "There is something you must know. You see me as a simple loving girl, *da*? But under this exterior of a happy party girl, I am dedicated to my goal of changing my country to make it better. I can love you and work to make a difference at the same time. We will change my country for the future, you and I. Now let's go join my family and celebrate our success while we are able." She kissed him again. "And let's be happy tonight."

They rejoined the others at the tavern. They had decided that they should all go out to eat at an Italian bistro that had just opened near the Mariinsky Theatre. On the ride over to the restaurant, Eric talked to Nadya a bit about the joys of the book business. They all had a pleasant evening during which both Lena and Nadya drank too much for their own good.

Afterward, they went back to Lena's apartment. Misha told funny stories of his younger days on his father's farm before coming to Leningrad. Lena and Nadya both passed out and had to be put to bed. Katya and Eric assumed this duty after the two men carried them into the bedroom and lay them on the bed. Katya stripped Nadya of her clothes, leaving only her panties and a cotton undershirt that barely covered her large breasts. When she was tucked in, they removed Lena's clothes and dressed her in a nightgown.

Katya said to her sleeping sister, "You see, sometimes it is the loyal younger sister who takes care of her older, wiser sister when she has too much to drink. Sleep well, my dear." She kissed Lena on the forehead and tucked her in.

Eric chuckled at her display of sisterly love.

"You will have to sleep in the bed with them too," Katya said. "There is no room in the living room, and Misha and I will be making unusual noises still tonight, if you know what I mean." She raised an eyebrow and left the room.

Eric undressed and crawled under the covers on Lena's side of the bed. It was a tight fit, but the other two occupants didn't notice.

***

The next morning, they all arose late. There was some concern about breakfast because there was no real food in the apartment. Eric got up first and made coffee. Everyone else remained in bed to stay warm, as the heat in the apartment couldn't keep up with the cold front that had blown in overnight. Katya and Misha were spooned in a tight fetal ball in the living room. They woke up when Eric started making noise in the kitchen, and they requested coffee to sip in bed. Lena placed another blanket on top of the bed, and she and Nadya snuggled under it to stay warm. Eric returned with three cups of hot black coffee, two with milk added. The girls let him crawl into bed between them, where it was warmest, and they all drank the coffee.

They called back and forth to Katya and Misha in the other room, making jokes involving sex and cold weather. Soon Katya and Misha got busy in the living room, and the bedsprings of the pullout sofa rocked with rhythmic sounds. Realizing that they were trapped in the bedroom for a while, Nadya, Lena, and Eric slipped down under the covers and waited them out. Nadya made dirty comments about what was occurring on the sofa bed. They finally all got up and went out to find a cheap diner for breakfast.

Nadya left for the day to see her uncle's family across the city. Katya and Misha had friends to visit too. They arranged to rendezvous later at the Northern Lights. That left Lena and Eric on their own. They had planned to tour several small monuments in the city, but the cold and windy weather precluded that. Instead, they wound up sitting in a coffee shop in her neighborhood, she reading the newspaper and he reading a novel by John Hersey, *The Child Buyer*. Later, they went to a Russian movie that he didn't understand at all, even with Lena's translation of the humorous scenes. They whiled away the rest of the day in Lena's apartment.

Lena and Eric were the first to arrive at the Northern Lights at nearly 7:00 p.m. They drank beer while they waited for the others. When everyone was present, they left to have dinner at an inexpensive Hungarian restaurant they knew. They were all a little tired from the previous night's activities and called it an early evening. They dropped off Nadya at her apartment and then drove to Eric's hotel. Lena and he were going to stay there tonight for a little peace and quiet.

As they approached, they noticed unusual activity at the front door. Two black sedans were parked in the drop-off area in front of the Nevskiy Hotel. Two men in trench coats were talking to the doorman, with their notebooks out, scribbling what they heard. Misha, alerted by the presence of the cars, drove slowly past the hotel so that they could see what was happening.

"The black Lada is a city police car, and the Czech Skoda is the make of car used by the security services—you know, the KGB. They like Skoda and Mercedes cars," he said.

"Something has happened if they are here at the hotel. You should not go in until we know what has occurred." Lena threw Eric a worried glance.

Misha drove around the corner and continued on for two blocks. He pulled the car over and parked in an alley.

"You all wait here. I will walk back and see what I can learn by listening. I can go into the hotel and buy a newspaper in their shop and snoop around a little."

"I am coming with you," Katya said, as she started to get out of the car.

"No, Katinka! You must stay here." Misha held up his hand to stop her. "It is perfectly safe for me to go. Anyone would be curious about the police presence at the hotel, so it will not look strange for me to ask a few simple questions of the shop owner. If they see you with me, there may be questions because you are so young." He cast her a stern look. "You know what I mean. Please just stay here and wait." He kissed her and then walked away briskly.

They waited patiently in the dark for his return. Katya decided that she should move the car so they weren't sitting in one place too long to attract attention. She moved it over one block and walked back to where Misha had parked to meet him and show him where the car was now located. Lena and Eric sat inside and speculated about what could have happened.

"Maybe it is because I didn't return to the hotel last night. I should have been more careful and come back before we went to your place," Eric said. "Now there will be questions. How do I explain being out all night? I can say I met a girl, but then the police will want to know who I stayed with." He paused and took in Lena's worried features. "They will follow up and find out that you have a security clearance, so I can't say I was with you. You will get in trouble for consorting with a foreigner. It could jeopardize your job."

"It is now complicated," Lena said, her voice quiet, her hands nervously clasping and unclasping Eric's.

"I've really screwed things up, haven't I?" He was beginning to see many problems coming their way.

"No! This is not cause for the police," Lena responded. "If they were interested in you because you missed a night at the hotel, only the local police would be involved. Besides, many tourists come here and spend the night with other people and with rented women. It is not so unusual." She stopped speaking and thought a moment. "But this is special because the KGB is involved. Maybe they have found out you are a courier or something like that. Maybe they have found out that I made the copy of the database and are here because of that."

Eric shook his head. "No, that doesn't make sense either. It is too soon for anyone to find out. And if they knew about the copy, they would have been at Nadya's apartment waiting for her too."

Lena sat up straight. "Oh God! We must warn her."

Just then Misha and Katya came back and climbed into the car.

"It seems you are person of interest to the police. At first, I thought maybe hotel clerk notified the police because you not return to the hotel last night. But that was not it." Misha started the car and pulled onto the street slowly. "I went in and noticed that is definitely the KGB in charge of investigation, with the local police helping them. I browsed the newspapers and asked desk clerk what all fuss was about. He whispered to me—you know—like he knew all about it. He says to me, 'They looking for an *Amerikanskiy* that may be smuggler.' Then he said the man did not return to the hotel last night and police want to talk to him. They are holding your passport . . . will lay a trap for you when you return."

"It sounds serious," Eric said as he tried to control his emotions. He was shocked at this turn of events.

Misha continued. "This fellow could not keep secret if he was paid to. He just talks and talks. I had to leave because he went on so long that I was afraid police would come over and tell him to shut his mouth." He laughed out loud. "But I'm afraid you are in big trouble for some reason, my friend. The fact that KGB is involved could mean that it is security issue and not related to smuggling."

"You are truly fucked, Eric," Katya said. "I do not know what has happened, but you can never go back to the hotel. And they have your passport, so your goose is cooked." She peered over the seatback at him, her face grim.

Misha kept driving carefully along back streets. "What will you do? You know what is going on? Are you smuggler?" He turned around in his seat and stared at Eric. "You don't look like smuggler, and I know few of them too. They have big guns and scars on their faces!" He laughed at this description.

They headed to Nadya's place to see if there were any police there, but everything appeared normal. They drove by her apartment building twice, and Misha walked back to make sure that no one was surveilling the place from the shadows. Lena decided to go in and warn Nadya that something had happened but not to worry, because it concerned Eric and not the computer tape.

They returned to Lena's apartment and carried out a similar check there, but no one was watching her place either. They were all flabbergasted by this turn of events.

Katya thought she had it figured out. "Somehow one of the people you have been dealing with on your sales visits must be involved in a sort of illegal trading or smuggling operation and the police found your name in his records. That would explain why they want to talk to you."

"Yes," Lena said slowly. "It may all be a mistake because you met with this person. Maybe the police ensnared one of your book contacts and found out that he was smuggling in books from the West." She turned to Eric. "They control everything here, even books and magazines. But somehow we can buy them if we know who to ask."

"In which case," Misha said, "Eric is not innocent bystander. He is a bookdealer and may be one conducting documents into the country." He stopped a moment. "At least, that is what police can think."

Eric didn't contribute much to the conversation. He spent the whole time retracing his moves over the last few days. How did the police get onto him? Did he make a mistake when he was doing a dead drop? Did he act suspicious at any time to draw their attention? Or did one of the book agents who gave him information get caught and turn on him? Or was it something entirely different that he couldn't possibly guess?

After much discussion, they all agreed that Eric couldn't go back to the hotel, no matter what the cause of the police inquiry was. They told Eric that once the KGB suspected someone of a crime, they usually just locked them up until they had time to resolve the case. That might take months or even years. It would take a large effort from the Swedish and American governments to get him released. In the meantime, he would be interrogated by the police and the KGB.

"This is not be pleasant either way," Misha said gloomily. "It not matter whether you are guilty of crime or not. In Russia, prisoner is presumed to be guilty."

"Eric," Lena said as she reached out and took his hand, "I think the best thing would be for you to lay low for a while and then try to get out of the country."

"But how can I do that without a passport?" He turned to each of his new friends. "I can't get another passport without going to the US embassy in Moscow. To do that I would have to come up with a story as to where I have been and who I was with. The embassy would have to report that I have been located. They might have to turn me over to the police anyway."

"The other possibility," Katya said, "is to get forged documents to travel out of the country. From what I know, it is very difficult and expensive to get a false passport."

Misha thought about that while waving his arms about to get their attention. "Your only real choice is find people who sneak you out of country overland through forests into Finland or small boat at sea. But these options are only practical in summertime when the weather is reasonable."

"Is that even possible?" Eric thought it sounded dangerous.

"There are those who are smuggling as profession, although few I have met smuggle only contraband into country." Misha hesitated. "I know shady people who supply auto parts on the black market." He paused and looked at Lena. "If you want, I ask them if they have any ideas."

Smuggling was big business in the Soviet Union and in the other Eastern Bloc countries. Maybe Misha could learn something useful.

Misha and Katya decided to go to Misha's place for the night. He would make inquiries the next day. Lena and Eric stayed at her apartment.

"Whatever the case," Eric said quietly, "we need to do some serious damage control to protect anyone I have contacted."

They went to bed late but didn't fall asleep for a long time as they turned over the events of the evening in their minds again and again.

Eric's last thoughts were that he was screwed no matter what had happened.

Chapter 16

Leningrad, Russia
Sunday, May 7, 1972

The following morning, Eric went with Misha to retrieve his trunk from storage. Even though it was a Sunday, the storage facility was open for business. Misha went in to get it and presented the claim check. That way if anyone asked, the clerk wouldn't remember an American claiming it.

They took the trunk to Misha's garage, and Eric removed all sensitive items from it while Misha dealt with a customer. He took out several small packages and a hoard of cash from a hidden panel in the floor of the trunk. He also set aside several books that he had to retain and take out of the country with him. The remaining books and promotional materials were strictly commercial and no longer needed.

"Do you have a way we can dispose of these books and the trunk?" Eric asked.

"I have furnace that I use to heat my shop, if you really want to burn books," Misha replied. "Trunk is too nice to destroy."

"But it will lead to trouble if the police find it. It has special qualities."

Misha raised an eyebrow and frowned at that reference.

"I see," he mumbled. "A smuggler's trunk."

They carried the trunk and books down to the furnace room and began to break up the trunk with an ax. Misha opened the furnace door, and they threw in the trunk pieces along with extra coal to make sure it burned well. Finally, they tossed in the books and printed matter after tearing them into sections.

The very last book to be destroyed was the only remaining Adam Smith copy, and in a moment of weakness, Eric held it out from the flames to take with him. They made sure everything else had burned completely before Misha dropped Eric off at Lena's place.

Eric spent the rest of the day in the apartment while Lena went out to visit Nadya to make sure she hadn't received unexpected guests. All seemed well on that front. Meanwhile, Misha made contact with the black marketers he knew, who said they would see what they could find out for him.

Eric sent a message to Turner through their secure channels, even though he knew it would take a few days to get a response. To do this he had to leave a message at one of the dead-drop sites and then flag the notice site that there was a message waiting for pickup. In the meantime, he had to look for a means to exit the country.

They held a somewhat somber gathering that night as they prepared dinner in the apartment. That gave them a chance to exchange tales of close calls with police that they had each had in various situations in the past.

Eric told the others about growing up in the American Midwest. They were surprised at how similar it was to growing up in rural Russia, except for the obvious differences in the government and the economy. They made it a short night and turned in before 10:00 p.m. for a change.

The next day was Monday. Lena went to work to avoid suspicion and worked the full day. She and Nadya both double-checked the tape logs to make sure that they had left no trace. Nothing unusual happened at the university, and they followed their normal routines, including making the tape backups they always did at the end of the day. No one had noticed that an unauthorized copy had been made.

Monday was also the day that Misha hoped to hear something from one of his sources regarding exit possibilities from the country. He and Eric met at the Northern Lights to discuss what he had learned. Misha's contact had returned with a single name.

"Yuri told me there is fisherman named Rasputin in Vyborg," Misha began. "What obvious alias, *da*? Anyway, this man is known to bring certain things into the country from Finland in his boat. It rumors that he also takes people out of country to Finland on some occasion." He looked around the bar, which wasn't busy at this time of day. "It is considered very risky and expensive. He took some Jews out of country last year. My friend Yuri said he can be trusty, but he would want lots money to do such thing."

"How much is a lot of money?" Eric asked.

"This could be problem," Misha said. "I not know how much exactly, but for such trip, it might be five thousand rubles." He spread his arms out wide, almost knocking over his beer. "That is fortune! No one can afford to pay such amount!" He had raised his voice, attracting attention from a man farther down the bar. Misha glared at the patron and he returned to nursing his beer.

Eric didn't react but settled back in deep thought.

"He said we must meet the man and ask him ourselves," Misha continued, whispering once again. "He arranged meeting for us tonight at bar by Neva north docks. He gave me directions—said we should go to bar if we want to talk. The man will find us."

"Tonight? That's fast." Eric was impressed.

"Yuri gave man my description, but said we should both wear green caps as mark we have talked with him. If we do not go, that is sign we not want to meet." Misha looked at Eric to see if he wanted to follow through with the meeting.

"I may be able to come up with that much money," Eric said quietly, almost to himself. "If I use the money I have on my expense account for business purchases, I can pay the money back to my company when I get home." He finished his Peter's pivo and ordered them both another. "Yes, let's go to the meeting tonight and see what this man has to say. When would we have to leave?"

Eric tried to sound uncertain about the money, but he knew he had at least that much in cash now that he had emptied the trunk of his operational funds. His hopes were raised for the first time since the police had interceded.

Misha looked doubtful. "I do not know man we will meet—this Rasputin. Yuri said be careful but he can deliver. We should leave here at nine o'clock to arrive there on time. There is no set time for the meeting. We wait, and if not contacted by eleven p.m., then meet is off for unknown reason—or he does not like our looks."

***

Misha and Eric set off by car to the designated meeting place on the north bank of the Neva River west of downtown Leningrad. It was an area where commercial fishermen docked their boats and where smaller Baltic trading vessels also loaded and unloaded their cargoes—definitely an older, rundown part of the city. As with many dockside business districts, there were several greasy spoon diners and bars where sailors and wharf workers could eat and drink or seek out female companionship. The bar they were going to was named Rasti Del'fin, the Rusty Dolphin, or so Misha translated the name. They had trouble finding it at first, but a few inquiries and suspicious looks brought them there.

The Rasti Del'fin wasn't located directly on the wharf but set back behind the other buildings, as if it were an afterthought. It was a long and narrow tavern, with a straight bar along one wall and tables at the front and back of the establishment. Misha opted for a defensive location at a table near the rear door, in case they had to make a hasty departure. He even stepped outside to see where the exit led as a precaution. The door opened onto an alley that ran back toward the wharf.

They ordered two mugs of ale when the stout barmaid came to the table. She looked them over, squinting her eyes, and decided that they didn't belong there. But she kept bringing them more beer as soon as their mugs needed refilling. They waited until 10:30 p.m. and then began to get nervous that they wouldn't meet anyone.

Misha told Eric what he knew about this area. "I worked nearby here for few months in shop that repairs small marine engines. So I learned much on job, about engines and about dark side of business. Marine mechanics is an entirely different business from automobile repairs. You see, marine engines often worn out from prolonged use. There are no longer any replacement parts available for these engines, so I guess is the same as many older cars too. There are shops in area that specialize in fabrication of replacement parts from scratch in small foundries." He looked at Eric to see if he was interested. "I learned more here in three months than my mechanical school in whole year."

Eleven o'clock came and went. They ordered more beer and continued to talk.

Then the barmaid came to the table and said in simple Russian, "There is a man who will talk to you in the storeroom." She nodded toward a doorway at the side of the bar.

Misha handed her some money and thanked her. When she walked away, Misha and Eric slowly worked their way over to the door. They carried their beer with them as if they were just shifting around the room a bit.

Once they stepped into the storeroom, a man's gruff voice whispered hoarsely, "*Zakrey dver.* Shut the door."

They did so, and Rasputin walked out from behind the storage shelves. He motioned for them to move over to a small table at the side of the room.

In a very heavy Russian dialect, he said, "So you are the ones who need to get to Finland, is it?" He stood in the shadows but in such a way that the small light bulb illuminated their faces for his examination. "I may be able to help you find a ride in that direction for the right reward. It has been done before and that's the truth. Is this the case then?"

Rasputin was a large, swarthy, bearded man who looked like he had lived a very hard life of forty or so years. He was dark skinned from grime and sun and had shadowy, confident eyes. *Not the kind of man I would want to trust with my money,* Eric thought. He wore two or three layers of wool clothing, all of which looked well used, and a black leather slouch cap that matched his stained teeth. He smelled of stale herring.

"Only one of us will be traveling," Misha said as confidently as he could. He indicated Eric with a shift of his eyes.

The man drew closer to Eric to look him over, then he said in Russian, "So you are the one, is it? When is it you need to leave?"

Eric tried to answer him in the man's native tongue, but Rasputin stared at him and swore. Misha corrected Eric's words and explained that Eric did not speak Russian, only English or Swedish.

Rasputin exclaimed loudly, "That he does not speak Russian is clear!" He spat on the floor.

"He needs to leave as soon as it can be arranged safely," Misha continued in Russian. "We understand that you may sail from Vyborg, is that correct? How certain are you that you can get my friend out safely?"

The man spoke quietly. "There is supposed to be a very heavy fog tomorrow night, which is the sort of thing we need to slip by any coastal patrols. At this time of year, there is a lot of ice floating around, which can be a problem if we have to move fast. My hull is only wood, but I have sheathed the bow in steel to protect it from ice floes." He seemed proud of this fact.

For some reason he stopped to stare at Eric and Misha carefully before continuing. "We have to travel far in the fog to make a clean getaway, but once at sea in the gulf, we can run faster. Then we go straight out to the fishing banks and make a showing there." He eyed Eric to see if he understood. "If all looks good, then we will turn north and go straight in by Hamina in Finland the next night." He turned to Misha. "That is when I am planning to go. Can you leave that soon?"

Eric and Misha looked at each other. Eric said, "Da."

The tricky subject of money came up, and Rasputin sized them up. He probably wondered how desperate Eric was to get out of Russia and how much he could pay.

"Six thousand rubles is the price. That is a very good price for you—especially because I think you are an American." He laughed in a guttural manner and smiled, revealing his black, rotting teeth.

Eric said nothing but listened grimly.

"I wonder what you have done to be on the run? It cannot be good. I suspect you are in trouble with the police already." He stopped and looked back and forth between Eric and Misha.

Eric flinched, even though he was trying to show no response to the man's words.

"No," Rasputin said and his eyes widened. "I would suspect that our friends at the KGB might be after you too." He grinned savagely, showing his black teeth again. "Now those are some real bastards to deal with, and so my price is a bit more because I take an extra risk if politics are involved." He smiled in a toothless way. "It's not that I care for those bastards, but I am a businessman. I must get paid for my risk. You understand?" Again he displayed that dark smile and stroked his beard as he studied Eric.

"I don't have that much money in rubles, but I can give you four thousand rubles and five hundred American dollars," Eric said slowly, with Misha correcting a few words. "That is a little more than the extra rubles, if you will take it. Is that satisfactory?" Eric inquired, expecting that it was. The ruble wasn't worth so much these days. And dollars were harder to come by in the USSR.

"*Da!*" Rasputin barked loudly, then laughed. "We have a deal. I will need two thousand rubles now for my preparations and to be sure you are on time." He stared at Misha. "Now I will tell you what you must do and where to meet."

He became all business then and turned to Misha, making sure that he understood the arrangements. Eric listened carefully.

Misha and Eric left the bar a short time later. They weren't certain that they could completely trust Rasputin, but they had no choice. They drove back to Lena's place and told her and Katya what had happened. Then, over drinks, they prepared for the next day.

Eric lay awake much of the night beside Lena, who slept with her head on his shoulder. Tomorrow would be a dangerous day. He hoped he would survive it.

Chapter 17

Leningrad and Vyborg, Russia
Tuesday, May 9, 1972

Tuesday morning, Lena stayed home from work and spent much of the time in bed talking with Eric. In all the excitement, they hadn't considered the very real fact that they wouldn't see each other for a long time. They could possibly write through an intermediary, but that would be risky. It was very unlikely that Eric would be able to reenter Russia any time soon, even if the issues with the police were somehow straightened out. It would only be possible to see each other if Lena could get permission to travel outside the country for a holiday. They spent as much time together as they could, snuggling under the blanket and making love.

That night, Lena told her family, Katya, Nadya, and Misha, that she was going along to Vyborg to say goodbye to Eric. Misha would drive because he knew the roads to Vyborg and how to circumvent the police checkpoints along the way. Only Katya and Nadya would stay behind in case something went wrong. Katya wasn't happy with this but realized that was how it would be. Her sister was firm on this point.

Eric bade a warm goodbye to both Katya and Nadya. "I will miss you two ladies," he said as he gave each a warm hug and kiss. "I hope to see you again someday."

"Oh, Eric," Katya whispered as she hugged him. "I will love you forever too, just like my dear sister."

"We will miss you too, Eric," Nadya whispered as tears ran down her cheeks. "Be careful and go with God."

He walked to the car, carrying his briefcase containing the few remaining packages and the last book he was supposed to deliver. They left for the north.

Their first stop was Lena's aunt's house in the Petrogradsky district, where they had to retrieve the steel tape canister from beneath the neighbor's house. It was already dark, so nobody saw them.

As Misha drove carefully, Lena pulled out a roll of adhesive tape in the back seat of the car. Eric lifted up his shirt so that she could arrange the steel tape canister flat against the small of his back. He held it in position with one hand as she securely taped it in place. This was the one spot where it could be concealed on his person without it showing under his winter coat. Once the canister was affixed to him, he pulled down his shirt and tucked it in as well as he could.

They drove out of the city along back roads. Misha turned onto a minor highway that ran north along the edge of Ozero Sarzhenskoye, a small lake. There were no checkpoints this way because there were no places worth driving to, according to Misha. They came to the small town of Vaskelovo, and passing through it, they approached the intersection with the A-141, a moderate-size highway. Misha drove carefully forward out of the edge of the woods. When the traffic was completely clear, they quickly crossed the highway and turned onto another small gravel road.

"We go west now. Avoid checkpoints. We be on small roads for minutes now," he said. They crossed another large highway and continued along roads that ran through the forest. After three hours they passed a large lake that Misha said was close to Kamenka, a town where he had spent some time a few years ago. His circumspect route was taking several hours, but it was necessary to avoid any police roadblocks.

Eric wondered how Misha knew of this circuitous route. He must have had an interesting story to tell. After a little while, they joined a larger highway and drove northwest directly toward Vyborg. It was nearly one thirty in the morning as they neared Vyborg.

A few miles south of the town, they turned off onto a small dirt road and drove southwest. "This is road Rasputin told me about," Misha said quietly. "It leads to small fishing port southwest of Vyborg and lies farther out along the channel. The road not used by many people. Let's hope it not too muddy for passing."

It was extremely dark now, with no moon and low-lying clouds. Fog had settled into depressions in the earth, drifting off the marshes that surrounded them. There was still snow on the ground in places, and Misha swore as he had to keep his speed up to avoid getting stuck. They traveled this way for a few miles, occasionally passing an isolated farmstead. At two o'clock some vague lights silhouetted the trees ahead.

Misha switched off the car headlights, and they crept forward in the gloom, steering only by the depth of the shadows and the distant light.

"Are you sure this is the way?" Lena asked as they bumped along in darkness.

"Da," Misha said. "Look—the fence Rasputin said would be along the side."

A wide area opened up approximately one hundred yards ahead where the road turned into a boatyard. They could see a small guard shack near the gate. A dim light emanated from the building, indicating that someone was inside. Misha backed the car into a space between the trees away from the fence and behind some brush. He cut the motor.

They silently got out of the car. Misha turned on a small penlight. "Follow me," he whispered.

He led the way along a narrow foot trail through the marshy area that surrounded the boatyard. They shuffled along a slight rise for sixty yards to a gap in the boundary fence, which they could barely make out through the fog. Misha snapped off the penlight. There was just enough ambient light from the mercury vapor lanterns of the boatyard to see the way.

Fifty yards ahead they spotted the first of several piers projecting out from a low wooden wharf, with numerous watercraft tied up alongside for the night. Most of them looked like small local fishing boats, with a few large vessels moored farther along the wharf. At the near side of the pier, two men were loading supplies onto one of the bigger boats, which was flying a small white pennant on the spar. One of them was a large fellow with a black leather cap.

Eric and Misha were ready to step through the fence when they saw a figure walking along the wharf with a flashlight. He was one of the guards Rasputin had warned them of, so they crouched down and held their breaths. The guard did a sweep of the rest of the wharf and then walked back up the road toward the front gate, apparently to enjoy a warm heater in the guardhouse.

Eric turned around, reached for Misha's hand, and looked him in the eye carefully. "Thank you for your help, friend. Without you I couldn't have made it this far, let alone get out of the country. I hope we meet again someday."

Misha grinned. "And on that day, I buy the vodka." They shook hands firmly.

Eric looked at Lena, who had tears welling up in her eyes. She was so kind and loving. How could he ever say goodbye? He set his briefcase down and held her with both arms. They kissed for a long time and then she began to sob quietly.

She whispered, "I will always love you, Eric."

"I love you too, Lena," he said. "Someday we will be together again."

Misha interrupted, "They ready to sail now. You must go."

Eric pulled away from Lena, and in doing so, he knocked over the briefcase. The top of the leather case flopped open, and a couple of packages fell out on the wet grass. He knelt down and replaced the items, then rose and said one last goodbye. He turned and struggled to hide his feelings as he checked around him for the guard. He then walked briskly down to the wharf. Rasputin saw him and motioned for him to hurry.

Rasputin's boat was a low-slung craft approximately thirty-five feet in length with a raised cabin and a working spar structure for fishing. It was designed for an inboard engine but also had two large Volvo outboard engines mounted aft. The rear of the boat was clear except for a winch and several tanks used to store whatever fish they would catch. Nets were piled in one corner of the aft deck by the cabin door. Two oars stood ready by the ladder to help push away from the dock. The boat was colorless in the dim, murky fog, appearing as a phantom in the night. An outboard motor was running, quietly purring like a muffled cat.

Eric handed Rasputin the briefcase, and he tossed it down the ladder that was nailed to the side of the pier to his first mate, a small, compact man who merely grunted. Then Rasputin held out his hand for the balance of his money and smiled at Eric.

"Business," was all he said.

Eric dug in his pocket and pulled out a fat envelope stuffed with bills that were banded together in two groups, rubles and dollars. Rasputin felt the thickness of each bundle with an experienced hand and said in English, "Good! Good! Ve mus' go." He began to release the aft line holding the boat to the pier.

"Eric! Wait!" Suddenly Lena appeared out of the fog, running to catch them before Eric descended to the deck of the boat. "You dropped this. It is a book." In her hand she held the copy of the Adam Smith book that he had kept for himself. She gave it to Eric and hugged him. "Why do you have to go?" she asked mournfully.

The first mate didn't know what was happening and now appeared on deck with a revolver in his hand.

"It's OK!" Eric exclaimed. "OK!" Fortunately, *OK* is a universally understood word in almost any country. The first mate lowered the weapon.

Rasputin barked something at Lena in a hoarse whisper.

"*Chto ty zdes' delayesh?* What the hell are you doing here?"

"*Ya za nego.* I am with him," she explained, and he motioned for her to go away before the guard came back. He came up to Eric and pushed him toward the ladder.

"Mus' go! Mus' go!" he said in a low but stern voice.

Eric said goodbye to Lena again and quickly started down the ladder to the deck. She volunteered to cast off the bowline and rushed toward the front of the boat to do so.

Then they heard a loud demand in a deep Russian voice. "What goes there? Who are you people?" The guard had heard Lena and had returned. He raised his rifle in Eric's direction and barked at Rasputin, "Why do you have these people with you? They do not look like fishermen."

Lena backed away down the pier toward the sea.

He turned to Eric. "*Pokazhi dokumenty!* Let me see your papers."

Rasputin replied that he could explain everything. But the guard looked suspicious now. He pointed his rifle at Rasputin. "Raise your hands."

The guard walked closer to the boat while keeping them all within sight. "Are you going fishing or something else? You had better tell me something good right now." He took a step past the ladder toward Lena. "Get away from the boat. Move where I can see you."

Lena backed away from the bowline.

Just then the first mate pulled out his revolver and shot the guard in the arm. Rasputin shouted for him to stop, but the guard had already fallen on his side with his rifle in hand. Rasputin shouted at Lena, "Cast off that line quickly!"

She bent over the bollard and lifted the rope free, tossing it onto the foredeck of the boat. Rasputin had already dropped the aft line onto the deck and scrambled down the ladder, pushing Eric ahead of him.

The guard began to get to his feet and raised his rifle toward Lena. He shouted, *"Suka,"* the equivalent of "bitch" in Russian, and aimed his rifle at her. Lena responded, but he clearly didn't like the words he heard. She backed away from him, moving farther down the length of the rough planking, until she reached the end of the pier.

Before he knew what he was doing, Eric had climbed back up on the pier with an oar in his hand and came upon the guard from the rear. As the guard shouted a final order to halt and pulled back the bolt on his rifle, Eric made a wild swing at the guard's head with the oar. The blade of the oar sailed a bit on the air, resulting in only a glancing blow to the back of the head. But it was enough; the guard went down.

Suddenly Eric was pushed off his feet and into the boat, still holding the oar in his hand. Rasputin had seen him climb the ladder and had thrown him back on board roughly. He shouted, "Ve mus' go!" in a harsh but muted voice. The first mate engaged the engine and started the second outboard.

Lena looked down sadly from the pier, her hands held to the sides of her face like the girl in Edvard Munch's painting *The Scream*, and exclaimed, "Go!" She watched the fishing boat slip away toward the fogbank.

As they slowly pulled away from the shore, headlights appeared on the road leading to the wharf. A black sedan screeched to a halt, and two guards ran out with AK-47s ready. They saw that their comrade was down and went berserk. One of them began to fire at the boat as it was only fifty yards away and gaining speed. The other rushed toward Lena with his weapon raised. She turned and watched the boat depart, waving her hand in a fond farewell. Eric was standing in the rear of the boat and waved back at her. Rasputin shouted for him to get down and pulled him toward the cabin.

Suddenly Eric felt a heavy blow to his lower back as one of the AK rounds struck him, and his knees buckled. He fell forward onto the pile of nets but struggled to turn around and watch the action on the wharf.

Rasputin appeared with an old bolt-action rifle in his hand and took up a firing stance aft. He sighted in on the guard who was shooting sporadically at the boat. He fired twice, and the guard jerked backward onto the pier.

The remaining guard shouted at Lena as she stood at the far end of the dock, screaming with a hand over her mouth. She didn't do what he wanted, and he fired a shot. Suddenly she fell sideways onto the wooden deck of the pier, and as Eric watched helplessly from the boat, she rolled off the edge of the planks into the icy water.

Rasputin took one final shot, and despite the growing distance between him and the pier, the fog, and firing from the deck of the moving boat, he hit the guard. They saw the man fall onto the pier as they disappeared into the fogbank.

Chapter 18

Gulf of Finland, Baltic Sea, Helsinki, Finland
Wednesday, May 10, 1972

Eric passed out for a while after that. When he came to, he was in such a state of shock that he couldn't remember all the details of the night. The sight of Lena falling into the sea was so upsetting that it left him startled and confused. It had happened in an instant and yet as if in slow motion. In his mind, he could see Lena falling onto the pier, her head bouncing off the wood decking, and then the sickening roll off the edge of the planks, her body limp as it fell into the freezing water of Vyborg Bay.

The scene kept replaying in his head, over and over. It seemed to be the reality that his recurring dream had foretold. All he could do was try to keep breathing as Rasputin lifted his jacket to inspect his back for blood.

He said, "*Vezet vam*. You are lucky."

Eric's back hurt a great deal. The blow he had suffered during the firefight came from one of the guard's bullets, a round that had struck the tape canister strapped to his back, but it had not penetrated through the heavy steel can. He *was* lucky.

They motored slowly through the fog for a long time. The central channel of the bay was marked every so often by buoys, a few of which had beacons flashing in dull red.

Rasputin soon shut down the outboards and started the inboard engine, perhaps because it was quieter. There was still a lot of ice on the water, even though it had been swept by a small icebreaker recently. They encountered little traffic on the embayment at this time of night, but Rasputin listened carefully for the sound of other motors. He steered the boat farther out from the main channel whenever he heard another boat approach.

The channel became wider as they moved farther down the embayment, swerving to avoid ice floes. They began to run faster where the channel was wider and deeper. Finally they reached the open sea at the east end of the

Gulf of Finland. They powered on more quickly now, as the fog began to thin and they noticed a slight northerly wind. Their westerly course ran nearly parallel with the waves, causing the boat to roll in a sickening manner with each swell.

Eric stayed out of the way and let the crew work. They spoke no more than a few words of English, and his Russian was equally limited. When they left the channel, he went below deck to the small crawl space-like cabin and stretched out on one of the bunks for a few hours of sleep. The only sound was the thrumming of the inboard engine as they motored along through the waves. Rasputin rested on the other bunk and later relieved the first mate.

Dawn came, and the fog gradually lifted. They navigated far out into the gulf to escape Russian national waters, and there Rasputin stopped the boat.

"Why are you stopping?" Eric asked.

His question was answered when Rasputin and his first mate broke out fishing gear and cast three seine nets out into the water. He told Eric, using signs and broken Russian-English, that they had to make a show of fishing for some time. Meanwhile, the first mate took a nap. They spotted a couple of other boats out on the fishing grounds. Rasputin waved to the captain of one of them and floated closer to get within shouting distance. They talked for a few minutes, both complaining about their catches, then went their separate ways again.

They had a small lunch of beer, bread, and cheese after that. Eric asked Rasputin, "How did you get to be such a good shot?" He pantomimed holding a rifle to clarify his question.

Rasputin shrugged and said, "*YA okhotilsya i byl v armii.* I hunted and was trained in army." He smiled, revealing his black teeth. "Good shot? *Da?*" Then he looked grim as he added, "It was bad luck to shoot the guards. They were good fellows." He spat into the sea. "But this business." That was all he said.

In the afternoon, they pulled in their catch, peeled the fish off the nets, and stowed them on ice in the wooden tanks above deck. Eric guessed that this would provide the evidence that they were simply fishing for the day.

"Finland!" Rasputin pointed to the north as he brought the boat around and headed in that direction. Now he opened the engine up, and they motored along at several knots against the wind and chop, the boat bounding and twisting on the waves. Eric worked hard to keep his lunch down.

This part of the Gulf of Finland was strewn with small picturesque islands, some having a few trees on them and others being just bare granite. No one lived on the islands, but they sheltered the sea to some degree from the wind and made the going easier as they threaded their way through them. Eric realized that the islands provided cover and dozens of potential landing spots for enterprising smugglers trying to reach Finland.

Late in the afternoon, they caught sight of the Finish mainland. They adjusted course and headed toward a rocky promontory. There were no other boats in sight and no signs of civilization on the land ahead.

The sun went down as they cut speed and paralleled the rocky shoreline. Rasputin guided the craft with certainty, knowing exactly where he was going. Sure enough, they came around the point, and a small gravel beach appeared. They steered directly toward the beach and banked onto the gravel. The first mate jumped down with a line and ran up the beach to tie the boat up to a tree. The water was calm there, and they simply bobbed up and down on small swells for nearly an hour.

After darkness fell, they detected headlights far back in the trees. The lights grew nearer as a truck threaded its way along a rough road toward the beach. It stopped and the lights went out. Rasputin looked pleased and flashed his spotlight in the direction of the headlights. They flashed back and the vehicle rolled forward. A two-ton truck loaded with boxes and small crates came into view, pulling onto the upper part of the beach to park. Two men got out of the cab and shouted a greeting to Rasputin. He returned the greeting and went ashore to shake hands with the men. They talked and Rasputin pointed to Eric, saying something to them that he couldn't follow. They nodded in agreement.

The men began to unload boxes from the truck and carry them to the waterline. Rasputin motioned for Eric to help them, so he did. They set up a relay, in which the older of the two men took boxes off the truck and passed them to Eric, who carried them to the shore and handed them to the younger man standing in the shallows, wearing rubber waders. He in turn carried the boxes to the boat and passed them up to the first mate. The mate shifted the cargo down to Rasputin, who stowed it away below deck. The unloading operation took more than an hour, even though only twenty-nine boxes and crates were involved.

When they had finished, Rasputin and the older man stepped aside and held a brief discussion. Money traded hands. They shook on their deal and laughed at a few jokes.

Finally Rasputin came up to Eric and said, "Here Vaslav. You go with him now. To Hamina." He shook Eric's hand vigorously and climbed aboard his boat.

Vaslav untied the line and tossed it in the water. Within minutes, Rasputin backed the boat out into the bay, turned, and drove into the dark sea.

Vaslav and his companion tied down the few crates left on their truck. When they had finished, Eric and the other two men squeezed into the cab of the truck. The younger man drove, and they slowly followed the dirt track through the forest. A half hour later, they emerged from the pitch black of the trees onto what looked like a gravel country road. They followed that for a while in the foggy gloom and then turned onto a two-lane highway.

No one talked. Vaslav and Eric nodded off from the monotony and the lateness of the hour. Eric was too exhausted to worry that his fate was in the hands of these two unknown smugglers. His final thoughts before falling asleep was that he was in Finland and Lena was dead.

***

Vaslav shook Eric awake. The truck had stopped in a parking lot. Vaslav got out and retrieved Eric's briefcase from the back. He handed it to him and shook his hand. He pointed to the building nearby and said simply, "Choo choo." Then he got back in the truck and they drove away into the night.

Eric watched them go, turned, and walked toward the railway station.

The station was locked up for the night, but Eric could read the name from the marquee. He was in Hamina, Finland. They had dropped him on the main rail line to Helsinki. *What good luck that was,* he thought.

A posted schedule said that the station opened at 5:00 a.m., and at 6:12 a.m. the train from Hamina to Helsinki was due to stop. He checked his pockets to see if he had enough Finnish marks for a ticket. No, he would have to use a combination of marks and Swedish kronor to pay his way.

He found one door to the waiting room unlocked and entered the station. There he curled up on a bench and fell asleep.

Horrible dreams came to him. The image of Lena falling into the sea kept playing in his mind over and over. It was like watching a movie clip on a repeating loop. Only this scene was real. Lena had fallen into the sea and was gone forever.

He was awakened by a man who attended the station restrooms. He said something concerning the time in Finnish. Eric responded in Swedish, and he seemed a bit puzzled. He didn't speak Swedish, so he just pointed to the clock on the wall and to the bathrooms. It was 5:00 a.m. and the restrooms were now open.

Eric stood up, stretched, and walked into the bathroom to clean up. His first glance in the mirror told him that he looked like death warmed over. His hair was unkempt, his face was dirty with grime, and he smelled of herring. He washed his hands and face and combed his hair so that he no longer looked like a complete derelict. It was a luxury to have warm water. He couldn't do much to improve the appearance of his clothes, but maybe he could pass for a Swede who was down on his luck. His eyes betrayed the sadness that was beginning to fill his soul.

He entered the station proper and bought a one-way ticket to Helsinki when the clerk arrived in the office. Then he sat on a bench, alone with his thoughts, as other people began trickling into the station.

The train came right on time and he shuffled on board, seeking out the second-class seats. He didn't have the fare for first class and had decided that he might pass as a Swede better in second class anyway. A Swede would likely not be asked for his identification within Finland. There were very few people on the train in the second-class coach, so he settled in for the ride, sprawled out on the bench seat. The conductor came along soon after departure and asked for his ticket. He was half asleep, so the man punched the ticket and moved on with no questions.

Eric couldn't get the scene at the dock out of his head. It was almost surreal—the splash in the water, the sickening feeling. He felt sorry for her. All she had wanted to do was help him—and be loved. He could not register the loss yet. Somehow it couldn't be real. It seemed like something that could be undone if he could just go back and change it. He was exhausted and fell asleep with these thoughts flashing through his mind. But through his dreams, he felt that he had failed—lost something. Only now was it becoming clear that he had lost his lover forever.

It took nearly eight hours to reach Helsinki. Upon entering the railway station, he immediately rushed to the telephone banks and made a collect call to Turner's office. He left a message; luckily, Turner returned the call soon afterward. Eric gave him the briefest of summaries of what had happened but didn't use the names of places or people involved. Turner told Eric to proceed directly to the American embassy on Itäinen Puistotie Street to pick up temporary traveling papers there, which he could arrange in an hour or so.

It took Eric nearly that much time to get a bite to eat and walk over to the embassy. He arrived just before the passport office closed. The staff had received word that he had misplaced his passport and needed temporary papers, which they were happy to provide. They gave him a lecture about how not to lose a passport and how this had better not happen again. Then they took a rather unflattering photo that was attached to an official document with Eric's name and status printed on it. He was told that he should clean up his act and try to be a better representative of America.

What they didn't tell him was that he also smelled like herring, which would have been a fair comment. Eric was free to go.

The first thing he did after leaving the embassy was to stop at a department store to buy a change of clothes, a small travel bag, and toiletries. Next he rented a room at a hotel near the train station. There he was able to change into clean attire. He took off his shirt and tried to find a way to dislodge the tape canister from his back.

Lena had applied the tape with abandon, which had successfully held the can in place for two full days, but now the adhesive had bonded permanently to his skin. He used a pocketknife to separate the can from his back and then pulled off several pieces of the tape. The remainder of Lena's handiwork would stick to him indefinitely.

Eric dressed and examined the tape canister. It looked fine, but there was a deep dent in the metal where the bullet had hit. He opened it up and found the tape inside to be intact and dry. The bullet had cracked the center of the tape reel, but otherwise, the tape itself appeared unharmed. He repacked his possessions into the travel bag he had purchased and stowed the tape canister under the mattress for the evening.

He called to make reservations for a flight to Stockholm the next morning, scheduled early enough to attend a meeting with Turner at 2:00 p.m., as planned. He went downstairs to have dinner at the hotel cafeteria and then retired to his room to turn in early.

Lena came to him in his dreams. First she appeared as the living, loving Lena he knew. Then the scene changed to the one of her being shot and falling into the frigid sea. She lingered as a shade-like being drifting beneath the surface of the dark water—a ghost with no color, no face, and no warmth.

Chapter 19

Stockholm and Uppsala, Sweden
Friday, May 12, 1972

Eric arrived in Stockholm nine days after he had departed for Leningrad and on the same day he had originally planned to return, if his travel plans hadn't been interrupted. He was exhausted and his spirits were crushed. He was beginning to understand how much he had loved Lena, and her death was sinking into his psyche.

He met with Turner at an office rented for just these types of meetings. It was a nearly vacant space in an otherwise abandoned building; sterile and empty, just the way Eric felt. He had never been to Turner's real office, if he even had one. For that matter, he had never met anyone else who worked with him, nor had anyone else made contact with Eric. It was an odd relationship but one that was derived from necessity.

The debriefing dragged on for five hours because Eric had to go through the sequence of events that had taken place several times. Eric took Turner through every detail, explaining why he had done things the way he had and what all the factors involved were. He confirmed that his primary mission was intact and that he had made most of his designated contacts, pickups, and drop-offs as planned and on schedule. Every time he recounted the scene at the boatyard, he broke down and had to stop speaking. Turner seemed to understand that it was hard for him, but he pressed on to get everything out in the open.

Eric explained that he hadn't returned to the hotel on Friday night, and when he went back on Saturday night, the police and KGB were there. He told Turner that he didn't know why they were there and that he had racked his brain to think of any possible slipup he had potentially made. He described how he had cleaned up any evidence in the hotel room and how he had destroyed the trunk.

Turner said, "You know, I only received your message that something had gone wrong today. I guess you did what you had to do using alternate means to get out of the country."

"Do we have a problem?" Eric asked.

"No, I don't think so. You followed procedure up to a point. And it was an emergency." Turner paused, then added, "I did receive notice that one of our other contacts in Leningrad was compromised last week. I don't know why."

"Sorry. I wonder what went wrong."

Turner looked grave. "We have shut down our network for the time being to ensure that there is no further damage. Everyone is staying in place but keeping their heads down until we know what happened."

"The KGB must have gotten my name from your other asset somehow?" Eric asked.

"So it seems." Turner glanced at Eric. "In any case, you're out."

"Lucky, I guess."

"Look, I'm going to think about what happened and try to put together a cover story explaining Eric Larson's disappearance." He made a note on his tablet. "It will help the KGB close the case on his whereabouts."

"Really? Can you do that?"

Turner grinned in a conspiratorial manner. "Maybe Eric was kidnapped by smugglers or robbed and killed by criminals in Leningrad. Maybe we can spin it into a missing person case that could embarrass the Soviet government. You know, use it to America's advantage in some way."

Next they discussed the tape. Turner took it from Eric and examined the steel canister, running his fingers over the deep crater in the metal where the bullet had hit.

"It's lucky for you that the Russians put so much steel into these cans," he said, raising his eyebrows. The tape inside was in good condition except for the reel itself.

Eric told him what Lena and Nadya had written on the tape and he whistled. He made Eric repeat all the details concerning their copy routine and what the contents were several times to be sure he had it right.

"I have to pass this on to the technical guys to evaluate. We can read the Russian files OK, and the programming language they use is probably similar to one of ours, either FORTRAN or COBOL." He looked thoughtful for a few moments. "If what you say is true and the data is undamaged, this could be a huge breakthrough for us. Imagine if we have the unadulterated economic records for their major industries—what an advantage that gives us. We have been trying to get that level of information for years."

"I certainly hope so," Eric said. "Lena gave her life to get it out to the West." Eric looked grim.

Turner continued. "The computer model is a different matter. It may reveal how their economy is interconnected in ways we don't yet understand. We have to see how useful that will be."

Turner then scowled at Eric. "Now that we have all the easy stuff out of the way, we can review how you got into this mess in the first place."

Eric looked up and saw what was coming. "Oh shit."

"First," Turner said in a loud and stern voice, "you failed to follow protocol by contacting Lena directly without my permission. You may have compromised an important asset that wasn't even in my network." Turner slammed his fist on the desktop. "That's going to piss a lot of people off."

Eric didn't know how to respond. He just sat there and took the blows.

"Second, you involved outside personnel in your little exit operation. That may have been necessary, but it was very undesirable." Turner stared at Eric as he spoke. "Third, you got them and yourself involved in a wild gunfight that could cause all kinds of trouble in itself. You know that killing policemen and security guards isn't allowed in the spy business! That's an unwritten rule."

"Wait a minute," Eric objected. "I didn't cause all this to happen."

"I'm going to catch hell for this little screwup of yours," Turner said. "And you crossed networks to use an asset from another network for your self-extraction. You also used that poached asset to steal data that was in the purview of the other network. This is a big no-no in the agency. You don't trespass on someone else's assets." He glowered at Eric. "Third, or fourth—whatever it is—you don't stir up a hornet's nest by killing personnel on the other side. This could lead to retaliation by the Soviets on our people." He pounded the desk again with his fist.

Eric jumped up. "That's not fair. First, it was *Lena* who contacted *me*. I knew it was a bad idea, but it happened anyway. We were discreet and practiced good tradecraft in our meetings."

Turner just stared at him as he spoke. His face twisted in an unpleasant manner.

"Second, it was Lena's and Nadya's idea to make the tape copies. I advised them to wait until we could contact you before they executed their plan. However, conditions in the field presented an opportunity they couldn't pass up. Namely, the office was unusually deserted on the days they made the copies, thereby greatly reducing the risk of detection." Eric felt that he had the right side of this argument. He stopped to look at Turner to see if he was listening.

"Go on." Turner's face was neutral, but he still had his hand clenched in a fist.

"Conditions could have changed," Eric continued, "and they might have lost their access if they had waited for instructions. And the fact that I was there, a trusted courier, provided the missing element to their plan—how to get the tape outside the country and into the right hands." He stared at Turner's face and thought he saw his lip twitch upward. "Third, because of these enterprising female assets, you have in your possession two of the most valuable pieces of information that you could have possibly obtained in a lifetime of running networks." He stopped and raised his hands in the air in front of him. "Why hadn't the manager of the other network realized what was available? And why had that manager failed to take advantage of this resource?"

Turner smiled at the thought. He made a *keep rolling* gesture with his finger, indicating that Eric should continue.

"Fourth, as far as the Soviets are concerned, the guardsmen had a shootout with an unknown smuggler. Vyborg is teeming with smuggling activity, which is why the government stations armed guards at small fishing ports such as the one I used. If anything, they will retaliate against the smugglers and not even know we were there. Fifth, I didn't in any way want Lena to be hurt, or killed . . ."

Eric stopped moving and stood by the window. He couldn't go on. He was overwhelmed by emotion. The room fell silent. His life was shit without Lena.

Turner took up the list of counterarguments. "And sixth, you may have found another mechanism that we can use to get people and goods into and out of the country. Overall, I'd say that you did good."

Eric looked at Turner, his face now streaming with tears. "What?"

"Look, kid, there's no way that you are responsible for Lena getting shot. She shouldn't have come down to the dock like that. She knew the risks—at least theoretically. She lost her head for a minute because you two were involved." A sympathetic look came over Turner's face as he spoke. "It happens, in spite of protocol. After all, agents are human beings, and we often forget that."

The room seemed stuffy in the uncomfortable silence that followed. The sun poured orange light on the walls as evening approached.

"Go home and get some rest," Turner said, then stood up from his desk. "Look—tomorrow I need you to go to the safe house in Uppsala and write up a summary for me using only code names for yourself and Lena—LARSON and VERNA—and initials for Misha, Katya, and Nadya. I'll meet you there. Tomorrow at ten a.m."

"OK, sure."

Turner shook hands with Eric and said, "Go on. Get out of here."

Dejected, Eric took the train back to Uppsala and the bus home from the station. When he arrived at his dorm room, Eric didn't want to talk to anyone. He poured himself a glass of Black Label on the rocks and looked out the window at the advancing sunset. He wanted to be left alone. He didn't go out to eat but just sat there and sipped whisky all evening. Finally he fell into a guilty sleep filled with images of Lena plummeting into the icy sea.

***

Eric prepared his report and went over it with Turner the next day as planned. Turner was scheduled to meet with the other network manager and their superiors on the following day. Hopefully, everything would work out the way Eric had suggested, and the gunfight could be passed off as a smuggling operation gone wrong. In the meantime, the Eric Larson identity was deactivated and so was Eric's involvement in any Russian operations.

"It means that you're basically finished as a courier, except for occasional jobs that don't involve Russia. I want to keep you available and on the payroll for a while until this mess is all cleared up." He paused. "After that you'll be on your own, but we'll keep in touch."

Before Turner left, he added one more thing. "The technical boys tell me the tape was good. Hell, *good* isn't the word. They said that what Lena, Nadya, and you brought them is spectacular. One of our economists said that it may be the key to understanding the Soviet economy and their economic thinking. It could be as useful as another division of tanks in taking them down. I thought you would want to know that Lena didn't die in vain."

He left Eric in the safe house. Eric couldn't bring himself to depart for another hour. *So that's how it goes. Things happen—some good, some bad,* he thought.

***

Eric spent the next few days getting his Uppsala life back in order. In the short week that he had been gone, Tika had been summoned to return to India by his family. It was very sudden, but his parents had threatened him to return or be cut off from all family funds. He had little choice.

Eric was also shocked to learn that Sabrina had left Uppsala with her father to return home for an unspecified period. All he had was a short note.

Dear Eric,

My parents demanded that I come home as soon as my last class was finished. My father came to Uppsala personally to force me to comply. I had no choice. I am not running away on you. I love you very much and will find a way to come back to you as soon as possible.

I must go. My father insists that I stop writing and never see you again. He cannot do this to me. I am my own woman. I will write again soon.

Love,
Sabrina

While Eric was away, his grade for one class had been posted. It was a B—not good for graduate work. The professor for his other class demanded that he rewrite his eighty-page final report with more clarity and fuller documentation. It would take a few weeks to redo the project.

The next several days went by quickly. Turner met with Eric to go over some more questions. Eric asked, "Did you hear anything about what happened that night? Did they find Lena's body? Did Misha get away safely?"

"We don't know much as far as the police reports go. It looks like the guards said they encountered a smuggling ring and two men died performing their duty in fighting crime for the glory and people of Russia. There was no mention of any bodies or other people being seen at the dock. Apparently the guard you hit on the head couldn't remember what had transpired except that he had seen a woman smuggler there too."

"That's not much, is it?"

"No," Turner said. "It seems they don't know how many people were involved or what the boat looked like. So there was little need for concern that the event would ever be traced back to our people."

"That's a relief," Eric said.

"Look, Eric, I know that Lena's death is a tragedy and that it's hit you hard." He appeared concerned and spoke in a fatherly manner for a change. "I've arranged for you to be paid the equivalent to five Helsinki trips for your trouble and to keep you in the loop." He handed Eric a large envelope full of American dollars. "I'll be in touch from time to time, and I want you to keep me informed of your whereabouts. Maybe you can help me out once in a while."

Eric agreed and they shook hands.

***

Eric had the nightmare again that night. In it he and Lena were back at the marina. He was on the boat moving into the fog, and he saw Lena get shot again. She fell onto the wooden planks of the pier and, while lying on her side, looked at him with her blue eyes and said, "Go! You must go!" Then, with blood oozing out of a wound on her head, she rolled off the wharf and into the water.

Then it was over, only to return three more times during the night.

After the last nightmare, he sat up for a while, wondering why things happened the way they did in life. Eventually he went back to sleep, safe from the dream for the rest of the night.

He had another version of the dream the following night, but this time when the woman fell to the dock, he saw Sabrina's face for a moment, then Lena's blue eyes came to him again. That woke him and kept him up for the rest of the night.

Lena was still haunting him.

***

The next weeks were hectic for Eric as he tried to focus on the class project that he had to revise. His professor made it clear that his work so far hadn't met expectations and that he would likely receive a grade of C. That was incentive enough to throw himself into it.

Most of the other students he knew were on summer holiday, and Uppsala seemed like a veritable ghost town compared to the party-filled days of the winter term. He had to buckle down to fill in gaps in his research and to rewrite three sections of the report. The benefit of this activity was that it took his mind off the other problems in his life.

He still had dreams of Lena during the night. Now some of them were remembrances of the good times they'd had together in Leningrad, although the nightmare returned to him once or twice a week. He dreamed of Sabrina as well, pleasant dreams that were much less intense and revolved around the various parties they had attended that year. But, all in all, he was too busy to socialize, and his daytime hours were filled with academics.

A short time later, he received a letter from Sabrina postmarked from Barcelona. She said she couldn't return to Sweden anytime soon. Could he come to Spain? She could sneak away from her family to meet him in Barcelona. She would call him soon. He felt torn by all the pressures in his life. He wrote her back but never heard from her again.

The third week of June, Eric received a letter from the granting agency that had provided him with meager funds for the current school year. The auditors were concerned because they had not received the proper documentation that he had enrolled in the required number of classes during the year. In fact, they had proof that he had completed only one class during the spring semester. They wanted him to submit evidence of any other classes he had attended by the end of June or they would have to pull his funding for the following year.

That put pressure on him to finish his project quickly so that his professor could record a grade and provide proof of completion by the end of the month. He wrote like fury for three days and completed his final report by June 27. Unfortunately, his professor had gone on vacation for a week and wouldn't be able to evaluate the report until the first week of July. Eric resigned himself to losing his grant for the next year and returning to Minneapolis in a few weeks. He felt like a failure.

Part 2
Gambit

Chapter 20

It was cold and dark, as if the whole world was a chilled and silent coffin. She could not breathe.

Lena opened her eyes as the shock of cold water on her face brought her back to consciousness. Her instinct was to take a deep breath as she came awake. But another automatic response delayed that action. She was terrified. Her mind quickly perceived that she was in the water and that she must reach the surface for breath. Perhaps it was her swim training that dictated her response. Perhaps it was a primal instinct. In either case, she sensed in which direction the surface was and pulled herself up to take in a desperate gasp of air.

She was floating just beneath the water. It seemed that air in her thick winter clothing had kept her from settling rapidly. Her head throbbed at the temple and something was wrong with her left arm. It hurt when she made the breaststroke to stay afloat. She also realized that she was getting very cold. She was floating near the end of an old wooden dock. Gunshots came from the boat that was vanishing into the fogbank, and additional gunfire came from overhead on the pier.

The boat disappeared into an ethereal cloak of Baltic vapor.

Then her memory flashed back and she remembered what had happened. Something had hit her head and she collapsed on the wooden deck. She must have fallen on her side before rolling off the end of the pier and into the water. Her mind reeled with understanding, and she began to swim around the corner of the dock toward a boat moored nearby on the dark side of the pier. She quietly pulled her way through the water and away from the shooting as icy cold seeped into her being. A heavy thud on the wharf sounded nearby. The shooting stopped.

Her body was weakening as it cooled in the freezing water, and she realized that she would not be able to swim very far. Her clothes were getting wetter and wetter as water soaked in and weighted her down. She pulled past another moored boat and decided that she had to climb up on the small jetty to which one of the boats was tied up. She looked for a ladder. Even though the jetty was only a meter above the waterline, she was too weak to pull herself onto it without a ladder. One was close to shore. She tried to swim to it, but she felt very heavy by that time.

She reached the ladder, but her arms wouldn't respond any longer. She took a deep breath as her head began to slowly sink below the surface of the freezing black liquid. She couldn't make it. She was too tired, and her mind accepted that this was how she would end.

Her last thoughts were of Eric. She had seen him get shot, and he was gone. She had no reason to live now.

***

Misha watched from the fence line as Lena ran recklessly to the wharf to intercept Eric. He tried to stop her because the guard might see her. But once she started, he had no choice but to hide behind the low shrubs and hope for the best. Then the guard emerged from the shack and walked to the wharf with a rifle in hand.

Lena made it to the pier and gave Eric the book he had dropped. She and Eric embraced, and several seconds passed as the boat captain yelled for him to get on board. She hurried along the pier to cast off one of the boat's mooring lines, but it was too late.

Although Misha couldn't hear what words were exchanged, he knew that the guard had confronted Lena and the others. A gunshot cracked through the crisp air, and the guard fell to his knees. He must not have been badly hurt because he staggered upright and leveled his weapon at Lena as she released the rope. Then Eric climbed onto the wharf and hit the guard with an oar. Incredible! This simple escape was getting dangerously out of control. He ran down to his friends.

As Misha stepped across the dilapidated fence, a dark car pulled up to the guard shack. *Hurry,* Misha thought. *The guard is coming.*

The changing of the guard was happening earlier than expected. Men in uniform, marina guards, got out of the car and started for the shack before they noticed their comrade in trouble at the wharf. They unslung their AK-47s and headed down the hill to help him. One guard began to fire in short automatic bursts at the accelerating boat as it pulled away. Misha saw Eric get hit by a round and go down in the boat. The men in the boat returned fire with rifles, and one guard was killed outright. The second guard farther up the wharf fired at Lena, and the single rifle shot reverberated through the night air. Lena, then at the end of the wharf, spun around at the impact, fell onto the pier, and rolled sickeningly into the water. A final shot came from the boat, which was now invisible in the fog. The last guard collapsed onto the wooden planks.

The night became quiet.

"Oh my God," whispered Misha as he sprang from his hiding place. He raced down the slope in the darkness, stopping momentarily to make sure that no more guards were near the shack. Seeing no movement, he continued down to the wharf. The first guard that he came to was clearly deceased and didn't argue with Misha as he took the rifle from his hands and pulled a semiautomatic pistol from his holster. He ran to the guard who had just been shot. He checked for a pulse but felt none. He stripped the man of his weapons and threw all the guns over the edge of the wharf and into the water. The third man was still alive and moaning as Misha approached him. Misha threw his weapons into the sea also, keeping one pistol for himself.

The injured man was just recovering from the blow to his head from the oar and wasn't bleeding seriously from the gunshot wound to his arm. Misha looked down at him and decided that he could not kill him. He was only doing his duty, but Misha couldn't let him scramble to the shack and call for help either. He would have to hit the man on the head to gain a little time before he could send out an alert. Then he noticed that the guard had handcuffs on him, so he instead rolled the man toward the nearest mooring post and cuffed him to the iron tie-down on it. As the guard began to moan again, Misha dug through his coat pockets in search of a key for the handcuffs. He found it and threw it into the sea.

The man was slowly waking up. *Should I hit him again to knock him out?* He decided that he didn't know how hard he should hit him without killing him, so he would leave him as he was. Help would probably come soon enough.

Then Misha realized that he had lost valuable time dealing with the guards. *What was I thinking?* In those few minutes, he should have been helping Lena if she was still alive. He raced to the end of the wharf and slipped on the wet planks as he stopped where he had last seen her. He fell down violently and crawled quickly to the edge of the pier on his hands and knees. He looked into the dark water and saw—nothing.

"*Bozhe moy!* Oh my God!" he mumbled in despair.

I am too late! She is gone!

Overwhelmed with grief, his eyes clouded with tears. He had let them down. Eric and Lena were now gone, and there was nothing he could do to help them. Maybe he should dive into the sea and look for her body. But she could be very deep now, and he wasn't a good swimmer. *How would I find her in the dark?* he asked himself in despair.

He heard moaning from the downed guard. He could not stay here any longer or the man would see him. Then he heard the crackle of static from a radio and a chill went through him. *The guard has a radio on him! How could I have missed that?* He spun around and quickly got to his feet. He walked briskly to the guard, and before he could think it through, he kicked the man in the head.

"It's your fault. You have murdered my friends!" he shouted. "I could kill you." He sobbed and fell to his knees again.

The moaning stopped when Misha kicked the man. He searched him for the radio and threw it into the sea once he found it. He got to his feet and walked slowly away toward the shadows and the site where the car was parked. He had failed.

As he passed the row of small watercraft on the far side of the pier, he heard a splash in the water to his right. He thought he heard a muffled voice call out, "Eric!" A shiver ran down his spine. *Was it a ghost?* he wondered. *Or could it be?*

Misha carefully stepped along the narrow jetty between the boats, searching the dark, quiet water for a sign. At that moment a glimpse of moonlight crept through the fog and reflected on a single ripple on the water's surface. *There is something in the water!* He hurried over and slid down onto his belly to reach into the water to retrieve it. It was a piece of cloth floating just at the surface. He closed his hand over it and tugged. It was the hood of a jacket. As he lifted it out of the water, a head appeared and then shoulders.

"Lena!" he cried.

With a burst of adrenaline, he pulled Lena from the water and dropped her onto the narrow wooden jetty. She hit the planks hard and gasped almost immediately.

She writhed on the deck of the jetty as she alternately breathed in air and coughed up vile-looking water. After many seconds, her breathing settled down to a more labored effort and she began to shiver. She stared up at Misha in the darkness and whispered, "Oh, Misha! How will I go on without Eric?"

Without answering her, he lifted the water-logged woman onto his shoulder and staggered up the hill to the fence line.

"We must get you to the car or you will freeze to death. How will I explain to your sister that I pulled you from the sea only to let you die of the cold?" They disappeared into the shadows and struggled back to the car.

"Misha—thank God you are all right!" Her teeth chattered as the cold set in. "My Eric is dead. How will I go on?" She could barely speak now. "Maybe you should have left me in the water." She began to shake violently and could not speak again.

Misha stood her up against the car and pulled off her cold, wet jacket and found her soaked to the skin. He opened the trunk of the car and threw the coat inside. He quickly unbuttoned her saturated blouse and began stripping her of the rest of her wet clothing and removing her boots. He threw the items into the trunk piece by piece as he removed them until she was completely nude. By then she was shaking uncontrollably and nearly fell into the trunk. He pulled a large dry towel from inside it and quickly dried her icy skin. He retrieved two coarse wool blankets and wrapped her in them from head to toe. Thank God he had placed his winter fishing supplies in the car recently or he would have had nothing dry for Lena to warm up in.

He carried her to the passenger side of the car and carefully placed her unresponsive form in the front seat. Then he rubbed her vigorously all over to help get her circulation going. He asked her if she was all right. All she could do was shake her head, but her eyes signaled recognition.

Misha closed her door and the trunk, then started the car. Fortunately, the engine was still warm and the interior began to heat up quickly. He turned the feeble heater to maximum and directed all the vents toward Lena. He began to drive cautiously along the dirt road, keeping his headlights off. They retraced their route through the forest in the darkness and fog as he spoke to her to keep her from falling asleep.

"Lena, you must stay awake," he said loudly. "Do not sleep. We will be home soon."

They turned onto the main road from Vyborg and headed south. He looked carefully through the thick fog for the turn onto the small gravel track that would lead them through the woods and around the checkpoint. He mistakenly passed it at first, quietly cursing himself for the error, but backed up, making the turn off the empty highway. They drove east toward Kamenka under a dark and cloudy sky.

After a while Misha pulled over alongside the road to check on Lena. She had stopped shaking violently, but her body continued to tremble and she still couldn't speak clearly. He was afraid she was becoming hypothermic, as he had seen happen before when people fell through the ice while skating on frozen lakes. He felt her skin temperature and found that she was icy cold on exposed areas, and when he felt her belly, it was also cold to the touch, a sure sign that she needed to warm up very soon. He rubbed her roughly all over again, moving the dry wool blanket back and forth against her skin. He knew from experience that he had to get her home as quickly as possible.

Misha raced as fast as he could along the dark provincial roads. He took a few risks at being seen by authorities to save time but soon managed to reach a small village near Kamenka. There he saw workmen standing around a campfire next to the road drinking hot tea.

He pulled over and asked if they would sell him a little warm beverage. He said he had been driving much of the night and was about to fall asleep. They agreed for a few rubles and poured some tea into two paper cups for him to take away. He thanked them, then carried the blistering hot cups back to the car. He managed to pour some of the liquid into Lena's mouth, making sure that it wasn't so hot as to burn her throat. She was able to swallow, and before long she had drunk both cups. He rubbed her all over again and was rewarded when she stopped shaking and opened her eyes briefly.

He drove on more carefully as he approached Leningrad. Now he encountered a few other vehicles on the road—probably people on their way to work in the forests nearby. The first rays of golden sunlight began to streak across the sky as he parked the car behind Lena's apartment building. He carried her up the stairs and unlocked the door.

Katya was already awake and fully dressed. Her first words were "Thank God!" when he entered the room. "Misha," she cried as she eyed her wool-wrapped sister, "what happened to Lena? Is she all right?"

"She fell into the sea and is freezing to death," he blurted out in Russian. "We must warm her up fast. You put on the kettle and boil water in all the pots. I will fill the tub so we can put her in a hot bath. We have to get her warm soon. If . . ." Misha stopped before he said more.

"If what?"

"Let's just get the water going, *da?*"

They ran hot water into the cast-iron tub. At least it was supposed to be hot water, but it was only as hot as the building's boiler ever produced. They unwrapped Lena, who had started shivering again, and placed her naked body in the warm tub, adding extra hot water from the stove to keep her warm. Katya held her head up so that she wouldn't submerge, talking to her the whole time.

Lena looked passively at her sister and tried to reply, but she made no sense. They fed her warm cocoa from a mug and massaged her arms and legs.

Finally, Lena opened her eyes, looked directly at Katya, and murmured, "So cold." But she had stopped shaking.

After three hours Lena could talk, and they decided to help her out of the tub before she was completely cooked. They wrapped her in blankets and laid her down in her bed to sleep.

Misha stayed with Lena as Katya left the apartment to use a public telephone. She called her employer to say that she would not be in for the day. She also called Nadya to let her know that Lena had fallen into the sea and wouldn't be going to work again today. She asked Nadya to come over that evening so that they could talk.

When Katya returned home, she found Misha in bed next to Lena, fast asleep. He woke up long enough to say, "Crawl in bed on her other side to keep her warm. I must sleep now."

He fell into a deep slumber as they all lay under the covers on the cold winter's day.

Chapter 21

Leningrad, Russia
Saturday, May 6, 1972

Major Ivan Ivanoff sat in his office and watched snowflakes lazily drift past his grimy window. The glass provided him with a dull reflection of his face, displaying his longish features accented with blue eyes and a well-trimmed mustache and beard. He stared at himself now and wondered if others saw him as a bright but quiet man—or simply as another bureaucrat in a dull, faceless agency that as often as not brought despair to his fellow citizens. He hoped they had a more optimistic view, perhaps seeing him as one who worked to right some wrongs of the past and perhaps direct his agency to change for the better. Only time would tell such things.

He was one of the three new inspectors to join the security services in Leningrad. He had arrived six months before from the desolate city of Perm, glad to leave the misery of the central provinces. He had grown up in a small town near Perm, and after elementary school, he had been selected to attend gymnasium based on his test scores. A good student, he gravitated toward discipline and logic as he grew up.

He had an interest in criminology that grew from a class field trip to the offices of the municipal police force in Perm. He excelled in school and was recommended by two of his teachers to attend university there in criminology. After he graduated, he had quickly worked his way up in the local police force from patrol to detective because of his abilities in solving organized crime cases.

After several years, he had been recruited by the KGB for the current post in Leningrad. There organized crime was heavily involved in smuggling and black market operations. Sometimes these sorts of crimes had a national security angle, and that was what interested him about the present case.

He sipped a cup of black tea that tasted more bitter than it should if it was really the product that the label claimed it to be. Perhaps it was another creative substitution that state vendors were so good at making.

He added another small teaspoon of sugar and mixed the tea with the spoon while he mulled over the facts of the new crime that had been brought to his attention.

It seemed that a small-time illicit book smuggling operation he had uncovered might also involve the laundering of illegal currencies as well. Not a major operation, but who knew where it would lead? *Whenever foreigners were involved, there was potential for a crime against the state,* he told himself.

Earlier in the day, one of the local police sergeants had tracked down a bookdealer who sold limited amounts of contraband books and magazines from the backroom of his legitimate bookshop. Ivanoff found that this wasn't so unusual, and if it was the first time a dealer was caught with a small black market operation, he was usually fined and his illicit property was confiscated.

Ivanoff savored his tea and watched the snow shower intensify as he considered the situation. Such an infraction was frequently a lucrative opportunity for the local police who conducted the raid because they often pocketed a portion of the dealer's cash and stole any pornographic magazines the dealer had. There was some first-class German pornography available outside the country that made the domestic porn industry look like a religious order. Often the local police would simply take bribes of materials and cash from the small-time crooks and play dumb if any other policemen raided the place.

The bookseller whom the local police had stumbled on was a dealer in intellectual books and Western economic journals. This was unusual in itself because bookdealers usually carried a range of subjects. Of course, economic and political materials were considered especially dangerous by the Communist Party operatives, and so they had to be suppressed. The party would not want any poor citizen to learn the right way to manage a factory, how to make a profit, or how to manage personnel efficiently because that would draw attention to the fact that the state and party members had no idea how to do these things.

The search of the bookshop had turned up a few additional oddities. The bookdealer had a significant amount of cash in his possession, more than you would expect for a small shop. A portion of the cash was in foreign currencies, itself not unusual, but the dealer had Swedish kronor in some quantity. That was curious, as US dollars and West German marks were the typical currencies of the foreign book markets.

The dealer had said, "But I went to a bookseller's convention in Stockholm recently." He had that look on his face that lawbreakers often did. "I came home with much more leftover Swedish money than usual."

A plausible explanation perhaps but still unusual, since mere possession of large amounts of any foreign currency was forbidden by law.

The fact that the bookshop had recent foreign journals also caught Ivanoff's attention. This suggested that someone at the Leningrad Technical Institute or in a government position may have had a standing order for specific materials. It also suggested that the dealer had a regular supply from a foreign source or sources. This was troubling because it meant that several people who were in responsible and influential positions were importing subversive information from the West. It also meant there was the potential for information and materials to be conducted illegally in the opposite direction.

Ivanoff smiled to himself and then said quietly, "Such is the nature of espionage."

Further investigation by local police and more forceful questioning of the bookdealer had revealed a small ledger that included the names of several university staff. The dealer wouldn't yet admit to contact with any foreigners other than several bookdealers who occasionally visited the city to sell their wares. Perhaps more information would be forthcoming after the dealer had spent a few nights in the city jail.

It was too early to discuss the possible consequences of his illegal activity, especially how it might affect his family. That would all come in good time, and no doubt the poor man was very aware of some of the possibilities. Ivanoff wanted to keep the interrogations largely friendly and hoped to gain a degree of cooperation from the hapless fellow. Therefore, he allowed the city police to keep him in their custody. He could always tighten the screws later.

Ivanoff smiled to himself at the thought of that phrase. It was so archaic, and yet the term described exactly the modern science of interrogation and the mind games that an interrogator could employ. One of the things that Ivanoff detested about many of the senior members of his organization was their quick use of physical violence to intimidate and interrogate suspects. The method was old fashioned and often unreliable. It might be useful against hardened criminals when time was limited, but there were easier ways to extract information.

He had demonstrated a better means of interrogation already with the bookdealer, achieving a level of success that had surprised the local police captain. Ivanoff hoped to continue with a measured plan of questioning to find out who the man's suppliers were. To Ivanoff, a planned interrogation was like a game of chess in which you tried to maneuver the subject into a position where he would give up a piece of information with each of his moves. He would cooperate more each time he lost a piece or was placed in check, until you finally had him where you wanted him. *Checkmate!* He would then give up his most valuable secrets.

On a hunch, Ivanoff had searched through records of foreign commercial agents who had visited Leningrad in the last thirty days. Surprisingly, there were only seven Swedish businessmen currently visiting the city. And only one of them was a bookseller. This fact struck Ivanoff as too coincidental to result from serendipity. When Ivanoff learned of the Swedish vendor, he had decided to locate him and ask the obvious questions.

But he was stymied.

Captain Pronin of the local police had arrived at the Nevskiy Hotel before Ivanoff. This occurred partly because the police knew the city streets much better than he did, being a relative newcomer. It was also because the car that Ivanoff had been issued by the local KGB office was a piece of crap Skoda that no one else in the office wanted. It was difficult to start, and it stalled frequently in the cold weather. Ivanoff hoped to upgrade to a more reliable vehicle soon—perhaps to one of the Mercedes sedans—if he solved this case quickly.

The police had entered the hotel, obtained the room number, and had already contaminated the room before he arrived. That was unfortunate because their obvious police presence was sure to scare away any businessman who might be returning to the hotel late in the evening.

He had the police ask the usual questions of the hotel staff. The man hadn't returned to his room last night, and no one had seen him since yesterday morning at breakfast. The room contained a few clothes but no commercial materials like books and catalogs. There were no notes, appointment books, or anything useful to the investigation. It looked like the man had gone out to conduct his scheduled meetings and simply not returned.

The man was named Eric Larson and he lived in Stockholm. He apparently visited Helsinki, Turku, and a few other towns in Finland, as well as Leningrad, on a regular basis. He had been in the city for a few days and had a return train ticket from the Finlyandsky station in a few more days. One unusual fact gleaned from the passport was that Mr. Larson was an American citizen by birth, even though he was now a registered permanent resident of the Swedish state. This was a red flag perhaps but not evidence of any wrongdoing.

The snow was now coming down in oblique, heavy flakes, harbingers of a significant storm. Ivanoff finished his tea and decided to leave the office, before the snowfall mired the city in icy chaos.

Larson might simply have completed his appointments yesterday, been invited out to dinner at someone's dacha, and stayed overnight as a guest. Still, Ivanoff would have the hotel watched to see when he arrived. Most likely, he would return and provide a logical explanation for his absence. He might be the source of a portion of the bookdealer's contraband, but only time would tell. He would hold off on further investigation of the man until he learned more from the bookdealer. In the meantime, he could pay visits to the bookshop's clients at the university to determine whether there were more leads there.

Mr. Larson would soon turn up. After all, his passport had been held at the hotel. Now he would have to talk to Ivanoff to get it back and make his train trip home. Ivanoff left a plainclothesman at the hotel to wait for the businessman to return.

Leaving the office, he managed to get his aging auto running and left for his apartment. As he crept along the slippery streets, he thought of how he might spend his night. He hoped that the single young lady who lived in the apartment down the hall from him had not eaten dinner yet. Maybe she would be inclined to keep him company for part of the evening. Everything else could wait.

***

By Monday, Ivanoff was becoming suspicious of the American, Mr. Larson. He hadn't returned to his hotel for three days now. There was still the possibility that he had gone off with someone for the weekend and would return today to continue his business. Perhaps he had been lucky and had befriended a young woman whom he had spent the weekend with. In which case he had been luckier than Ivanoff in the personal relations department.

Ivanoff had spent a miserable and lonely Sunday on another investigation that should have been handled by the local police. As the junior investigator with the department, he had been assigned as the liaison with the local police force. As such, he had spent an entire day with a local police sergeant chasing down a liquor shipment that had been intercepted at the docks. It was all routine police work and had nothing to do with state security. It was a complete waste of his time, with no leads of interest and no reason for him to be there at all.

The only good thing that had happened was that he had met a rather attractive woman named Larisa at the shipping office that had reported the anomalous cargo. She had seemed interested in his questions and had encouraged him to call her if she could help him in any way. Perhaps he would follow up with her in a few days.

Ivanoff decided that if Mr. Larson didn't return today, he would put out a lookout request with the police as to his whereabouts. He had also asked police Captain Pronin to review any accidents that had occurred last Friday night involving foreigners. Perhaps Mr. Larson had an accident or an encounter with local criminals. Everyone knew that foreigners traveled with a lot of cash, and he would be an easy target for robbery. A thief might assume that he carried more valuable wares than books in his sample case, which could seem inviting.

Meanwhile, he had begun to interview many of the people who were on the list of the bookdealer's clients. So far there had been little of relevance there. Most of them were simply interested in foreign economics and business. These were minor infractions punishable most likely by a fine or a simple warning to behave. The prisons were already overflowing with real criminals and political detainees, so why bother these poor fools and sentence them to incarceration. The bookdealer didn't seem to know very much concerning the missing American, and he appeared to be a minor fish.

But the American remained a problem. If he had been robbed or killed, the American consulate would get involved, and he would lose time answering questions that the police should handle. He hoped the businessman resurfaced soon. He stared at Larson's passport photo and wished for a development.

***

Ivanoff sat at his desk and looked out the window at the freezing rain that was coating the city in a thin layer of icy, gray misery. It was now Thursday, and the American had not returned to his hotel. No one had seen anyone matching his description, and no bodies matching his description had turned up either. Ivanoff had already begun three other cases that were more interesting and higher priority and that had actual leads he could work on. The missing American was put on the back burner for now and perhaps forever.

The only interesting crime to occur in the last week had been the reported shootings at a small marina near Vyborg very early on Wednesday morning. Two security guards had been killed and a third seriously injured. The Vyborg police cataloged it as a smuggling operation gone wrong. Three men had been boarding a fishing vessel when the surviving guard became suspicious of their boat. One of the boatmen had shot at the guard, wounding him, but he was also struck from behind and had blacked out for the remainder of the incident. A half hour later, he awoke to find himself handcuffed to the pier and his two replacement guards shot dead nearby.

This could easily have been a drug or tobacco smuggling syndicate that the guard had encountered, although there had previously been little such activity at that particular marina. The fact that the smugglers didn't simply kill the remaining guard while he was unconscious was unusual. Hardened criminals would have willingly put a bullet in his brain to eliminate him as a witness.

The guard had been shot by a medium-caliber handgun according to the ballistics lab. But the two dead guards were shot with heavy-caliber rifles, most likely older-model hunting rifles or old black market military weapons. More analysis would better define the type of weapons used. The smugglers were experienced enough to be armed but not ruthless enough to execute an unconscious policeman. Or they were fishermen who carried weapons to avoid robbery or hijacking at sea, which occurred often enough to justify having a rifle or handgun on board.

The other detail in the report that had caught Ivanoff's attention was that, according to the guard, a light-haired woman had been at the pier, apparently seeing the fishermen off. Again, this could simply be a wife sending her man off on a fishing voyage. She didn't speak to the guard, so he could say nothing more about her. He added that the people were not regulars at the marina.

On the surface, the whole affair seemed to be a mistaken encounter between the guard and the fishermen. Because of the shooting, the woman would have fled the area, and perhaps she had the kind heart and presence of mind to handcuff the unconscious guard so that he couldn't wake up and create trouble. Perhaps one of the fishermen had been arrested before or had an outstanding warrant out on him, and he had panicked and shot the guard. In any case, the boat and the people on board would never return to the marina, and they were unlikely to be seen again. The incident appeared unrelated to any of Ivanoff's cases, so he would not follow up on it. He placed the Vyborg police report on top of the Larson file and put the folder in his desk for possible later action.

He had too many other things on his agenda to lose more time on Larson.

But still he hesitated.

The nagging point was that the guard had insisted that the woman was too well dressed to be a fisherman's wife. Maybe they were smugglers after all. He would telegraph the lead investigator in Vyborg and ask him to be kept informed of any new developments in the investigation. That would allow Ivanoff to rest easy because he had covered his bases, an important necessity in these days of internecine competition and backstabbing that infected his department.

Now he had time to make an important meeting with the charming Larisa for coffee at a café near her office. There were a few small points concerning the cargo case that she could perhaps clear up. He hoped for a pleasant meeting and perhaps a happy future liaison.

Chapter 22

Leningrad, Russia
Wednesday, May, 10, 1972

Late Wednesday morning Lena awoke with a headache as bad as any hangover she had ever had. But this throbbing centered on her left temple, where a large welt had formed just above her hairline. She managed to greatly increase the pain by probing it with her fingers and found fresh blood on her fingertips.

She gasped at the scarlet stain.

Katya, who was preparing a simple lunch of toast, cheese, and coffee, came over to look at the injury. She cleaned the wound while Lena leaned over the sink. There was a deep horizontal and bloody gash in Lena's skin at the temple where she had been shot. The flesh wound began to bleed again after washing, and Katya bandaged it with a gauze strip to stop it.

The pain caused Lena to feel sick, and she vomited in the sink. "Katie, I don't feel good at all," she muttered. "I feel the nausea all the time now when I stand up."

She ate a little bread and went back to bed. She fell asleep, and it worried Katya that she was sleeping so much. Maybe the head injury was worse than they thought.

After lunch, Katya walked to the Communist Party clinic twelve blocks away and purchased another roll of gauze and more tape. Thank God they had joined the party to keep their jobs, or they would have no place at all to go for such supplies.

The young pharmacist who worked there had always been friendly to her, so she asked him for advice. She explained that a friend of hers had fallen into the Neva Canal while fishing and had breathed in some of the fetid water after hitting her head on the gunnel of the boat. Would the pharmacist recommend that she see a doctor, especially if she was vomiting from the pain of the bruise?

After asking for more detail about the bruise, the young fellow recommended that Katya's friend should come to the clinic and see a practical nurse or doctor. He told her that head injuries could be serious and the fact that she was vomiting might mean that she had a concussion. In any case, she should check out whether they would give her penicillin for the infection. He was also concerned that she had inhaled canal water, which could be very foul indeed.

Katya thanked the pharmacist and left the clinic with her supplies. After walking a block or so, she decided to go back and ask a nurse what her friend should do. Once there, she received much of the same general advice and made an appointment for Friday afternoon, the earliest that the clinic could see her sister. They had just had a cancellation for that date, otherwise the wait would have been two weeks, even for a simple consultation. Katya slipped a few rubles into the receptionist's hand to reward her for her help. Lena would have to suffer through the next two days until Friday arrived.

***

Katya took off work early on Friday in order to escort Lena to the clinic for the appointment. She was very concerned about her sister, who was getting more ill with each passing day. Katya was afraid that she might be getting pneumonia. She coughed a good deal and had a fever. Although her headache was largely gone and her head wound was healing nicely, she had dizzy spells and felt sick to her stomach every day. She vomited sometimes and had to be careful about what she could eat. Perhaps the continued vomiting was the result of a serious concussion.

They braved the twelve city blocks of rainy weather to get to the clinic by 3:00 p.m., where they waited until nearly six o'clock to see a practical nurse named Kosomov. Katya accompanied Lena into the examination room and helped her disrobe for the nurse.

Kosomov had Lena sit on a cold wooden bench while she checked her head wound. She asked Lena to repeat the details of the fishing accident. She commented that usually such falls resulted in a simple bruise and not a linear tear to the skin.

Lena cautiously said, "I think I grazed a bolt on the gunwale when I fell. Maybe that scraped away a piece of skin."

Kosomov looked doubtful. "The wound is healing well enough, but I am concerned about your lungs, my dear."

She told Lena to take deep breaths as she listened to her chest and back with a well-refrigerated stethoscope. Lena couldn't keep from violent fits of coughing, which produced colored phlegm each time. The nurse put on a mask and examined Lena's nose and throat carefully.

The nurse had Lena lie back on the bench, asking her if she wanted her sister to be present for the inspection of her lower body, something of a surprise to Lena. Katya observed in silence as Kosomov poked at Lena's belly, her breasts, and, finally, her private parts for a couple of minutes.

The nurse told Lena to get dressed and then she made a few notes in a notebook. She turned to the sisters, removed her spectacles, and told them her conclusions.

"First, let me say that I am not sure I believe your boating story, as it seems a bit 'fishy' to me. The type of laceration on your head looks more like those I see from people who have been in a fight or on women whose boyfriends or husbands might have hit them in some way. I don't see other signs of violence on your body other than the bruises on your arm and hip, which may be from a fall."

She eyed the two sisters carefully before proceeding. "In any case, I do not think a man is abusing you or your body would show the signs." She moved closer and examined Lena's temple again. "The swelling on your temple is healing, which is good."

She stepped away and looked Lena in the eye. "You have a bad case of bronchitis and almost certainly early signs of pneumonia. This is very serious at this time of year and is consistent with a fall into cold water, so I will not judge you further. I am going to give you a full course of penicillin to fight the respiratory infection." Kosomov made a note on her notepad. "I will count the pills out for you myself when we go over to the dispensary next door. You are lucky you came in today so soon after we received our allocation of medicines or we might not have had any penicillin left to give. We often run out of our useful drugs in a few days." She rolled her eyes in exasperation. "I can give you the full dose due to your special condition. And if you were wondering why I had to examine your feminine parts, it is because if you had gonorrhea or other venereal disease, I couldn't give you any medication."

"But I don't have such diseases," Lena protested. "I don't even have a man any longer. How would I get a disease?"

Kosomov chuckled at her response. "We often encounter these diseases in women who are abused by men for profit in prostitution. In those cases, we are required to refer the women to a special clinic in the city for treatment. I am certain that this doesn't apply to you, so I can dispense the medicine." She paused and stared at Lena seriously. "You must take all the pills per my directions, and in two weeks you should be well again. But I want you to come see me again at that time for a checkup. Now come with me to get the pills."

Kosomov stood up and led them next door into a small storeroom. She counted out twenty-eight capsules and placed them in a plastic bag. "Sorry, we are out of plastic medicine vials. Do not lose these pills, and be sure to take them all. If you stop early, the pneumonia will return. It's not worth the few rubles you might earn selling the extra pills on the black market." Kosomov proved that she had a keen understanding of how the real world worked.

The girls prepared to go, but Lena turned back and asked, "But what about my queasy stomach and vomiting? Do I have a concussion or not?"

Kosomov stared at Lena a moment and began to chuckle out loud.

"No, young woman. You do not have a concussion at all." She had a surprised look on her face. "Do you not understand? That is the special condition I mentioned. You, my dear girl, are very happily pregnant!" She paused and patted Lena on her shoulder. "Now go home and get some rest. And be sure to come back to see me."

***

That night, Lena sat with her friends around the kitchen table while they ate a meager dinner of boiled cabbage, onions, and beets. Lena couldn't consume any solid food with her queasy stomach, but the others supplemented with bread and cheese to help fill their hunger.

"I always hoped to have a child someday," Nadya muttered. "As I grow older, I wonder if I will ever be so lucky. So in this I am happy for you, Lena." She looked at her friend with sad eyes. "I only wish that you could have your Eric here with you."

A tear ran down Lena's cheek as she stared into her bowl of borscht. Nadya put a hand on her shoulder.

"Finally, I fall in love again and then he is taken from me," Lena sobbed. "But at least I have a small part of my Eric within me now. Maybe that is all I will ever have of love."

"Dear sister," Katya said in a serious tone. "It is true that we all loved Eric and that he has been killed. But he died doing something dangerous and courageous. He is gone now and all we have of him are happy memories . . . it is sad, but life must go on. At least you are alive and you will have a child to remember him by." She paused and placed her hand over Lena's. "I, for one, am happy that you were not lost too. I don't know what I would do without you." She began to tear up as well.

Nadya tried to keep her emotions in check. "But you must go on. Eric would want that. And you'll have a son or daughter whom we will all help to raise."

"But how will I go on without Eric? I will be alone."

"No, you won't," Nadya said. "We are all here to help you—your family. You will simply be a single mother whose husband died one day before you could be married. That is all. He was a Swedish businessman who died at sea. That is all we can say to avoid questions."

"But he was American," Lena said.

"Yes, but in our country we can't admit that to anyone. The government that treats us so badly would only make your life and your child's life miserable if they knew the baby was half American."

Lena cried openly.

***

Three weeks after Larson's disappearance, Ivanoff received a letter from Detective Resinsky of the Vyborg Police Department. It was a brief update concerning the investigation into the marina shootings. Further debriefing of the injured guard, confirmed by one of Resinsky's colleagues on the police force, had yielded a few new details that might be related to the incident. Resinsky apologized for waiting so long to contact Ivanoff, but at first the additional information appeared inconsequential.

It seems that a guard had walked around the marina's perimeter and found a gap in the boundary fence. He did that five days after the incident and found footprints in the wet earth and tire tracks in a largely unused dirt road nearby. It had rained two nights after the incident, obliterating any detailed impressions of the tread on the shoes and the tires and, quite frankly, everything else that might have been useful. But a few imprints of a woman's shoe were still visible next to those of men's shoes. The gap in the fence and the roadway may have been used by local fishermen who lived nearby, so this might not be important.

The guard had also found a couple of sheets of blank notebook paper in the mud. They were soaked, but it seemed strange to find them there. When the policeman dried them out at the station, he noticed that they were prepunched and of an odd size.

Following due diligence, Resinsky had taken the paper to a stationer in Vyborg to see if he was familiar with the size and punch-hole pattern. The stationer said he was sure that it was not of Soviet manufacture. He noted that the size and pattern were distinctly foreign, perhaps of Swedish origin, and the quality of the paper was far superior to any notebook paper made in Russia that he had encountered. Resinsky thought it was unusual, but he couldn't justify spending more time on the matter. In any case, he had promised to contact Ivanoff if there were any further developments.

Ivanoff wondered if the Swedish stationery was somehow related to Larson's disappearance. He pulled out the Larson file from his desk and thoughtfully added the letter to its contents. He then replaced the folder in the drawer. He mused to himself, "So it is not yet a dead case. We will see if Mr. Larson reappears someday."

He closed the drawer and turned out his desk lamp for the evening.

Chapter 23

Leningrad, Russia
Wednesday, June 21, 1972

It was Midsummer's Eve, the longest day of the year and a time for celebration. Lena had gone out with her sister, Katya, and with Misha, Nadya, and another woman from work named Irma, with whom Lena often ate lunch in the coffee room. Lena and Irma were both pregnant and due close to the same date, near the middle of January. They had begun to hang out together once they learned that they had pregnancy in common and because it was less lonely to be with someone who also could not party like they used to.

"How can I have fun if I must drink water?" Lena asked gloomily.

Lena was happy to sit with her friends and sip a vodka and soda water in which one would never suspect there was any vodka in the drink—it was so little. Now she watched her crazy sister celebrate and consume enough vodka for herself, Lena, and Irma combined. Katya was a wild and happy child, but Lena worried that she would not be able to moderate her vices if she, too, became pregnant someday. Lena reasoned that she was young and would become more sensible when the time came . . . maybe. She rolled her eyes at the thought.

Nurse Kosomov was very clear that Lena had to start a new regimen. She told Lena that she could still have fun in moderation, but she now had to behave herself for the sake of her baby, or in her words: "Less drinking, less fucking, less eating, no drugs at all, and less smoking." Lena had been lectured that she always had to think of her baby in all activities. Then she would have a strong, healthy child. Kosomov was happy to hear that Lena would keep the baby, even though the father was not in the picture. Most unmarried girls had an abortion in these modern days. Kosomov told her that she would be a great mother.

Lena was lonely without Eric and a little bored at work. Her handler, VLOSTOK, had been reassigned in May, and she had a new handler named RURIK. He had told her to lay low for a few months. She had heard nothing to indicate that anyone at work had noticed a change or knew that any data had been compromised. With the summer vacations occurring now, there was much less work on the model going on anyway. It was a good time for her to stay healthy and enjoy the season. RURIK told her that they would begin actively collecting information again later in the year. She thought that it was kind of him to not push her and allow her to continue her small regular stipend.

**

Lena and Irma had their babies within a week of each other in mid-January 1973. Lena had a boy who she named Eric in honor of his father. Irma named her daughter after her mother, Irina. They spent much time together after that, taking four weeks off from work to recover and adapt to their new lives.

"You are lucky, Irma, that Irina's father is interested in his little girl," Lena mused.

"Yes," Irma said. "I'm lucky to have a man who can help with the costs of raising my child. I'm hoping that we might get married soon—if he could find a steady job in the city."

The women still got together once per week to share their mothering experiences and to laugh at the antics of their babies. Lena had her own support group, especially Katya, who showed an unexpected interest in her little nephew, Eric. Life went on in the crowded apartment.

Lena's work had become more exciting during the winter months. She was made part of a working group that performed quality assurance on the data sets and model code. This allowed her access to most of the data and part of the model source code itself. The working group had to conduct constant testing of new data sets to be sure that they were verified and well documented. She even wrote a portion of the subroutines that compiled the data files and interfaced with the main economic model. This was a big step up for her, and she was happy that she could now really use a portion of the computer training she had received at university. It also meant that she was included in discussions of changes being made to the model itself.

Nadya was now in charge of all backup and equipment maintenance operations and was assigned two technicians who helped her with the maintenance. She was also in charge of the tape and disc library. It was a lot of responsibility, and she enjoyed the challenge.

Lena's handler now encouraged her to make copies of documents and data files when she could do so safely. Over three months, Lena made several copies of documents and passed them along her contact channels to the West. RURIK rewarded her with an increase in her stipend.

Lena maintained her hope that someday her work would prove meaningful and that it would lead to real change for the Russian people. In the meantime, it earned her extra money that she needed to support her little family. Raising a child was now the most important thing in her mind, and her quest to change Mother Russia was shoved to the back burner of her life.

Chapter 24

Time flew by as Lena watched Eric grow into a very active little boy. Raising him and working long hours filled her time every day. Little else had changed in her life in the last five and a half years. Katya and Misha lived with her full-time now. They had constructed an unauthorized partition in the apartment so that Lena and Eric had their own little room and Misha and Katya had a separate bedroom for privacy.

Misha had been provided his own apartment by the state but he didn't use it, preferring instead to stay in the loft above his auto-repair garage to save money and to protect the premises when he wasn't with Katya. So he "sublet" his apartment to another family and received rent for the space. It was strictly illegal to do so, but money was tight and the housing authority rarely checked on the vast number of small, dilapidated apartments under their control. He used his extra income to supply the whole family—Katya, Lena, and Eric—with additional food and clothing. In a general way, they were happy with their simple lives.

One thing had changed recently for Lena. She had found that one of the economists at work named Dmitri Lachinov was very friendly toward her and pleasant enough to spend time with. He was good looking, with wavy brown hair, brown eyes, and well-formed features anchored by a strong chin and prominent cheekbones. He was tall, dark, and intelligent as well.

Dmitri was an accomplished academic who held dual positions as a lecturer at Leningrad Technical Institute and a researcher with the economic modeling project. His area of specialization was the interface between the theoretical concepts of markets and the reality of how they actually worked. He was considered one of the bright young men on the project and contributed to portions of the model logic. Although not a major programmer himself, he developed a few of the algorithms on which the model was constructed. He was familiar with current economic theory in Western Europe, and so he was very influential among the modeling theorists. He had recently been allowed to attend a major economic conference in London, a rare privilege in the communist state, and had gained new insights into trends in economic thought in the West.

They had developed a friendship that seemed to have long-term potential. He even liked little Eric and occasionally had dinner with the family at Lena's place. Lena had spent a few nights with him and found that she was beginning to care for Dmitri in a fundamental way. She wasn't sure that she would ever be over her love for Eric, but she felt that Dmitri might soon own a place in her heart too. Their relationship was still new and tentative, and only time would tell where it went.

Not everyone in the modeling group found Dmitri to be as likeable as Lena did. He was considered by a few of the elder, more traditional economists to be a little too arrogant for someone with so few years in academia. He had made enemies among the theoretical types by arguing against them and their old socialist concepts, often trumping their arguments by referring to recent economic developments in the West. This angered some people because he somehow had more access to Western ideas than they did. Many groused that he had too much faith in Western dogma and that it was unpatriotic.

Lena worried that Misha wasn't enamored with Dmitri, since he found him arrogant and perhaps spoiled by his professional status. Part of this resulted from Dmitri's behavior toward working-class people who weren't as well educated as he was. Misha, who had never qualified for university, took offense at this attitude, and Dmitri did not hide the fact that he felt auto mechanics were necessary but boring people.

***

Lena was late for the meeting today, and she hurried along the corridor of the economics building. She arrived at the door of the conference room and was surprised to see a queue of people lined up in the hallway. She approached the end of the line just as Dmitri appeared from a side door.

"They have increased security today because of the meeting," he said. "They must have something important to tell us if they think we need to be frisked before we enter the conference room." He joined the queue behind Lena. "What can be so important?"

Everyone attending the meeting had to place their outer clothes, coats, and hats on hooks and shelves along the hallway. They were frisked by plainclothes security officers, and their briefcases and papers were searched. Everyone's credentials were checked against a list of authorized attendees. Finally they were allowed to enter the meeting room.

Lena and Dmitri found seats around the far end of the conference table, and the project leaders took up the prime seating near the head of the table where the project director was to make his presentation. Lena and Dmitri prepared to take notes as the last of the twenty or so attendees scrambled for the remaining wooden benches. A slide projector and large screen were arranged nearby for use in the lecture.

Lena noted that while she knew most of the people present, there were three new faces near the head of the table. They were sitting close to the director and appeared very intense.

The director stood up and called for attention. "Thank you all for coming here on what seems like short notice. We have important new information to share with you. I will get straight to the point since our time is limited." He waited for a few moments for a late arrival to find a seat.

"As most of you know," he said, "we have been planning to perform a major rewrite of the modeling code at some point. Our reasons are that as we have developed the economic model, we have added more and more capabilities to it. This has led to many problems over the last year." He stopped and looked at a few people in particular before continuing. "The impact of all these changes and issues is that our model is performing slowly. That limits our ability to use it in a practical way to predict outcomes from different economic trials."

Dmitri leaned over to Lena. "Finally, they will do something about the speed problem."

"Last summer," the director continued, "I met with a few of our lead modelers, and we began a review of the model from a fundamental perspective. We realized that we needed to find a faster, stable means of solving the various sets of equations that we have constructed. We called in a few of our colleagues from the Department of Applied Mathematics to seek any insight that they could lend."

The director looked around the room at the audience and cleared his throat before continuing.

"After several discussions, we all realized that we needed to simplify many of our equations. We decided to linearize them so that they were easier to solve and had similar characteristics to the equations used in other scientific fields. By doing so, we found that our equations could be solved using advanced matrix solution methods from the field of aerodynamics."

He looked hopeful and smiled as he turned toward an elderly gentleman seated at the table.

"At that point I conferred with Comrade Bolokov here, our assistant secretary of economic planning, and asked him if we could apply methods that are used in other disciplines. Our inquires at the Defense Ministry led to several people who could assist us with our situation. As we suspected, the aerodynamics engineers at the National Defense Laboratory had a quick and reliable solver for this type of problem. The defense secretariat offered to make people and methodology available to us."

Now the director practically beamed with enthusiasm.

"I am happy to announce that one month ago we conducted a test of these concepts. And for the first time in the field of economics, we were able to solve a simple system of economic equations using a purely matrix solving mechanism."

Cries of amazement were uttered by several of those assembled in the room. Dmitri raised his eyebrows and glanced at Lena for her reaction. She looked at him and nodded.

"Please, please," the director called out. "Let me finish. I know it sounds remarkable, and it *is* remarkable!" There was still some talking in the audience.

"Let me introduce to you now the members of the mathematical working group who are new to our project." He indicated the three people sitting next to him at the head of the table. "First is Dr. Gregori Markov of the Defense Ministry. His area of specialization is the mathematical solution of matrices and tensors in the area of aerodynamics. He has conducted breakthrough research for aeronautical design and has worked for the space directorate. Second is Dr. Minuri Semelov, Gregori's attractive assistant and a well-respected mathematician in her own right. And third is Colonel Vasili Chayka, a member of the Defense Ministry who has overseen security during the development of the computer code used by that agency for these sorts of problems."

The director clapped his hands and looked around at members of his staff who soon joined his applause.

"Let me now turn the floor over to Dr. Markov, who will discuss the solving mechanism." With that, the director sat down but talked briefly with the young man with dark rumpled hair and penetrating eyes.

After a minute or more, Markov stood and looked around the room. His eyes briefly paused as he looked at Dmitri, apparently surprised by his presence. His gaze next lingered briefly on Lena's face before he focused on his notes. He pressed a button on the slide controller, and the first image appeared on the screen. The slide contained the title of the presentation: "The Markov-Semelov Inversion Method."

"I was remarking to your director that I came prepared to make a detailed presentation of the method that I invented, assuming that I was speaking to a group of my peers." Markov paused and a crooked smile appeared on his face. "But I am afraid that a comprehensive explanation of my work would not be appreciated by this particular audience. I do not think that many of you would understand the theoretical concepts involved. I do not want to waste your time or mine presenting concepts that you cannot grasp." His face settled into an expression similar to a sneer. "A few of you with advanced mathematical training can talk to me in future days so that we may discuss the methodology at a level that is more useful for your applied work."

Markov sat down abruptly, and a pall fell over the audience. People began to whisper among themselves, and several shot menacing glances in Markov's direction.

Lena thought that Markov couldn't care less that he had just insulted a roomful of people who he was going to work with. He looked at Colonel Chayka and tapped his wristwatch. The colonel nodded and turned to the director to say something. After a hushed discussion, the director rose to address the now outraged audience.

"I am sorry, but we must end the meeting so that Dr. Markov, the colonel, and Dr. Semelov can leave for another appointment. If my project staff will stay behind for just a few more minutes, I have further announcements to make. And now let us thank our speaker." He clapped his hands together briefly without enthusiasm and was joined by only a few staffers.

As Markov hurried from the room, several unflattering catcalls followed. He didn't seem to notice.

After Markov and company had exited, the director stood up and looked embarrassed. "I simply must apologize for Dr. Markov's behavior. He was quite rude." He looked around the room at his colleagues. "Let me explain that Markov will not be here working among us very often but will function only in an overview capacity. We will instead be working daily with Dr. Semelov—a much more agreeable person. She will be our interface as the work progresses."

The director went on to explain that the colonel had an important role in the project now. The solver that they would use for the model was a highly classified invention used only by the Defense Ministry. The ministry had not wanted to help the economists at first because its solver was considered unique and extremely valuable to the defense design apparatus. They thought it was a new technique far beyond anything used for aerodynamics in the Western nations. Therefore, it was top secret and must be protected by the highest levels of security.

"Our modeling project will change in some respects. From now on a high level of security will surround the model and especially the solving mechanism. It has been decided that while the solver is being adapted for use in the economics model, it is most vulnerable to possible loss via espionage. Once the model has been fully implemented, the economics team will have access only to the compiled code for the solver and not to the raw computer code itself. At that time security levels for the project will return to the normal classified level we apply now."

He went on to explain that the concern of the state was not that the economics team was using the solver but that any mention of it or any copy could fall into the hands of a foreign agent. People had apparently already died to protect this secret. That was one reason why Markov had refused to discuss the method without a thorough security verification of all audience members.

The meeting ended with loud complaints from nearly everyone present. The grumbling did not begin to describe the emotions that were expressed. The staff dispersed back to their offices and duties.

Lena and Dmitri were excited that the model would be revamped to be more efficient. They were aware that the model ran very slowly and limited the number of test runs they could perform each day. After all, that was the whole purpose for developing the model. A more rapid solver would certainly be an improvement.

***

That chilly night Lena, Nadya, and Dmitri were the first to arrive at the Northern Lights for cocktails. Nadya had not attended the meeting, so Lena and Dmitri summarized the high points. Lena explained how arrogant Markov had been and how he had insulted everyone there. Then Lena remembered how Markov had stared at Dmitri during the meeting and asked, "Why did Markov look at you like that today? Do you know him?"

"Yes. I know him . . ." Dmitri hesitated for a moment. "Well, I used to know him back in university. He and I lived in the same hostel for one year, and we were both competitive then. That led to a bit of ugliness at times."

"What do you mean?" Lena asked.

"We were both in the same calculus class, and he was the prevailing boy genius. The professor really liked him and had him explain to us our errors on examinations and class demonstrations." Dmitri winced as he recalled those days. "Markov loved the attention and enjoyed pointing out the mistakes we made. He called one boy a fool and caused him to flee the room. Markov was really cruel to many students and to me especially."

"Why was he against you? Did you cross him in some way?" Nadya asked.

"I was the unfortunate student who was the best chess player in our hostel. I was very good in those days. Markov was not so good, but he thought he was a grand master or something." Dmitri slugged down the rest of his vodka, as if to wash away a bad taste in his mouth. "One night during a championship competition at our school, he and I happened to play against each other and I won—quite easily, I must say. In any case, he knew me from class and told everyone that I must have cheated somehow."

"But how do you cheat at chess with everybody watching?" Lena asked.

"The faculty member in charge of the competition declared that Markov and I must play a set of three chess games to settle the issue, and we had to do it right then and there. Everyone in the competition wanted to see such an unusual exhibition, so soon the whole meeting room was filled with students."

"What happened, Dmitri?" Nadya asked. "There must have been great pressure on you to win."

"We played three games, and I beat him soundly each time. He was furious and knocked over the table at the end of the last game. He tried to hit me, but the students booed him for being a sore loser and a bad chess player."

"My God," Lena said. "He made a fool out of himself."

"He has hated me ever since," Dmitri continued. "It was so bad that the calculus teacher stopped asking him to critique problems in class."

"I know that many people at work think I'm arrogant," Dmitri said. "But I'm nothing compared to Markov. He is hopelessly intolerant of others. I mean, I agree that in mathematics he is some sort of wizard, maybe even a genius, but he has a very big ego too." He shook his head. "In any case, today was the first time that I have seen him since my undergraduate days. And I could still feel the hatred. Much of the arrogance he displayed in the meeting was directed at me, I'm afraid. I would sure like to see him pulled off his high horse one day."

Lena poked Dmitri in the arm playfully. "If you were such a good chess player in university, why is it I beat you in two games of chess last week? Why, smarty boy?" She laughed.

"I think that during those games I must have been asleep. Did you see if my eyes were open?" He chuckled and bumped his shoulder against hers. "That must be how you managed to win a game or two." They all laughed and made small talk until other friends joined them for dinner.

Chapter 25

Leningrad, Russia
October 1978

The transformation of the economic model began in late October and continued into the New Year. Lena and her associates worked hard to do their part to make it a success.

Lena found Dr. Minuri Semelov to be a very competent and helpful coworker. She was pleasant and quite attractive, an athletic blonde with keen blue eyes the color of the arctic sky, slightly rounded features, full lips, and perhaps some Siberian heritage. The men in the department noticed her as soon as she arrived. She was cheerful, and that set her off from her grim associate, Markov.

After a few days of working with the group, she relaxed and became friendly to Lena, Dmitri, and several others. She spent most of her time with the code writers advising them how to revise the model to be consistent with the new solver module. The main portion of the model that directed all other operations and the solver together were referred to as the *core* of the model. All the other parts of the model had to be made compatible with the core, which took a lot of recoding work. Semelov wrote portions of the code as well, but most of it was written by other programmers under her watchful eye.

Lena dreaded the days when Markov came to meetings to comment on model progress. He rarely found anything up to his standard and often commented on the sloppy code writing done so far. He actually could write elegant and efficient code when he showed a staffer how he would structure an algorithm. He even smiled once when a coder had done very good work. Otherwise, he kept his visits short. He took the time to march around the computer room with the director in tow as a show of force. But he never stayed more than a few hours.

Markov went out of his way to look for Dmitri on a couple of occasions to gloat about his great success. One day he found Dmitri sitting at lunch with Nadya and Lena. Markov walked directly to their table.

"So, Dmitri," he said, ignoring the two women, "I see you managed to find a position in spite of your shortcomings. How could you have worked your way into a classified modeling project such as this?" Markov grinned malevolently while looking down on his foe. "I suppose there is a shortage of people who can read and summarize old journal articles, so you would meet the minimum standard." Markov smirked as he made sure that everyone in the lunchroom could hear. "Well, I must go now. I am expected at the Defense Ministry where my time is more valuable on matters of national importance."

With that, he looked down at Nadya and made a quick evaluation of her dark good looks and voluptuous figure. "Hello, my dear. It's Nadya, is it not? Perhaps we could have time for lunch when I am here on my next visit on Tuesday? If it would please you, I will be in touch soon." He smiled at her and offered his hand, which she surprisingly took in hers. She smiled and he returned the favor. Then he simply walked away. The trio of friends glared at him as he retreated. Lena stood and left the table.

***

"You smiled at him, Nadya," Dmitri said after Lena departed. "What is wrong with you? You are not actually thinking of having lunch with him, are you?"

Nadya grinned at Dmitri. "I don't know. He caught me off guard. You have to admit that he is very direct, isn't he?"

"Direct indeed," Dmitri said. "He is as direct as a horse's ass."

"Women like men who are confident. Perhaps he isn't as bad as he used to be in his college days."

"Nadya, be very careful," Dmitri said in a low voice so as not to be overheard. "He's a very strange fellow, and he will not treat you well. If you don't believe me, ask Minuri about him. She knows him very well. Perhaps she can warn you of his temper."

Nadya perked up at this. "So it is Minuri you have been seeing, is it? I thought you have been hanging around her a lot lately."

"It's not like that," he said. "We are simply colleagues—friends. And we have had lunch once or twice. It is nothing special."

"She is very good looking, and I have seen you staring at those long legs of hers." Nadya grinned at Dmitri in a knowing way. "You, too, should be careful, my friend. We may be in dangerous waters together."

***

As part of the quality assurance group, Lena was kept informed of any significant revisions to the model. She sat in on many meetings that covered changes and problems with the model rewriting process. Often she was asked to report on the progress her team was making on the changes to the data input modules and on the modified data sets themselves.

Lena's team reworked the raw data structure so that it could be read into the model. This put Lena in an uncomfortable situation of having to revise code for input whenever there was a significant rewrite of the core code. It also meant that she and Nadya had to modify the data sets to match these new changes. It became very frustrating to revise their work so often.

At a meeting in mid-November, Lena objected to one of the changes called for by Markov. Lena stood up and aimed her comments at the director.

"The current request for changes undoes a good deal of our recent work and is very similar to changes that we made three weeks ago. Why must we undo all that work now just because Markov has a new idea?" She paused to look at a few other people around the table who she felt would support her statements. "Can't the core modelers hold their requests for changes until they are very certain what their requirements will ultimately be?"

This brought a volcanic eruption from Markov. "I will not stand by and have my work criticized by a mere data entry technician who shouldn't be allowed to interfere with the most important work on the model—the core." Markov lost control and made many rude and personal remarks, degrading Lena in front of the meeting attendees.

Lena left the meeting in tears as Markov ranted on for several minutes, complaining that most members of the group were simply not up to the modeling task at hand. The room was strangely silent after his rant, as people looked awkwardly around and finally fixed their gazes on the director. Nadya left the room to find Lena and offer her encouragement. She located her in the room next door to the meeting where she could see and overhear the rest of the discussion.

Nadya ran up next to her friend and put a hand on her arm.

"Lena, I'm sorry. The man is an ass."

Lena said, "Hush. I want to hear what is decided." They both listened in silence, peering in on the proceedings from the doorway.

Surprisingly, Minuri Semelov was the first to speak. She stood, fixed her gaze on Markov, and said vehemently, "That was uncalled for. I, for one, agree with Lena on this matter. Every time the core code changes, it has repercussions throughout the model subgroups." She fixed her stare on Markov. "Markov, you cannot expect everyone to jump through programming hoops each time you want to make an improvement in the solver code. It's not reasonable." She crossed her arms over her chest. "And you have no right to complain about the work that these people are doing. We are all working hard to make the model successful. Don't blame *us* if *you* have difficulty with the solver stability."

Markov glared at Minuri, then said loudly, "You are a moron to defend these people."

Minuri somehow retained her composure and made a suggestion.

"I know it has been an obstacle lately, so why don't we come up with a simpler data set for you to focus on until you work out any bugs in the new code? That would save everyone a lot of work and give you a test data set that could be easily revised if need be."

The director, who wanted to avoid conflict among his modelers, leaped at this idea and seized on it as a way to both defuse the situation and find a solution to the solver problems that now bedeviled the project.

"I think this might be a reasonable approach to settling data input problems for now," he said, "and it may help you isolate any little glitches in the new version of the solver. What do you think, Markov? Could it be done?" They were anything but glitches.

Markov was at first furious that anyone, especially his old lover and possibly only real friend, Minuri, should question his statements. It was obvious when he looked around the room that no one at the table would support him now that he had attacked their little favorite, Lena. He looked at Minuri. Her face showed a trace of concern he had seen before. She had offered him a way out of the cul-de-sac into which he had so foolishly backed himself. He looked at her again and then at the director. He swallowed hard.

"Yes, Minuri. You are right and point out a useful option. I, too, am growing frustrated with the small glitches that we have with the solver. I am sorry for my outburst. It was uncalled for."

He looked around the room to see if his apology had resolved any of his problems with the staff. He could see that he had made new enemies today.

"Perhaps a test data set would allow us to make progress on the core without causing so much work for everyone else. And yes—I now admit that we are having some difficulties with the stability of the solver. It is usually very stable with fluid dynamics models, but the equations involved in the economics model are different in many ways."

"What do you mean by instability?" the director asked. "It can still solve the equations, can't it?"

"The solver can sometimes drift toward an invalid solution." Markov defended himself. "In most cases, it will reevaluate and come to the proper solution, but the excursion can lead to hundreds of iterations lost while chasing a faulty answer. That all takes time." He huffed at the others but then his expression changed. "Maybe we should discuss how to make a representative data set to work with until the glitches are fixed?"

The director was relieved. He refocused the rest of the meeting on defining what the test data set should consist of and how it should be structured. The meeting went on for hours on that subject.

Afterward, Lena, Nadya, and Dmitri agreed to meet at the Northern Lights for drinks later in the evening. Dmitri went out of his way to speak to Minuri and invited her to join them.

At the end of the day, a somewhat repentant Markov came by Lena's office to offer an apology. Nadya hurried over to make sure that Lena would be all right. She entered the room as Markov, standing opposite Lena across from her desk, offered a very stiff and indirect apology.

Lena sat at her desk and looked like she was being confronted by a spotted hyena.

"Perhaps I should not have been so sharp in my comments," he said. "I understand that you people are struggling very hard to make things work. I did not mean to attack your efforts directly, but you people don't know how difficult it has been to salvage a semblance of order from the chaotic model that you have been fumbling around with here. People do not understand—"

Nadya had heard enough, watching Lena pull farther away from this rude man.

"No, it is you who doesn't understand! We're not your servants, and you cannot treat us as such. You attacked Lena viciously in the meeting, and by doing so, you attacked all of us."

Nadya marched up to Markov and stood toe to toe with him, her face inches from his. He backed away when he saw the fury in her eyes.

"We were 'fumbling around' here with a model that was working just fine," she said, "until you and your wrecking crew came along. Now we have chaos, and the only part of the model that doesn't work is your delicate little solver. We should all be shouting at you, you rude, arrogant man!"

Markov was clearly taken aback by Nadya's direct and loud attack. Several people emerged from down the hall to see what was happening and arrived to hear the end of her remarks. Nadya went over to Lena and put her arm around her friend.

"Well, ladies, I see that I am in the wrong here. I am sorry. I didn't mean to offend you so badly. Perhaps I can make it up to you by taking you for coffee now or to lunch?" He looked at Nadya hopefully. "Perhaps, as we discussed a few weeks ago?"

"No!" Nadya shouted. "I will not eat lunch or have drinks with any man who is so rude to my friend Lena. You can have your lunch alone, you awful fool!" The onlookers seemed to approve, as several snickered or clapped their hands at her moxie.

Markov could see that he had no friends here, so he simply excused himself. He put on his hat and walked down the hall.

***

Lena packed her things and said goodnight to several people before bustling out into the cold and blustery night air of the Leningrad winter. She walked across campus to the commons building where the staff day care center and primary school were located. As she entered, she saw little Eric already dressed and waiting for her to pick him up and go home. She smiled at her always happy little boy and his cheerful greeting.

"Privet, Mama!" he said as he ran to her. He immediately showed her a drawing he had made and chattered on enthusiastically. She could feel all her troubles of the day quickly fade away as they walked and then rode the bus home.

At their apartment, Lena cooked an early dinner, washed some clothes, and made a little time to play with Eric. She took him down the hall to see "Auntie Olga," the older woman who babysat for him in the evenings. Lena was lucky to have the friendly old babushka living so close by and so willing to take Eric on a moment's notice. She settled him with Olga and took the bus to meet her friends at the Northern Lights.

As often happened, Lena was the last of the little group of friends to arrive. She waved as she saw them in a large padded booth at the back of the bar. She slid in next to Misha, hugged him, and then greeted the others. She would have sat on the other side of the booth, but Dmitri was already tightly packed in next to Minuri, and Nadya was tucked in the corner, chatting across the table to Katya, who was seated on Misha's right side. Nadya commented that they had a shortage of men at the table. Dmitri and Minuri were heavily involved in conversation that centered on work, so Lena joined in the discussion of a new book that Nadya was reading.

The evening passed by rapidly as they all talked and drank vodka and occasionally a beer or two. Minuri turned out to be very entertaining and friendly, fitting comfortably into the clique of old friends. She regaled them with stories of how badly Markov had behaved on several projects, during which he angered many of the people he was supposed to collaborate with.

"Early in my career, Markov and I were lovers for a short time," she confessed. "He is a very aggravating man to live with, but then he wasn't as arrogant as he is now."

"I disagree. He has always been an ass," Dmitri argued. "That is based on my experience with him at university." He retold the tale of the chess match.

"You are the one who embarrassed Gregori at chess? He told me about that, of how he was convinced that you cheated and made him look like a fool in front of all those people. He is still quite angry about that . . ." Her features suddenly brightened. "Oh my God! Now I understand. That first day when we came for the meeting, he became very agitated and told me that there was a snake in the room. He must have meant you." She went on to say that Gregori was a truly great mathematician but that he had no people skills at all and a huge ego.

At ten o'clock the party broke up, and the friends parted company. Misha and Katya offered to drive Lena and Nadya home. Dmitri volunteered to take Minuri back to her housing unit, and she gladly accepted. She walked down the street arm in arm with Dmitri toward his car.

Nadya looked at Lena's face to see if she had noticed. Lena caught Nadya's glance and looked away with glistening eyes. It had been a difficult day. Nadya sat in the back seat with Lena and asked to stay at her place overnight so that she could see Eric.

Later they sat together, and Lena cried out her woes on her best friend's shoulder. After a nightcap, they crawled into bed to sleep next to each other and stay warm. Eric slumbered blissfully in his cot nearby.

In the middle of the night, Lena awoke when the little boy climbed into her bed on the side opposite Nadya's heavy wheezing. She put an arm around him, and soon they were both sound asleep again.

Then, as sometimes happened, Lena was visited by her true love, Eric, in a dream. They were lying on the lawn at the Embankment near the Admiralty Building on a sunny spring afternoon, watching the waters of the Neva River flow past. She had her head on his shoulder, enjoying the sunshine and the sounds of people picnicking nearby. She was so happy as she watched little Eric—only three years old, running on the grass, gleefully chasing a pigeon.

She closed her eyes in her dream and the warmth of the sun faded. When she opened her eyes again, the clear blue sky had been replaced by low, threatening snow clouds. No longer resting on Eric's shoulder, she saw him at the river's edge, stepping into a small fishing vessel. As she watched, he waved at her and turned away. A rifle shot cracked through the air, and he fell forward onto the deck of the boat. The craft sailed away into a dark fog bank.

She suddenly sat up in bed. The nightmare had returned.

Chapter 26

The next morning Nadya waited until Dmitri appeared at work. She marched into his office and closed the door behind her.

"You are no friend of mine this morning, you foolish man. Why did you take Minuri home and waltz down the sidewalk like two lovers? Did you think Lena would not see?" Nadya stood upright in front of his desk, with her arms folded over her chest. "You hurt my friend very much last night, a night when she needed to be loved after a very bad day. *You* are on my shit list."

Dmitri sat at his desk with his head in his hands. His eyes were bloodshot and his skin was sallow. When he looked up to face Nadya, his collar fell open to reveal a large, fresh love bite on his neck.

"Oh my God! You slept with that woman, you slutty ass. Oh, you are in big trouble now." Nadya opened the door and stormed out into the corridor.

"But wait! I have an awful headache, and I didn't sleep at all. How was I to know she could drink like a soldier and be so demanding? Nadya, come back and let me explain . . ."

***

The modeling project proceeded well for several days. Lena had prepared the test data set, and the core programmers seemed happy with it. After a few modifications, they worked on their own trying to correct problems with the solver. They made good progress, and other components of the model were coming along well also. Soon all groups were waiting for the core to be ready. At that time, the pressure was on Markov for a change.

The holidays came and Lena attended several parties with her colleagues. Work slowed to a near halt as people took time off and visited their families. Lena and her family of friends celebrated a quiet Christmas at her apartment, and Eric's eyes lit up at the sight of the small Christmas tree that they had cut down in a nearby forest.

The New Year's celebration was held at the Northern Lights, where new and old patrons welcomed in 1979. Dmitri wasn't invited to the party, and needless to say, Minuri wasn't present.

During the holidays, security relaxed because so few people were in the office. Lena was able to copy several documents concerning different aspects of the modeling project. She passed the information along through the usual dead-drop channel.

Her handler, RURIK, pressed her to take advantage of any lapses she found in protocols or security. She had, of course, kept him apprised of the work being done on the model and the trouble they were having with the solver. He told her that any information she could acquire regarding the Markov solver would be extremely valuable.

RUKIK rarely met with his agents, but Lena demanded that they meet in mid-January to discuss a strategy to gain access to the solver. They met at a café near Nevskiy Prospekt in the early afternoon. Lena took some personal time off from work and did a little shopping to cover her tracks on the way to the meeting. There was nothing like narrow shopping alleys to screen out anyone following her.

RURIK was already waiting at a small table at the back of the room near the rear exit. He was a rather small man with gray hair and a short goatee. He was sitting alone drinking tea and reading *Pravda*. His bright gray-blue eyes occasionally peered out from beneath an old brown fedora. After an established protocol, Lena sat down at the table and they talked cautiously.

Lena explained that before long the solver would be finalized, and the computer code for it would no longer be available as raw code but only as a compiled, unreadable form. She was concerned that the higher security now in place would increase the odds that she could be caught making a copy of the model.

She was worried about what would happen to Eric if she were captured. Until now she hadn't needed to worry so much regarding his future. But now the risks were very high, and she required assurances that Eric, Katya, Misha, and Nadya would be protected if things went wrong. The Soviet authorities would most certainly take out their revenge on her family and close friends.

"There is another topic we must discuss," she said quietly. "I want to know what will happen to me after this—if I obtain the model for you."

"What do you mean?" RURIK asked, looking a bit puzzled by her question.

"What will I do next?" she asked, eyebrows raised. "I cannot go on leading this double life forever. What happens when you no longer need me?"

"But we always need information."

"But what if I get caught? What will happen to my son, my sister, my friends? They are all part of this equation now. I need protection."

"You mean if you get the model code? What can I do to protect you?" RURIK seemed surprised but then acted like he understood her concerns.

"Yes, you fool." She felt that he was being obtuse. "Can you get my family and me out of the country if everything goes to hell? If I get caught or have to go on the run?" She felt her face harden.

There. She had said it out loud. She felt a sense of relief after finally stating her greatest concern.

She had to think of Eric's future. Would it be possible for her to someday live in the West, maybe in Scandinavia, where Eric could grow up free and have more opportunities? If she did this risky, nearly impossible thing—copying the solver code—could RURIK protect her and get her out of Russia? If he could, then it certainly would be worth any risk.

RURIK was taken aback at first; perhaps he didn't expect agents to be so direct about outcomes—or, at least, not to be so determined. He stared at her and then smiled. He asked, "Do you really think that you can make a copy of the model code and the data sets? And not get caught? And leave no trace like you did last time?" RURIK rubbed his goatee with his hand.

"I believe so. But it will be dangerous. There are many obstacles."

"VERNA, if you could do that, which sounds to me like a miracle given the new security, then the answer is yes. I think we would owe you a great favor indeed." He raised his steely eyes to her face, and she sensed that he was sincere.

Lena was almost elated with joy to hear these words. She had suspected that RURIK would say she was asking too much. She thought that he would only offer her more money to cover her risk.

"Are you certain? I will need assurances," she said seriously. She had assumed that any need she had to flee into a life of hiding and running from the KGB would be beyond his caring.

"I have to verify my position, but I can assure you that we would protect you—and your family."

Now she had reason to be hopeful. She was surprised and could hardly breathe. She would have to make an absolutely foolproof plan to copy the model and data. She already had the beginnings of an idea. Now she would prepare in great detail.

The meeting ended and Lena walked away. When she looked back at the table, RURIK had already vanished, as if into thin air. She wondered if his promises would vanish in the same manner if she needed his help.

***

Lena spent time preparing for her upcoming mission over the next few days. She planned the operation in three parts. First, she would obtain materials and establish patterns so that no actions were out of place and no activities seemed amiss. Second, she would make copies of the code and data and leave no trace while doing it. Third, she would get the file copy out of her possession as quickly as possible and into RURIK's hands. If she could do all this seamlessly, then all would be well.

Based on the last time she made a copy of the model nearly seven years ago, she had insight into how to carry out the task. Previously, she had needed to find a magnetic tape that wasn't in the catalog and write the copy on it. She was lucky enough in those days to find an uncatalogued tape. Now there were no blank tapes lying around on a shelf she could access due to the tight record keeping protocols currently in effect.

But there were factors working in her favor now that hadn't existed then. The tape drives on their new computer system were much faster than before and the data being stored was written at a much higher density than on the earlier tapes. This meant that she could copy everything onto a smaller eighteen-centimeter diameter tape reel instead of on the big and heavy twenty-five-centimeter diameter reel that she had adhered to Eric's back all those years ago.

She stopped for a moment. She hadn't thought of that day for a long time. It still saddened her to think of losing Eric. It reminded her of how dangerous this work could be. But since then she had become even more determined to bring change to her government. She had turned this goal into her own challenge, her own *taynaya voyna* or "secret war" to bring freedom for herself, her little Eric, and the Russian people.

She fought to keep those deeply buried emotions in check. She had to concentrate. It might be the only way to keep what was left of her love for Eric alive. It would let her protect her little boy—and give him a future.

Lena returned to planning the operation. She had requested that RURIK provide her with not one but two magnetic tapes identical to those used by the project. If he supplied her with the tapes, she didn't have to cover up a missing reel or leave a trail on the tape logs. The two tapes would come on plastic reels and in plastic cases to avoid detection.

She had also come up with a clever means to transport the tapes one at a time into the office when blank and to remove them from the office when the copies were made.

She created a diversion.

She had begun to practice throwing discus—an old sport that she had been quite good at in gymnasium and had tried to do competitively in university. She was no longer at the university, but last year she had enjoyed practicing with a few of the university athletes. To implement this strategy, she had struck up an acquaintance recently with one of the new Leningrad Technical Institute team players and had shown so much interest in practicing again that the player invited her to train with the team once in a while.

She made it known around the office that she was trying to get back in shape by meeting the team after work for practice as they began their early-season workouts. Even though competition wouldn't begin until March, the coach had the team start strength and endurance training early, and every once in a while, they got to practice their throws in the training field nearby.

Every day Lena came to work with her gym bag and the big metal hand case that contained her practice discus. She had shown the discus to several people at the office who had been impressed by its size and weight. It was quite heavy for a round piece of polymer that measured only eighteen centimeters across. The first time she brought it in, the security guard had thoroughly checked the disk and the box. He also marveled at the high-density polymer used to make the disk itself. Now whenever she came or went from the office, the guards, out of habit, asked her only to open the box so that they could look inside.

Lena had of course been careful to select a discus that was of exactly the same dimensions as the magnetic tapes the computer used. It had been expensive but was marked as an official Olympic specification discus and matched those used by the university team. She was able to modify the plastic interior of the case to create a secret hiding place for a tape under the discuss where it would be difficult to discover.

Lena was in a higher-level position now than she had been seven years ago. She was in charge of the data input modules of the model, so she had access to the data sets, and she herself wrote part of the model code. She was therefore able to temporarily disable the read-write counter in the tape control software when she needed to. That would allow her to make a copy of the database any time without leaving a trace.

The database would require much more time to write to tape than the model code, simply due to its size. That was why Lena had requested the two tapes. She decided to copy the data as the first part of her plan because the operation would take three or four times longer than the time it would take to copy the model. Time would be her enemy once she began to write to tape. Anyone could come in and find her waiting for the tape to write. If she was making a copy of the data set only, she could explain that away as an extra backup procedure. But if she was caught copying the model, that was a different matter altogether.

Copying the code required a more circumspect approach because she did not really have authorization to access that portion of the computer's memory. She needed a higher-level pass code to log on to the computer for that. She had a strategy but now only waited to gain access.

The easiest way to obtain a password was from one of the programmers themselves. There were only a few people who had such passwords: Markov, Minuri, Dmitri, Alex, Yusef, Vladimir, the system administrator, and the director himself. Each person had a personalized password unique to them so that the system administrator could tell who was logged on to the computer at any given time. This presented a problem for Lena because if she used someone else's password and she was caught, that person would be implicated and thought to be a possible coconspirator. She thought about this and decided that the only person she would consider risking was Markov.

The core programmers worked in a separate room from the rest of the staff, where they accessed the computer via several specialized workstations. The room had a secure door and glass windows in the wall facing the main computer room. The system administrator's office was located next door and also looked out onto the main computer room but not into the programmer's work space.

The computer room contained the main computer and all its peripheral equipment. The operations console for the computer was where the administrator usually worked, retreating to his office when he needed a little peace and quiet. Sometimes he held small meetings in his office, but he preferred using the conference room down the hall for those. His office was his private retreat, where he often lowered the blinds on the glass windows to get uninterrupted privacy.

The data management group, including Nadya, worked in a suite of rooms located on the upper floor of the building. There they had their own small computer, computer terminals, tables, and a file room where they kept incoming data sets organized. The other programmers, those who didn't work on the core, were also stationed at offices on the second floor. While the programmers had direct access to the computer for their work, the data team had to shuttle their data sets back and forth to the tape drive room on the first floor next to the main computer room. This wasn't an efficient arrangement because they had to organize their files on the small computer, write it to tape, carry it downstairs, and load the data on the main computer via its own tape drives.

The model and database had grown rapidly over the last year, and the main computer did not have sufficient random-access memory, or RAM, to accommodate the program and all the data at once. Therefore, it was necessary to operate the model by reading subsets of the data from one tape as needed and writing the final results to a second tape. In that way there was enough available RAM memory for the model to run unimpeded.

The conversion of the model to use the matrix solver placed increased demand on memory. The system administrator had recently tried to address this problem by increasing the number of RAM memory modules attached to the computer to help improve operations and run speeds. Those sorts of upgrades seemed to be a constant challenge. As soon as he added additional RAM memory online, the core programmers would use it and ask for more. They supplemented the RAM with external hard memory drives that were the size of washing machines.

The problem for Lena was that only terminals in the programmers' workroom, the administrator's office, and the main computer room were authorized for core programming. If she obtained a core password, she would have to use one of those core terminals, most of which were occupied during the workday. After normal office hours, some people stayed behind to get work done when the computer wasn't in such heavy use and more memory was available. It wasn't unusual for a programmer to work late or even come back to work after dinner if they had a deadline to meet. Sometimes the person would forget to log off the computer when they left for lunch or dinner. In that case, the computer would automatically log the terminal off if it was inactive for an hour or longer.

Lena had two options if she was to accomplish her mission—obtain one of the programmer's passwords or wait for someone to leave their computer unoccupied but logged on when they left the room. Either way, she would have a small window of opportunity to copy the model file. It would be risky.

Chapter 27

Leningrad, Russia
January and February 1979

The end of January was very bleak as a mass of extremely cold arctic air lingered over Leningrad. People said that the weather was even worse in the eastern provinces near Perm and the Ural Mountains where ferocious winds swept the landscape. The cold weather kept most people indoors much of the time, and the city seemed like a windswept wasteland for days on end.

During this time Lena and Dmitri had tried to recover their friendship after the Minuri incident, as Nadya called it. They didn't spend nights together anymore, but they tried to be colleagues and even friends at work. Nadya was much less forgiving and chastised Lena whenever she thought that Lena was becoming too close to Dmitri.

It was a good time for the modeling project. After weeks of frustrating work, the core programmers finally fixed the problems with the solver, and it began to behave itself. It also began to demonstrate how superior it was at speeding up computer runs. Model simulations that had taken seven or eight hours before could now be completed in less than an hour. The only slow operations left were the reading and writing of data to tape, which were still necessary. Plans were made to add even more RAM memory and hard drives to the computer system to provide more buffering of the tape read and write tasks, which would speed up those operations as well.

The modelers decided that it was time to test the model using real data sets instead of the test data set they had been working with up until then. In order to do that, the data sets would need to be restructured one last time.

The director called a meeting to discuss what the final data structure should be, and both Lena and Nadya attended. Lena was tasked with writing any new code needed to make the files compatible with the model. Nadya and her staff were assigned the preparation of the actual data sets. Dmitri was asked to assist them by telling them what the structure and input sequence would be.

After the meeting they set to work on their respective tasks. Lena and Dmitri decided that the easiest way to discuss the structure required was to sit down at a terminal to scroll through the data sets. To do that, they went to the core workroom and used one of the specialized terminals. There Dmitri could access both the code and the data.

They worked on the model until the end of the day, when Lena had to leave to pick up Eric at the day care. She and Dmitri realized that they would have to spend more time together over the next few days, so they agreed to spend two to three hours after work each day to achieve the results.

On the third day, Nadya took Eric home so that Lena could stay late when the computer wasn't busy and they could work more efficiently. Nearly everyone was gone by four o'clock, and they had the workroom to themselves. That was when Lena noticed that a few of the programmers had left their terminals running after they had left. She knew that this was against security protocols but said nothing about it. She did not want to get anyone in trouble, and she immediately saw how she could use the laxity to her advantage.

At six o'clock, Dmitri said that he was going to the lunchroom to make tea. He needed a jolt of caffeine to stay alert. He and Lena both left the workroom and were gone for close to ten minutes preparing the refreshment. When they came back, the terminal was still logged on to the same file they were using under Dmitri's password.

They worked until 6:30 p.m., when Dmitri had to leave. Lena asked, "I have another hour before I must go home. Do you think I could stay here and continue with the work?"

"You could stay, but if the security people come by, you might be in trouble. But if it's the data file you want, I can make you a copy to use at your terminal."

"Should I get a tape so that you can write a copy on it?"

"No. There is a simpler way. That is a big advantage of all the new memory we have added to the computer. We can store lots of data and files in memory now, at least temporarily." He pointed to the screen. "You see on the screen there is a list of the files we use. All the ones with a star at the end are the secure files. See, here is the test data set and next to it is its file size in kilobytes. And here is the new model code, which is approximately the same size. The other files are older versions of the model or results." Dmitri continued pointing to the screen as he talked. "I can use the copy command to create a new copy of the data file and write it into a section of the memory that you have access to. This is much like you do to write files to your tape drive. Where should I write the file?"

Lena looked thoughtful for a moment, then said, "Put it in the project temporary data directory. I can access it from my terminal upstairs. But if it is a secure file, I won't be able to do anything with it anyway. I need an unsecured file to work with."

"That's no problem. Because of my clearance, I can make an unsecure copy by writing the copy command with these extra parameters." He copied file TDAT009*.RVX to the temporary data directory as the unsecured file labeled TDAT009.RVX. After two minutes the screen confirmed that the write operation was done.

"My, that was fast! I'm impressed." Lena was surprised at the speed. "Why is it so much quicker than the tape operations I do?"

"We just wrote from one memory stack to another memory stack. It was completely electronic with no moving parts. So it is very rapid indeed."

Dmitri got up to go. He and Lena went up to her terminal on the second floor to verify that she could read the file. Sure enough it was there, and she could open the new file called TDAT009.RVX. He told her that she should copy it to tape for use on the small computer. He also said that it might not be there in memory tomorrow because if the model run required more memory, the computer would overwrite that part of the memory stack.

He left for the night, and Lena made a tape copy that took ten minutes to write. She sat at her desk and looked through the data file structure and took notes. She decided that she was too tired to continue beyond 7:00 p.m.

She rode the bus home and held her briefcase on her lap. She smiled as she realized that she now had the final component of her mission in hand. Now she only had to execute the plan.

***

By that Wednesday Lena had worked out the changes needed to the model's data input code. Nadya and the others in the data group worked diligently to assemble the latest data sets into a final set of files for use in the model. It seemed that everything was ready for a model test run using real data sets.

On Thursday a model run was made using real data for a five-year period—only a fraction of the duration of the data in the database. Markov came to the building early to make sure that nothing had been overlooked. To everyone's surprise, after an initial glitch, the model ran through the data set in less than one hour. Using the old solver, that same run would have taken at least four hours and possibly longer. Markov was both relieved and encouraged. Even *he* smiled as he reviewed the results.

The director was ecstatic and kept saying over and over, "It runs like a wildcat, it is so fast!"

At the end of the day, the director called the assistant secretary of economic planning to announce that the model was working well but that they needed a few weeks to complete work on it. Then it would be ready for the secretary to visit the university and see a demonstration of the model's performance.

The month of February was spent on model calibration and testing under a range of conditions to make sure that it was indeed stable. No major problems were encountered. By the end of the month, the data set was certified as final.

The director designated March 14, a Wednesday, to be a celebration day. He invited the secretary to attend a ceremony at the project offices and organized a series of events for the day. He also instructed his staff to have the first complete model simulation finished before the ceremony.

Markov went further and insisted that they time the simulation to finish during the ceremony. He thought that would surely impress the secretary.

To that end, a complete model run using all the years of actual economic data was started on Saturday, the tenth, and ran to the end of the day on Sunday. It was a twenty-nine-hour run. Nearly everything worked as planned. Preliminary evaluation of the results indicated that the model could match the known calibration data set well and a short verification data set within an acceptable range.

Markov and the core programmers were very pleased with themselves. The economics experts were also happy with the results so far.

The director told the staff who had worked on the weekend to take Monday off and to come in late on Tuesday to begin the official computer simulation that would end during the celebration ceremony.

Chapter 28

On Monday morning several of the economics project staff came in as usual, but most modelers who had worked on the weekend stayed away. Among those who worked were Nadya, Lena, Dmitri, Minuri, and Markov.

Markov and Minuri were the first to arrive just after noon. Markov wanted to make one more small change to the code to improve its performance. He and Minuri worked on it for three hours and then left the building.

Nadya came in to make backup copies of the data files that had been used over the weekend. She logged two copies into the tape catalog. She admitted to Lena that she was afraid something might happen to the data and she wanted to be absolutely certain that it was protected. When she was finished, she stopped by Lena's office to chat for a while before leaving for home and taking little Eric with her.

Lena and Dmitri kept working and didn't realize how late it was getting to be. Dmitri found Lena at her desk, going over a printout from the weekend model run. She was trying to verify a small portion of the results suggesting there might have been an error in the manner in which one specific data set was read. She showed Dmitri what she had observed, and he also thought that it might indicate an input or output error. On further checking, he agreed. They decided that the irregularity Lena had seen was not really a reading error but that the program was writing the results incorrectly. Dmitri said that he would make a small change in the code and all should be well.

It was 6:00 p.m. by the time they finished, and only the cleaning staff and a few guards were left in the building. Dmitri went to the core workroom to make the code change and to finalize some other tasks.

Lena went down to the lunchroom, slowly walking along the corridor and confirming that no one else from the data or programming groups was around. She had hoped that she would have free run of the computer room for the evening. It had occurred to her on the weekend that today would be the perfect day to copy the data set onto her own tape.

Once she confirmed that all was clear, she went to her office and placed her discus case on her desk. She opened the case, lifted out the disk, and removed the thin plastic panel below to revealed a blank eighteen-centimeter magnetic tape on its plastic reel. She pulled it out and replaced the panel and the discus, setting the case back on the floor.

Next, she went down the hall to the tape drive room where she loaded the tape onto the drive. She used the terminal in the room to log herself on and to command the computer to make a backup copy of the entire database plus the model input data files. The tape began to whir as data was transferred to it from memory.

Lena now had nearly forty-five minutes to wait while the tape drive did its job. She walked into the computer room to look at how the administrator had managed to pack all the computer equipment, mostly the bulky memory modules, into the room. She went over and looked at the administrator's control station and sat down nervously to examine the console.

"You are still here?" Dmitri asked, startling her as he came out of the workroom. Lena bolted up from the console and began to turn red in the face.

"Aha!" Dmitri smiled at her. "I caught you trying out the administrator's chair for size. Beware, someone tried to switch chairs with him once, and he now has written his name on the bottom so that no one will do it again."

"Dmitri, you surprised me. I thought you would be done by now."

"I have several things left to do it seems and will be a little late tonight. I was just going down to the lunchroom to make a pot of tea. I have a bit of coffee cake with me I could share, if you are interested. Would you like to join me?" He smiled benevolently at her.

Lena began to decline his invitation but then paused as she stared through the glass windows of the programmers' workroom. There was no one inside. "Dmitri, are you the only one working tonight? I thought Minuri or Markov would be here tending to their special baby."

"No. I seem to be the only one here except you." He turned to walk away.

"Wait! Yes. I would like to have tea and maybe a bit of coffee cake too. I am getting a little tired, and it would help perk me up so I can finish and go home . . . Oh. But I need to check on my tape run. Why don't you go ahead and I will catch up with you?"

Dmitri seemed pleased that she had changed her mind and started down the hallway. He had been trying to make things right with her for weeks.

Lena stopped by the tape room for a second to make sure that the tape was on track. She went to look down the hall and saw no one. She decided that she must act now. She may not get a chance like this again soon.

She walked quickly back to the core workroom. True to form, Dmitri had left his terminal logged on before leaving to make tea. Without hesitation Lena sat down and scrolled through the computer screen to see what the new model file name was today. It was the file Dmitri had just closed, so its name was clearly labeled: MARKOV39*.RVX. Her hands started to shake as she began typing in the key sequence to tell the computer to copy the file to an unsecured portion of memory under a different name, TDAT049.RVX. She used a phony data file name that only she would recognize. She had planned the exact syntax of the command line so that she couldn't get it wrong. Still, in her haste, she mistyped the write parameters and had to edit the line. She pressed the enter key, and the computer began the operation.

She looked around as she waited. The sound of footsteps came from the hallway. Without thinking, she ducked beneath the computer desk to hide. It was the same reflex that she had when she was a child. She heard a radio crackle and realized that one of the security guards was making his rounds. She looked at her watch. It was 7:14 p.m., the time when the guard usually came by this area. How could she have forgotten the guard's schedule? She began to panic. She could not be found in this room. *The guards know that. What can I do?*

"*Svet v komnate no tam nikogo net.* The lights are on in the computer room but no one is here." The guard spoke into his radio, then paused. "Just a second. The tape drive is working. Let me look down the hall. Wait a minute. I hear someone in the lunchroom. I'll check on it. Out."

Lena heard his footsteps receding down the corridor. She raised her head to look around the room. No one was there. The computer terminal made a beeping sound, and she looked at the screen: COPY OPERATION COMPLETE.

Breathing hard, she slipped into the chair and verified that the new file was where she intended. Then she scrolled back up and erased the last few lines of commands and responses. She returned the screen reading exactly as Dmitri had left it.

She hurried out of the workroom and into the hall. She started down the corridor and realized that the guard was in the lunchroom talking to Dmitri, who was in the process of telling him that Lena was supposed to join him for tea.

"Didn't you see her in the tape drive room?" he asked.

"No. I didn't see her," the guard said. "I'll look for her now." Then he began to back out of the lunchroom into the hallway.

Lena was at a loss to explain where she had been. She would have to lie and think of something clever to say quickly—very quickly.

Now!

Just then she came to the door of the ladies' room, and with animal instinct, she ducked into the bathroom as the guard turned around. He walked down the hall. She waited two seconds and opened the door. She stepped out and nearly ran into the guard. He reacted with surprise.

"Comrade! You have startled me," he said in Russian and began to laugh at the near collision. "I was coming to account for you but didn't expect to find you so dramatically. Are you all right? Did I bump into you?" He was quite amused and friendly.

"I am sorry. Yuri, is it not? I was in a hurry and you scared me too. I get a bit nervous when I have to work here at night. I am glad you are looking after me."

The guard ambled away to finish his rounds, and Lena hurried to the lunchroom.

"I'm sorry I took so long, Dmitri. I had to stop at the bathroom. But I wasn't so long that you had to send a guard to find me!" She and Dmitri both laughed at her joke.

They sat down for a few minutes to drink their tea and make small talk. The coffee cake was rich and gave Lena the energy she needed to get through the night. She had a hard time focusing on the conversation and Dmitri noticed.

"Are you still angry with me for being so stupid? I swear I didn't mean to harm you, Lena."

Lena realized that he had mistaken her quietness as anger over the whole Minuri affair.

"No, Dmitri. I'm not so angry with you," she said quietly. "But you hurt me deeply that night." Then she grinned devilishly. "But you were a cad. Is that what they call it in the West?" She laughed.

She went on to tell him about her training with the discus team. They chuckled at how out of condition she had found herself. Finally she looked at her watch and said that the tape must be finished.

They both went back to work, Dmitri to the workroom and Lena to retrieve her tape. She confirmed that the entire database was copied and checked the amount of space left on the tape. There was ample room left to write the model file on it too.

She went to the terminal, but instead of rewinding the tape, she typed in the command to write the model file onto the end of the tape. That took close to ten minutes. She verified the copies, then went to the tape drive and pushed the manual rewind button to rapidly rewind the tape onto its original plastic reel. She removed the tape and walked to her office. After a last-minute check of the hallway, she set the tape back in the secret compartment in her discus case, ensuring that the plastic panel was firmly in place.

Next, she needed to make a data file backup on an official project tape in order to justify her activities that evening. She checked out a tape from storage and took it to the tape room. There she mounted it on a drive and began to make another copy of the data file. That took nearly forty minutes, so in the meantime, she went to talk to Dmitri in the core workroom.

When she entered the room, Dmitri looked surprised and acted as if there was something wrong.

"What happened? Did I startle you this time?" she asked jokingly.

He responded with a flurry of rapid typing on the terminal before she could step to his side.

"Yes! You startled me, and I think I erased something. I was just falling asleep." He got to his feet right away and put his hand on her shoulder, blocking her view of the screen. He moved closer, and before she could react, he leaned in and kissed her on the cheek.

"Dmitri! We are not going to do that." She backed away, surprised.

He gave her a sheepish smile. "You can't blame me for trying, you beautiful computer girl!" He laughed and shepherded her toward the door. "I need more tea. I am getting silly."

That she could agree with, and she smiled back at him. *Maybe he is not so bad after all,* she thought to herself.

"Come with me to make tea," he said. "I need the company."

She sauntered to the lunchroom with him, and they talked pleasantly while they waited for the teapot to boil. They took their cups back with them to the computer room. Just then the tape drive finished its operation, and Lena looked at the drive. Dmitri said that he had to get to work in order to finish before it got too late. They both returned to their tasks.

Lena verified the copy and prepared to rewind the tape. She stopped with her hand near the rewind button. She hesitated while she thought. Maybe she should make another copy of the model file from the temporary memory while she had access. She didn't have her other secret blank tape with her tonight, but she could possibly write the much smaller file onto the end of the official tape for now. She could bring in the other blank tape tomorrow and copy it over using the small computer upstairs. Or even do it from tape to tape here in the tape room if no one was watching.

She decided to risk it. She realized that her palms were sweating and her hands shook from the tension. She was terrified but fought to contain her fear.

At the terminal, she typed in the command to copy the model file to the end of the tape and hit enter. The drive whirred into action.

Dmitri entered the room just as the tape drive had finished writing. "You must be ready by now. I am done, and if you like, I can drive you home. It is too cold to wait for the bus tonight."

Lena leaned against the terminal to face Dmitri and to hide the screen that was blinking her commands in bright-green light.

"Dmitri, that would be very nice if you behave yourself. Yes. I accept your offer. Let me put the tape away and log it back in." She stepped up to the tape drive. "How about meeting me at my office in five minutes, *da*?"

When Dmitri left, she pressed the rewind button and erased the last lines in the terminal record. She went upstairs and returned the tape to storage, logging it back into the catalog. In her office, she bundled up in the wooly layers of clothing she wore to protect against the frigid night air. She picked up her discus case and prepared to leave. She walked with Dmitri to the security station. She opened her case for Yuri to look inside and passed through the metal scanner. Dmitri followed.

They said goodnight to Yuri and stepped outside as heavy snow began to fall. Lena took a deep breath of fresh, cold air and felt a huge weight lift from her shoulders.

Chapter 29

Leningrad, Russia
Tuesday, March 13, 1979

Lena had disturbing dreams that night. She was in a long line at the market, waiting for hours it seemed. Finally she came to the head of the line, and an officious woman in a crisp brown uniform asked her what it was she wanted. She couldn't remember and was sent back to the end of the line. This was repeated three times until she was once again at the head of the line.

"What did you forget this time, comrade?" The uniformed woman was now leaning right into her face in an aggressive manner.

In her dream she asked herself, *What did I forget?*

Lena bolted upright in bed. "The file! I forgot to erase the file!" she exclaimed out loud.

"*Mamochka*, Mummy! You scared me." Eric, on his small bed nearby, began to cry.

"*Mne zhal'*, I'm sorry, darling. I didn't mean to frighten you. I just had a bad dream and it startled me," she said in a soothing voice. "But it is all right now."

The boy whimpered and said, "I'm cold, Mummy."

"Why don't you come to Mummy and sleep in my bed tonight? I can keep you warm." She coaxed him over, and he snuggled in beside her. She put his head against her breast and whispered calming things to him as he quieted down.

Lena lay on her back wide awake. She was doomed. She knew it now. She had forgotten to erase the temporary model file from the computer memory. She had been startled by Dmitri and had simply forgotten to do it. Now someone would find the file and there would be no explanation for it.

She would be caught. She would be questioned without mercy. They would put her in a dark gulag somewhere. They would take Eric from her, and she would never see him again. She began to sob silently.

She hugged Eric to her breast. He had stopped crying now but was awake, sensing the tension in her body. He snuggled in and mouthed her breast through her nightgown, always content while suckling. He was too old for that now, but she still fed him occasionally. It calmed him and it calmed her as well. She reached down and unbuttoned the top of her gown and gave him her nipple to suck on. *This might be the last night we have together*, she thought despairingly.

They both fell asleep that way. Mother and son together.

***

Lena arose very early in the morning and saw two inches of new snow on her windowsill. The sky was clear, suggesting there would be frigid conditions at the bus stop.

She dressed warmly and made a breakfast of eggs and toast, ensuring that Eric ate until his belly was very full. While he was getting dressed, she removed the tape from her discus case and placed it in a plastic tape canister to protect it. She wrapped the canister in cardboard and taped it closed to make a sturdy square package. She wrote "for Mr. Cerny" on it and dropped it in a paper shopping bag. She then hid the second blank tape in the discus case.

She hurried Eric along and packed his things for the day. She called through the door to her sister to say that she was leaving already. Katya opened the bedroom door, dressed only in her flannel nightgown, rubbing her eyes with a fist, to see what was happening. Lena explained that she had to be in early, and she embraced her sister for a long time. Katya was surprised but hugged her back sleepily.

Lena left with Eric and walked down the hall to Auntie Olga's apartment. She hoped the old woman was awake at this early hour. She pounded on the door until she heard angry shouting from the other side. She called to Olga through the door and asked her to open up.

Olga did so and gave Lena the evil eye. She was dressed only in a bathrobe over a tattered cotton nightgown.

"Olga, I am sorry to wake you so early. I have a small emergency at work and the day care facility isn't open yet. Can you take care of Eric for most of today?"

The old woman smiled when she saw Eric standing beside his mother.

"Yes, I suppose," she said huffily. "But dear. I have a weak heart and wasn't awake yet. You need to be more considerate of old people."

Lena left Eric and the package with Olga. "A friend, a Mr. Cerny, will come by to pick up the package later, if it is all right with you. I am sorry for the short notice, and I will make it up to you."

She felt awful about leaving her son so abruptly and for imposing on her elderly neighbor. But she was desperate. She gave Olga extra money for food for Eric, something she never did before. She rushed down the hall.

Lena was lucky and caught a bus right away on the street. She had to get into the office before anyone noticed the extra file on the computer. Maybe she could erase it before it was discovered. And if she was lucky—very lucky—she could write another copy of the file on the secret tape. If everything went as she planned, she would have a second copy of the model for safekeeping. RURIK would have his file for sure and all would be well.

She got off the bus three stops before the university. She walked down a side street for two blocks to a small convenience shop that was just opening its doors. She went inside to buy an apple and a pastry, as she did some mornings. She greeted the shop owner and asked how she liked the snow from last night. After a few pleasantries, she paid and took her little bag of food with her. As she walked away from the shop, she made two diagonal marks with chalk on the side of the nearby streetlamp as she stopped next to it, rearranging her case and the bag. She walked back to the main street just in time to catch the next bus to the university.

Everything appeared normal at work, with very few people in the building. Markov and Minuri were talking to the system administrator in his office, preparing for the start of the long model run. They planned for it to begin just before 10:00 a.m. so that it would finish at 3:00 p.m. the next day, midway through the official ceremony.

Lena entered her office and closed the door. She quickly removed the blank tape from the discus case and hid it in her handbag. She opened the door and hurried to the tape storage area to log out the tape she had made last night. She had to erase or overwrite the copy of the model file she had made there to avoid discovery. She decided to queue the tape up at the end of yesterday's data file and write a new copy of the data file over the model file. That would destroy the temporary model file. While no one was looking, she pried off the tape label from the official tape and stuck it to her secret tape reel so that it would look like an official tape.

She steeled herself against the risk she would now take. Once again her brow began to moisten as if she was in the summer heat.

She walked to the tape drive room and could see that the lead programmers were still meeting in the administrator's office. She might have enough time if all went well. To her relief, the temporary file was still on the computer's RAM memory as she had left it. She mounted her blank tape quickly and began to copy the temporary model file over to it from the computer memory. She wiped sweat from her face with the sleeve of her blouse.

The tape finished writing as the meeting broke up. She verified that the file was copied to the tape and immediately erased the temporary file in RAM. No one would find the file now and she would not be sent to a gulag—at least not yet. She erased the terminal command line records. She went to the tape drive and prepared to rewind the tape but decided to remove it instead just as Minuri came out of the meeting. Lena placed the tape in her handbag as Minuri leaned into the tape room doorway to say good morning.

"Hello, Lena. Why are you in this morning?" She seemed genuinely friendly. "Most of the staff took the morning off and will come in after lunch." She smiled as she watched Lena work. "How did you like the snow overnight? Doesn't it make everything look like magic?"

"Yes," Lena replied. "The snow is beautiful, but I would rather that spring came early this year."

"I can agree with that. Winter seems to last longer each year."

"I came in to make one last copy of the data file before the model run begins," Lena said, "just to be safe. Once the model begins, the computer will not be available for tape operation."

Minuri looked mischievous. "This is a good idea. And Markov would be angry if he had to share even a little bit of the computer with anyone else."

The women laughed as Minuri puffed out her cheeks and made cross-eyes to mimic the expression of a red-faced and angry Markov.

Lena decided that she could make an extra data copy if she did so immediately. She reloaded her secret tape and queued it to start a new write operation at the end of the model file. She gave the command to copy the data file to the tape, and the tape whirred.

She had time to kill, so she went to visit Nadya at her desk. The data team was busy verifying that the modelers had the correct data file for the simulation. Apparently Dmitri had asked her to recopy the file and save it under a new name. She wasn't sure why they had changed the file name at the last minute, but she was not one to argue about it.

"Lena," she said, "I'm a nervous wreck. I am afraid something will go wrong and the director will be disappointed."

"And if that happens," Lena grinned, "Markov will throw a tantrum in front of the entire meeting tomorrow. I would love to see him taken down a notch."

"Yes, but still. It terrifies me," Nadya said. "I think Markov is grandstanding by wanting the model run to be timed so it would end during the ceremony. His ego is always involved in his decisions." She had made her opinion widely known to the staff on the second floor. Many people there shared her views on Markov.

Lena shuffled back to the tape room, where her copy operation had finished. She rewound the tape, removed it, took off the label, and stuck it back on the official tape. She hid the secret tape in her handbag. Then she loaded the official tape on the drive and began to copy the data file to it as well. While the tape drive whirred, she went back to her office and hid the secret tape in her discus case.

She finally had a chance to breathe easy. Sitting in her chair, she closed her eyes for a minute. *Maybe God has favored me today*, she thought.

She went back to the tape room but heard voices coming from within. As she entered, she saw Markov standing at the terminal with the administrator. Markov was pointing to the tape drive that was still operating.

"Why is someone using the computer here?" he demanded in his loud and irritating voice. "I made it clear that there should be no interference with the model run. Who is doing this? It must stop now."

Lena entered the room in time to hear all of this. "I am making a final backup of the data file for safety. What is the problem? I am almost done, so stop complaining." Lena went right over to face Markov and prepared to be yelled at.

"So it is you who is trying to ruin my model run," he glowered. "I should have known it was one of the data technicians who would do something stupid."

Lena was getting angry enough to respond in kind when the tape operation stopped.

"There! You see. I am done," she said angrily. "You can have your damned computer to play with all by yourself." She stepped over to the drive and pushed the rewind button. The administrator looked sheepish and began to apologize for Markov's accusations. But she cut him off, took the tape, and left the room.

"I don't need this much stress," she called back to the administrator. "Tell the director that I am taking the rest of the day off. There is too much testosterone and ego here to work." With that, she stormed away to the tape storage room.

She logged the official tape back into storage, packed her things, and left the office. By the time she passed through security, even the security guards had heard of Markov's outburst and expressed their sympathy. They told her that he had already unloaded his wrath on them, on Nadya, on the director, and on the administrator that morning. He was living up to his reputation as a world-class ass. Secretly Lena thought, *We all despise this man.*

Lena took the bus along the main road to the third stop and got off there. She walked to the convenience shop and looked at the lamppost. Her marks were still there with no additions. She went into the store to buy a juice drink and sat on the bench by the street corner to eat her lunch. She decided that she couldn't wait for the usual protocols to transfer the tapes to RURIK. She would ask for a direct meeting again. With this in mind, she sauntered over to the lamppost and leaned back, taking in the morning sun. She made two more marks on the pole and casually walked away.

Lena took the bus home and retrieved Eric and Mr. Cerny's package from Auntie Olga. She spent the day with her son, going to the park and enjoying two hours in the sunshine. Somehow everything had changed for the better after all.

She had survived another day.

Chapter 30

The next morning the blue sky held only a few cirrus clouds overhead, meaning that there would be frigid weather all day. Lena bundled up in her heaviest coat with a hood and wore wool long underwear under her thick trousers. She dressed Eric in his winter coat and a warm rabbit fur hat. They set off for the bus stop and felt chilly all the way to the university.

Lena dropped Eric off at the school and walked to a little coffee shop near campus at 9:00 a.m. The usual assortment of students, staff, and locals was present at tables or standing in line for coffee. She found a small table at the back of the shop and sat with a cup of rather good-quality coffee. Somehow the cafés and restaurants could still purchase premium coffee through their special suppliers, better than the masses could buy. It was refreshing to sip the brew slowly while she waited for her contact to arrive.

After a few minutes, a young man with a heavy woolen coat and a shock of blond hair entered the shop. Lena recognized him by the book he was carrying. Finding no free table, he ordered a coffee to go and waited for it, standing by the counter. Lena got up to leave, and the man brought his coffee over to see if her table was now available. As he approached, he appeared to trip and spilled a little coffee on the table.

"I'm sorry. Did I splash coffee on you?" He handed her a napkin in case she needed it.

"Oh no. I am fine. The coffee missed me." She laughed. "There was no harm done. In any case I am just leaving, so you can have this table if you wish."

"Thank you," he said and sat down.

She put the napkin in her pocket and left the shop.

When she was a block away and saw no one following, she removed the napkin and unfolded it. A small strip of paper with an address and a time was inside. She memorized the address and put the strip in her mouth, where it dissolved.

Eleven a.m. was only two hours away. She would have to hurry to get to the meeting place on time. There was no time to go to work first or to create a cover story. She just had to do it.

She caught a bus home and quietly climbed up the stairs to her apartment. She stowed both of her magnetic tapes in the discus case, placing one in the secret compartment and the other plastic canister on top. There was no room for the discus in that arrangement. She repackaged the second case in the "Mr. Cerny" cardboard wrapper and assembled the discus case to hide only one tape as usual. She placed the package in her oversize handbag so that she could carry both tapes at once and set out to meet RURIK.

She took the bus that traveled to the nearby shopping district, such as it was—a few shops along one side of the street. She rode one stop past the district and stepped out into a rundown neighborhood filled with gray houses dilapidated by age or lack of care. She walked for several blocks, glancing around her frequently to make sure that she wasn't being followed, and then she returned to the shopping center. She walked past several stores, searching for the address designated for the meeting on the pretext that she was doing some shopping. No such luck, she commented to herself, as there was little to purchase from their meager inventory. When 11:00 a.m. arrived, she entered an apartment building and proceeded to number 21 on the second floor. She knocked lightly on the door four times and went in.

She stepped directly into the living room of the small, empty apartment. No one was there, so she closed the door and waited. Soon she heard four knocks on the door and it opened. A small man in a long winter greatcoat entered and removed his wool hat, revealing a gray beard and clear eyes. It was RURIK.

"Were you followed?" he asked perfunctorily. Seeing her shake her head, he continued. "Are the tapes in the case?"

"One is in the case and one is in this package. They would not both fit with the discus inside."

RURIK put the metal case on the floor and opened it. He examined the layer of plastic at the bottom of the case. He pulled out a pocket knife and cut around the outside of the material, which caused the bottom to drop down a few millimeters. He tried stacking both tapes beneath the plastic panel and replaced the panel and the discus on top. The case closed tightly. Only the empty cardboard packaging remained.

"OK. This is good. Now, how are you?" He was all business, his sharp eyes glancing at Lena and the door alternately, as if expecting they would be discovered. "Tell me quickly how it all happened. Were there any problems? Suspicion? Did you cover your tracks?"

Lena summarized her exploits over the last two days, including the fact that she had forgotten to erase the model file on the first night. RURIK stopped her frequently to provide more details. When she finished he seemed satisfied that her cover was secure and that there were no known traces of her activity.

He breathed a sigh of relief. They both stood in the center of the room thinking of what came next. Lena stood absolutely still, anxious to hear what he would say now. Finally, RURIK smiled thinly.

"When I got your notice that you wanted to meet," he said, "I at first thought that something was the matter. I feared that maybe you had been discovered."

"I don't think there is any suspicion," she said nervously.

"Good, VERNA," RURIK said reassuringly.

Lena smiled back nervously, wondering what he would tell her next. *Good news? Or bad news?*

"I have set up arrangements for a safe house in case you and Eric need to disappear. I have the address and protocols for the location here in case there is still a problem. You must read this information now and memorize it. Burn the paper and this packaging material before you leave here."

He extended his hand and a small folded note in her direction. Lena took the slip of paper and put it in her pocket.

"Thank you."

"Notice that if there is an emergency, you cannot contact me or use the usual channels. That would risk the network. There is a number to call from a pay telephone and a protocol. An agent named VICTOR will help you then. He can protect you and will contact me, if necessary." He placed his hand on her shoulder to show comfort. "I will warn you that many times things seem as if they went well, with no hitches. But later you find out something, a little thing, went wrong. So you shouldn't feel safe yet."

Lena didn't need him to tell her that everything could still fly into pieces. She was terrified.

He saw the fear creep into her face. "No. No. It's not certain. But only a possibility. Everything is probably fine, but you must be prepared, just in case. It is like we always do. You must have a plan ready in case you need it at a moment's notice."

Lena relaxed a little. He smiled and held out his hand to her.

"I must go. I must leave and secure the tapes. I will be in contact, indirectly. VERNA, you have done well here, extremely well. We will talk soon." With that, RURIK took the discus case, opened the door, checked the hallway, and left the premises.

Lena had difficulty focusing on her task. She had to read the address and phone numbers several times before she could remember them clearly. She went to the small woodstove in the kitchen and found a few matches there. She tested her memory one more time before burning the paper and packaging.

She checked the apartment to be sure that there were no traces of her or RURIK's visit and left the room. She repeated her careful and circuitous route after leaving the building and business district. After two bus changes, certain that she hadn't been followed, she went to work.

***

Later that afternoon, everyone at the office was energized by the upcoming ceremony. Extra chairs had been placed in the conference room to accommodate all the senior management of the project, the university administrator, and the assistant secretary of economic planning with his staff. It would be a tight fit, and after trying several arrangements, the director decided that some people would have to watch the ceremony from the hallway. A long cable ran from the computer room to a computer terminal that had been set up in the conference room. Everyone could watch the progress of the computer run on the terminal, and the screen would flash a banner when the simulation was completed.

All this was part of Markov's grand plan—he would finish his short speech just as the model run finished. He apparently thought it would really impress the secretary.

Lena had lunch with Nadya and Dmitri in her office. They laughed about all the hoopla surrounding the ceremony. Dmitri joked about how angry Markov would be if the model run did not finish on his exact schedule. He and Nadya made fun of their boss and exchanged office gossip until it was time to go to the conference room.

At 2:45 p.m., many people gathered outside the conference room in the hallway, awaiting security screening.

Colonel Chayka was in his element—in charge of security and in overall control of the meeting. His tanned face with deep brown eyes set wide over broad cheekbones showed that he was fully engaged in this presentation. He wore his usual khaki uniform with gold braid and epaulets over highly polished black regulation shoes. He was very proper toward the few dignitaries who had arrived for the ceremony and seemed more nervous than usual. Lena thought he perhaps realized how much was riding on Markov's lecture—even his own reputation could be affected.

***

Before long most people were seated, and the ceremony got underway only a few minutes behind schedule. The director and Markov sat at the head of the table flanked by the assistant secretary and his aides on one side and the system administrator and economics faculty on the other. Lena, Nadya, and Dmitri sat next to the other programmers at the far end of the room. Everyone else was seated around the room on wooden or folding chairs, except for a few staff members and Colonel Chayka, who looked in from the hallway.

The director extended a warm welcome to the attendees, thanked them for coming, and immediately introduced the guests in the room. He gave a brief summary of the project in general terms. He talked about the exceptional work carried out by the economists who first envisioned such a model and who formulated the general theory behind it. Then he introduced the head of the economics department of the university and explained how the project came into being. Finally he lamented the fact that so much of this work was classified and would therefore not qualify for publication for years, if ever. Next, the head economist said a few words, and the secretary talked about his role in the project and how important the work was.

The director stood up. "Comrades, we seem to be running a little late, but Dr. Gregori Markov will now speak. We are excited because we can watch the model's progress on this terminal as it performs this historic calculation." He waved an open hand in Markov's direction and sat down.

Markov rose and prepared to speak, but a frown crossed his face. He looked down at the terminal. "This isn't normal. The computation is almost finished, but it is taking longer than it should." He tapped on the keyboard to verify that the model was solving the final step in the long simulation.

He gave a short presentation, emphasizing that none of this would have been possible without the Markov solver. He stated this boldly and preened as he did so. Several guffaws and a few muffled complaints erupted from the audience. But he continued and explained that the model would be finished in only a minute or two. He completed his presentation, but the model kept on running. He became agitated and sat down at the terminal to see what was taking so long. He swore under his breath.

The director stood up again, unprepared for the delay, and commented that even the best-laid plans sometimes went awry. He said that the model might be running slower because of any number of variables—memory availability, processor efficiency, and so on. He stalled for time as the secretary and many others looked at their watches and people began to talk among themselves.

Markov, who had never been a paragon of self-control, was typing away furiously at the terminal. He muttered under his breath, swearing out loud on occasion.

"There is something wrong. This cannot be taking so long to solve. It finished in one hundred twenty-six iterations on the last run. And now it is taking four hundred seven iterations. That is not possible!"

He issued the last statement in a loud outburst that silenced the whole room. All eyes were suddenly on Markov as he frantically pounded on the keyboard. He talked out loud as he searched for an explanation.

"All the steps until the last one ran normally. Why is this step not finished? Look at these results. The solver is oscillating. It has become unstable! How can that be?" By then he was on his feet and shouting, oblivious to the people around him.

The director didn't know what to do. He conferred with the administrator a moment and then with the secretary. "I think that we are finished with our presentation now. I know that many of you have tight schedules and need to leave. But I want to thank you for attending. Thank you, everyone, for your contribution and for coming today." He rose and shook hands with the dignitaries as they exited the room, all a little unsettled by the circumstances of the meeting.

People rose from their chairs, many of the staff snickering at Markov's lack of composure. He was sweating now and swearing loudly enough to be heard throughout the room and in the corridor. People began to leave the room as the administrator came to Markov's side and tried to help him.

"Stop! Stop, everyone!" Markov shouted as he leaped up from the terminal. "It's not the model at fault here. I can prove it now. Someone has changed several numbers in the last data set and that has made the solver unstable. Look here. You can see." He pointed at the screen. "There are a few nine hundred ninety-nines where there should be small real numbers—nothing larger than ten. That was deliberate!" He turned and stared at the computer screen.

People stopped moving and gazed at the Markov spectacle.

"This is sabotage!" He nearly screamed the accusation as he pounded the table. His face was red and distorted with rage.

"And I know who must have done it!" he shouted, looking wildly around the room. His eyes found Lena, Nadya, and Dmitri as they moved toward the door. Suddenly Markov pushed his way around the table until he was looming over Nadya, glowering and spitting.

"You! You bitch! You are the one, the only one to handle the final data. You did this to the model. You did this to me!" He grabbed Nadya by the blouse and shook her, tearing her clothing and frightening her.

Nadya pushed at his hand and twisted away from him. "You are insane, Markov! You're a crazy man and a pompous fool. Leave me alone and don't blame me because your ego is so easily bruised."

Markov tried to grab her throat, but he in turn was grabbed from behind by Chayka. The colonel wrestled him against the wall and told him to calm down and stop acting like an idiot. Then he turned and waved at the security guard by the door to block anyone from leaving.

"Ladies and gentlemen, please stop where you are," Chayka said loudly, taking command of the situation. "No one is leaving this room until I determine what has happened to the model. And if there was any sabotage, I will soon know who is responsible."

Chapter 31

Leningrad, Russia
Wednesday, March 14, 1979

Lena, Nadya, and Dmitri stood clustered together while everyone was forced to wait in the conference room. This whole incident was unprecedented, and the director seemed confused about what should be done. He argued with Chayka and the system administrator.

"Now what will happen?" Lena asked. "They are arguing about what to do."

"This is something new to our staff and the director, I'm afraid," Nadya said.

"I'll try to talk to the director, if I can get close," Lena said and then began to work her way through the crowd of anxious scientists.

Chayka had prevented the project staff from leaving the conference room. He declared that because the incident involved the model and potentially the solver code, he would launch an investigation as the project security officer. This raised some concerns among the staff because Chayka was an officer of the military intelligence agency, the GRU. If he took control, any investigation would not fall under the jurisdiction of the Leningrad Police Department or university authorities.

"I don't understand," the director said. "This is university property. Shouldn't the Leningrad city police conduct the investigation?" This was a new development for the director, who left to notify the university administration.

Meanwhile, Chayka told everyone in the room to take their seats and prepare to be questioned about what had happened. Lena pushed her way over to Chayka and asked, "But what exactly has happened? Why are we being held here like this?"

Markov overheard her and shouted, "Because one of you imbeciles has sabotaged my model! Was it you, Lena? Did you put impossibly large numbers in the data set?"

234 • Fred G. Baker

The director returned and announced that the city police were on their way to the economics department. The university had taken the position that they were in charge.

Chayka said that he understood the university's concern but that this was a state security matter and the police didn't have clearance for such a "sensitive" issue. He would execute the investigation per his authority from Moscow.

The director and system administrator objected in a loud and public manner.

"Wait! Wait!" the director said. "No one knows what really happened yet. It is possible that the solver code wasn't involved in the incident at all—except perhaps tangentially." He paused. "In fact, this all appears to be some sort of foolish prank intended to embarrass Markov. The only tampering of the model that we are aware of so far is the fact that someone added fictitious data to the last data set to deliberately cause the model to stall."

"That may be true," Chayka shot back, "but it is still interference with the model run."

"But it may not involve tampering with the code itself," the administrator pointed out.

"If that was all it was," argued the director, "and we can find out who has done it, then maybe there was no security breach." He had the attention of the others. "It appears that there is bad blood between Markov and one of the staff. Are you surprised? That isn't worth building into a major investigation that could possibly taint the modeling project and embarrass many people, like Markov, the university, the secretary, and the three of us."

Chayka was about to say something but stopped; he was overcome by a pensive look.

The administrator saw an opening. "After all, why make a problem for us all if it is a tempest in a teapot. And, of course, because you, Colonel Chayka, are in charge of project security, any investigation could only reflect badly on you." This caught Chayka's attention.

Chayka agreed that they should contain the scope of the investigation until they found out what had happened. He conceded that if it was just a prank, then the city police should be involved. He would not contact Moscow until they had completed their preliminary questioning.

Lena edged close to the men as they carried out their loud discussion of what to do. She tried to add information where she could, and the director pulled her in as an ally during the ensuing verbal battle.

Captain Pronin of the Leningrad Police Department arrived at just after 5:00 p.m. to head up the investigation. He was a smallish man with a waxed mustache and black hair that appeared oily and was combed straight back from his forehead. He had dark yet intelligent eyes, an aquiline nose, and a narrow face. He looked like he could have some French heritage but said that he was entirely Russian in his background. He wore a gray wool greatcoat to withstand the glacial weather and a dark-brown fur hat with earflaps he unfolded for subarctic conditions. He was very professional in his bearing and approach to police work. He wouldn't be bullied by any GRU functionary.

Pronin said that he was surprised to find Colonel Chayka of the GRU involved in a university matter. He pulled the director aside, and Lena listened in from a distance. Pronin said that he would telephone his old friend Colonel Ivan Ivanoff, who was now assistant director of the KGB's Second Chief Directorate in Leningrad. He would ask him to join them to provide a counterweight to the GRU presence. Lena thought this was a clever move because it offered them administrative cover. As much as he detested the KGB, the director agreed.

Pronin told the director that he didn't know whether he could trust the GRU after many of the rumors he had heard regarding them. He had heard the same rumors concerning the KGB and didn't trust them either, but at least involving the KGB through Ivanoff was a known risk. "It is simply a matter," Pronin said to the director, "of choosing what, at the time, seems to be the lesser of two evils. Or at least the evil I know versus the evil I do not know."

Pronin, Chayka, the system administrator, and the director formed an investigatory committee to begin interviewing people. They discussed who the likely perpetrator could be. They agreed that it was someone who had gained access to the final data set in order to modify its contents. But it could also be any of the core programmers who all knew that large spurious data values would cause the solver to become unstable. The committee decided to question Nadya, the only person accused by Markov; Lena, the input programmer; both Minuri and Dmitri, who worked on the final model run; and Markov himself.

When Lena's name was added to the list, the director said it couldn't be her. Besides, he needed her to sit in on the initial questioning to assist him as necessary.

They began the questioning with Markov, since he insisted on going first. He argued that he couldn't have sabotaged his own model because he was the person most likely to be embarrassed by the incident, not to mention that his reputation would be severely damaged. But they argued that he could just have easily done the data manipulation because he had full access. He responded angrily by accusing Nadya again, since she was the last person to work with the data file and had personally loaded it.

Next, they questioned Nadya and verified that she had prepared the final data file. They were aware that she disliked Markov intensely because of his mistreatment of Lena and herself. Yet they weren't certain that she knew that inserting spurious data would lead to such drastic results. In any case, she had lost her temper before and now told them in no uncertain terms what she really thought of Markov and what he could do with his precious solver.

Finally, they questioned Minuri and Dmitri, who had access to the model and knowledge of the serious impact that large data values would have. But neither of them had been directly involved in preparation of the final data file yesterday or today.

After completing the interviews, the committee decided that Nadya was the most likely suspect based on her animosity toward Markov.

Dmitri and Minuri were eliminated, and Markov, they decided, was unlikely to have sabotaged his own model.

The system administrator recommended that no one be allowed to access the computer until the investigation was complete. He would deactivate everyone's passwords for now to prevent further tampering with the evidence. He suggested that he, the director, and Markov should review the results of the model run to search for any internal clues. They should also examine the actual data tape that Nadya had delivered for the final model run.

In the meantime, Pronin and Chayka insisted that Nadya be held in custody while the investigation continued. The administrator and director, who knew her, objected, saying that they could not believe she had committed such an act deliberately. To hold her would be to punish her before there was any valid reason.

Pronin argued that, as a single woman, she was a flight risk. Chayka wanted to take her to a secure GRU holding facility, and the director objected to that strenuously. Pronin proposed holding her at the city jail on a temporary basis, at least until matters became clearer tomorrow. In the end, it seemed to be a reasonable compromise they all could live with.

Nadya was arrested amid protests from all her coworkers, especially Lena. The director repeated that it would only be temporary and not to be overly concerned. Pronin ordered his sergeant, Babichev, to take Nadya to the central police holding facility used for witnesses and petty crimes.

At six o'clock, Colonel Ivan Ivanoff arrived on the scene. He apologized for taking so long to get there. Pronin brought him up to date quickly and was surprised when the colonel became angry.

"Captain Pronin, I demand that you assemble the investigative committee immediately." He gave Pronin a look that would allow no questions.

When they were all together, Ivanoff stood up and spoke with great authority. "What you have done tonight is a good start to the resolution of this situation. But let me take the time to straighten out how this investigation will proceed. We don't know yet whether this incident was an accident or a crime."

"Yes. We already know all this," Chayka said curtly. The corner of his mouth curled downward.

Ivanoff looked around the room to be sure that he had everyone's attention. "Now we must discuss the matter of whose jurisdiction is involved here. Let us assume that this was a crime. In that case, it was committed on university property involving university staff working on an economic project. The nature of the crime suggests that it was motivated by a personal vendetta, so far as we know. Ordinarily, it would be considered a police matter. The fact that it interfered with a project of national importance makes it a matter of state security. Because the Defense Ministry is involved in the project in only a peripheral way, the investigation falls under KGB purview."

Chayka jumped up. "This is exactly the point, Ivanoff. It is a state security matter, and I am already in charge because security for this project falls under my purview."

Ivanoff wasn't intimidated by the GRU. "Colonel Chayka has an interest here because a secret militarily important computer code was used in the project, but we don't know whether the code was compromised. I strongly suspect not, because if someone wanted to steal the code or a spy wanted to make a copy of it, he would be a fool to create an incident to draw such attention to the matter." He stared Chayka down and noted that most of the committee were nodding their heads in agreement. "I think in the end, we will find that this is a vendetta, not espionage. Although still serious, it is not a national incident by any means."

"I am still the most directly involved in this matter," Chayka insisted. "Therefore, I will be in charge."

"But, you see, the incident occurred on the university campus here in Leningrad," Ivanoff replied. "Therefore, it should be up to the city police force unless and until a more sinister crime is indicated."

Captain Pronin spoke up. "I feel that the city should be in charge."

"Pronin and I will take over this investigation with the full cooperation and involvement of the GRU representative. If we find that the computer code itself was compromised, then we will inform Colonel Chayka, and his office will become fully involved." Ivanoff smiled and now turned to the grim-faced Chayka. "For now, we will proceed as you have all planned and reconvene here at nine o'clock tomorrow morning. Captain Pronin will bring the suspect, Nadya Michaijlovich, here for a further interview, and we shall see where we stand at the end of the day. Pronin, you have custody of the prisoner. However, I trust that you had all our best interests in mind when you arrested her; therefore, you will retain custody of the woman until tomorrow. We will sort it out then."

Chayka protested again. "I will call Moscow in the morning about this and we will see." He was overruled by the others.

Finally, he acquiesced and they all called it a night. The rest of the staff were allowed to leave the building but were told to report to work as usual the next morning.

***

Dmitri wished that he had driven his car to work. He didn't expect that he'd have to walk home at this late hour of the evening. He decided that everything would seem brighter if he ate something substantial at the cafeteria on campus. He helped himself to a large portion of the fish casserole and a glass of milk. He would have a real drink when he returned to his apartment.

He staggered back into the cold, clear night and trudged along his usual route to the university-subsidized housing block of aging and partially dysfunctional apartments. The snow was so cold that it crunched under his boots as he walked. Soon he was lost in thought about the day's events.

He arrived at his concrete-panel apartment building and was surprised to see a man wearing a long coat standing at the front door. The man saw him and approached as he turned toward the entryway.

"Dmitri Lachinov, is that you?" The man pulled out a leather wallet and held up his government credentials for Dmitri to see.

Dmitri had been lost in thought, and the last thing he expected was to find a state security officer at his door. "Yes, I am Dmitri Lachinov. Can I help you?"

"Yes, you can. Someone wants to talk to you. An old friend." The man pointed in the direction of the street.

Only then did Dmitri see the large black Mercedes sedan parked at the curb with its engine running, clouds of smoky vapor curling up from its exhaust. Dmitri swallowed hard as his mind raced through all his worst thoughts. *What is this? What have I done? What do they think I have done?*

The officer led him to the side of the car, where he opened the back seat door and motioned for him to get inside, as if he had no choice. Dmitri's throat suddenly went dry as his eyes probed the darkness within the vehicle.

A familiar voice called out. "Good evening, Dmitri. It has been some time since we last spoke."

Dmitri entered the car and sat down next to Ivan Ivanoff, saying nothing. He decided that it was best to let Ivanoff do the talking, at least until he knew what he was being accused of.

"Dmitri," Ivanoff said in a light tone, "you must be surprised to see me again after so many years. Perhaps you have forgotten of our encounter regarding those foreign economic journals that you like to read so much. You may also have forgotten our previous conversation in which I agreed to let you continue to obtain such potentially subversive materials." He smiled and looked at Dmitri to gauge his level of shock at seeing his old acquaintance.

Dmitri stared at Ivanoff. He was afraid to say anything.

"But only if you kept in touch with me on any other matters involving state interests." He paused. "You have not contacted me in two years. I cannot believe that nothing of interest has caught your attention at the university, with its foreign visitors and social idealists."

"I have been busy, comrade. That's all." Dmitri felt trapped like a rat.

"Imagine my surprise when I was brought here tonight on a matter involving the economics department." Ivanoff turned carefully in his seat within the cramped interior of the car to eye Dmitri. His voice took on a harder edge now. "It is probably just a personnel matter but may in a tangential way involve state secrets. Yes? Imagine how astonished I was to look at a list of suspects and see the name of my old friend there. Yes, you!" He raised his arms in front of him to show his surprise. "You are listed as one possible saboteur in this model nonsense." Ivanoff leaned forward in his seat, bringing his face close to Dmitri's. "And you didn't think that I might be interested to know that an officer of the GRU was working here at the university? Here in my district? I am interested in such things, and you should have contacted me about it. That was part of our arrangement."

"I am sorry. I didn't think."

"Yes. You didn't think." Ivanoff paused long enough to light a cigarette. "Now we must speak concerning today's catastrophe with the computer model."

They sat in the car for more than half an hour as Ivanoff questioned Dmitri about the economics modeling project and its goals. They talked about Markov and Minuri and their involvement with the model. Dmitri told Ivanoff he didn't believe that Nadya had anything to do with the so-called sabotage.

"I simply cannot imagine her doing it." He paused. "I am quite sure that we can prove that in the morning. All we have to do is check the data file Nadya supplied to Markov just before the model run. If she had changed the data, it will be evident on the tape." He stopped and searched Ivanoff's face for his reaction. "If not, she is in the clear."

Ivanoff was silent for a full minute as he considered this information. "Then we will test this idea first thing in the morning."

When they finished talking, Dmitri crawled out of the car and Ivanoff's man drove him away, leaving Dmitri dazed from the encounter. He saw the curtains in one apartment window move a little.

Fine, he thought. *Now my neighbors will be convinced that I am working with the KGB or that I am in trouble with them. That is all I needed. A night visit from the secret police.*

He retreated to his apartment and looked through his limited belongings to make sure that Ivanoff's men had not searched the place. Somewhat reassured, he took off his boots and went to sit by the radiator with a bottle of vodka and a small glass. He fiddled with the radiator valve to coax additional heat into the room. If there was a slight improvement in the temperature, he couldn't tell the difference. At least the radiator was warm, which wasn't something that he could count on every day. He settled into his comfortable upholstered chair and sipped his vodka.

He had just begun to muse about the day's bizarre events when someone knocked lightly on his door. He wondered if it was Ivanoff, returning to ask more questions.

He dreaded the notion. Maybe he could just not answer the door. He thought better of the idea as soon as he realized that, with his lights on, it was obvious that he was inside. Besides, Ivanoff would enter anyway. He went to the door and hesitated, his hand on the doorknob.

"Dmitri! It's me, Minuri. Open the door. I know you are home." He complied and let a shivering Minuri into the apartment.

"Oh, Minuri," he said, surprised. "What are you doing here?"

"I have been standing outside for an hour." As she stepped inside, she said, "I was waiting for you, but a man came and stood by the door. I hid behind the building until the car drove away and I was sure they had not arrested you." She shuddered as she tried to warm up. "Who was that, and why did they make a night visit? Are you in trouble?" She asked the last question sincerely. "Before you answer, let me stand by your radiator to warm up. I am freezing to death."

She took off her gloves, coat, and hat and shuffled over to the radiator by the window. "My God! You don't really have heat, do you?" She felt the radiator with her hand. "Do you have chocolate or tea? Maybe we could make something hot to drink."

They went into the kitchen and set the kettle on the stove to boil. Dmitri pulled two ceramic cups out of the cupboard and ladled light-brown cocoa powder into each one. They waited for the water to boil, and Minuri held her hands near the gas burner to warm them. "It is damn cold tonight. I thought I would die out there."

Dmitri poured the hot water into the cups and added a shot of vodka to each one. They sat at the table and sipped the cocoa while Minuri's cheeks regained a bit of color.

"I was thinking about what happened today and how terrible it is that Nadya was arrested. I don't believe she could or would do something like *that*. Sure, she disliked Markov and thought him an ass, but so did everyone else in the building—even you, I think." Dmitri gazed at Minuri and waited for her acknowledgment. She looked up and nodded slightly.

"Yes. I agree that he is a first-class horse's behind. And I, too, do not believe Nadya would do such a thing. I am awfully sorry this all happened." She looked down at her cup and wrapped her hands around it for warmth. "But first, tell me who that was in the car. Was it the police? Did they have questions for you?" She watched for his response. "Why did they come here to see you instead of talking at the office in the morning?"

Dmitri knew she suspected that it was Chayka in the car. He didn't want to lie to her but thought it better not to admit who he had talked to. After all, he didn't know Minuri that well.

"The authorities had questions about the incident this afternoon," he said reluctantly. "They asked how such an event could happen. I told them that Nadya almost certainly had done nothing wrong. I think they were convinced. I told them that we must check the data file in the morning to see if it had been changed. If it was not tampered with, then Nadya is in the clear and can have her freedom back." He stopped talking and drained his cup of cocoa. "What do *you* think happened?"

"I don't know what to think, Dmitri. You know Nadya better than me. You have known her for a long time." She raised one eyebrow in interest. "But she doesn't strike me as someone who would do this action. It must be someone else. You are right that the data file should tell us if she was involved." She looked at Dmitri a little mischievously. "But I couldn't blame her if she did it. Markov has treated her badly and even more savagely today at the meeting with his wild accusations." She became angry and clenched her fist. "And then he tried to choke her! What an idiot."

"Why do you think he got so angry with her?" Dmitri asked. "Why so vile?"

"Because she will not go out on a date with him," Minuri said calmly. "He has asked her two or three times, and she always says no. The last time she told him to go away and proclaimed it loudly in front of several people." She finished her cocoa and held out her cup to Dmitri. She turned and leaned close to him. "He was outraged. He thought she was mocking him, but I was there. I think she just wanted him to stop asking."

"That would explain why he was so vicious to her. But why blame her for the problem?"

"He just reacted without really thinking." Minuri raised her hands in front of her in a questioning gesture. "He saw a problem with the data set and put two and two together to make four. But you can get four by other means." She stopped speaking and stared at her cup again. "Can we make some more cocoa? The vodka is warming me up. And now that I am warm, I don't wish to go back out into the cold night to return to my lodging. Besides, Gregori might be looking for me, and I couldn't bear his ranting at this late hour. "

"What do you mean?" Dmitri asked innocently.

Minuri stepped over next to him and ran her fingers over his shoulder. He took her hand in his.

"You wouldn't send me out into the cold, would you? When we can keep each other warm here in your bed?"

Chapter 32

The next day the investigative committee reconvened at the project offices to begin interviewing witnesses. Ivanoff took charge while the others directed their attention to the data files. He had the system administrator produce the command log for the model run so that they could recreate the sequence of events involving the data in question. By lunchtime they had already examined the data file that Nadya had provided to the modelers and determined that there was no corruption of the data recorded on the tape. That fact exonerated Nadya completely.

"So you see, Chayka," Ivanoff gloated, "it appears that she is not the culprit in this incident. It also appears that the accusations made by the volatile Dr. Markov were unfounded. Perhaps we will have to discount his wild theories from now on in order to make progress in this investigation." Ivanoff enjoyed pointing out the GRU officer's mistake from the previous evening.

Chayka agreed that Nadya had not caused the computer glitch. Everyone glanced at one another as if they knew that he was covering his behind, but they kept their opinions to themselves.

Ivanoff continued. "Pronin, I think that we can recall this Nadya Michaijlovich from the city jail and bring her back here for questioning as a witness rather than as a suspect." He stared at Chayka. "An apology would also seem appropriate." He raised his eyebrows.

Chayka replied, "It is true that Markov has a mercurial temperament. He appears to have been wrong in this instance."

Ivanoff then directed the committee to look at other possible ways in which the data file used by the model could have been modified. He looked around the table at the investigators, expecting suggestions.

The administrator said that it was possible to introduce anomalous data points by revising the source code to write new values into the data set after the data file was read in from the tape. He suggested that they examine the model code itself to see if such a change had been made.

The committee broke for lunch, and everyone resumed their duties during the hour-long intermission. Ivanoff telephoned his office to make sure that other irons were still in the fire. Chayka conferred with Markov and Minuri to discuss what other avenues they should investigate. Pronin sent his sergeant to release Nadya from jail and then went to the cafeteria to eat. The administrator and director began reviewing the code while they ate their sandwiches in the administrator's office.

They reconvened after lunch. The administrator directed two of the other programmers to continue reviewing the model code. They couldn't find any evidence of tampering within the code. No changes that could have corrupted the input file had been made. The administrator reported that a review of the command line log indicated that only Markov, Minuri, and Dmitri had accessed the source code in the two days before the model run. He suggested that the committee interrogate each of them carefully and create a timeline of all activities involving the model during that period.

They began with Markov, who was outraged that they should question his actions. Next they interviewed Minuri, Lena, and Dmitri. By four o'clock they had a good idea of everyone's role in the setup and execution of the final model run, and they had established a detailed timeline based on the command line log and the witness testimony. They still needed to question Nadya, but she had not yet returned from jail with the sergeant.

The committee took a break, and Ivanoff secretly sought out Dmitri to ask him for anything he could add to the investigation—off the record, of course.

"Dmitri," Ivanoff said, "we have considered that someone could have modified the code after the data file was read into the computer. Correct? But the administrator found no changes to the actual source code." He stopped and stared at Dmitri, putting him on the spot. "How could this be? What are we missing?"

Dmitri replied that he found this to be an intriguing problem. He thought about it silently and then caught Ivanoff's attention. "There is another way."

"Tell me about it."

"It may be possible for someone to make a change in the source code, compile it for the model run, and then erase the change from the source code afterward. There would be no trace of the modification. But there should be evidence of a change in the compiled file itself."

"Can this really be done? Can anyone do it?" Ivanoff was immediately intrigued.

"Many people have the skills to make the change, but they would need access to the source code," Dmitri said.

"How can we determine whether this has happened?"

"I think I can detect a change if we can access the computer."

After he explained his idea, Ivanoff had him write down the key points to take to the committee. He did not want to show any semblance of favoritism toward Dmitri or even acknowledge that they already knew each other.

The committee reconvened, and Ivanoff asked the project administrator what he thought of the idea of checking compiled files. The administrator was impressed by the prospect and thought that it was a logical extension of their inquiry.

"We have a copy of the compiled model as used in the model run," the administrator said. "All we need is to make a fresh compiled version of the model code that we have already reviewed."

"I see," said Ivanoff, with an air of determination. "Then we must make the comparison."

"Give me a few minutes to execute the compilation, gentlemen, and then we can reconvene." The director rushed to the computer room.

He returned in a few minutes and said, "I have compiled a new version of the model and compared it with the version used in yesterday's model run." He paused for dramatic effect. "There is a noticeable increase in length of yesterday's file. This indicates that someone has indeed tampered with the source code. The only question is who made the change?"

The director said that he and the administrator would check their records to determine the time when the code was last recompiled. That might give them a clue as to who was involved.

They were close to wrapping up the meeting for the afternoon when a policeman rushed into the room and whispered something in Captain Pronin's ear. The captain looked puzzled and asked the man to confirm what he had said. Then he leaned over to talk to Ivanoff in hushed tones.

After a brief exchange, Pronin stood up and told the group what he had just learned. "Excuse me, gentlemen. I have just been informed that the witness, Nadya Michaijlovich, is not in the central holding facility but has somehow been misplaced within the prison system. My sergeant is trying to locate her now, so therefore she will not be available for questioning this afternoon. If you will excuse me, I must return to headquarters to facilitate the search." He turned to Ivanoff. "I will let you know as soon as we have found her."

The meeting concluded, and the parties dispersed for the evening. Captain Pronin summoned his driver and left the building immediately.

Ivanoff merely shook his head in disgust and wandered off to locate his Mercedes, in which he had stored a flask of vodka in the back seat. It was useful for washing away the taste of bureaucratic bungling such as he had just experienced. Perhaps a drink and a good night's sleep would repair his current exasperation.

Chapter 33

Ivanoff and Pronin stood outside the dismal and disreputable Kresty Prison the next morning. They entered the expansive hospital ward together and wove their way through the crowded rows of beds. This was where the sergeant had managed to locate the missing prisoner. The men had been shocked to learn not only that she had been lost in the prison system for two days but also that she had been abused by guards at Kresty Prison in that time, having been processed into the jail with several prostitutes.

"I tell you that this has not happened on this scale before, Colonel," Pronin said sourly. "At least not in my experience."

"I have seen it happen in the military prisons that are managed in a haphazard manner," Ivanoff said briskly. "But not with these consequences. Let us see what the damage has been, shall we?"

On hearing that special visitors had arrived, a matron approached to greet them. She led them through the rows of white-sheeted beds to the one occupied by the current victim of prison violence. Nadya Michaijlovich was handcuffed to the frame of the bed.

"We were very concerned when the patient first arrived," the matron muttered almost to herself, "because she had lost a good deal of blood overnight. Thank God the woman's cellmate was so persistent in trying to get the attention of the guard staff. Someone finally heard her banging on the cell door when the new shift came on duty at six a.m." She looked up at the two men. "The guard responded immediately and called for a doctor. I tell you that had another hour gone by, she surely would have bled out on that dingy cot."

The bed was occupied by the brutalized form of a battered woman. Her face was black, blue, and, in some places, a strange yellow color, all swollen out of proportion. Two of her front teeth were missing. She wore a white gown that had red-brown, dried blood spattered in two or three places. A tent had been created with a sheet draped over the woman's lower torso and legs to prevent contact with her most egregious wounds. Several intravenous fluid bags were elevated above the bed delivering antibiotics, whole blood, and nutrients to the stricken form.

"She was beaten savagely on her face, head, and belly. As you can see, her face is virtually one long bruise, her nose is broken, and she has suffered a concussion. She has been unconscious since that night. The most severe wounds and ones that are life-threatening are those to her lower body. She was, of course, raped many times by the looks of it. There is much vaginal damage—much more damage than one usually expects, even in a gang rape event." She paused. "We see many of those here in the prison," she explained. "We found flecks of what look like black paint and wood fibers in the clotted mass of blood inside her."

"Paint?" Pronin asked.

"*Da*, inside her," the matron continued. "The cellmate also suffered repeated rapes, but she showed only normal levels of abuse. She said that the victim fought her assailants, and they beat her for resisting. They did the most evil things to her, even using a nightstick on her. Is that what it is called?" She winced at the thought of what had befallen the prisoner. "That would explain the deep penetration damage we see. The men were animals!"

The matron lifted the sheet that formed the tent to reveal a large mass of bloody gauze between the victim's legs. "Oh dear! She is bleeding again. I will let the doctor know so that he can see to her on his next round." She replaced the sheet and prepared to leave them at the bedside, eager to get away from the reminder of such violence.

Ivanoff grabbed the matron's arm and spoke in a calm but forceful voice.

"No. You will go directly and find the doctor. Tell him this is his priority-one patient. This woman is an important witness in a case involving state security. He will give her whatever medicines, blood, or attention she requires. I will arrange for her to be moved to a private clinic later today. And remove those handcuffs now. She is a witness, not a criminal."

The matron's eyes opened wide when Ivanoff showed her his credentials. She scurried off to find the doctor. Pronin and Ivanoff took one last look at the unfortunate Nadya and left the ward.

In the hallway, Ivanoff placed a hand on Pronin's shoulder, his face grim.

"Tell the warden that I will see him in his office in thirty minutes. He must have the lead perpetrator and whoever was in charge of the women's wing of the prison last night present for interrogation." He paused briefly, his eyes closed for a moment. "I will call my office to arrange the patient's transfer to a better facility than this meager hospital ward. I will find my own way to the warden's office and meet you there in half an hour."

"Yes, of course," Pronin responded.

Ivanoff turned to go but stopped and gave Pronin a weak smile. "Thank you, Pronin. I know that you are as outraged by this incident as I am."

Pronin left as Ivanoff stepped into the prison yard to smoke a cigarette. He pulled in a long draw from the strong, unfiltered Belomorkanal that he had lighted. He had always favored this brand because it had a strong flavor and much nicotine. Somehow the smoke helped him focus his mind as he tried to forget old memories that had flashed into his head at the sight of the unfortunate prisoner, Nadya.

He had witnessed just such a brutal scene years ago when he was a young officer on the Perm police force. At that time his sister, Ivanka, had been a wild and crazy young woman who embraced alcohol and the urban lifestyle too freely. She had associated with a rough young crowd who were envious of the skinheads they heard about in Germany. They resented control and all conventional ways, riding old motorcycles and wearing black leather in defiance of society. Ivanka began to date one of the gang's members and traveled with a few members of the gang for a while. Then one of the members was killed in a robbery in Perm, and she was accused of ratting out the gang to her brother.

The gang took retribution, using her as an example of what they did to informants. She had been beaten and raped, even though she had never talked to Ivanoff. She suffered in a hospital for four weeks before her body gave out.

The family was traumatized. Ivanoff's mother never recovered from the sight of her tortured daughter lying in a coma.

The experience had changed Ivanoff. For a while he had descended into a primal state of rage and revenge that he later regretted. He and a few of his patrol colleagues had savagely avenged his sister's death. They had systematically worked their way through the gang's membership, beating and in two cases killing those responsible for the assault on his sister. The Perm Police Department had initially granted their actions considerable leeway out of respect for Ivanoff's family. But after a few weeks, the carnage had become too blatant even for the authorities. Ivanoff and his friends were reigned in, and he was assigned to a burglary squad. He had released his rage and later regained his self-control.

He had buried that anger deep inside his psyche, and for years he had fought to keep his police work strictly professional. He had managed to keep his emotions on a tight leash, even when working the most troubling of cases. But now he found that the old memories had sprung back, too raw and near the surface for him to control much longer. He felt that he owed this young, innocent woman, Nadya, all his energy to bring her the justice that the legal system, such as it was, could not provide.

Ivanoff looked at his wristwatch and snuffed out his third cigarette on the concrete wall beside him. It was time to talk to the warden.

He needed to make someone pay for all the Nadyas and Ivankas in the world.

Ivanoff and Pronin entered Warden Zarubin's office and found him sitting behind a large wooden desk, wearing a good-quality wool suit.

The warden rose to welcome them and shook hands as Pronin introduced Ivanoff to him. The warden was impressed. He offered both men a chair and asked if they would prefer coffee or vodka for their meeting, being as agreeable as he could be for a man who knew he was in trouble.

Pronin and the warden began to sit down but rose again when they noticed that Ivanoff had remained on his feet and refused any drink. There was an awkward silence that Pronin filled by expressing their shock at learning that their prisoner—witness, really—had been so gravely mistreated under Zarubin's care.

"How could this happen in this contemporary age of criminal justice? We want to know," he said.

The warden admitted that he was at first caught off guard by yesterday's violence. He now realized the extent of his failure and attempted to share their outrage that such an incident could happen at the "modern" Kresty Prison. He said that he had ordered an investigation and would punish the men involved severely. He made a good show of it, pounding his fist in his other hand and raising his voice in indignation.

Ivanoff's only reply was, "Bring in the responsible persons now." He leveled his eyes at the warden's face, letting him know that he would not be fooled by any amount of late-offered contrition or feigned outrage.

Zarubin signaled his male secretary, who was seated at a side desk, to bring in the man and woman who waited in the antechamber. The secretary returned with a large, muscular, defiant man and a small, ordinary-looking woman having no notably favorable features. They were both in guard uniforms, and she wore a supervisor's crest on her shoulder patch. They lined up along the right side of the room. The woman was the first to sense that something was wrong when she looked at the warden's face.

"You two stand at ease. We were discussing the unfortunate incident that befell the female prisoners last night. These gentlemen are here to ask you several direct questions. You must answer truthfully to aid in this investigation," Zarubin said.

Pronin stepped forward and addressed the woman, Supervisor Marina Denikina. "You were in charge of the women's cellblock of the prison last night. Is that correct? And you were here last night, *da?*"

"Yes, sir. I was here all night."

"And you were present when a busload of women arrived from the city station and were registered to cells in your block?"

"Yes, sir. I supervised their entry into the system."

"When did you become aware that there had been an attack on the women of cell 9-139?" Pronin asked.

"An attack?" She seemed surprised by the question. "No, sir. There was no attack. I understood that when the busload of prostitutes were assigned to cells, the two women in cell 9-139 became unruly and had to be restrained. They began to fight with the guards, and as a result, they received some minor injuries." She ended with a catlike smile on her lips, as though she had successfully pulled off a neutral yet sly evasion.

"And did you know that the two women were raped by several guards as well?" Ivanoff asked.

"Raped? Of course not!" She sneered at Ivanoff, obviously detesting such women. "You don't understand, sir. Those sorts of women always want the sex, you know. And sometimes the men are willing to oblige them. If it happened, then it was surely not rape." She set up her face. "They said the big girl was asking for it."

"Look at these photos and tell me if you think that consensual sex was involved here." Pronin showed the woman two photos of Nadya Michaijlovich that were taken when she was first removed from the cell in the morning.

Denikina glanced quickly at the photos, at first pretending not to see anything out of the ordinary. She stared at them for a while longer and her face blanched. Sure, the guards would occasionally force themselves on a few of the women, but they were not usually very rough with them.

Causing bruises maybe, blackened wrists where the women's arms were held down, or minor pelvic bruising if they were not careful.

"But this isn't normal," she said. "This is like the poor woman was attacked by a wild beast, beaten to a bloody mass."

Apparently, even she was surprised by what she saw. She no longer continued to look at the photos. Instead, she turned to stare at the man next to her.

"You said you had to teach her a lesson, Boris." Her face was filled with revulsion as she continued loudly. "But this is no lesson; this is butchery! What sort of animal are you?"

Zarubin, who had not yet seen the photos, reached over and snatched them away from Pronin. At first he squinted, as if trying to interpret what he was looking at. Then he pulled out his handkerchief, held it to his mouth, and looked away.

Ivanoff now stood facing Boris and noted that he was wearing his full weapons belt, including his baton. The baton had seen a lot of use judging by its battered appearance and its chipped and missing paint. He asked to see it, and Boris handed it over. Ivanoff ran his fingers along the weapon, paying particular attention to its blunt end. The black paint had worn off, and the red hue of dried, caked blood was clearly visible.

"Boris, is it? You say that sometimes these women make themselves available to you? Is that right? And sometimes they like to be treated roughly?" asked Ivanoff, his face a foot away from the guard's.

"*Da.* Yes, sir. You know the type, sir." His face formed a twisted grin. He apparently didn't sense his own danger. "They want us to use them sometimes, the really hard ones. Like the big girl in cell 9-139. Oh yes. She wanted it. She put up a show, but she wanted it."

"And you had to teach her a lesson. Is that it?" He held the nightstick up close to his face to inspect it. "And she liked it, you say?"

"Well, yes. She resisted our orders at first but came on to me and Oly. Sometimes these whores play hard to get. But this one, she kicked and bit. So we taught her a lesson."

"Did you teach her a lesson with your baton? Is this her blood on your nightstick?"

Sensing a trap now, Boris became cautious. He did not notice the warden's furtive hand signals to stop talking. "I don't know. There might be a little blood on the stick."

"I think that when I test the blood on this stick, I will find her blood on it. And that will be unfortunate for you, Boris. You see, she was not a prostitute at all. She was a state's witness in an important security investigation." Ivanoff's voice changed dramatically, as did his features, taking on a harder edge. "Now she is in a coma and may never wake up, you imbecile." He brought his face to within inches of Boris's surprised visage. "You have sabotaged my witness, you fool."

Ivanoff began to slap the nightstick in the palm of his left hand as he held it in his right. He stopped talking and looked at the floor as the anger built inside him, rising to the surface like red-hot lava in a volcano's caldron. Finally he snapped and glared at Boris.

"I think I will also find some of your blood on this stick when I test it," he whispered so that only Boris could hear.

Then with no warning, Ivanoff raised the heavy nightstick and brought it down on Boris's head. Not once, not twice, but seven times—harsh, punitive blows to his head, his neck, and his jaw. His rage was unbounded. But in thirty seconds, he was finished. The big man simply fell in a heap on the floor, blood spewing from his skull. Ivanoff stopped when the man went down. Like a large, dull ox, he had somehow remained standing while receiving all the blows.

The others in the room had not moved, aghast and shocked by what had happened. Pronin started to speak but stopped before a single syllable left his lips. The warden fell into his chair. The secretary backed toward the door, ready to run away.

Supervisor Denikina stood at the side of the room, with her head turned to look at Boris slumped on the floor. Her jaw dropped to expose several steel teeth in her open mouth. Was this to be her punishment as well?

Ivanoff walked over and stood in front of her. He leaned toward her and said, "You were responsible for my witness. You will rue the day when you neglected your duty and let your prisoners be abused by men like him. You will never serve in a command position again." He poked her in the neck with the gory, blood-spattered baton.

Denikina's eyes opened wide and her mouth even wider. Then her eyes rolled up and she fainted. She crumpled to the floor, her head making a loud impact on the floorboards. Ivanoff dropped the nightstick on her body.

"Warden." Ivanoff stood before Zarubin's desk and leaned forward to glare directly into the man's face. His stance reflected the gravity of the situation. "This incident will go on your record, but you will not be punished further if you severely tighten the ship that you run here at this place called Kresty Prison. I expect you to deal harshly with the other people involved in the rapes." He swung his head around to look at his colleague. "Pronin, you take custody of the other woman who was raped in cell 9-139 for her own protection and get her out of here immediately. Charges against her should be dropped, and the warden here should pray that she does not file a complaint because that would cause a scandal if it happened. I will ensure that she is treated with respect."

"Now, Warden. Clean these two up, pack their bags, and dismiss them from their employment immediately. I will have my man collect them so that they can join a convoy of convicts headed for the new railroad project in our northeastern forests. They will find themselves at home there with other vicious animals."

With that, he turned for the door.

"Pronin, let's go." They marched out of the office as Zarubin's secretary jumped back to get out of their way.

***

The black Mercedes sedan was parked in front of Dmitri's apartment as it had been two nights before. A man wearing a long black wool coat and dark fur hat paced back and forth on the sidewalk nearby, on guard but also keeping himself warm in the frigid night air. Inside the car, Ivanoff spoke in hushed tones about the day's events.

"Dmitri, I must suspend the investigation for two or three days, as my duties take me to Moscow on other matters. Pronin has agreed to wait for my return, as we seem to have reached the end of our preliminary investigation." Ivanoff paused and lit a cigarette. Dmitri sat silently, afraid to respond.

"But I am concerned that Chayka will feel he must press on with his own inquiry. He is getting pressure from Markov to arrest Lena Kristoff. Apparently, Markov now thinks she changed the code to make him look foolish. I am afraid that if I am not here to act as a counterweight, Chayka will do something stupid, if nothing more than to appease Markov and his superiors in Moscow."

He looked at Dmitri to judge his reaction. In a quiet, friendly tone, he said, "If I were a friend of Lena's, I would caution her to avoid Chayka or Markov for a few days. In my absence they may pounce and create another spectacle like the one involving your other friend Nadya Michaijlovich. If the GRU is involved and Chayka's ego is also in play, then such an action may not be reversible."

Dmitri was simultaneously overwhelmed and agitated. "Poor Nadya. I hope she will recover. She did not deserve to even be arrested. You must admit, Ivanoff, that our police state does not treat its citizens well."

"I must agree in this case, as in many others." Ivanoff's lips curled upward incrementally. "But let us keep my opinion a secret for now."

Dmitri shook his head and raised his eyes to study Ivanoff for a moment. "I will keep you informed of any rash decisions I hear about while you are gone. But I must see Nadya and will warn Lena to stay away from work until you return."

Ivanoff nodded his understanding.

"I have had the woman moved to a clean and well-run clinic outside the government system. She will be well cared for there by excellent medical staff. I understand that she regained consciousness after being transferred there this afternoon. That is a very good sign in cases with coma. You can visit her at this address. I have listed you and Lena Kristoff as permitted visitors. I have also left explicit instructions that no one else is to see her without my permission. That should keep Markov and Chayka from doing any more damage."

He handed Dmitri a slip of paper bearing the clinic's address as well as a telephone number.

"The telephone number will find me wherever I am, should you need to reach me." He put his hand on Dmitri's arm. "This whole incident is not a state security matter any longer but an act of pique by an offended party. I am beginning to wonder if this Minuri Semelov may bear Markov a grudge. Keep all information concerning the investigation to yourself. I know you and she are involved, but keep our secrets between us, *da?*"

Dmitri exited the vehicle, and Ivanoff sped off into the night.

Chapter 34

"Poor Nadie! Poor, poor Nadie. Why did this have to happen to you?" Lena sat next to Nadya's bed at the clinic on Saturday, alternately sobbing and trying to comfort her dear friend. Nadya was deep asleep after regaining consciousness twice in the previous afternoon. Instead of going in to work as the administrator had asked, Lena had maintained a bedside vigil, holding one of Nadya's hands, ever since the doors had opened.

The clinic was very modern, clean, well equipped, and professionally staffed. It was unlike any of the government clinics that Lena had ever visited. Nadya had a bright, cheery room with two windows decorated with white lace curtains, unlike the drab, plain wards of the state.

A nurse stopped by the room to check on Nadya. "Ah. You are the friend—Lena?"

"*Da*, this is true. How is she today?"

"We gave her a full transfusion yesterday, and the persistent internal bleeding has been stopped with a surgical procedure." The nurse, a middle-aged and sympathetic soul, touched Nadya's forehead with the back of her hand to check her temperature. "She is receiving the best antibiotics to fight infection, and she is being fed intravenously, as you can see. At first we were concerned that her jaw was broken, which could present future feeding problems. But that wasn't the case. Her broken nose was reset, and a fracture in her left eye orbital will heal naturally. She is expected to make a full recovery in time, but there are still concerns about her internal injuries." She stopped and placed a reassuring hand on Lena's arm. "They might interfere with pregnancy in the future. Do you know if your friend planned to have children one day?"

"Yes," Lena whispered. Then she began to cry, and the nurse withdrew from the room.

Lena felt guilty about what had happened to Nadya. She wasn't responsible for her predicament, but she felt that she should have better protected her lifelong friend. She knew that whatever happened in the days ahead, she would tend to Nadya, nurse her back to health, and find a way to care for her over the long term. How she would do this wasn't clear, but Lena owed Nadya so much. She would find a way.

"Lena! Thank God. You are here."

In her reverie, Lena had not noticed that Dmitri had entered the room. "I have been looking for you everywhere. I went to your apartment, and Katya said you were here. I am glad I found you before you went in to work. How is Nadya doing?"

Lena told Dmitri what she had learned about Nadya's attack and her injuries. They mourned their poor friend's suffering, both trying to talk to her in her sleep. After some time Dmitri spoke. "Lena, you should stay away from work and especially Chayka and Markov. They are on some bizarre warpath, and I am afraid they may have you in their sights now. Maybe you could say you had to stay here to care for Nadya. Anything—just stay away from the office."

"Why, Dmitri?" she asked. "What have you heard?"

She did not take him seriously until he finally admitted that it was Ivanoff who had told him to warn her.

"Ivanoff? He came to you? What does this mean? How does he know you?"

"He knows me from a foolish mistake I made years ago. I bought several foreign journals that are considered contraband by our all-knowing government. He has kept tabs on me ever since, although not too often. Lena, we all have our secrets, you know? He is one of mine."

"Yes. We all have our secrets." She looked at him warily. "Your secret is safe with me. But if I were you, I would not let anyone else know that you have a connection with the KGB." She stared at Nadya's bandaged face for a moment. "But it worries me." She wondered what else he knew. What other secrets did he have that might affect her? As a friend, she was sympathetic, but as a foreign agent, she was on her guard.

Dmitri held Nadya's hand in his as he searched her brutalized face for any indication of a reaction.

"How did you obtain the foreign journals?" Lena asked.

"It was nothing, really. You know how I try to keep up with foreign economic literature if I can find articles or books from abroad. Sometimes I bought journals from a bookshop in the city." He looked at the floor as he spoke. "You understand—when they had something of interest. Then one day a few years ago, the shop was raided by the police and they got my name from the shop owner who kept a list of clients." He spoke slowly, as if he was choosing his words carefully.

"This was a bookseller in the city?"

"*Da*, Ivanoff came to see me at the university to ask about my purchases," he continued. "He was just a junior officer then, and he did not seem to care very much about economic articles. But he has asked me on occasion about a few specific things going on here at the university. That is all." He tried to make it sound innocent enough. "Then this Markov thing happened, and he recognized my name on the project personnel list. He came to see me to get background information regarding what had happened. He asked me to explain how the computer files could be altered, and I told him what I knew. That is all. I even told him that Nadya could never do such a thing, even if she didn't like Markov. I think he believed that from the start."

Lena stared at him and wondered how much of this story she should believe. "Is that all, Dmitri?" Her face hardened. "All that you know and are keeping from me?"

"Yes, I swear." He looked as if he had been caught in a lie. He tried to act as if he had not heard her accusation. "But now he is concerned that the politics of the GRU and the Defense Ministry may cause trouble. That is why he wanted to warn you. He wanted to prevent things from escalating while he is out of town for the next few days." Dmitri finished and looked at Lena for a sign that she did not hold this confession against him.

Lena's face was fixed in a neutral expression. She honestly did not know what to make of this information.

"Lena, I must go to work. Please heed what I say. It is for your own safety to stay away. I will tell the director that you will not be in today, if you like. I can tell him you are helping Nadya. Is that all right?"

She nodded.

"Good. I will try to see you tonight after work at your apartment, yes?" Dmitri left the clinic.

When Dmitri had told Lena about his first encounter with Ivanoff, she had winced at his account of the bookseller being caught. She could not reveal that she knew anything about the incident, but her mind went immediately to the night that Eric Larson found the police and a KGB agent at his hotel.

Could the two events be related? Could Ivanoff be the KGB agent on Eric's trail? If so, did he know about Eric and her? She did not think it likely, but she would have to be even more careful around him than before.

She stroked Nadya's fingers with her own as she submerged herself in thought. A plan of action had formed in her mind. She decided that she must act immediately or lose any small advantage of surprise that she had.

She badly needed sleep. The last days had been difficult and stressful, and the strain was beginning to show in her attitude and level of alertness. She began to doze but was suddenly awakened by a movement.

Wait a moment! What had awoken her? She looked down and felt Nadya's fingers moving in her hand. She looked up and saw that Nadya's one uncovered blue eye was looking at her and that just the corner of a smile showed on her face.

"Lena," Nadya whispered.

Tears welled up in Lena's eyes as she clutched Nadya's hand, raised it to her lips, and kissed it.

"Nadie, you are back. Oh, I am so glad. You are safe here and in good care." She leaned in to talk to her friend in a soft voice. "Let me tell you where you are, yes?"

Lena spent the next fifteen minutes telling Nadya what had happened and reassuring her. When she was finished, like clockwork, Nadya's eye closed and she slept again.

Lena sat at Nadya's bedside for a long time. She had much to consider. There were many practical things she must do now. Things to do to care for Nadya. Things to do for the long term. The situation at work would now enter into her decisions. There was much to plan, and there were actions to take.

Chapter 35

Lena rode the bus to the little square more than a mile from her apartment. She walked directly to a pay telephone that had seen better days. She deposited her coins and dialed the number from memory. The phone rang five times and she hung up. After three minutes, she redialed the number and listened carefully. After five rings the phone was answered but no words were spoken. Then someone recited a telephone number, a series of ten digits. Lena replied with a different set of numbers, a false telephone number.

"Yes?"

"VICTOR. It is VERNA. I have four for dinner and one late arrival."

"I cannot seat four for dinner. Make it four for lunch tomorrow and one late arrival."

The phone went dead. Lena hung up and wiped the receiver off, replacing it in the cradle. Then she boarded a bus and returned home.

She entered the apartment and Eric ran to greet her. She picked him up to hug him as Katya came out of her bedroom.

"Lena, I told Eric that we are going on a vacation for a week and that we have to pack our clothes and things." Her voice sounded light and casual but her face told a different story. There was fear in her eyes, so she tried not to look at Eric, lest he see that something was wrong.

"Look, Eric!" Lena said in a relaxed but upbeat manner. "I brought you a cookie and a new toy to play with. Isn't it fun? Here, you use it like this." She pulled the toy out and placed it on the kitchen table. "See! It is a little fire truck, and you can make the ladder go up and down. Now come over here and you can play while I talk to Katie, yes?"

Lena pulled Katya into the bedroom and closed the door. She hugged her little sister and squeezed her as tight as she ever had to reassure her.

"Katie. It is as I have told you. I have not done anything wrong and yet now they will come for me for something I did not do. I cannot tell you what all happened. Not yet, but I will in a few days." She pushed her sister back far enough to look her in the eyes. "But now I need your support and Misha's. We have to pack our things because we will probably never be able to come back here to our little home. Well, maybe someday, but not for a long time."

"Lena," Katya said, then began to sob as she pulled Lena in for another hug. "I love you, my sister, but what have you done? Why must we leave? Who is after you? Did you steal money at work?" She pulled away to examine Lena's face. "Did you cross somebody there? Lena, tell me something so that I will not go crazy."

"Do not worry about these things now." Lena pulled away and paced back and forth across the room. "We have work to do. Did you call Misha? Will he be ready?"

"Yes. I did everything we talked about on Saturday night. This morning, I took everything from work. I told them that I was taking a few days off to look after a sick friend. I even got them to give me my pay for the week." She pulled a wad of rubles from her pocket. "It is not much, but we will need all the money we can get if we are to leave. I picked up Eric and told Auntie Olga, the caretaker, that he would be home for a few days and not to worry. By the way, that older lady is very nice but seemed too nosy to me. I hope she isn't a problem." Her face turned pale as she searched Lena's features for a reaction.

Lena said, "Olga is nosy to be sure, but she will not be a problem. We just need to start packing." She stopped at the bedroom door. "I bought three soft suitcases and four duffel bags so that we can pack more easily. I got one suitcase each for you, Eric, and me. One duffel for each of us and one for Misha's things. We have a couple of old bags we can use also. We cannot take everything, just some valuables, keepsakes, and our better clothes—toys for Eric too." Lena looked around the room sadly. "Put all of Misha's things in one of the duffels for now. Leave no papers that reveal our names or his name. We must be sure to clean the place of all information that could be used to follow us."

She set her shoulder bag on the bed to show Katya that she had retrieved all their important papers and identification cards from her secret hiding place under the kitchen floor. As she pulled the documents out of the bag, it leaned sideways and several items fell out on the bedspread. Among them were three bundles of United States $100 bills and a cascade of loose ruble notes.

"My God, Lena!" Katya whispered loudly. "You robbed a bank. Oh my God!"

"Keep your voice down, Katie! Eric and the neighbors will hear you through these paper-thin walls of ours."

Katya sat on the bed and pulled the bag over to inspect its contents. "Lena? Where did you get all this money? What have you done?"

"I can't tell you, Katie. Not now. Don't you see? We have to pack." She sat on the bed next to Katya and took her hand in hers. "I will tell you later, but we need this money to travel." She paused. "Do not worry. I have a plan—a good one. Everything will be all right."

Lena put the money back in the bag and pulled Katya to her feet. "Now. No more questions. We must pack. Here is your suitcase and two duffel bags for you and Misha. Remember, take only what we will need for a week or two at most. I will start in my room for Eric and me." She opened the bedroom door.

"Now let's get moving. Our lives may depend on it."

The women sprang into action. Lena collected all other papers that had no real value, like newspapers, bills, and other printed matter, and dropped them in a separate shopping bag for disposal. She packed her good clothes in one suitcase and Eric's clothes in another. Then she stuffed keepsakes, toys, and other valuables into the duffel bags. It was sad to see that all she owned filled only four pieces of luggage, even with shoes included.

Lena stopped packing periodically to check on Eric and keep him busy. She also checked on Katya's progress. Her sister had an alarming number of clothes and shoes for someone of small means, but she managed to get all of it into her suitcase and Misha's duffel.

Lena made a point of ensuring that nothing of Misha's was left behind in the apartment. No one could know that he had been there or what his name was. That was important for her plan to succeed.

Misha arrived at the apartment later that afternoon. He wasn't in a good mood. He stared at Lena.

"Why are we doing this? I do not like it one bit." He pulled Katya into their bedroom, and Lena could hear his voice rise in protest as Katya tried to calm him down. The conversation went on for several minutes until the anger in his voice began to fade away.

Lena went to the kitchen and prepared a quick and meager meal, the last they would have together in their cozy home. She thought of all the memories hidden within these simple walls. She remembered when she had first convinced Katya to move in with her. When Katya first introduced Misha one summer evening long ago. When she had first met Eric and told her friends about the mystery man from Helsinki. The many happy days that she and Eric had spent together. All the dinners and parties and sleepovers with Nadya and other friends. And now it would all be gone—locked away in her heart.

When the food was ready, she called to the others to come and eat. She opened the last bottle of wine she had and poured it into three glasses. She called out again and realized that Katya and Misha were, true to form, involved in some intimate moment. As she had done so many times before, Katya giggled and replied that they were on their way.

Lena went to get Eric, who had wandered into the bedroom. She found him on the bed, where he had pulled out a shoebox containing photographs and postcards from the top of the duffel. He had managed to spill them across the bed, and a portion of the contents had fallen onto the floor.

"Eric? What are you doing? I just packed those things away. Now put them back in the box and come to dinner." She helped him to gather them together and return them to the box again.

They all converged in the kitchen to eat. Lena held up her glass of wine and proposed a toast. "To new beginnings, wherever they may lead us."

She said it bravely and then began to cry. Soon every eye around the table was wet with tears, including Eric, who did not yet understand.

"But, Mummy, we are only going on a holiday. It should be fun!"

"Yes, my dear. You are right." She wiped away her tears and held up her glass again. "To our holiday. May we all have fun!" They laughed, and Eric squealed with delight.

After dinner, they carted the luggage out to Misha's car. Katya made one more sweep around the apartment to be sure that they'd left nothing important behind. They drove away, leaving their happy home forever.

***

Misha drove the car to his workplace and pulled into one of the garage work bays. He closed the overhead door so that they could all disembark from the car without being seen. The main order of business was to unload the car and get Eric settled down for the night. Lena set him up on one of the cots in the office and tucked him in. Katya curled up in bed with him and read one of his favorite stories.

Misha and Lena drove out again on a short mission to Nadya's apartment and quietly entered the premises. They quickly collected clothing that Nadya would need when she was released from the clinic. Having grown up together and been friends forever, Lena knew what Nadya valued most and where she kept things. They again took the time to gather keepsakes, photos, and papers. Lena emptied Nadya's hiding place in the wall by the stove where she kept all her money, her other valuables, and her few important papers. They limited what they took to what would fit in one suitcase, a duffel, and a few smaller bags. They tiptoed out of the apartment building and drove back to the garage.

When they arrived, they found both Katya and Eric asleep on the cot. Lena pulled Katya out of bed and took her place, nestled in beside the unconscious boy. Katya undressed for bed in the dark and squeezed into the second cot with Misha on the other side of the office. Soon all the exhausted parties fell into a deep sleep.

Chapter 36

Colonel Vasili Chayka was a man of great stature. He was a solidly built six-footer who stayed in shape by running five kilometers every morning. He had trained for special services in the army before joining the GRU, the security apparatus of the Defense Ministry. He was very experienced in investigations, military secrets, and the politics of his department. He was savvy to the ways of his organization and aware of what was positive for one's advancement within the ministry and what was the sort of thing that could stifle one's career.

Now he found himself in a difficult situation. Although he had been agreeable to let Ivanoff and the KGB take the lead in the preliminary investigation of the modeling incident, he could not let the investigation appear to be stalled. With Ivanoff gone, the investigation had come to a complete halt. Chayka had continued to wrap up details such as completing the timeline and following up on security issues. But to interested parties, such as Markov, it appeared that nothing was happening.

And an unhappy Markov was a dangerous thing.

For the first two days of the investigation, he had been satisfied with the progress. He had not done more than tell his superiors that a preliminary investigation had begun but that there was no apparent security issue. The unhappy Markov went over his head to his superiors in Moscow and complained that Chayka was not doing his job. Markov was a spoiled child and an ass, but he had influence.

On the third day of the investigation, the first day Ivanoff was gone, Chayka received a telephone call in the morning. He suffered through a long and searing lecture about his dereliction of duty and was told that the undersecretary of his branch of the Defense Ministry was asking questions: Why was the KGB directing an investigation that should be headed by the GRU? Were defense personnel and methodologies not involved? Why was there no progress? Why had Chayka made no arrests? Did his superior have to come up to Leningrad and lead him by the hand?

Chayka hated this sort of pressure and the foolishness that usually resulted from such histrionics. He also hated the people who caused such political theater—people like Gregori Markov. That vain imbecile was producing a lot of waste and damage. All because he seemed to have no end of means to alienate everyone he worked with. Chayka had in the past covered up one other debacle Markov had created, and he had heard of other messes caused by the department's golden child. But Chayka would not let his own career suffer because of Markov. He would take measures to protect himself. He knew the only thing that would satisfy Moscow was a quick arrest of a patsy and a rapid end to the investigation.

With this in mind, Chayka arrived at the modeling project offices that afternoon with a specific purpose. He first inquired of the director whether Dmitri, Lena, Markov, and Minuri were all present. He was told that all except Lena were at work. The director explained that Lena was taking another day off to be with her sick friend at the clinic.

Chayka was visibly disappointed and asked the director for a moment of his time for a conversation. They stepped toward one corner of the computer room to have some privacy.

***

Dmitri had been on alert for just such unusual activity. He saw Chayka enter the computer room, so he eased into a chair at a terminal nearby and pretended to busy himself reviewing a file on the computer screen. He was just barely able to hear what Chayka had to say.

"We are not going to wait for Ivanoff to return. I, under the authority of the GRU, have made a decision regarding the perpetrator of the computer incident. It is clear that Lena Kristoff was responsible, perhaps with others, for the code changes. Therefore, I will arrest her today. Where can I find this woman, if she isn't here?"

"Lena! No, not Lena!" The director reacted in a loud and angry voice. "You cannot arrest her. The investigation is not finished. This is premature and a mistake." He leveled his eyes at the colonel. "Does Ivanoff know you are doing this?"

"It is my decision. Ivanoff isn't involved, nor should he be. This has always been a GRU security matter."

Several people had overheard the director. They all reacted against Chayka. Word spread through the building, and work came to a halt as everyone began to talk about it.

Dmitri was shocked by what he had just heard. He rose and left the computer room. He walked to his office, collected his briefcase and coat, then marched down the small hallway to the front door. He exited the building and was glad that he had taken his car to work today. He drove directly to the clinic to warn Lena.

When he arrived, he was told that Lena had not stopped in to visit Nadya today. He drove recklessly to her apartment, parked on the sidewalk, and ran up to her floor. He pounded on the door for several minutes with no response. Where could she be? Defeated, he wrote a short note for her to contact him, which he began to slide under the door. On second thought, he decided that if she did not find it, Chayka surely would when he began searching for his unfortunate friend. He stuffed the note in his pocket and drove away.

Chapter 37

On Monday morning, Katya prepared a tasty breakfast of blini, a crepe-like pancake, and sausages for them all. She was used to cooking in Misha's small lunchroom from the many times she had stayed overnight with him during their relationship. She was reminded of all the fun times they had had in this garage over the years. She, too, wondered what would come next in their uncertain lives.

They spent the morning sorting through the papers and clothing they had retrieved from the apartment. Lena made a point of burning everything that they would not carry with them. She did this in the large coal furnace that Misha had to heat the garage. She was ruthless in overseeing that everyone reduced their possessions. She made sure that they had only the amount of luggage for convenient handling on a train ride. She was even harder on herself because she would have to carry her own things as well as Eric's. She reduced Nadya's belongings to one suitcase and a backpack. She was surprised to find that Nadya owned only three pairs of shoes and five dresses to her name. And she thought she knew everything regarding her friend. When they got where they were going, they could all buy new things.

Lena had a long talk with Misha and convinced him that he would need to pack up the essentials of his trade to take with him. That meant his tools and other materials he would need to start a garage afresh elsewhere. He had begun this task the day before and had narrowed down his selections to a few hundred pounds of gear.

Lena was shocked by the sheer number of tools a mechanic needed to operate his business and asked him to try again to reduce the amount. She thought in terms of the hand tools he must have and he thought in terms of those—plus gear pullers, belt tighteners, alignment tools, electronic timers, and many other instruments. It became clear that his basic tool set wasn't going to fit in a couple of suitcases or toolboxes.

Misha stressed that much of what he needed would be hard to replace in the Soviet Union without great cost, and in a small town, he might not be able to replace some things at all. In the end, she agreed that he could bring it all with him, but she would need to change part of the exit plan.

The other thing that Misha had done the day before had caused him to run late in getting to Lena's apartment. He had finished working on a large Lada sedan that one of his customers had left with him for a starter repair. The owner had been told that he would need the car for a week to get the necessary parts for the repair. But yesterday Misha had switched starters with another car to make it operate reliably. This gave them a second car to drive when needed.

Katya and Misha now began to execute part of Lena's plan. They each drove one of the cars, Katya in Misha's old Lada and he in the newly appropriated one, to the parking facility at the Finlyandsky railway station. Katya parked the old car, made sure that she left no papers behind, except one, and rode back to the garage with him. The car was an attempt to throw the police and GRU off their track, if only for a short while. Hopefully, it would be discovered abandoned. The paper left behind was a note written by Lena listing several departure times for the train to Helsinki. In addition, they would leave a partially burned train schedule next to Misha's furnace at his garage. That was planted there to mislead the police if they found out about his involvement with the Kristoff sisters.

At 11:30 a.m., they had the large sedan packed with all the tools, luggage, and people it could hold, and they left the garage for the meeting with VICTOR. Lena and Katya squeezed into the front seat next to Misha in the big black Lada. Eric sat on Lena's lap. The back seat was full, as was the trunk. Katya held one of the duffel bags on her lap as well.

They drove to a warehouse that matched the address Lena had been given. They had to take an indirect route to be sure that they were not followed. The aging building was located in a sparsely occupied area on the east side of Leningrad in the industrial Kalininsky district. Only a few people appeared to be working at the businesses nearby, no doubt because some factories worked only half days on Mondays due to the slow economy. They parked behind the building and waited.

Noon came and went. Lena began to worry that something had gone wrong. The meeting was supposed to take place at 12:00 p.m. sharp. At 12:15 p.m., a black Mercedes sedan appeared from around the corner of the building. It stopped a few car lengths in front of them and flashed its headlights three times. Misha responded in kind. Then the car pulled up next to them.

The driver's window rolled down, and the driver asked a simple question concerning the weather. "Will it rain today?"

Lena leaned over and called out the expected response. "It will snow at three o'clock."

"I am VICTOR. Please follow me. We must drive slowly for several miles."

VICTOR pulled his vehicle forward and cautiously drove through the northern edge of Leningrad. They took a circuitous route obviously designed by VICTOR as a foil to ensure that they were not being followed. He executed his tradecraft for a good half hour, and they all watched for any signs of surveillance or tracking. They followed carefully as he entered a suburb northeast of the city, a sign that VICTOR was satisfied that they were in the clear. On the outskirts of town, he turned onto a country lane that led to a modest dacha.

It was the sort of weekend house that many middle-class families could afford for summer vacations. This one was a cheery little cottage set in the woods for privacy with a wood-shingled roof and a small front porch. It had a two-car garage attached to the back of the house so that people could enter without having to face inclement weather outside. The layout was not uncommon for dachas used in the winter.

VICTOR pulled up to the garage, opened one of the overhead doors, and motioned for them to drive in. He closed the door behind them and left his car outside. He led them into the house and showed them where they would be staying.

"Welcome to your temporary home. I already know your first names and that is all that is necessary. You will be staying in this dacha for several days to a week while we prepare your papers and make other arrangements. I have stocked the kitchen with food that I hope will meet your standards. But if you need other food or items, especially for the young man here, let me know. There are two bedrooms upstairs and a little bathroom on this floor. It is small but everything works." He laughed because most homes had at least one plumbing fixture that needed repair.

They all stared back at him deadpan.

"Please do not go outside during the day. If you must smoke, do it in the garage and open one of the windows. All the windows in the house are closed and most have the shades drawn. We don't want the neighbors to see your faces or even to know how many people are here, whether man or woman or child."

"We will remain indoors and be careful," Lena said quietly.

"Do not go out anywhere, even if you need supplies. I will come to resupply you, to check on things, and to keep you informed once a day, if not more often. Now, please get settled in and make yourselves at home. Make yourselves lunch."

VICTOR pulled Lena aside. "VERNA, can we talk in the other room? I have some questions about the delayed guest."

***

Chayka and his men had already searched the apartment from top to bottom by Monday night. What they found was of limited use. All the furniture, pots, pans, eating utensils, bedding, clothes, and books made the apartment seem quite furnished. Even the dishes in the sink rack had been washed and left to dry. There wasn't a scrap of paper in the place. A few books to be sure, but nothing personal at all. Clearly some clothing and all personal effects had been removed, along with any suitcases or baggage the occupants had owned.

Chayka was furious that he had missed the woman. He should have come here immediately instead of trusting that old fool, the director. He had caused a delay by talking Chayka into waiting a little longer to arrest Lena Kristoff because he said she would come to work in the afternoon.

Clearly she had misinformed the director, and now she was nowhere to be found. She had fooled them all and *that* he could not allow. He paced back and forth across the small room, hands clasped behind his back, head down in anger.

Chayka had his men interview the neighbors, most of whom were home, but only a few of whom were foolish enough to answer the door when the police or security services knocked. They did find an old woman who lived down the corridor who sometimes looked after the little boy. She was of no help and did not even know they were gone.

Chayka left one man to finish searching the apartment and set off to examine the home of Lena Kristoff's only close friend, Nadya Michaijlovich, in case she was hiding there. On his way out of the building, he ran into Ivanoff and one of his officers coming in and they chatted briefly. He asked Ivanoff how he knew he was here at the apartment and Ivanoff merely shrugged.

He muttered under his breath, "Fucking KGB prick."

***

Ivanoff entered the apartment and looked around casually. He felt the stove top and found it dead cold. The dishes in the sink rack were dry. There were too many dishes for a breakfast. A wine bottle in the trash and wineglasses were neatly arranged in the rack. They had eaten dinner here, not tonight but probably last night. The small refrigerator contained nothing of interest except yogurt, milk, and other essentials. The cupboards looked like those of any household, containing only meager supplies. These people did not live well, only commensurate with their mediocre jobs and salaries. Nothing suspicious at all.

Ivanoff wandered through the apartment, poking here and there at clothes and in drawers. They had left behind older, worn clothes and used bedding. There were two sets of women's clothing, consistent with

Lena and the younger sister who lived with her, as well as clothing and a few knickknacks belonging to the little boy. They had been smart not to take everything the way most outlaws did. The extra things and baggage would merely slow them down.

He sat on the sofa and let his man take a look around in case his eyes caught anything he might have missed. He turned the evidence over in his mind. The people had left last night, apparently, after dinner and when most people were tucked in their own homes for the night. But why did they leave so quickly? Chayka had only made his decision to arrest Lena this morning and had practically announced it to the entire staff at her workplace. Why did she decide to leave yesterday?

Dmitri had clearly seen her a day earlier and given her the warning that Ivanoff himself had suggested. That must have been what initiated her decision to leave. She must have anticipated the worst case and moved her family to safety.

He could not blame her after her friend's disastrous arrest by Pronin at Chayka's insistence. How could she know whether she would be subjected to the same malicious treatment? After seeing the condition that her friend was in, who wouldn't hide from the security forces?

Then, of course, there was the matter of her child. Ivanoff knew that the boy would most likely have been taken to live in a domestic services home, a nightmare that no parent could contemplate. No, he understood why she ran. He probably would have done the same thing, given the circumstances.

Chayka has certainly screwed this up. Now what? The GRU man was in a difficult spot with all the pressure being put on him to solve this foolish little case. He was in a position where he had to find Kristoff or lose face with his department. Now it did not matter whether she was guilty or not. He had to assume that she was and that was why she had run. After all, she had been convicted by Chayka's bumbling and Markov's shrill accusations. People had gone to the gulag or died for much less in this country.

Ivanoff's man came up to him holding a photograph in his hand. "Excuse me, sir. I have talked to the GRU sergeant on the subject of the evidence they found here. He told me they only found this photograph under one of the beds. Chayka said that it wasn't important and so they dismissed it and agreed to share it with us." He handed the photo to Ivanoff, who looked at it quickly.

It was a simple black-and-white snapshot of a man and a woman standing by the railing somewhere along the Neva River. The woman was clearly Lena with a brown-haired man, taken a few years ago. He flipped it over and read the few words written in pencil on the back.

"S Erikom na Nevskom beregu. With Eric on the Neva bank." He must have missed the boy in the photo. He put on his reading glasses and inspected the image again. No, there was no boy in the photo, only a man and a woman.

Wait! he thought. *I have seen this man's photo before.*

Just then the GRU sergeant came and told them that he was finished, and if they were also satisfied, he would close up the apartment and place a seal on the door to preserve evidence. Ivanoff tucked the photo in his pocket and rose from the sofa. He and his man stepped into the hallway. They watched the GRU officer seal the door and depart from the premises.

Ivanoff asked his man to bring the car around front. When the officer had left, he walked down the hallway to the door of the apartment where the little boy had often been taken for childcare. He knocked on the door.

When it opened, he smiled at old Auntie Olga and inquired whether he could ask her just one more question.

She replied, "Yes, you have good manners—not like that other policeman. I would be pleased to help in any way."

He realized that she was terrified of the police, as were most citizens, but then he wasn't the police, was he? Of course, she did not know that he was KGB.

"Yes, madam. We found this photograph in the apartment, and I wondered if perhaps you recognized the people in it?"

Olga took the photo and scrutinized it. "Oh yes. That is Lena with her boyfriend a few years ago. A very pleasant young man. Oh, they were so in love. It was like magic that spring. And Lena. I have never seen her so happy."

"And what else can you tell me about him? Have you seen him lately?"

"Oh no. He died shortly after this photo must have been taken. It was strange." She stopped and put her fingers to her lips as if she fought to remember. "He died in one of those boating accidents years ago. I don't know the details, but it was at nighttime." She looked at Ivanoff with sad eyes. "She was completely crushed by it all. And she was very sick right after that and then she had the baby to raise all by herself, poor girl." She hesitated. "That is how I got to know her and little Eric so well. I have helped raise the little boy since he was a baby."

"And the man's name?"

She turned the photo over. "It is written there. He was the baby's father—Eric's father. She named the boy after his daddy. Eric . . . Eric . . . His last name was one of those Scandinavian names, like Jensen or Swensen. He was Swedish, you know?"

"Could his name have been Larson?"

"That's it." The old babushka's face lit up in recognition. "*Da*, Larson. He was Eric Larson."

Chapter 38

Leningrad, Russia
Tuesday, March 20, 1979

On Tuesday morning Chayka called a meeting of the investigative committee and announced that he had solved the crime. Lena Kristoff was the culprit and her guilt was confirmed by the fact that she had run away from justice. If she was innocent, why would she not stay and defend herself? She was now a fugitive, and it was only a matter of time before she would be apprehended and brought to justice to answer for her crime.

He announced that detailed examination of the incident involving the model run had revealed no compromise of state security. It was only the work of a disgruntled employee who had an issue with Markov personally. The GRU would cease all further investigation and focus on her capture. As far as he was concerned, the case would be closed once she was apprehended.

Ivanoff simply shook his head. He looked over at Pronin and saw the same reaction. He did not think that Lena was at fault either. But perhaps there was potential political benefit to be derived from Chayka's announcement. Ivanoff felt that there was no profit in keeping this issue or the investigation active. Whatever crime had been committed had done no real damage except to a few egos. Why pursue it? It was costing his office time and resources that could be better employed elsewhere.

He knew that Pronin and the Leningrad Police Department wanted the whole incident and prison scandal to go away. The university wanted to get back to work, and the assistant secretary of economic planning wanted to get the modeling project back on track. He had apparently told the project director and the university chancellor that the sooner they got Markov off the project, the better. He saw him as a loose cannon who could only embarrass them all.

"I agree with Colonel Chayka that we should conclude this investigation," Ivanoff said. "I am sure that the director and the modeling staff, as well as the departments involved, would like to move on with their business. My only request is that the colonel continue to keep my office apprised of the GRU's progress in pursuit of the suspect." He refused to call her more than that. "Perhaps your sergeant can keep my assistant informed?" He smiled grimly at Chayka. "Pronin, do you have any comments? Or others around the table? Comments?"

Pronin quickly concurred and looked like a man released from the gallows. Everyone agreed to end the investigation, including the director, who still maintained that he could not believe that Lena could do such a thing.

They were all willing to play the game and end the misery.

After the meeting, Ivanoff waited for a chance to speak to Pronin in private.

"The two criminals from the prison are on a train with a work party headed east. I assume that the others have been seen to?"

Pronin confirmed that the other prison guards involved in the rape had been reassigned to new duties more becoming to their skills and temperament. The warden had also been warned that the Citizens' Oversight Committee, an ironic euphemism for the prison enforcement bureau, had gotten wind of abnormal conditions at Kresty Prison and would likely begin a review of his facility.

The director made an announcement to the staff over the public address system. He said that the investigation was over and that everyone should get back to work as usual. He then went on to relay the news to his superior at the university and called the undersecretary. He met with the system administrator to discuss how to compile the solver code so that it couldn't be tampered with. The sooner that happened, the sooner he could get rid of Markov and Chayka. Then things could begin to return to normal.

Chayka's superiors were pleased that he had closed the case so rapidly and that the problem was alleviated. So far he had dodged a bullet. In this country, dodging a bullet carried a more literal meaning than in Western democracies.

**

That evening Minuri came over to Dmitri's apartment for dinner. It was a somber occasion. The news that an arrest warrant had been issued for Lena disturbed the entire staff. Everyone liked the woman and regretted the last few days of turmoil at work. They knew that she was innocent and were horrified by what had happened to Nadya. In a rare display of solidarity, the director had granted Nadya unlimited paid sick leave as soon as he heard of her condition. Her coworkers took up a collection to help her get back on her feet when she was discharged from the clinic. They all planned to do whatever they could to help her.

Dmitri made his version of spaghetti for dinner, accompanied by a bottle of inexpensive wine, supposedly from Italy, but suspect nonetheless. The government liquor store was quite inventive in the labeling of products they sold. They finished eating and sat at the table sipping the last of the wine.

"Poor Lena. Poor Nadya," Minuri remarked. "They have suffered so and they do not deserve it. What will Lena do?"

"I don't know. What will any of us do now? Things have changed drastically at work. People are depressed and afraid. Who will accuse them of something next? I just want that ass Markov out of there. He has done so much damage."

"Yes, Markov is at the root of this. I have finally had enough of his vain and angry tirades." She spoke with great emotion, her eyes on the verge of tears. "I have decided I will not work with him anymore, even though he is assigned to interesting projects."

"What will you do then?" He was surprised. "I thought you two were a team on these types of projects?"

"We have been for years, and I have usually done the majority of the work on them too. He is very good with ideas, but his ego and bizarre personality drive even the best people away. I have lost a lot of opportunities because of him. I feel that I finally need to break free."

She looked at Dmitri for understanding and slid her hand across the table to cover his. "But what is more important is what will happen to us. Can we stay together somehow?" She paused and looked down at her plate. "Or am I like Markov, part of the same pot of turmoil?"

Dmitri looked up when she said this. He squeezed her hand. "Minuri, I think I am falling in love with you. But it would be difficult to maintain a relationship if you are working in Moscow and I am here in Leningrad. I have seen people try to make such arrangements work, and few have been successful at it."

Minuri brightened up at what he said. She smiled and even giggled. "You love me?" Suddenly her cares seemed to slip away. "Oh, me too! I love you too."

She came around the table, squeezed onto Dmitri's lap, and kissed him. It was a sweet moment.

"Well, mister," she said playfully. "I have been hoping this would be true. And ..." She paused. "And I have been inquiring about the possibility of finding work here in Leningrad at the university. The Department of Applied Mathematics said they could make a position available for me in a few months. And the director asked me to stay on the project for the time being to help with the model. He specifically asked me to do whatever is needed to compile the model so that he can get Markov 'the hell out of my hair,' as he put it. He said he could get the university to sponsor such a move."

She kissed Dmitri again and they both laughed. "I would be pleased to share my apartment with such an esteemed university colleague," Dmitri declared in a jovial tone.

They went to bed and made passionate love.

Afterward they snuggled together under the thick feather comforter and talked while sipping vodka from a flask. "Dmitri, there is one more thing that you must know about me if we are to live together. It is of my history with Markov."

Dmitri pulled his head back to give her a dirty look.

"No, Dmitri, it is not that. You men are always so competitive."

She started again. "It involves my work with him over the years. You see, when we were dating, we collaborated together on many projects. It was for one of those projects that we began to think of a better way to solve the complex problems we encountered. That was when we developed the solver. Markov had a few ideas, but he could not find a way to put them together in a useful form. Then, one day, it came to me." She closed her eyes as if visualizing that moment. "I wrote down my idea and tested it with a few lines of code that worked very well. I even verified the approach on a trial data set to be sure that it arrived at the correct solution. I was so happy." She opened her eyes and smiled.

"You must have been very proud," he commented.

"Then I showed it to Markov, and he was also certain that it worked well. He added a few coding changes that made it a bit better. We worked on it together." Her expression changed to one of anger. "But one day at a meeting when I wasn't present, he announced that we had developed a new solver that was extremely efficient. Soon everyone assumed that he had invented the solver, and he never corrected them. His damn ego was there again."

Minuri grimaced and took a sip of vodka.

"Up until then, I thought we were in love, but I began to see another side of him."

"What happened?"

"I should have said something then. But when you are in a relationship, you sort of let things happen. I did not want to undercut him or make him angry." She rolled her eyes. "But he took advantage of me. Because I did not correct him, he began to pretend more and more that it was his idea and that I only helped him. That is why it was called the Markov-Semelov solver with his name first."

"What an ass," Dmitri said.

"But then we broke off our relationship, and he began to treat me like an underling, not like a partner on our projects." She stopped, and her face took on a distant stare. "Oh, I began to hate him then. But I still had to work with him. I guess I just decided to settle for what I had, which was interesting work and a good job. With time he treated me with respect again. We just moved on from there. But it has always bothered me that he took credit for what was really my idea. It should have been called the Semelov-Markov solver after all."

"I am so sorry to hear this."

She took another slug of vodka. "Sometimes, when I have been drinking and feeling sorry for myself, I wish I could kill the man. Or at least ruin that awful ego of his."

Dmitri interrupted. "How did he get away with this for so long? No wonder you want to get even."

"Yes. When we were assigned to this project, and it was Markov this and Markov that, I wanted to wring his neck." She glared at Dmitri as if he was to blame. "Then he started to treat people badly again. I think he hates women, especially smart women who challenge him. And he is paranoid too." She sat up in bed and pulled the blankets up to cover her naked body. "He started to mistreat Lena and Nadya, and I couldn't stand it anymore. I knew I had to do something to make him fail in front of many people. I had to act." She reached out for the flask and finished the vodka in one long guzzle.

Dmitri raised his head and propped himself up on his elbow to look at her. He could see that her face was set in an angry and determined glare.

"My God, Minnie. What did you do?"

"Dmitri, don't hate me for this." She began to sob drunkenly and deeply into his shoulder. "I am responsible for what happened to Nadya and Lena. I did it. I am the one who changed the code."

Chapter 39

Lena and the others began to prepare themselves for a new life. They discussed what they wanted to do and where they would go. Much of this was dictated by what was possible versus what was desired. VICTOR helped lay out several options and said they needed to come up with a final plan soon so that he could facilitate travel papers and identification documents. With that in mind, he took fresh photos of the five of them for use in passports and other IDs.

The main point that they all had reservations about was how they could stay together. This was a forgone conclusion for Lena. She would never leave Eric, and she could not imagine a life without Nadya either. Nadya and Lena had already discussed what they would do if they had to flee Leningrad years ago when they helped smuggle Eric Larson out of the country. They had decided then that they were inseparable, and now their lives seemed even more intertwined. Nadya loved little Eric as much as Lena did, and she would do anything to keep him safe.

Katya was a different story. She told Lena that she had always expected to live her life with Lena directly involved. She said she loved her older sister in no uncertain terms and would stay with her to the end. But she was also madly in love with Misha, and they planned to marry one day and raise a family. She admitted that he was the only reason she had some doubts about what to do. She could not leave Lena and she could not leave Misha either. It all depended on him. If he agreed to follow Lena, then Katya said she would have no reason to decide otherwise. For he had the most to lose because of his business and garage.

"Given a choice, I do not want to leave Leningrad," Misha announced, looking first at Katya and then at Lena. "I have spent my entire life here and have no desire to go anywhere else. Besides, I have done nothing wrong." He stopped, and Katya came to stand beside him. He continued. "I love you, Lena, and Eric and Nadya. You are my family too, and I wish to keep you with me always." He looked at Lena with a flat stare. "But you have gotten us all into mischief before, and it isn't fair for you to unbalance our happy lives like this. I, of course, know you are innocent of the crime you are accused of. But look at what has happened, and now you are a fugitive. I would rather live a quiet life and just be happy with Katya." He put an arm around his lover and pulled her to him.

Lena lowered her head and sadness overcame her. "It's my wish to leave Russia and move to the West—maybe Scandinavia," she confessed. "We all know what our circumstances are in Russia." She paused to search Misha's eyes for any sign of understanding. "We have a limited future here. I want to give Eric the opportunities that we did not have as children. I want him to grow up in a free society, to go to a good school, and to have a real future. Only a life in the West can provide that." She looked at Katya to see how she was reacting, then continued. "Nadya and I discussed these ideas long ago when Eric was killed and we feared that we would have to leave home. We were willing to give up what little we have here for a chance to start over where there were more opportunities. So the concept of leaving our country is not new to us."

Katya and Misha were shocked at hearing this news. They said they had never thought about escaping to the West except in their dreams. Leaving home was too big a leap for them. They had discussed going to Minsk or maybe Kiev but not leaving the Soviet Union. That was too wild an idea.

They were silent for a while, and Lena understood why they were having trouble deciding what to do. For all their lives they had been told by their government officials that the West was an illusion. How could it be so special? Americans were especially bad people, not all of them perhaps, but the leaders to be certain. The few images of life in the West they had seen were smuggled in from Europe and seemed so different from the diet of misinformation they were fed by their own leaders that they were hard to believe.

At the same time, they had heard rumors from people who had traveled abroad. Many of the good and seemingly fantastic things they had heard were, in fact, true. People in the West, in Europe and in America, were ordinary people who were, by and large, happy with their lives. They were free to live as they wished and become prosperous if they worked hard and seized the right opportunities. And yet to most Russians, it was difficult to accept such rumors as reality. They seemed like happy and shining dreams that they could never obtain. It was too good to be true—this fantasy called the West.

Katya was the first to entertain the idea of leaving. "Suppose, just suppose," she said to Misha, "we were to get married and have a family. Wouldn't it be wonderful to raise our children in a place where they could be free?"

"For me, the concept of freedom is a vague and uncertain thing, an unknown option that is unreal and elusive," Misha said. "I have never considered it a possibility." He looked at Katya as he spoke. "The idea of freedom may warm to me, if it is what you want."

He saw a glimmer of excitement build in Katya's eyes. It was as if something they had dreamed of was now very real and possible. Suddenly their horizons seemed to expand with new opportunity.

Katya said, "If that is what is best for our family, then I will consider going to the West but only if Misha wants to go too."

"I am sorry, my friends, but it sounds too good to be true," Misha said in a quiet voice. "All my life, things that seemed so good turned out to be disappointing." He stared at the floor and then looked at Katya, perhaps searching for her approval. "Maybe the West is too much to consider. I cannot decide on something so important so quickly. I need more time to think—more time to decide."

When Lena brought up Misha's reservations to VICTOR later in the day, little did she know that VICTOR would be the one to help them through the decision. He said that he had assisted many people to relocate and had sometimes encountered the hesitancy Misha had. He said that every person had to decide for themselves how much change they could adjust to. It turned out that for Misha, there were two areas of concern: one, he had never even dreamed of such a drastic change, and two, he had not learned any other language besides Russian, except for a few words of English that he had picked up from Eric years ago.

"I do not know if I can adapt in a country where Russian was not spoken."

VICTOR said that people had this fear of the unknown frequently and that he understood the uncertainty. He said it was a given that Misha must move from Leningrad, but had he ever been interested in living somewhere else in the Soviet Union? Misha said that the only possible alternative was the Crimea—as a boy he had been fascinated with the region.

Finally, with much help from VICTOR, they decided that Lena, Nadya, and Eric would travel by train to East Berlin and from there be smuggled to the west side of the formidable Berlin Wall. VICTOR would arrange everything. Katya and Misha selected a different route. They would drive south across Belarus and the Ukraine to Odessa on the Black Sea where they would be near Crimea. By driving, they could take all of Misha's tools and be prepared for him to find a job as a mechanic there. VICTOR said that he would inquire about job prospects in Odessa. In the Ukraine, people would be less likely to be suspicious of a Russian couple with an unknown history, even though Ukrainians did not trust most Russians.

All of them would travel under assumed names, and Katya and Misha would pose as a young married couple. When they arrived in Odessa, they would keep their false identities. One year later, if they decided to move on, they could still travel to the West. But the offer wasn't open-ended. They had to decide by then.

The only decisions left to be made were those regarding the "delayed guest." By this time VICTOR had dropped the deception and spoke directly of how the agency would extract Nadya and bring her to the dacha.

"I had someone inquire about her condition," he said, taking the time to look each of them in the eye. "The nurse said that Nadya is doing very well. All signs of infection have vanished, and she is getting stronger every day. Her bruises are looking better, and the swelling in her face has improved."

"Oh," Lena said, "that is wonderful news."

"I think with some heavy makeup, she could travel without drawing too much attention." VICTOR continued. "But her mobility is an issue. They have gotten her up on her feet, and she walked up and down the corridor for exercise. Aside from being in pain, she still tires easily. She will not be able to carry any weight and will need to rest often."

"So we will have to carry her?" Misha asked.

"The other trouble is that it is painful for her to sit down— considering her injuries," VICTOR said calmly. "It will be difficult for her to travel by train."

"You are saying that she needs more time to heal," Lena said, showing concern on her face.

VICTOR nodded. "But we have to move her in the next few days before she can be released from the clinic. We'll have to arrange to collect her under false pretenses."

"How can we do that?" asked Katya.

"I am working on a plan, but I need Lena to write a note that my men can present to Nadya. It will let her know that we are helping her on Lena's authority." He turned to Lena now for her input.

They discussed the plan for an hour, and they all agreed that it was audacious but that it would work. VICTOR left the dasha to prepare for their travel.

Chapter 40

On Tuesday, Chayka obtained a warrant for the arrest of Lena Kristoff on suspicion of malicious damages to state interests. He had chosen an innocuous-sounding allegation to avoid suggesting that state security had been breached. The result was a relatively low-level charge that would not garner much attention from the police or other security services. He put out an all-stations bulletin for the greater Leningrad area to be on the lookout for a young woman, aged late twenties, 110 to 120 pounds, five feet seven inches tall, with blonde hair, blue eyes, and a slender build. She would most likely be traveling with a small boy, aged six, also with blond hair and blue eyes. If found, she was to be held for questioning on a state matter. A rather attractive photo of Lena was attached, probably the only thing that would draw the attention of any police or guard stations around the city. The bulletin had been distributed to all transportation stations—bus, rail, and air—and also to all border crossings.

He had set two men, his sergeant and a private, to work on locating her friends, family, and anyone else she might have holed up with. They had turned up an aunt who had lived in a northern district of Leningrad but who had died several years before. Otherwise, her only living family members were her sister and her son, both of whom had vanished at nearly the same time she had.

***

Chayka had his sergeant focus on Lena's only close friend, a friend she might seek shelter with, Nadya Michaijlovich, who was still undergoing care at the clinic. The sergeant learned that he did not have access to the patient due to Ivanoff's protective order. He was therefore unable to interrogate her and would have to wait until she was released. That would occur on Thursday afternoon, at which time she was to be transferred to her home for additional recovery. A nurse had been assigned to visit her there daily to check on her progress.

The sergeant had protested but left the clinic empty-handed. He informed Chayka that he intended to be at her apartment when she was released on Thursday.

Meanwhile, the private had tracked down the sister's place of work and found out that she had a longtime boyfriend, Misha. No one where she worked knew his last name or where he lived. She had mentioned a bar that she went to frequently, but no one could remember where it was. It was called North Star or something like that. Her coworkers had not been there, so they could be of no further help.

The sergeant had his assistant search through a list of bars, taverns, and nightclubs in the northern half of the city. After many hours, he had found three possibilities: Great North, Northern Lights, and Peter's Star. The next day they had visited all three and hit mild pay dirt at Northern Lights. The bartender remembered the two sisters, Lena and Katya, and Katya's friend Misha. He did not know Misha's last name but remembered that he operated a small auto-repair garage where he worked as a mechanic. He had not seen any of them for two weeks. After all that effort, the policemen had gained little new information.

The sergeant reported their progress to Chayka, who was greatly disappointed. There had been no sightings of the fugitive yet. They decided that, for now, all they could do was wait until they could interrogate Nadya after she had left the clinic. Chayka, being wary of slipups, had told his men to be at the clinic at the exact time she was discharged and not to wait for her at her home. One could never be too cautious.

On Thursday afternoon, March 22, the sergeant and private appeared at the clinic an hour before the time of Nadya's release. They walked into the office and made their presence known. The sergeant told the receptionist that they had come to escort Nadya Michaijlovich to her home.

The receptionist reacted with surprise. "Will you wait one minute, please?" She picked up the telephone and dialed.

In three minutes her supervisor came out of the office behind her. "How can I help you?" he asked.

"We are here to pick up Nadya Michaijlovich and drive her to her home," the sergeant said impatiently.

The supervisor looked pained. "I'm afraid that Miss Michaijlovich has already departed. An ambulance attendant presented the proper forms to take her into his custody. He spoke with the patient and loaded her into an ambulance not three hours ago."

The sergeant bristled. "Why didn't you say this to begin with?" He turned and paced across the room for a few moments, then he asked to see the release form and sign-out sheet. The signature was illegible but the paperwork was in order. The ambulance service was one he had heard of in the city. He grudgingly thanked the supervisor for his help.

They drove to Nadya's apartment and found no signs of anyone there. One neighbor who was home had seen no ambulance. When they contacted the ambulance company to find out the address to which Nadya had been delivered, they were told that the company had no record of any such appointment. There must have been a mistake. When pressed, the scheduling manager informed them that they may have been spoofed by one of the "bandit" ambulance services working in the city.

"If you are the police," the manager asked, "why don't you crack down on this illegal activity? It is your job, is it not?"

At the end of the day, the sergeant went home and washed his worries away with vodka before and after dinner. He didn't know how he would tell Chayka about the day's events. But it would definitely not be a pleasant experience.

***

Nadya's transfer to the dacha went smoothly. Using a wheelchair, she was taken by private ambulance to an address that was a storefront. VICTOR had specified that the operation be conducted with the utmost secrecy. The ambulance crew departed, and she was transferred into the back seat of a black Mercedes sedan. There, she was able to lie down in relative comfort for the remainder of her journey.

Lena and the family greeted her enthusiastically at the dacha. They were all happy to be back together and did not dwell on her attack, which still terrified her. She was set up with a cot in the downstairs dining room so that she could be close to the small bathroom. She napped until a late lunch was prepared and demonstrated that she could sit up for brief periods of time.

VICTOR arranged for a doctor to visit in the evening, who placed her on a course of oral antibiotics and examined her wounds. He pronounced her to be as well as could be expected, given her injuries. However, he cautioned, she needed at least two more weeks to recover before attempting any travel. Lena knew that would be difficult to arrange.

After dinner, they had a chance to talk and catch up on news from the modeling office and their present travel plans. Nadya was very excited about the upcoming journey to the West.

The next morning VICTOR and Misha drove back into Leningrad to take care of unfinished business. They needed to dispose of the Lada, which was now a liability they couldn't afford. Sooner or later the owner would call and, not finding Misha, report it missing. They did not want to be anywhere near when the police found it.

The same morning VICTOR and Misha picked up a used blue panel van that would become the family's new transportation. It had two special storage compartments built into its floor and other improvements to accommodate six travelers. It was much roomier and practical for their purpose than a sedan. VICTOR had seen to it that the van was registered in Misha's new cover name, Mikhail Dereshenko. They drove the van to the dacha, and everyone inspected it to see how it would suit their needs.

The rest of the day was spent with VICTOR issuing passports, other IDs, and papers to the five travelers. They discussed the travel schedule and arrangements for hours. Finally, VICTOR quizzed them on their new names and cover stories, which they had been learning and improving on for three days.

VICTOR went over the details for Misha and Katya one more time. "You two are a newly married couple named Mikhail and Katerina Dereshenko, a good Ukrainian name to be sure, don't you think? Your story is that you have been raised in Leningrad by Ukrainian parents and now are moving back to that country to enjoy warmer weather." He smiled as they reacted favorably. He looked at Misha. "You are a mechanic, and you hope to find a good job in the auto import business in the Odessa area. You will drive the van, all legally registered in your name, Mikhail Dereshenko, carrying all your tools and equipment with you. I have arranged a place for you two to stay initially in Odessa and am trying to find you a job, possibly at the German motors importer there. In that way you can get into a training program for BMW or Mercedes and have a very good and easily transferable job." He smiled. "That will also help if you decide to move to the West in the future. These are excellent skills to have."

***

After VICTOR left for the evening, Lena called Katya aside and gave her nearly all her thousands of rubles. She kept only what she would need for the next few days.

"Here, my darling sister, is most of my Russian money. If all goes well, I will not need rubles again."

"But, Lena, how will you, Eric, and Nadie get by?" Katya asked.

"I will have dollars. Don't worry about Eric and me."

She handed Katya a sealed envelope filled with US dollars. "This is for emergencies. You must hide it and not open it unless you are desperate." She put a hand on her sister's arm.

Katya, being who she was, tore open a corner of the envelope immediately to see what was inside. She gasped and put her hand over her mouth. She was ready to exclaim when Lena held up her finger and said, "Shhh! Not here."

Lena signaled Nadya to watch over Eric while she led Katya upstairs to one of the bedrooms, where she closed the door.

"Lena, where did all this money come from? What is going on?"

"Katya, be quiet and listen to me." Lena tried to remain calm and in control. "Remember how I helped Eric with certain things when he traveled back and forth to Finland and Sweden? He worked as a bookseller, but there is something else." She paused and locked eyes with her sister. "He worked as a secret courier for his government."

Katya's eyes widened.

"No, not for the Swedish government, for the American government."

Katya's mouth dropped open. "But I thought he was just a smuggler or a petty criminal. No wonder the KGB was after him."

"Remember how I used to do extra work for some people and when I made trips to Finland and other places? I started doing that long before I met Eric. It was a way to earn extra money." She watched as Katya sat down on the bed, her mouth wide open, her eyes as big as saucers. "Yes? You remember? I told you I was collecting information for other economists. Remember how I told you I met Eric in Helsinki?"

"Yes."

"Well, it did not happen just by chance." She sat on the bed next to Katya and held her hand. "You see, I was helping another girl who could not fulfill her assignment. I went in her place to deliver a package. It was an accident. I was to give the package to a courier and get a package in return." Her expression changed to one of hope and happy memories. "Eric was the courier. We were never supposed to meet, but because I substituted for that girl, it just happened." She smiled at the thought.

Lena looked out the window and recalled that first meeting. Her eyes welled up. Katya saw her tears and realized that the memories of Eric were still painful. She pulled Lena to her and sat with her sister's head on her shoulder. Lena wept loudly for a few minutes.

"Poor sister. It has been so hard on you to lose your Eric, your one true love. I don't know how you have been so strong for so long."

"Katie, I am tired of always being the strong one. I am just worn out by it all." She cried a little more but then tried to regain control of her weeping.

"The last time Eric was here, I had an opportunity to copy information about the model project and sent it with him. It was a copy of the model and the data sets. The information got through, even though I saw Eric get killed."

"No," Katya gasped as she breathed in deeply.

"The information went to the Americans, and they paid me for doing that. I have been sending them information on and off ever since. They have continued to pay me and told me that if I ever got in trouble, they could help me."

Katya threw her head back as if she had been hit by a fist. "*Bozhe ty moy*. Oh my God."

"Oh, Katie! There is so much more I could tell you, but I'm afraid there is no time to explain it all." She took Katya's hands, straightened up, and looked into her eyes. "This current business that the GRU says I did—it is not true—none of it. But now I must run away for something I did not do. When I needed help and played my card, the Americans came through for me like they said they would. They are the ones who are helping us now, the Americans and their associates in our country. They will help us settle in the West, in Europe or in America, if we like."

Katya held her sister tight and looked stunned.

Lena emphasized her next words. "So you see, we have a chance to be free. I want Eric to be free and to be all that he can grow up to be."

"Oh, dear sister," Katya whispered, "you have been so brave."

Lena began to weep again, muttering between sobs. "Oh, Katie. I hope you understand. I really do. I did this for us and so that one day it will be better here in our country."

The two sisters sat holding each other for a long time, both crying a little and taking turns trying to comfort each other. They continued to talk.

In the end, Katya whispered, "Dear sister, now I understand how much you have done for our family and why we all must move on with our lives."

Chapter 41

Leningrad, Russia, and Warsaw, Poland
Saturday, March 24, 1979

On Saturday they loaded up the van and bade farewell to the dacha, their safe house for nearly a week. When everything was ready, they said goodbye to VICTOR and simply drove away.

Misha drove south along the outskirts of Leningrad. Katya had wanted to drive through the city for one last look at their beautiful home, but VICTOR and Misha had both argued against such foolishness. It took more than an hour to bypass the city and merge onto the provincial highway to Pskov. The road was a wide two-lane highway that had heavy long-haul truck traffic. They were unable to travel faster than fifty kilometers per hour. They stopped at a fueling station to refill the gas tank and to use the meager bathroom facilities. Then they were back on the road again.

The travel went quite well all day. They encountered a few police checkpoints along the road where Misha had to show his papers. At one such place, the guard asked to see everyone's ID cards, but he had no further questions. They stopped at 1:00 p.m. at one of the fueling stations to eat the big lunch that Lena had prepared.

For the last four hours of the drive, they talked about what lay ahead and agreed to find a way to get back together as soon as they could. Everyone except Misha cried from time to time. As captain of the ship, he had to keep his emotions together and focus on getting them to safety at Pskov. Katya told him that she was starting to have second thoughts about going their separate way to Odessa.

They pulled into the parking lot of the Pskov railway station just before dark, and they unloaded three suitcases, a backpack, and Lena's shoulder bag. Lena ran into the station to buy tickets while the others waited in the van. She returned a half hour later with the news that she, Nadya, and Eric were on the 8:00 p.m. train and could board at 7:00 p.m., possibly a little earlier. She had purchased a sleeping compartment, a luxury that few Russians had ever experienced.

They decided to wait in the van until 7:00 p.m., since it would be more comfortable than sitting on the wooden benches in the train station, especially for Nadya. This created an awkward situation in which they had to say goodbye but did not leave right away. To pass the time, Katya told a long story about the first trip she and Lena had made to the countryside to visit an uncle's farm. The story was funny and got Eric giggling. Finally the time came for the real goodbyes.

They huddled together in one last group hug and Lena said, "Take good care of each other. Misha, I count on you to look after my baby sister for me. We all love you both. I promise we will see each other again someday."

Misha and Katya drove away in tears to find the road south toward Minsk.

***

Lena led Nadya and Eric into the station, noting that there were police posted at all exits and patrols next to the trains themselves. They had to show their ID cards twice before they could proceed to the platform where their train was waiting. Lena carried the backpack and wheeled two suitcases behind her while Eric dragged one suitcase and Nadya carried her shoulder bag. Nadya walked with a pronounced limp, which she tried to hide when they were checked in by the police. They descended a few stairs to the platform and were allowed to board the train a little early. A steward showed them to their sleeper compartment and pointed in the direction of the dining car forward on the train.

They entered the compartment and got organized. Lena set up a bed right away so that Nadya could lie down. Then she pulled out a few toys for Eric and gave him a cookie. She looked at Nadya and became concerned.

"Does it hurt much to walk?"

"It is worse than I thought," Nadya said, "but I will be all right. Maybe you and Eric should go to the dining car and I will stay here. You could bring me something small to eat and drink. Take your time. Let Eric enjoy himself in the fancy restaurant."

Lena and Eric walked down the narrow corridor to the dining car and had a small table to themselves. The food was very expensive, but Lena spoiled Eric with everything he wanted, including an apple tart and a soda drink. When they came back to their compartment, Nadya had already gone to bed for the night, but she rallied to eat her meal. She propped herself up on pillows and relished the pierogi that Lena had brought her. "These are really good, and the beer is top notch."

Lena took Eric to the bathroom at the end of the railcar before they turned in. While she waited for Eric, she examined Elena Kuzuch, her new persona, in the mirror by the sink. She was at first startled by the dark-haired woman who stared back at her. She had cut her beautiful, long blonde locks and dyed them a shade of auburn brown, but she had never imagined herself as a brunette. What caught her attention now were her brown eyebrows, which were never as noticeable as when she was blonde. It would take some time to get used to this look. Little Eric had mistaken her for someone else the first time he saw her after her makeover, and it had frightened her. Thanks to VICTOR, she had her ID photos shot with her new look. It was good insurance because the police would be looking for a single blonde woman her age traveling with a young boy.

She and Eric returned to the compartment, made up the second bed, and went to sleep. They were awakened once during the night at the Vilnius railway station in Lithuania, where border police entered the train to check papers and passports. This happened again at the Polish border but was over quickly. They slept until morning.

When Sunday came, they ate the bread and cheese they had brought with them. Lena went to the dining car and came back with hot tea and a glass of milk for Eric to drink. They put away one bed and looked out the window at the Polish scenery as they rode along the rails.

They arrived at Warsaw's main railway station, Centralna, after noon. They collected their baggage and asked a porter if there was a good hotel nearby. He recommended two and gave them general directions. He did not know their rates but said that they were clean and safe for children. Lena offered him a small ruble note for helping them with their luggage.

The porter refused the rubles but then explained why. "You have not traveled before, I think. Most Poles do not like Russian money." He saw Lena's face squint in confusion. "It isn't very useful here and not worth as much as in the Soviet Union."

"Oh," she said. "I did not know this. But I have only rubles to spend."

"If you like, you can exchange some rubles for Polish zloty. That is, if you stay here in Poland any length of time."

He took them to an exchange kiosk where Lena changed part of her money. She tipped him, and he stepped outside with them to point out the way to the closest hotel. They rented a room and walked up three flights of stairs to get settled. By that time, Nadya was worn out and had to lie down. She crawled into bed immediately to keep warm.

Lena walked over and placed her hand on the single lukewarm radiator in the room. It appeared that warmth was in as short supply in Poland as it was in Russia.

***

The Lada had been noticed by a guard at the Finlyandsky railway station on Tuesday, March 20. The car was obviously abandoned because it had no paperwork left inside, and it was parked in an area where it should not be. A routine report was filed later that day with the local police post, the one in the station itself. Careful checking indicated that it had been parked there the day before. The suspicious car was reported to headquarters the next day as part of a routine summary of stolen or abandoned vehicles found in the city. A technician followed up on the vehicle's chassis identification number and requested that the records department check for ownership based on that number.

On Friday the records clerk reported that there was an address associated with the current owner, one Mikhail Petrovich, who was an auto mechanic by trade. At the end of the day, this information was passed to Sergeant Babichev.

The sergeant had immediately walked upstairs to Captain Pronin's office, just catching him as he was preparing to leave for dinner at home.

Pronin was surprised by the discovery for two reasons. First, he was astonished that they found anything at all that might relate to the disappearance of Lena Kristoff. Second, he was amazed that his department had analyzed and reported the information in only a few days instead of weeks. That most certainly was some sort of miracle.

Now he had to make a decision. This might be important information that should be followed up on immediately. But should he personally follow up on it, missing a home-cooked meal and probably invoking the ire of his wife? Or could he delegate the duty to Sergeant Babichev and ruin his evening instead?

He elected to bestow the honor on Babichev. He asked him to take a man and go to the address for this Mr. Petrovich to determine whether it was his car and anything else he could discover. Then Pronin drove home to await a phone call from the sergeant regarding his findings.

***

A downhearted but loyal Babichev recruited a patrolman, and together they drove to the address on the east side of the city. After much confusion, they located the address in a warehouse district. It was an auto repair garage. No one answered the steel door after repeated and increasingly loud pounding. But the ruckus did draw out a man from an adjacent shop who asked what all the noise was about. When police badges were shown, the man said that he was just asking and had to go back to work. Babichev delayed him long enough to find out that Misha had been gone for several days, but he knew not where. He was clearly afraid to say more.

The sergeant decided that he had grounds to break open the door, and he got the patrolman busy doing just that. After a few minutes, the door responded to pressure from an applied crowbar. They entered and found evidence that several people had occupied the premises recently, but nothing incriminating, just the type of records one would expect to find in a repair shop.

The only items of interest that they discovered was a child's toy and, near the furnace, a page from a partially burned schedule for the trains from the Finlyandsky station to Vyborg to the north.

The sergeant used the shop telephone to call Pronin at home. He told him what he had found and agreed to await his arrival after he finished dinner. He sought out the man in the adjacent shop for more questioning.

That interview, involving a few serious threats to investigate his small business, produced additional information. The man confirmed that two women and a boy had spent a night or two with Misha at the garage. One of the women was Misha's girlfriend, Katya. He did not know her family name.

When Pronin arrived, they searched the garage again, this time very carefully. Not turning up anything more of value, they sealed the place for more examination by the evidence team the next day. Pronin telephoned to the KGB office and learned that Ivanoff had already left for the day. A desk sergeant agreed to leave him a priority message and to alert his assistant to call Pronin immediately upon receipt.

Pronin congratulated Babichev for breaking the case, and in a rare show of camaraderie, offered to buy him a drink at a nearby tavern. Babichev was surprised by his boss's largess but accepted the invitation. He hoped that perhaps this breakthrough would be a strong point for him to emphasize when he pressed Pronin again for his long-overdue pay raise.

They discussed what to do next at the railway station and who to contact at the Vyborg Police Department to see what they might turn up. It was a long night.

***

Ivanoff did not receive the message until he arrived at his office on Saturday morning. He immediately called Pronin for a situation report and listened with great interest as the captain briefed him on the ongoing investigation at the Finlyandsky station and his contact with the Vyborg police. He agreed to meet with Pronin over lunch near his office to go over the evidence. He asked his assistant to give Chayka's sergeant a heads-up.

Ivanoff was surprised that anything had turned up on the case at all. At least now they knew who a few of the other people were who were helping Lena disappear. Her sister and her boyfriend, Petrovich, were involved. And he knew through Chayka's sergeant that they had collected Nadya from the clinic somehow. Now there were five of them on the run, one of whom required a doctor's care. That was a liability because Nadya would slow them down and necessitate at least a modicum of medical attention.

Lost in thought, he looked out the window as yet another snowstorm swept into the city from the north. He reviewed all the data systematically. Something about this Lena suggested that she was a careful planner and meticulous enough to not leave evidence behind. So why would she leave a car at the train station without sanding off the vehicle chassis identification number? She might not have been aware of the number's presence, but certainly this Mikhail knew. And why abandon the vehicle? And why travel north?

He decided to telephone his only contact at the Vyborg Police Department, Captain Resinsky. It had been years since he had talked to him, but if he was still there, he would be a senior man. He found the telephone number in his index and dialed.

The conversation with Resinsky was short. Captain Pronin had already talked to him regarding the same matter, and he was freeing up several men to work on it. He said that if the fugitives had legitimate papers, they had probably passed into Finland days ago. If they did not have good papers, then they would need to avoid the train to Finland and travel across the border by either land or sea. That would be difficult at this time of year because of the unusually cold weather. He said that the extreme cold was providing the Vyborg district with a

308 • Fred G. Baker

relatively crime-free period because even the smugglers were staying inside their warm homes for many weeks now.

Only a crazy person would try to travel overland through the forests in this weather, and it would be next to impossible for a boy and a sick woman to make such a trip and survive. The sea wasn't an option either. Many of the inlets and marinas were completely frozen in this month. There were no boats moving on the water except icebreakers and a few fishermen. But his men would check the train records. That was the most likely route the fugitives would have taken.

"Who were these people?" Resinsky asked. "Did they have false passports available?"

"I don't know that, my friend," Ivanoff replied.

"They could not get them made in Vyborg. We do not have any good forgers here that I know of."

Ivanoff completed the conversation and hung up the phone. He sat at his desk and puzzled through this new but limited information.

He opened his lower desk drawer and pulled out a bottle of his favorite vodka and a glass. He hesitated then. Yes, it was early for vodka. But the alcohol always helped bring things into better focus. To show moderation, he poured himself a short one, settled back into his chair, and stared at the falling snowflakes.

This is an inconsistent picture, he thought to himself. If the fugitives had all the papers necessary to flee the country, they could simply travel by train directly to Helsinki or catch an airplane. In that case, they could just abandon the car at the train station and go. They would not care if it was found a few days later. Or if they wanted to make a clean departure, they would get rid of the car in another way so as not to leave a trail. There were areas within the city where they could abandon the vehicle and it would disappear overnight.

Perhaps they did not have papers but expected to travel by boat or land and did not realize that it could not be done at this time of year. And since they could not get papers in Vyborg, they would have to return to Leningrad for those.

In addition, they had somehow extracted their friend from the clinic a week later. It made sense not to leave her behind as a witness or as someone who could be used for leverage against them. The police and security agencies were well known to use relatives as bargaining chips in different criminal and state cases. But why so much later? Did they come back for her after finding that they could not flee via Vyborg? Why not reclaim the car in that case? This Lena was too smart for that.

No. There was only one reason to leave the car at the train station.

Ivanoff sat up straight and shouted.

"*Moy Bog! Eto krasnaya sel'd'*. My God! It's a red herring."

Chapter 42

"Lena! Wake up. Something is wrong with me."

Nadya shook Lena awake and whispered in her ear so as not to wake Eric, who was tucked in the bed on the other side of his mother. Lena's eyes opened, and she gradually took in what her friend had said. Nadya pulled back the bedcovers to reveal her nightgown, now red from bleeding between the legs.

"It isn't the time for my period, and I do not bleed like this," she whimpered. "I feel like something is tearing loose inside me. Please, hand me a towel so that I don't get more blood on the sheets."

Lena jumped out of bed as fast as she could without waking Eric. She gave Nadya a hotel towel, which she used to soak up the blood. She helped her put on a coat, her only means to cover up and not freeze to death on the short walk to the bathroom in the hallway. By then, Eric was awake.

"Mummy and Aunt Nadie are going to use the bathroom down the hall and will be back soon," Lena whispered.

Eric was asleep in an instant.

Nadya cleaned herself up in the bathroom. She said she thought that the bleeding had stopped. She carried a few large absorbent pads with her for this eventuality, and they seemed to work for her now. They went back to the room so that Nadya could rest until it was time to leave. Finally, they got themselves and Eric dressed and then packed their humble possessions.

Nadya lay down on the bed.

Lena left the hotel and walked to the station to buy tickets on the 9:00 a.m. train to Berlin and Prague. They had to be on that train in particular because someone would meet them on arrival. She bought some sweet rolls and coffee to take back to the room.

By chance she ran into the same porter who had helped them the day before. She asked him if they had wheelchairs available at the station for passenger use. He said they did but only for use at the station. However, he could be persuaded to bring one to her hotel for a favor. When they agreed on the amount of the favor, she paid him and went back to the hotel to get the others ready.

They had eaten and were waiting downstairs in the hotel lobby when the porter arrived with the wheelchair. They proceeded to the station, with Eric and Lena pulling the suitcases and Nadya riding in the wheelchair. The porter took them directly to their platform and helped them onto the train.

The train wasn't overly crowded, but their first-class compartment was. They claimed the three empty seats along one side of the space. Nadya sat down but was in such obvious pain that Lena had her lie down across the seats with her head on Lena's lap. Eric sat on the floor at Lena's feet. She tried to explain to the German man and two other women in the compartment that her friend was ill. Even with her heavy makeup to cover her bruises, anyone could see that Nadya was suffering a great deal. They all looked sympathetic, and one of the women offered to let Eric sit on the edge of her seat.

The train left the station quite late. They picked up speed outside of Warsaw and sped directly to Poznan, where they stopped for only fifteen minutes before the locomotive raced to the East German border. Nadya didn't look at all well, and Eric asked if Auntie Nadya was sick. Nadya bravely said that she didn't feel well but would be fine.

Lena was worried. As the time passed, it appeared that Nadya was becoming more and more pale.

They crossed into East Germany and received the most thorough examination of documents they had yet encountered. Everyone in the compartment tensed up notably during the inspections. The border agents also randomly picked pieces of luggage to check and pawed through purses and bags. Then they moved on to maraud the next compartment.

The train finally entered East Berlin. As they moved slowly along the tracks, Lena was surprised to see such wanton devastation. Whole tracts of land were still lying in rubble from the horrors of the last Great War—what the Russians called the Great Patriotic War. Although Russian cities had also suffered much ruin, most of the damage had been repaired or buildings rebuilt. Here it was different. It was as if the destruction in Berlin and the other cities of East Germany were left as eyesores to punish the German people for their great evil during the conflict.

One woman pointed out the train window at the Berlin Wall separating East from West Berlin. It formed a long gray barrier across the landscape, with a denuded no-man's-land on the east side providing the soldiers posted in guard towers overlooking the wall with a clean shot at those unlucky souls trying to cross. The communists thought that any citizen who wanted to run away from the totalitarian regime should die rather than be free.

They pulled into the East Berlin station, the Ostbanhof, located only a few hundred meters from the wall itself. The train came to a stop, and people began to open doors and climb down the stairs to the platform. Everyone in the compartment got up and grabbed their luggage.

"Auntie Nadie! You are bleeding," Eric called out in Russian and pointed to Nadya's leg. A thin stream of dark blood trickled down her left leg. She sat down immediately, feeling woozy. The younger of the German women saw the blood and fainted dead away. The man with her just barely caught her and placed her back down on her seat.

The older woman looked at Nadya and said in broken Russian, "I, too, had that done a long time ago. I never wished it on anyone to go through such an ordeal." She apparently misunderstood what was causing Nadya's bleeding. Then she pushed her companion's head forward between her knees until she came to and was ushered out of the compartment by her friends.

Lena shut the door and told Eric to face it and close his eyes. She helped Nadya lift her skirt to clean herself up. There was a great deal of blood, and the pads were saturated. They wiped her legs with a handkerchief, and Lena pulled out the last of the absorbent pads for Nadya to use. The blood was a bright red now and flowed at a slow but steady trickle. Lena put the bloody pads in a plastic garbage bag in the small trash can in the compartment.

"Nadie, can you walk?" Lena asked.

Nadya tried to smile and said *da*, but it came out only as a sigh. She stood up and walked to the corridor. Lena and Eric brought the bags. There was a backup at the stairs, but the man who had been in their compartment said something in German, and people stepped aside to let Nadya, Lena, and Eric pass. He helped them down the stairs to the platform, handing their suitcases to another Good Samaritan on the platform, where his two companions stood waiting. Lena thanked the man profusely in both Russian and English and ushered Nadya to the nearest bench. Nadya rested for several minutes.

As they stood to go, a porter arrived with a wheelchair and helped Nadya into it. He spoke to them in German.

"The older woman said you might need some help."

He pointed up the platform where the three traveling companions were watching. They waved before they turned and continued toward the exit.

The porter helped them along the platform to where it ended in a staircase. He was able to slowly pull Nadya up the stairs in the chair going backward. As he did this, Lena scanned the observation area that overlooked the platforms. She saw a man standing there in a brown wool coat with a felt hat and a red scarf. He stared back at her.

At the top of the stairs, the porter began to walk toward the main exit, but Lena asked him to wait a moment. She thought she recognized a friend. Could he wait while she went to speak with him? Nadya tried to talk to the porter in English, but he did not understand her.

Lena went over to the newsstand and picked up a newspaper from the rack. She paid the kiosk owner in zloty, which seemed to be acceptable. She opened the paper and stood for a moment looking at the article on page ten. The man she had seen on the platform sauntered over holding the same newspaper open to the same page and article.

"The train from Dresden is running late," he said,

"The train from Minsk is always on time too," she responded,

Most people would recognize this as a complete impossibility, she thought.

"You are VERNA? You can call me Hans," said the man as he stepped away from the newsstand. "I am confused. I see three of you, not just two. I am to take VERNA and one boy through the wall. My orders are very strict. Only them." He seemed determined to keep to his quota.

"But we are here. You must take all three of us."

"It is impossible. My compartment can only fit one person," he said sternly. "It is already very tight for the boy too. But we can manage if he is small." He looked over where the others were waiting. "Yes, he is a small boy, so he can go. The bags aren't a problem. The guards are really only there to control the movement of people."

"Why is the compartment so small?"

"To go into the sector that we use by the wall, they always check the car for passengers. I have a false compartment behind the rear seat where I can hide one small man or a woman and perhaps a little boy. When we pass the guard station, I drive to a garage and they get out. The rest I can't tell you. But the key is to get past the sector guards. Do you understand?"

"But my friend is bleeding badly. She must get help soon. What will we do?" Lena wrung her hands as she looked across the station to where Nadya and Eric were waiting. "Where is your car?" she asked.

"Out the side exit, over there. I am sorry, but I can only take one woman." He was sympathetic now but said that his hands were tied. "It is too bad. I am sorry."

Lena was overcome with emotion. She felt as if she had been hit in the chest and all her breath had been taken away. Tears began to form in the corners of her eyes as she gazed at the man's implacable face. She shifted her stare to take in the view of Eric standing next to Nadya, her face twisted in pain. Eric looked confused by what was happening. She made the difficult decision that she had to under the circumstances.

Lena waved at the porter and motioned for him to come over. Then she told Hans, "You will take my friend, VERNA, and the boy, Eric, as planned. Can anyone else help me follow across?"

"But I thought you were VERNA? You know the passcode."

"My friend Nadya will die if she doesn't get through. Do you understand? That is what is important."

"I see. If that is what must happen, so be it. I think you are a good friend indeed." He paused and gave her a serious look. "To answer your question, there is no other way now. If you don't have a place to stay already arranged, the police will arrest you as a vagrant as soon as you leave the station property. They are very strict and check at the station gate. Even in the dark, you wouldn't be able to climb the fence and get out. And with no friends here, you would not be able to cross the wall." Regret shadowed his face. "I am terribly sorry."

"What will I do?" Lena asked, earnestly beseeching Hans for advice.

"Go from here and try to make contact. Your ticket is to Prague, yes? I will pass a message with your friend that you continued to Prague."

The others arrived, and they went to the side entrance. There Hans dismissed the porter and his wheelchair. He tipped the porter and thanked him in German. A guard at the door stopped them and asked for IDs and their business. Hans told him that this woman was coming out only to say goodbye to her friend. She would come back inside in a few minutes. The guard acquiesced when Hans pressed a few East German marks into his hand. He waved them through.

They descended a long staircase to the parking lot. Lena pulled Nadya aside and told her of the problem. Nadya said she that wouldn't go without Lena.

"Yes," Lena said, squeezing her hand very hard, "you will go because you need a doctor, and I expect you to take care of Eric until I find a way to join you. You don't know the protocols and would soon be arrested here if you didn't bleed to death." Lena pulled Nadya to her for a bear hug. "Don't argue and upset my son. I need you to stay strong for

Eric. I will go to Prague and find another way to join you. Please, my friend, my dearest friend, go before you fall down."

They laughed and shed tears at the same time. They kissed each other on both cheeks and hugged again for a long time.

"We must go," Hans said in English, clearly very nervous.

"Listen, Eric," Lena said, speaking in her native tongue to her son, "you must go with Auntie Nadie now. Do everything that she and this man ask you to do. Be a good boy. You two go now, and I will come right away behind you, yes? Now be brave and do as I ask, please."

She enveloped Eric in a long embrace. After nearly a minute, she pulled away and grinned at Eric. "You are going to play a game of hide-and-seek now. Have fun!"

Hans pushed Nadya and Eric into the back seat of his car. Lena waved goodbye as she saw Eric's tear-stained face looking out the window. The car pulled away, and she turned to reenter the station. The guard let her through with her bag. She watched the car pass through the exit and turn onto the busy street.

Lena stood there crying for a long time, trying not to be noticed. It was the most difficult decision she ever had to make, separating from her lovely boy so that he would be free.

Will I ever see him again? she wondered. She could not know. All she knew now was that she had to go on with no plan, no real hope, and no contacts in Prague. She wiped her eyes, picked up her suitcase, and rushed to catch the train to Prague.

Chapter 43

East Berlin, Germany
Monday, March 26, 1979

Nadya was terrified as Hans drove through the black streets of East Berlin for nearly ten minutes. They motored away from the busy avenues near the train station through darkened, empty byways and decaying neighborhoods. Here and there were battered apartment buildings along the vacant streets.

Nadya and Eric rode in the sedan's back seat, with Nadya resting in a reclined position and Eric holding her hand. She talked softly to him as she tried not to panic. In the dark, with as much blood loss as she had sustained, she was feeling extremely weak, almost as if she could slip into a long-deserved sleep.

Occasionally Hans turned his head and told them what was happening. He spoke in broken Russian so that they could understand. Then he pulled into a dark alley and stopped the car.

"We stop now and put you in secret place, *da*? When you are in, we drive five or ten minutes to guard station. You hear me say be quiet and make not a sound. No talk, no move, *da*? Five minutes and you get out."

He asked them to step out of the car, and reached behind the back seat to release the upright portion of the seatback. It fell forward, revealing a narrow hiding place. Nadya looked inside it and felt afraid. She had never liked confined spaces. She looked at Hans, shaking her head, then at Eric. But she knew that she had to be brave for him and for Lena. She reluctantly crawled into the hiding place and felt the pain in her abdomen increase. Hans helped her turn so that her back was toward the trunk of the car. She nestled into the hideaway.

Hans saw her fear and told her to think of only good things—of her friend. She would be free in one hour in the West. It was worth it.

Once she was in place, he helped the boy get in on top of her. Eric had to lie down with his head at her feet and his feet on her belly. Hans took Eric's shoes off so that he would fit better. He pushed the seat back into position, and after a few adjustments, it shifted into place and he was able to close the latch to secure it. He opened an air hole behind the seat. "Keep open now. Close when I say, *da*?"

Nadya couldn't hold back the fear that overcame her. It was like being stuffed into an ill-fitting coffin. She could tell that Eric was afraid too. She tried to comfort him, partly to keep her mind off her confinement. She could hardly move one hand but reached for the air hole to be sure she could close it when needed.

She told Eric how nice it would be in the West.

"My dear Eric, what shall we do first in the West? Should we find some ice cream to eat? They must have many flavors for you to choose from." She tried to look ahead to a future that she hoped would be bright. "You just have to keep still for a while and be quiet when Hans tells us, you understand?"

***

Hans moved a coat and one suitcase into the back seat. He started the car and drove into the street, making several turns. As he did so, he spoke to Nadya and the boy in his broken Russian patter.

"We are doing good. Almost there. Are you all right?" He kept up the banter to help the time pass for all of them as the dilapidated auto bumped along potholed streets.

At last he said, "My friends, you hear me? We are here. Two cars in front. Close the hole now, yes. We are next. Be quiet now." Eric held his breath to be as silent as he could possibly be.

Hans drove cautiously up to the guardhouse at the checkpoint and stopped. He sat very still and talked to the guard. He reached into his coat and retrieved his papers to show him.

The guard asked for the keys to open the trunk. He hurried to the back of the car and tried the keys on it. There was the sound of metal clinking on the car body and a light pounding.

The guard came back and told Hans to get out of the car. Hans asked what was the trouble, and the guard asked him to open the trunk. Fearful, Hans went to the back of the car and tried to open the hatch. He pushed on it in a special way while he turned the key and it opened.

The guard looked relieved and peered into the trunk. He pushed the spare tire to one side, unzipped the suitcases, dug through them, and moved a blanket to one side. He closed the trunk. He glanced inside the vehicle and asked to open the suitcase lying on the back seat as well. While he did that, another guard looked under the car using a mirror on a pole. When they were satisfied, the guard gave Hans the keys back and waved him through. He raised the small rail gate to let the car pass.

Hans said, "*Danke*, thank you," and, as calmly as possible, drove forward. He picked up speed and turned a corner. Then he called out to his passengers, "All is good. Open air hole now. Are you all right?"

Only the boy responded. "I think my auntie fell asleep. Can we stop now?"

Hans told him to wait a few more minutes and they would stop. They could all get out then. He called to Nadya and she still did not respond. After driving faster than he should to get to the garage, he pulled up to its door and turned off his lights. He got out to open the door and inched the car into a completely dark parking space. Once inside, he turned off the motor and closed the garage door.

He opened the rear door of the car and unlatched the seatback. It fell forward and the boy crawled out right away. He put his shoes on and took a deep breath.

"That was very scary," Eric said. "Wasn't it, Auntie?"

Nadya didn't respond, so Hans got a flashlight to see how she was faring. He could tell that she was out cold, so he reached for her eyelid to see if she would respond. She didn't react to the flashlight or to shaking. This was serious.

He reached into the hiding space and pulled out a small medical kit. From it he extracted a small vial of smelling salts. He crawled into the back seat and opened it under Nadya's nose. She began to come around quickly, but she was quite pale. She tried to get out of the compartment but was very weak. When Hans reached around her hips to pull her out of the back seat, he realized why she had no strength.

His hand came away covered with blood.

He pulled her up and slapped her face lightly to rouse her.

"Are we here? I couldn't breathe," she whispered in Russian.

"We are here, Nadya. Can you stand up?"

Hans got her out of the car before closing the compartment and the car door. He sat her on a wooden box and went to the back of the garage. He moved several boxes to reveal a concrete hatch in the floor. He opened it and reached into the manway it covered. He flicked a switch inside, and dim light radiated from beneath the concrete floor of the garage. He went to the car, got the luggage, and dropped it down the hole.

He approached Nadya and got her to her feet. She could only stand by leaning heavily on him. He propelled her to the hole and showed her the ladder along one wall of the tunnel below. With him guiding her feet onto the top rung, she started downward. She began to fall, so he held her in place.

"Boy, can you climb down in front and move her feet on the ladder?"

Eric climbed over his aunt and down the ladder. Hans slapped Nadya again to keep her awake. Then he started her down the ladder. She made it halfway with their support but fell the last four feet. She dropped onto Eric and the luggage, narrowly missing the concrete floor. She moaned in pain.

Hans climbed down and stood Nadya on her feet again. He began to panic. He had no idea if she would survive this trip. But still, he must try to move her along the dirt floor to the tunnel.

"Boy," he asked, "can you manage luggage and pull it along the tunnel? I help your aunt." Eric looked about to go into shock, but he dragged the two suitcases on their little wheels along the musty track.

They started down the long tunnel, which was two meters high and only wide enough for a single person to pass.

"We must be quick. No time left. Hurry, boy!"

Hans tried to rush Nadya along. At one point he found a light switch and turned off the lights behind them.

"We are halfway now. Here—I will use flashlight." He turned on a headlamp.

They continued by the dim light of the headlamp. Eric needed both hands free to pull the suitcases. He tried to keep up but found that he could move only one suitcase at a time in the narrow passage. Hans kept going with the light and Eric fell behind.

Hans waited and called out, "Bring one, get second later." He was now practically carrying Nadya. She finally collapsed and he couldn't rouse her again. Without hesitation, he rolled her onto her back and grabbed her by her shoulders. Walking backward, he dragged her along the tunnel. She lost a shoe as her heels scraped over the uneven tunnel floor.

The tunnel ended at a small wooden door approximately a meter tall. Hans lay Nadya down and pounded on the door until Eric caught up with a suitcase. He pounded some more. He looked at his watch and swore bitterly under his breath.

"OK, boy. Come with me for last suitcase." Hans began to run back down the tunnel and Eric followed. They left Nadya in the dark. They reached the suitcase in a few minutes, at which point Hans pulled out a small flashlight and gave it to Eric. He grabbed Eric by the shoulders and shook him. "Go back to auntie and pound on door. Someone will open it when they hear you. I am late and must go."

Then Hans jogged away back toward the garage.

***

Eric watched Hans get smaller and smaller as he retreated along the tunnel, the rectangle of light around him shrinking as he went, framing his silhouette. Eric turned and hurried along with the suitcase back to his auntie Nadie.

"Auntie, wake up." He prodded her shoulders to rouse her, but she remained asleep.

He pounded on the door.

"Please! Help me! Help! Someone help me!"

He pounded for several minutes. All he could hear were the echoes of his own calls in the dark passage. He sat down and held Nadya's hand in his. He saw blood on her leg and became afraid. He cried a little and went back to pounding on the door.

Time passed and the flashlight became weaker. It seemed like hours dragged by as the light dimmed.

***

Eric was now terrified. It was like they were buried alive. He shook Nadya again, but she was completely silent. He didn't know what to do. He lay down next to his aunt and turned toward her with one arm across her chest, trying to comfort her as his mother had done for him many times before. He remained quiet, noticing that the sound of every move he made seemed magnified in the dark space. Even the sound of his breathing reflected back to him from the concrete block walls.

He listened to his breathing. That was all he heard.

Then he noticed another sound—a weak wheezy noise. He listened carefully and felt that the sound was near him. He realized that Auntie Nadie was just barely breathing too. A very slow, quiet wheezing. He hugged her tightly as his mother would when he was sick and trying to sleep. Auntie was very sick now. He would help her.

"It will be good, Auntie," he whispered. "We will be safe."

Then the flashlight winked out.

***

Eric must have fallen asleep because he had lost track of time. Something had awakened him. He heard a sound behind the door. A key turned in an unseen lock, and the door opened a crack to reveal a lighted basement room.

A voice boomed in German, *"Hallo, junger Mann. Wilkommen im Westen!"* Then in English: "Hello, young man. Welcome to the West!"

Chapter 44

Captain Pronin called Ivanoff on Monday morning to report that all attempts to find traces of the fugitives at Vyborg had come up negative. Even the train records provided no useful clues as to what had happened to their quarry. He had his sergeant contact Chayka's office with the same news.

Ivanoff told Pronin that now he was even more convinced that the car and train schedule had been planted to misdirect their efforts. He reasoned that if the suspects feigned north, maybe he and Pronin should look south. He confirmed with Pronin that Chayka's all-stations bulletin had included only the Leningrad area. He argued that there were only two other options. One, the suspects were lying low in Leningrad—a distinct possibly with a sick accomplice—or two, they had escaped the Leningrad district by means undetected by the police and security forces.

He suggested that they continue their current plan to locate any suspicious sales of medical supplies and also extend the range of their all-stations bulletin to include all of Federated Russia and a few adjacent Soviet states, especially to the west and south. If Pronin approved, he would suggest it to Chayka, since he was the one with real skin in the game, as the Americans say.

Ivanoff himself felt that the matter was probably not worth the resources it would take to capture these luckless people. And for what? The Lena woman's only real crime appeared to be that she fell in love with and was used by an American agent. She seemed to have suffered enough for that misplaced trust. In fact, he felt a certain empathy for her because she had been forced to give up everything she knew because of Chayka's false charges. He was convinced that she had been wrongly accused, as had her friend. Now they and their companions were wanted for crimes they had no involvement in.

Ivanoff thought that he should linger at the margins of the case. If nothing else he could keep Chayka from making a greater fool of himself. He would stay involved for now.

***

The next day Ivanoff learned that the revised all-stations bulletin had turned up three suspicious railroad transactions. One of these was in Novgorod on Friday, where a blonde woman with a small boy had boarded a train to Minsk. Further checking indicated that she was too old to be Lena Kristoff. The other two leads came from the railway station in Pskov. On Friday three young women, one of whom was blonde, and a small boy had boarded a train to Kiev. Chayka was looking into that group further. On Saturday, two dark-haired women and a blond boy had purchased tickets to Warsaw, Poland. Chayka was also checking that group. The local police were presently at the Pskov station interviewing workers.

Ivanoff's assistant knocked on the door to tell him that Colonel Chayka was on the telephone with an update. Ivanoff picked up on line two and heard a triumphant colonel report his findings.

"Comrade Ivanoff," he crowed. "The two women and boy who traveled to Warsaw were in fact our fugitives. They fit the descriptions well, except that the Kristoff woman must have dyed her hair to a brunette color. The second woman was unwell and walked with a decided limp." He seemed quite proud of this information. "I have people on their way to the station in Warsaw to interview personnel there, and I plan to go there also, as soon as I can free myself from my office duties."

"Congratulations, Colonel," Ivanoff said. "You made good progress in your investigation. Thank you for keeping me informed." He paused. "And let me know what you learn in Warsaw, yes?"

Ivanoff finished a memo and made time to reflect on the new information. Why in the world would you escape to Poland if you were on the run? Unless you had relatives or friends in Warsaw. But none of the fugitives had Polish backgrounds that he could remember. Time would tell.

He checked his watch. If Chayka was flying to Warsaw on a commercial flight, he could be there this afternoon. Giving him time to verify things on the ground meant that he might call Ivanoff in the evening with results. Ivanoff called Pronin just to keep him up to date.

He drove home to enjoy dinner at the unlicensed diner next to his boarding house. They served a delicious pelmeni dish that reminded him of his mother's cooking. He would continue writing two reports that were due at noon the following day. Next, he should have time to consider the latest move mailed to him by his longtime chess opponent in Moscow—black knight to king's bishop three. What an odd move. Perhaps his friend was really going somewhere else with this play? He sat back and wondered if maybe there was logic in escaping to Poland. Maybe Lena Kristoff was making a longer play.

Ivanoff finally finished his reports at 6:00 p.m., when Chayka called. He listened carefully.

"I tell you, Ivanoff, I have them now."

The two women and the boy had checked into a hotel near the Centralna station for the night. They traveled under assumed identities now: Elena and Eric Kuzuch, and Kalanoff, Nadya Michaijlovich's new name. The injured Kalanoff woman was having difficulties walking and had to use a wheelchair to navigate around the station.

"Her injuries are still quite severe," Ivanoff commented, wondering how the woman he had seen unconscious only a few days ago could travel at all.

"A porter helped them get on the nine a.m. train to Berlin on Monday morning. My people checked with the ticket master, and he recalled that a woman fitting Kristoff's description had purchased three tickets to Prague that day, all first class. She had the proper papers for that sort of trip. The man said that the train left on time, so they should have made the connection to the Prague train at Berlin's Ostbanhof that evening."

"That is illuminating. Perhaps they will cross to the West from Czechoslovakia?"

Chayka again seemed pleased with this progress. "I am taking the train to Berlin tonight. I have called ahead to have an officer I know in the East German Stazi ask questions at the Berlin station to see if they were seen there. Then on to Prague."

"Good luck and safe travels, Colonel."

"I will update you when I have more to report." He paused for a moment. "Can you relay this information to Captain Pronin for me? I must hurry to catch the Berlin train."

"Of course."

Ivanoff hung up the phone and considered the new data. First, it appeared that Chayka was tracking the correct people, from his description of the findings. The fact that they had obtained false identification and travel papers suggested either that they had underworld connections or that they had plenty of money to buy such documents. If Chayka could obtain any of these documents, especially the passports, they could tell what level of expertise had been employed. That would indicate who was assisting them. Ivanoff made a note to follow up on this matter.

Going to Czechoslovakia provided a reasonable place from which to exfiltrate to West Germany or Austria—or better yet, to Yugoslavia. *Those borders were as open as a fishing net is porous,* he thought.

But where were the other two persons? This Mikhail Petrovich and Katya Kristoff? They may have been traveling separately along the same route or, better yet, taking a different route to the West. They would be harder to find because he had no photograph of Petrovich on file and only a poor-quality employment photo from Katya's file. In any case, they were small fish and not worth much effort unless they could lead them to Lena.

He called his assistant at his office, surprised to find him still at work, and ordered him to contact Chayka's sergeant to double-check train records for the two other fugitives. He would now consider traveling to

Prague if there were any new useful developments. He asked his assistant to update Pronin's sergeant, Babichev. Next they discussed other pending cases.

After he hung up the phone, Ivanoff stared at his chessboard. Was it worth his time to travel to Prague? Probably not. But something about this Lena Kristoff intrigued him. He mused that she was executing a complicated escape strategy. He wondered what sort of chess player she might be.

Chapter 45

Prague, Czechoslovakia, and East Berlin, Germany
Monday, March 26, 1979

Lena boarded the 8:00 p.m. train to Dresden and Prague on Monday night. She had three tickets and thought that she should buy food for three people in the dining car to support the ruse that they were traveling together. She spent the last of her zlotys on dinner and a glass of wine. She took food back with her "for her traveling companions," she announced. Instead, she placed the extra dinners in her shoulder bag to eat later.

The train pulled into the Dresden station at 11:30 p.m., where it waited for a few minutes as new passengers boarded. After that delay, they continued to the Czech border, where everyone had to show their IDs and travel papers again. She was able to sleep for the next four hours of the trip.

She faced a logistical dilemma when the train arrived at the Hlavní Nádraží station, the main railroad station in Prague, at 5:00 a.m. on Tuesday, since no businesses were yet open. She asked a porter to recommend an inexpensive hotel, and he gave her directions to one within walking distance. But he reminded her that she would need Czech currency to register for a room. He told her that there was a money exchange kiosk in the station but that it wouldn't open until 6:00 a.m. She thanked him and walked outside.

Lena ambled to a side street and found an out-of-the-way place to sit and rest until 6:00 a.m. arrived. She ate some of her leftover food for breakfast. She would have waited inside the station, but thought she would have drawn the attention of any police patrolling the area. It was better to wait outside and reenter when shops were opening and she could exchange money. She dug in her purse to inspect all the money she was carrying and pulled out a few American dollars to keep handy, if needed. She counted it all up and found that she had just enough to rent a room for a couple of days and to buy food before she had to dip into the dollars. Then she would have to find someone on the black market to exchange those.

That is when she realized that most of her dollars were sewn into the lining of Eric's suitcase, which was now in Berlin somewhere. She didn't have a lot of money on her now when she most needed it.

What the porter had said concerned her now. He had reminded her that she would need to register at any hotel she went to, meaning that she would have to show her passport and possibly leave it with the hotel for security. Most hotels had to report any foreigners staying on their premises to the police, which would leave a clear trail for anyone following her.

How could she avoid the hotels? She could look for a guest room to rent where the owners probably might not want to report their guests. In Russia, most people who rented a private room did so *pod prilavkom*—under the counter—so as not to report their extra income. It was probably the same here in the Czechoslovak Socialist Republic.

Unfortunately, she wasn't supposed to be in Prague at all. The through tickets to this city were a ruse to throw any followers off her trail. She and VICTOR hadn't made any contingency plans for her to be in Prague. Therefore, there were no arrangements to contact anyone, no addresses of safe houses, and no exit plan from the country. She would have to improvise to remain ahead of her pursuers and to stay alive.

The other problem was that she had no exit plan. It would be best to establish contact with the Americans to get their help to leave the country. But how could she do that? They wouldn't know who she was. She couldn't go to the American embassy because if things here were as they were in Russia, the secret police would be watching to see who showed up there. If she was recognized by a Czech agent, she would not be safe when she left the embassy meeting.

Her best hope now was to blend in with other tourists so as not to draw attention to herself. She had seen vacationers on the train, many Americans and West Germans. Maybe she could pretend to be a tourist too. She would need to speak English in that case and not Russian.

Besides, she had heard that the Czechs resented Russians a great deal. Who could blame them after the Russian army invaded their country in 1968 to oppress the Czech people and their quiet revolution? English would be a good choice if she could remember her vocabulary. She had been able to carry on a conversation in English when Eric was with her.

She paused as her mind drifted to her *dorogoy* Eric, her dear Eric, and the love she felt for him. *I cannot think of him now,* she told herself. Instead, she thought of her little boy and how she missed him. *I hope my dear little Eric and Nadie are safe and in the West.* By now they would have had a night's rest breathing the air of freedom.

I wonder what that must feel like.

It was after 6:00 a.m. by now and the money exchange would be open. She wheeled her suitcase back across to the railway station and exchanged all her cash for crowns, speaking English as she did so.

She left the station and walked along the narrow cobblestone streets toward Staroměstské Náměstí, the Old Town Square. That was where the tourists would be.

She followed a group of German tourists through the medieval arch of the Prašná Brána. the Powder Tower, into what she thought must be the most beautiful town square in the world. Occupying the center of the square was a massive monument to Jan Hus, the great Czech reformer. The monument was surrounded by magnificent pastel-colored buildings—representing the architectural wealth of a city miraculously untouched by the last world war. A variety of architectural styles stood side by side in perfect harmony: Gothic towers, Baroque facades, and colorful hand-painted murals. She stood for a long time, gawking at the scenery, while her tourist group moved on to the west side of the square to gather around the Pražský orloj, the medieval astronomical clock mounted on the Old Town Hall.

"It's amazing, isn't it?" a young woman called out to her from the nearby outdoor table of a bakery. Lena looked at her, surprised that someone should talk to her.

"I looked the same way when I first saw this square," the girl continued. "I couldn't believe that anything could be so beautiful."

Lena, suspicious at first, realized that the woman was just trying to be friendly.

"So beautiful," she replied in English as she assessed the woman quickly and stepped closer. "It is my first time here. I did not know it looked like this."

Lena looked at the woman. She was quite young, in her early twenties, and rather thin to Lena's eyes. She had blonde hair swept up in a ponytail, green eyes, and a few freckles on her face. She had bright-red lips, which Lena thought to be too much makeup, and was wearing a short black skirt with a white blouse covered by a light jacket. She was eating a pastry and drinking coffee from a paper cup. She looked cold and had goose bumps on her legs.

Lena asked if the food was expensive there and the girl said, "No, just average, I think."

Lena decided to get something to eat from the bakery. "I will eat too, maybe. But inside there are tables." She smiled at the girl. "It is too cold out here."

She dragged her suitcase inside and found a free table to set her bag on. She parked her suitcase adjacent to it and walked up to the counter to peruse the menu, which was in Czech. She ordered a cup of hot chocolate and pointed to a pastry stuffed with ham and cheese. She sat at the table and began to eat the tasty pastry. *Ochen' vkusno!* Very good! The hot chocolate was the best she had ever had, very rich. She looked out the window and saw the woman—girl, really—get up and come inside. She went to the counter and ordered a cup of hot coffee, then looked around for a place to sit. All the tables were by then occupied, so she stood by the counter.

She looked at Lena and smiled, then hesitantly came over to ask if she could sit in the extra chair.

Lena said, "Yes. Please sit, miss." It sounded awkward, and the girl laughed; so did Lena. "My English isn't so good. I need practice, yes?"

She looked at the girl's bare legs, now red from the cold. "You are dressed for summer, not weather like this."

"When I got dressed, I saw the sun and thought it would be warmer." She held out one of her slender legs to inspect how red her skin was. "And these are not the best shoes to walk on cobblestones." She flexed her foot to show off the black high heels she had on. "I must be an optimist or a masochist." She laughed.

Lena asked what a masochist was. The girl explained and they both laughed.

They sat together and talked for an hour or so. The girl said that her name was Krista and that she was on a weeklong vacation from Copenhagen, Denmark. She had arrived by herself yesterday and was still exploring the city. She had a guidebook and had selected many sights to see. She told Lena a few of them—the town hall with its astronomical clock tower, the castle, the old library, and the cathedral.

She asked Lena about herself, and Lena was cautious in her reply. She said that she had just come in from Warsaw and didn't know anyone in the city either. But she needed a vacation, so here she was. Her name was Elena and she was not married—still single.

Krista asked Lena if she wanted to spend the day with her sightseeing. It would be fun to have a friend along. Lena hesitated but realized that she had nothing else to do, so she agreed and they spent the morning wandering around the old city. She had fun and they both laughed a lot, which took her mind off her worries for a while. The only real drawback during the day was that she had to wheel her suitcase with her everywhere.

They ate a sandwich for a late lunch. When they finished, Lena broke away to do "errands," like finding a guesthouse for the night that wasn't too expensive.

Krista pointed to a rustic building on the square. "If you like, we could meet there for dinner later. I don't know anyone here in Prague, so it would be fun to have a companion to eat with."

"Yes. That would be very nice," Lena replied.

They agreed on a time and went their separate ways.

Lena asked at a few shops where she could find a guest room for a reasonable price. Several places were suggested and she inquired at each. She quickly learned that nearly every guest room was occupied for the week because a special musical celebration was happening that had brought many people to the city for a few days. She learned that most guesthouses didn't report their clients to the police like the hotels did, which was good news, but she had to keep looking for a room. Unfortunately, when she finally found one, the price was extremely high, so she decided to save money and sleep on the street.

While searching she noticed that people were staring at her outfit. She realized that she needed better clothes that didn't look so worn and so Russian as those she was wearing. She looked in a couple of small shops, but again, the cost was too much for her.

She asked a person in a bookshop where she could find less expensive clothes. She was given an address several blocks away and trudged there, dragging her suitcase with her. She did find a few things she liked and could afford, so she tried them on and modeled them in front of the mirror. One of the salesgirls came over and told her that the blouse she had picked out fit her well but that she should try a brighter color. What she had on was very plain. She suggested a couple of things, and Lena liked them better so she bought them—a blouse and a pair of slacks. She also saw a pair of fashionable shoes but couldn't think to buy them given her low cash reserves. She wore the new clothes when she left the store.

Lena hurried back to the square to meet Krista for dinner. *At least I can eat a big meal before I spend a night on the street,* she thought.

When she got to the square, Krista was already waiting at the door of the restaurant. She waved when she saw Lena coming toward her. They went inside and found a table near the back, where a stove gave off a warm glow. Lena parked her suitcase next to the table. Krista insisted that they order wine with their Italian meal. Lena ordered simple spaghetti, and Krista had a veal dish. They had a wonderful time. Lena talked of her day shopping, and Krista described the ancient library she had visited.

"Did you find a room?" Krista asked.

Lena didn't answer at first, not knowing what to say. "No. I asked at many guesthouses, but no one had a spare room I could afford." She smiled wanly. "It seems the whole world has come to Prague for this week."

"None at all?"

"Well, there was one," Lena muttered, "but they wanted two hundred crowns for one night. I cannot pay this."

"I agree, it is too much money. It is twice what I paid for my nice room." Krista paused and scrutinized her new friend. "So you don't have a room? What will you do? Even the hotels are full this time of year."

"I will find a place to curl up out of the wind," Lena said as cheerfully as she could. "It's not so cold. I have done it before."

Krista's jaw dropped in disbelief.

"You would sleep outside on a night like this, when it is so cold? The police will arrest you if they find you. And if they don't, men will find you when the taverns close." She seemed shocked at the thought. "No. I cannot let you."

Lena said nothing and looked down at the top of the table as she tried to think of a response.

When Lena raised her head, Krista met her eyes. "Look," she said, "we are friends now. I have plenty of space in my room for you to stay for the night."

"No," Lena said. "I couldn't do such a thing. It is nice of you to offer, but no."

"Just until you find a room of your own, *ja?*" Krista said with kindness in her voice. "Come with me. Will you, please?"

Lena said no again but not convincingly.

Krista kept at it until Lena agreed. "Just for one night. You are a good person to be so kind."

It was late when they left the restaurant, after several glasses of wine each. Lena was quite drunk because she wasn't used to wine. Vodka was her drink of choice. They walked two blocks and entered a house, ascending the staircase to Krista's room. They took turns going down the hall to the common bathroom. When Lena came back to the room, Krista was standing next to the bed in a nightgown, laughing hysterically.

"I forgot to tell you that there is only one bed." She pointed to the double bed. "But I thought I had a couch in the room too. I am sorry!"

Lena was surprised and a little disappointed. "It is all right. I can sleep on the floor."

"No, no. You are my guest. I can sleep on the floor and you can have the bed."

Lena smiled at Krista and said, "Do not worry. Where I come from, we can get three women in a bed that size. I just hope you don't snore." They broke out laughing.

"It is settled then. You can pick your side of the bed, Elena"—Krista made a mischievous face—"as long as I get this one!" She leaped into the right side of the bed and crawled under the down comforter, a big smile on her face.

"Oh no you don't!" Lena laughed. Perhaps the wine was making her feel adventurous. She hurriedly climbed in and pushed Krista to the other side of the bed with her behind. They were both giggling as Krista got up and turned off the light. She slipped in under the comforter.

"Good night, Elena. Sleep well." She rolled onto her back and fell directly to sleep. She began to snore lightly.

Lena settled in and, also lying on her back, considered her good fortune to meet this funny Dane. She thought of Eric and Nadya and began to sob quietly. But she was exhausted and soon fell asleep.

***

Chayka arrived at the Ostbanhof at 6:00 a.m. on Wednesday morning, March 28. He was met at the station by Captain Hofstein of the infamous East German secret police, the Staatssicherheit, also called the Stazi.

Hofstein was impeccably dressed in a gray uniform with silver epaulets and the gold bars of his rank on his collar. He was wearing one of the high-fronted, billed caps that were typical of the East German armed forces and the Stazi. He was clean shaven, alert, and had the clear blue eyes of a conqueror. He spoke to Chayka in a friendly if formal manner.

"Colonel Chayka! It is a pleasure to meet you." He held out his hand to greet his Russian colleague. "Welcome to Berlin and the German Democratic Republic." He bowed his head to his honored guest as they shook hands. "I regret that my superior officer, Colonel Krautz, couldn't be here due to urgent matters at headquarters. But he has briefed me thoroughly, and I and my men are at your disposal. I understand that the criminals are wanted for sabotaging an important element of your government's economic apparatus." His eyebrows rose. "Is that correct?"

"I am also pleased to meet you, Captain." Chayka spoke forcefully to this younger officer. "Tell your colonel that I hope we can meet soon, perhaps under a less pressing situation."

"Of course, Colonel."

Then Chayka took on a serious tone. "Yes, they have interfered with part of our planning apparatus and perhaps have, in doing so, interfered with our security. We will know more when we can question them about the extent of their activities. They may be receiving aid from foreign agents in their escape, but that hasn't been confirmed. Based on our current knowledge, they appear to be headed to Prague, probably to make their exit to West Germany or Austria." He contemplated the situation. "That isn't yet clear."

"Very well, Colonel. My men have just begun questioning the station employees. Perhaps you would care for a cup of coffee while we wait for their results?"

The two men walked to a kiosk that had just opened and ordered coffee and pastries, eating while they talked. A sergeant approached and asked to speak to Hofstein. After a brief exchange, the captain returned to Chayka.

"A porter said he helped a young injured woman and her two traveling companions, a young woman and a small boy. The injured woman was in great pain and needed a wheelchair." He searched Chayka's face for any indication that this information might be helpful. "They met an older man who picked them up in a car. He didn't see the car but helped them to the side entrance near the parking lot. They left the building there. That is all he knows."

"I see," Chayka said. "It sounds like our conspirators."

Chayka and Hofstein discussed what they should do. All they knew was that Nadya and Eric had left the station with a stranger, undoubtedly an agent who would get them across the wall and into West Berlin.

"Many people still cross the wall or tunnel under it," Hofstein said, "or find a way through other means to escape to the West. We uncover at least one new tunnel a month and sometimes more." He smiled at Chayka, one professional to another. "And who knows how many tunnels we don't find."

"It is a difficult problem," Chayka said.

"Colonel, here is what I think happened. Two of your fugitives have been handled by a professional operation and are most likely across the wall by now. I can have my men make the necessary inquiries from the usual suspects, but the odds of finding those two are very small. If that is indeed the case, then we are only looking for the other woman, who most likely is on her way to Prague."

Questioning of the ticket sellers revealed that Lena apparently had not purchased any tickets. But why would she if she already had tickets to Prague? She likely just got on the train. Someone on the train might have seen her, or if she got off at Prague, she might have been seen there.

Hofstein said, "The last train to Prague that night left at eight p.m., and it was the only one she could have taken that late. The train would have continued on to Budapest following its usual schedule. This means that the crew will not be back until tomorrow evening when the train does its return route." He looked optimistic. "We will be able to question them at that time."

"Yes, that would be useful."

"Can you provide me with a set of photos to use when interviewing the crew?" Hofstein asked.

Chayka had anticipated the need and gave him a set.

"Thank you for your help, Captain," Chayka said, disappointed. "I think it is best if my men and I take the next train to Prague. I understand that it leaves at one p.m. That will put me in Prague nearly a day and a half behind this woman."

"That sounds reasonable. In that case you will be in Prague at eight p.m."

"Very well. That is what I will do. I can make inquiries and call you for your update."

It was agreed.

Hofstein set his men to work and then left the station.

Chayka bought a first-class ticket on the Prague train for himself and two second-class tickets for his men. He telephoned Ivanoff back in Leningrad with his news. When the time came, they boarded the train with their limited luggage.

They continued their pursuit southward to yet another country. Chayka was still hopeful that he would catch this fugitive. If he failed, he would have a difficult time justifying the costs he had incurred. Now he must find this Lena Kristoff, or he might face more questions from his superior than he would be comfortable with.

In any case, he was in a bad mood. He was running behind the insidious woman, Lena, who seemed to always be one or two steps ahead of him. He had to take drastic measures to find her and end this embarrassing chase across Eastern Europe.

Perhaps he would make real progress tomorrow. He settled into an angry state as he sipped brandy and watched the vulgar East German countryside glide past his window.

Part 3
End Game

Chapter 46

After he completed his PhD degree at the University of Minneapolis in the fall of 1978, Eric Barrenger was offered a postdoctoral position in the civil engineering department at the University of Illinois. His research into the characterization of soil engineering properties had led to the development of a field method to measure the ability of soils to support structures and underground voids, which could be applied to new types of construction projects. This had caught the interest of several faculty members who considered it a novel area of research that crossed over between the fields of civil engineering and soil science. Eric knew that with further testing, he would be able to demonstrate the efficacy of his invention. He could now fully develop his test equipment at one of the nation's best engineering schools.

When he had returned to the United States in the fall of 1972, the country was suffering through a long recession and jobs were hard to find. By chance he had run into a professor of geology at UM who had taken him on as a master's student on his research project. That had carried him through May 1975 when he received a master's degree in engineering geology. After that he had enrolled in a PhD program in the UM civil engineering department to conduct research in the testing of soil properties in the field. After three grueling years, he had completed his degree.

During that whole period, Eric had found himself too busy to do many of the things he used to enjoy, like fishing and camping. His social life was limited by the hours he worked and the need to spend time traveling to different field locations during the summer season.

The net result had been that he didn't have much of a life outside of work. He had gotten together with other students from the department, meeting them and a few other friends for the Friday Afternoon Club, or FAC, when he could, to drink beer and listen to music, but not much else.

To his surprise, a Swedish band that he recognized from his Uppsala days had achieved great success on the international music scene, and its songs were played frequently on the radio. He had known them a few years earlier as Björn and Benny. Later they had renamed their group as the hot new band called ABBA.

But his love life had been virtually nonexistent, since the only women he met were usually fellow engineers who were just as focused on their studies as he was. He was involved in a few relationships, but none of them lasted very long for a variety of reasons. In many ways he was limited by a fear that none of his relationships would work out. He also had never really gotten over Lena. In consolation, he settled into a confirmed state of bachelorhood and simply carried on with his everyday life.

Lena still visited him on some nights, not in the nightmare so often but in memories of happier times. He wondered why she still lived in his thoughts so vibrantly after all these years had passed. It was as if they were forever linked in some desperate spiritual embrace.

***

He had moved to Champaign in January. The postdoctoral position required him to land on his feet and promptly order equipment for the field season, which would begin sometime in May if the weather cooperated. Between searching for an apartment, getting settled, and trying to decipher the politics in his new engineering department, he had been extremely busy. He had moved, organized his research program, submitted a budget, and once that was approved, begun buying supplies. All that and planning for his fieldwork had occupied nearly all his time for three months.

Now that April was nearly upon him, his schedule was less chaotic. He was still unpacking his possessions—a low priority—but a month ago, he had started to construct part of the soil test apparatus he would need to kick off his upcoming fieldwork. He was also slowly beginning to make friends in the department and have time for a life outside of work.

Today was like any other day spent building his prototype equipment. He was in his laboratory lying on his back under an equipment trailer that would serve as the base for his field testing apparatus. As he worked on the chassis, he saw a pair of highly polished black Oxfords make their way across the concrete warehouse floor. He gave the bolt he was tightening one last turn before asking the unseen visitor, "Can I help you?"

"Yes, Eric, you can," said a familiar voice from the distant past.

"Who? What?" Eric hit his head as he slid quickly out from under the trailer. He stood up and looked for the source of the voice.

"Well, I'll be damned! I haven't seen you in a while, Mike." He smiled as he walked around the trailer to shake hands. "What are you now, an admiral or something?" He gripped Turner's hand and tried to interpret the new insignia on the collar of his khaki uniform.

"No. But I made full commander a couple of years ago," Turner replied. He grinned broadly. "Are you about done here? Maybe we can grab a beer somewhere and catch up on our history."

"Sure," Eric said. "I can finish this tomorrow." He was happy to see his old friend but was also aware that Turner didn't just show up out of the blue to reminisce and drink beer.

"Geez, it's good to see you, Mike."

They left the university campus and drove to a tavern Eric had discovered recently. They ordered beers and sat down at the corner of the bar to talk. Eric noticed that Turner was showing a little bit of gray in his sideburns and pointed it out to give him a hard time. They both laughed.

Turner gave him a thumbnail sketch of what he had been doing since they had last seen each other. He had been stationed in Southeast Asia for a couple of years and then in Washington as a liaison with the agency, which he wouldn't name, but they both knew what it was. During that period, they had talked on the phone once or twice, and Turner had been the one to help Eric find funding for his doctoral research three years ago.

By the time they had finished their second beer and ordered snacks to hold off their appetites, Eric had summarized his recent years. At that point, he turned toward Turner and said, "Mike, why don't you tell me why you're really here? It's not to just catch up on old times." Eric gave him a knowing smile, and his friend laughed in response.

Then Turner's face took on a serious cast, and he suggested that they move their drinks to a booth at the back of the bar where there was more privacy.

When they had taken their seats in the comfortable shadows, Turner started to explain his visit.

"OK, Eric. Here it is straight up." He paused to collect his thoughts. "One of our undercover people from Leningrad has had her cover blown and is being chased across Europe by the GRU and the KGB. The agent has made it to Prague, in an attempt to stay ahead of the Ruskies. There was a problem with a prior extraction plan in Berlin, and the person could not exfiltrate as planned but had to take the train to Prague. It was totally unexpected, you see, and there is currently no contact info, no protocol to come in, and no exfiltration plan. The agent is completely on her own there now, and we need to find a way to help with contact and exfiltration."

"Her? It's a female agent?" Eric leaned forward in his seat. "Boy, she must have been evading them awhile to make it all the way to Prague successfully. What happened in Berlin?"

"She was traveling with another woman and a boy. The other woman was badly injured when they had to exfil, but there was a problem and only one woman plus the child could make the escape. The agent sent the boy and the injured woman on to safety and had to continue alone to elude the Soviets and the Stazi by leading a trail to Prague. The two made it out OK because of her quick thinking. But she took a big risk by leading the trackers."

"That is one hell of a brave agent," Eric said. "It took some balls to stay behind to safeguard the others. You said she was from Leningrad."

Eric sipped his beer, eyes riveted on Turner. "Is she anyone I would
have met up with there when Lena was working for the agency?"

"Yes." Mike took a long pull from his beer before he continued. "It's
someone you knew there." Turner stared at the top of the table that lay
between them. "But first let me say something that I've wanted to get
off my chest for some time now. I feel pretty badly about it."

"Uh-oh," Eric said jokingly. He didn't know what Turner was going
to tell him, but he detected a vibe that he wouldn't like what it was.

Turner looked at Eric, searching for any sign that he knew what he
was about to say. He took another drink.

Now Eric sensed that he was going to hear something more than a little
upsetting. What could it be? The only other women he had met in
Leningrad were Lena's friend Nadya and her sister, Katya. Could they be
involved?

"Spit it out, Mike. For Christ's sake, just tell me."

"OK. OK. Here it is. Don't get mad at me. I have always been on
your side." Still, he hesitated. Another sip of beer. "Nearly a year after
you made your escape from Russia, I learned something that you should
have been told. But I didn't hear about it until then, OK?" He stalled for
time. "A few things we thought happened didn't occur the way we
thought they did. The people who ran Lena's network didn't let us in on
it because of their network security."

"I have a bad feeling about this," Eric said.

"When I found out, I was shocked at the news, quite frankly." Turner
continued hesitantly. "But it was too late to make a difference. Everyone
had moved on with their lives."

"Well?" Eric sat up straight in his seat. "What is it? Did something
happen to Lena's friends?" His face turned red as he processed the
story. "Her sister's boyfriend was there—Misha. Did he get captured or
something? Is her family OK?" He raised his voice and clenched his
fists. "Katya and Nadya?"

"Now, let me tell it in sequence so I get it right. Yes, they're OK. In fact,
Nadya is the woman who made it through the wall with the boy. She's

recovering in a hospital in West Berlin. And the sister and boyfriend have been assisted to escape the goons chasing them. They'll be OK." Turner sat back in his seat, increasing his distance from Eric. "What I'm trying to tell you is that on the night they saw you get shot and go down, they thought you were dead. The network people who ran Lena thought you were dead at first until they found out later from us that you had survived. So you see, it was just a snafu, with both groups misunderstanding what really happened that night. And they kept it to themselves for a good long while."

"What?" Eric said loudly. "They thought I died?"

Eric searched his memory of that night. Maybe they had seen him get hit in the back by the bullet that smacked him so hard. He had fallen down right away.

"So all these years Misha has been telling the others that I was killed? How awful!"

Turner swallowed a long draft of beer and waited for Eric's reaction to what he had said.

"And that's not all," Turner said softly. Again he was silent.

Eric didn't like the direction the conversation was going. This was too easy an explanation. Why hadn't anyone told him this before? Agitated, he stared hard at Turner. He could tell that he was holding something back and grabbed his arm in a firm grip.

"What are you not saying, Mike?" His voice rose. "You'd better tell me what you're leaving out, or there's going to be trouble right here and now." Then he had a thought. He retraced what happened that night.

"Wait a minute. You said *they*. Only Misha and Lena came with me that night. Who else is *they*?"

He increased his grip on Turner's arm until he finally dropped the last and biggest bombshell.

"Eric, I wanted to tell you most of this earlier." Turner's expression showed emotion as he dropped his formal military facade. His face was slack. Now he pleaded with Eric. "But there was no point. You had moved on with your life and career. And besides, you couldn't go back to Russia again. It didn't seem like it would change anything when it came out."

Eric jumped up from his seat and pulled Turner out of the booth. The bartender called over to see if everything was cool at booth number three.

"Tell me, Mike!" Eric shouted, but he was starting to put the clues together. "There's only one way that Lena's network could know what happened that night. Tell me now!"

"OK, Eric. Here it is straight." Turner's face seemed resolute now. He had decided to come clean.

"The agent who has gone to ground in Prague is none other than your Lena."

"You son of a bitch!" Eric yelled and punched Turner squarely on the jaw. Turner fell backward over a chair and landed on his back on the floor.

"You bastard!" Eric cried. "Why didn't you tell me? I had a right to know. I loved her. Don't you understand? I loved her." Eric stood over his friend, fists clenched in anger and rage mixed with loss.

The bartender came over with a baseball bat and stood next to Eric, poised to strike if needed.

"Are you done?" He helped Turner up. "Do you want to call the police?"

"No. We're old friends. I just told him some very rough news. He'll be OK in a while—make that a long while."

Eric sank back into the booth and put his head on the table, great heaving sobs releasing his anguish. Everything he had ever felt for Lena—and lost—came rushing to the surface. He was overwhelmed with emotion.

Turner stood next to the booth and put a hand on Eric's shoulder, which he quickly shrugged off. Then he called to the retreating bartender, "Bring us a bottle of whisky and two glasses, will you?" Turner sat down across from his friend.

The bartender looked back at Turner to see if he meant what he said. "Any special flavor?"

"Make it Black Label if you have it. And lots of ice. I think we're going to need to drown our sorrows tonight."

Chapter 47

Mike and Eric had spent the evening getting drunk. Stinking drunk. It was a sad and slobbering affair until the bar closed at 1:00 a.m.

Turner had felt that it was his duty to stick with Eric, serve as his wingman while he worked through the news that had rocked his world. If drinking was a useful way to drown your sorrows, then Eric had been a deep diver that night. He and Turner had finished off the bottle of Scotch before Turner got a little food into him, which didn't last long. They had gone back to Eric's place after one, and Eric had collapsed onto his bed facedown. He was out cold.

"Well, I've seen some sailors do a better job of it," Turner had commented, "but you made a good stab at being a world-class drunk. I bet you'll have a world-class hangover in the morning too." Then he had flopped down on the couch to collapse into his own oblivion of guilt and sadness.

***

On the morning of March 30, they both had hangovers, but Eric looked like a cast member from a zombie movie. They cleaned up and downed a few aspirins with a beer to cut the pain. They went out to a Denny's for a full breakfast—not a good idea. The chipper attitude of the waitstaff there and the din of morning conversation all around them were painful. But they began to feel like they might possibly survive the searing lights and gut-wrenching headaches after eating bacon and eggs with copious hot coffee.

"Have you come to grips with the news that Lena is alive? And that she is now in danger?" Turner asked between sips of coffee. "You'd think I told you that she was dead after all. You should be happy for her."

"I still can't believe it," Eric mumbled over the rim of his cup of java. "After so long, I had pushed all thoughts of her deep down in my mind so that I would learn to forget her." He cast Turner an evil glare. "I still don't understand why you kept it from me, you bastard."

"When I found out, you were no longer working for us, and I was told that you didn't need to know, that it was a security thing. I kept silent." Turner looked sheepish but then tried to add reason to the conversation. "But what really kept me from telling you was that it would do you no good because there was nothing you or she could do about it. And apparently she doesn't know you're alive either—even now. I didn't know if I could have done anything different from an operational point of view. I am sorry to have sprung it on you like that out of the blue."

They talked twenty minutes more and finished their meal. They exited Denny's and walked to the car, standing next to Turner's rental sedan.

"Do you have anything that you need to do here today," Turner asked, "or for the next few days? Can you free up your schedule? I have something I need you for." He winced as he asked.

Eric glared at Turner and thought, *So that's it. He really needs me for one of his cockeyed missions. And after telling me that the love of my life is suddenly alive.* Eric swore under his breath.

"Eric, we need you to go to Prague and bring Lena in," he said bluntly. "We need someone she will recognize and trust."

"You've got to be kidding!" Eric shouted. He began to step sideways around the front of the car, prepared to slug his friend again. Instead, he hit the rental car on the roof and immediately regretted it. His hand felt like he had broken a bone. He didn't say anything but winced in pain.

"Hear me out," Turner said as he backed away.

"We need you because there are no protocols in place for her there. It must happen right away too. The GRU and the KGB are tracking her, and she's in danger. It's only a matter of time before they find her. We have to locate her first and get her out of the country." He stopped and looked chagrinned. "That's the real reason I came to see you. You're our best bet to help her."

Eric stared at Turner after this new revelation.

"Fuck you, Mike."

Turner continued, hoping that Eric would cool off. "Here is a current photo of her." He held out a four-by-six-inch black-and-white picture. "She has dyed her hair brown and is using the alias of Elena Kuzuch on a Russian passport. We have our embassy people on alert if she shows up there. Our agents are quietly checking for her at hotels and guesthouses to see if she's registered anywhere." He motioned for Eric to look at the photo. "She would probably not stay anywhere that requires registration, but if she gets desperate, she might. As a last resort, she might come to the embassy, but that isn't a good option if the Czechs or Russians are watching, as they most assuredly are. They can keep her bottled up there indefinitely."

"So what happened? Why is she on the run?"

"We don't understand why they are after her. She has been accused of a low-level crime at her work that hardly warrants this level of effort from the Ruskies. We have to assume that her cover was blown somehow and that's why she arranged to have her family protected too. Her control in Leningrad helped her with new documents and the escape plan, but that went south in Berlin. We won't know the details until we talk to her." Turner stopped. He could see that Eric was taking it all in, and he gave him a minute or two to make a decision.

Eric looked at the photo of Lena. She was still the same beautiful woman he had met years ago. Maybe a little older and sadder. The dark, short hair made her look more mature. His emotions overwhelmed him. His eyes teared up. He stared at the picture as if he was mesmerized. He knew that he had to go and try to help her, but this was all happening too fast for him to process his feelings.

"Fuck you, Mike," he said again and glared at Turner. Then his face softened. "OK. I'll go. I owe that to Lena. But I don't know what to say after all these years."

"Let's worry about finding her first." Turner seemed hopeful. "Come on. We have things to do."

They climbed into the rental car and drove to Eric's apartment to pack. Eric made some phone calls to postpone the few appointments he had scheduled for the week and stopped at the warehouse to make sure that everything was secure.

In two hours he was ready to leave town. Turner had already set a plan in motion to get them to Europe, and the mission was underway. He had assumed that Eric would go. Why wouldn't he? He knew that Eric wouldn't turn him down. Not where Lena was concerned.

***

At noon Turner drove them to the local light aircraft airport where he had a Cessna 205 on standby. From there they flew directly to Midway Field near downtown Chicago. One of the agency's Gulfstream executive jets was waiting for them on the taxiway. It whisked them directly to Vienna, Austria, by Saturday night, with a refueling stop in Boston.

They were met at the airport by an embassy staffer who hustled them through Austrian customs and immigration quickly. They arrived at the Agricultural Economics Institute, the cover for the agency building on the outskirts of the city, by 2:30 p.m. There they were ushered into a room with their luggage and waited for their point of contact with the local office, Mr. Dunbar, to appear.

Dunbar arrived after fifteen minutes and showed them into a conference room where he apprised them of the current situation. He said that there was little news of Lena. She wasn't staying at any hotel or registered guesthouse in Prague under her alias or her own name. But there were plenty of unofficial guesthouses where she could be hiding. Preparations for Eric to enter Czechoslovakia were nearly complete and on schedule for his departure the next morning.

There was no time to create a new backstory and identity for him on such short notice, so the staff had reactivated his old identity, Eric Larson. It was the best they could do with a day's warning. They figured that he had been inactive for so long that there would be no reason for the Czechs to notice his name if he appeared in their country after six years of absence from the continent.

He would drive a rental car and cross over into Czechoslovakia at the southern border crossing station on the road linking Vienna and Brno, the second largest city in Czechoslovakia. If he crossed at 8:00 a.m. tomorrow, he could be in Prague by 2:00 p.m. or earlier if traffic was light. Local agents had arranged a room for him in a guesthouse near the Old Town Hall. That was where most of the tourist activity was centered. Because hundreds of vacationers had converged on the city for the holiday weekend, he would blend in as one more happy tourist.

There was no established recognition code to present to Lena and no real protocol for making contact with her. Therefore, they expected Eric to mix with the crowds and look for her. He would have to be careful not to arouse the suspicion of local police and possible opposition agents who were also searching for her. No contact with the embassy staff was recommended unless there was an emergency. He had to protect his cover at all costs.

He would take a false passport for Elena Larson with him so that Lena could pose as his wife, also from Stockholm, visiting in Prague as a tourist. He would bring her through Brno by car and across the border on the strength of their passports. Turner and Dunbar would meet them on the Austrian side if Eric could get word to them.

Agency personnel had already arranged to exchange Eric's ID, passport, and wallet contents for the Eric Larson identity: license, passport, credit cards, and even a receipt from a Vienna hotel and a car rental agreement in the same name. They gave him Czech crowns, US dollars, and Austrian marks to complete the cover. A survival kit had been stashed in the interior of the car for emergencies, including more cash, a Beretta semiautomatic handgun, and other tricks of the trade.

If all went well, he would be in Prague at 2:00 p.m. the next day, Sunday, April Fool's Day.

Chapter 48

Prague, Czechoslovakia
Wednesday, March 28, 1979

Lena awoke late on Wednesday, feeling strangely refreshed. She had fallen asleep swiftly, leaving her worries behind for the night. She pulled up the comforter to her neck to stay warm and stretched her entire body, enjoying the soft bed.

Then she became aware that she wasn't alone. She turned her head to the left and looked directly into the smiling face of her bedmate, Krista. She was lying on her side with her head on her own pillow, staring at Lena.

"I tried not to wake you, so I was just watching you sleep the last few minutes," she whispered. "Could you tell? I didn't mean to stare so much as to wake you up."

Lena looked at the sparkling green eyes of her friend and rolled on her side toward her. "Good morning," she said. With their heads close together, they began to talk.

"It's past eight already," Krista said. "You must have been really tired because you slept as still as a stone."

"I was very tired." Lena rubbed her eyes. "And the wine too, I think."

"Let's go out and eat breakfast." Krista giggled quietly. "I'm starving."

They got dressed and walked to a nearby café for coffee and croissants, something new to Lena. They were made from a very light flakey pastry, rolled into crescents, and were excellent with jam spread on them. They discussed what they would do all day.

Lena said, "I need to do a few things by myself for an hour or two. Maybe we could meet for dinner later."

"That would be fine with me," Krista said brightly. "I have to go to the travel office downtown to look for mail. I'm expecting a letter."

"What is this travel office?" Lena had never heard of the place.

Krista explained that it was a government travel agency where you could change money.

"It is called *cestovní kancelář* in Czech. It also acts as a post office for travelers—like if you came to do financial business and for tourists in general. You can use their address to receive mail."

Lena was very interested in this information and hoped she could use it in some way.

After their light meal, they went back to the guesthouse to get organized. Krista went to speak to her landlady while Lena went directly to the room to pack. While she was storing her clothes away, Krista came into the room, very excited, a wide grin on her face.

"Elena, I have good news," she chirped. "I talked to the landlady to ask if I could have a friend stay with me in the room for the week and she said yes."

"Oh," Lena said, unsure of Krista's intent. "What does that mean?"

"It means that you can stay here with me and not have to look for a room of your own. You'll never find one this week anyway."

"No, Krista. I would be imposing, and it would cost too much."

"Listen to me, Elena," Krista said warmly. "I want you to stay. It's too late to change now anyway. It's all arranged."

"But why do this for me?" Lena was surprised and also a little suspicious. "Why?"

"Because we get along well, and I would like to have a friend with me while I'm here in Prague. Besides, it doesn't cost much more than I already pay. I can treat you with it. It's only another twenty crowns per night, practically nothing."

"I don't know. It is still imposing." Lena hesitated. She was unsure how to respond to the sudden offer. "And I don't have much money."

Krista persisted, and finally they came to an agreement. Krista would cover the cost of the room but Lena would treat her for dinner tonight as payback. Lena agreed happily and it was settled.

Secretly Lena was very glad. Now she had a place to stay, which was her immediate concern. *And I don't have to show any papers.* Now she would go out and focus on her next move. Could she devise a way to make contact with the American agency? Or could she come up with a plan to leave the country on her own? She needed to sit somewhere quiet and think. After a few more minutes, they walked down the street, and Krista rushed off on her errands.

Lena looked on her map and decided to try the Strahov Library located by the Prague Castle. She thought it would be quiet there—a place to think and plan. She found her way through narrow cobblestone streets and arrived at the banks of the Vltava River. It was beautiful. And across the water, high on a hill, was the spectacular Prague Castle complex dominated by the Gothic steeples of Saint Vitus Cathedral. *What a splendor!* she thought. She walked across the Charles Bridge and wound her way through the Hradčany district below the castle and up the hill to the Strahov Monastery with its ancient library. When she approached the main entrance, she discovered what she should have suspected sooner—the monastery and all its services were closed to the general public by the current Czech government.

She walked down the hill from the castle and found a below-ground cafeteria tucked beneath a commercial building in which to sit and drink hot tea. She had to come up with a plan. She decided that she could wait in Prague for only a few days to try to make contact with someone who could help her. The longer she stayed in the city, the more likely she would be spotted by her enemies. She knew no one in Prague, except Krista of course, and so had no one to work with. Perhaps there was a way to contact the agency through the embassy. But how could she do that if she couldn't go there herself?

If only she knew an American, she could send a note directly to the embassy. Maybe the message would get through to someone who knew who she was.

She asked the young woman working behind the counter where the travel office was and made her way there. She reconnoitered it carefully to see if any undercover agents were staking it out. There were no secret police lurking in the shadows.

She watched as several tourists changed money or picked up their mail. It looked like a very simple procedure. It was like an underground post office at home where people sent letters to family when they didn't want the government snooping in their mail. This operation seemed less clandestine.

Next she walked to the American embassy located on Vlašská Street, a busy roadway outside the center of town. The embassy occupied an older building that had been a private palace at one time. It was set back on a large lot with a steel bar fence surrounding it. Entry to the compound was strictly controlled by a guard station and traffic barrier set up at the main gate. All visitors arriving by car had to stop, present their identity papers, disembark, and pass a vehicle inspection. Pedestrian traffic was directed through a smaller gate with equally stringent security. She watched for some time as people stated their business, showed IDs, and entered through the small gate.

She looked closely for any secret police who might be watching the entrance. She was careful to change her position and observe from far away so as not to be noticed. A table inside a café across the street presented a safe viewpoint.

After two cups of tea, she thought that she had picked out two men who looked suspicious. The first was a tall man in a long leather coat who pretended to read a newspaper. He was distracted by passersby and didn't keep his eyes fixed on the gate. Either he was very bored or he wasn't a real professional. After a long time, a woman came out of a shop nearby and joined him. They appeared to argue but walked off together. Not a problem.

The second man was very subtle, very professional. He was in a perfect position to watch the gate but not be seen by people approaching the embassy. He was plainly dressed and was sitting in the back seat of a car with darkened windows. His concentration was excellent. Once he lifted a radio to speak to someone, but he never took his eyes off the gate while doing so.

As she expected, the embassy was being watched by someone, most likely by the Czech secret police, the Státní bezpečnost or StB. She knew nothing specific about them but recognized that like all the Soviet Bloc countries, the government had a form of security force to conduct intelligence and counterintelligence operations. They were useful tools with which to oppress the country's people.

The result of her hours of surveillance confirmed that she would be spotted if she went to the embassy. She was careful to hide her face under a scarf as she left the area discreetly. She walked slowly, checking for anyone who might be following her, stopping at shop windows and changing directions to shake any tail.

She worked her way back to the old square to a restaurant Krista wanted to try because she had heard it was very popular. It was a more traditional Czech-style restaurant than the one they had eaten at the night before but with a few new cuisine twists. There was a long line to enter, but once in the door, they could order drinks while they waited. They met two other women in line and wound up sharing a table with them for dinner. It was nearly eight o'clock when they were finally seated, but the food was good and they had a wonderful time. Lena and Krista joined their new friends for drinks at a small nightclub after dinner and staggered off to find their guesthouse afterward.

They got to their room and prepared for bed, giggling frequently due to the many drinks they had consumed. They tried not to fall down as they undressed and laughed at each other's clumsiness.

Krista turned off her lamp, leaving the room lighted only by the warm glow of the lamppost across the street. Lena slid under the covers and arranged the comforter over her. As she lay there on her back, Krista scooted over next to her and put her head on Lena's shoulder and her left arm across Lena's torso. Lena responded by placing her left arm around Krista in a friendly gesture. They lay quietly like that for a minute or two, talking about their pleasant evening, until Krista fell asleep while they held each other.

Lena's last thoughts before falling asleep were of how much she missed Katya. She had held her like this when she was much younger and needed comforting. Finally she, too, succumbed to sleep.

Chapter 49

Chayka had been in Prague for two days. It was the end of the week, and he had little to show for his efforts. When he arrived in the city on Wednesday night, he had met his counterpart in the Czech StB and informed him of his mission and his quarry. He had been assigned Major Cusak of the StB to work with him and to interface with the bureaucracy in Prague. They had made copies of Lena's photo to distribute at major points of transportation around the city. With great energy, they coordinated their questioning of individuals working at the train station, at hotels nearby, and at money exchanges with no luck.

On Friday afternoon Chayka received word from Cusak that one of his security officers stationed to observe people entering and leaving the American embassy had seen Lena on Wednesday. The man had looked at the photo and recalled seeing a young woman who looked very much like her enter a café across the street from the embassy. Cusak was convinced that the information was reliable because his man possessed a near-photographic memory.

On hearing this news, Chayka was upset that he had learned of the sighting so late. He immediately dispatched one of his men to surveil the embassy too, positioning him across from the Americans. He hoped Lena Kristoff would return to the area and perhaps meet someone there.

Cusak had also reported that routine police work by StB agents had encountered a clothing store where a woman matching Lena's description had purchased slacks and a blouse on Tuesday. They had fanned out to try to find other places she may have visited in Old Town. Chayka felt that it was only a matter of time before they ensnared their target.

***

In the morning Lena and Krista had coffee and pastries at the small bakery on the square. It was a warm day, and they sat outside at a somewhat secluded table that Lena had suggested because it was set back from passing pedestrians. They had a pleasant conversation about what they would do for the day.

Lena took the opportunity to ask Krista for a favor. She said she needed someone to drop off a letter to the US embassy because she didn't want to do it directly herself. Krista asked why. She could see that Lena was holding something back.

"Hey, Elena. You can tell me whatever trouble you're in. I knew something was wrong the minute I met you." Krista smiled and reached across the table to take her hand. "It's like you are hiding from someone. What is it—a bad boyfriend or lover? I am your friend now. You can trust me."

"Yes, I can trust you. That is why I asked for this favor."

Lena told Krista that she was really Russian, even though she had arrived in Prague from Warsaw. She was escaping from an angry husband who would beat her if he caught her. She was unable to go to the police because in Russia they wouldn't protect her and the same was probably true in Czechoslovakia. But even worse, her husband worked for one of the national security forces in Leningrad, and they were helping him track her across national borders. They would probably look for her at places like money exchanges, travel offices, train stations, and the embassy.

Krista looked doubtful. "If your husband beats you, how come you don't have any bruises? You don't have any bruises that I could see." She raised her eyebrows.

"I have been hiding from him for some time. Friends helped me in Leningrad when I first ran away a month ago. Then I decided to try to escape to Poland. But they found me there before I could make arrangements. Now I came here, but I don't know anyone who can help me. Only you." She hated to lie to her new friend but felt that she couldn't tell her more.

Krista scrunched up her face as if this explanation didn't sound right to her. "I think you're still holding back on me, but I'll drop off the letter for you." She eyed Lena carefully. "I can change money at the travel office for you if it's dollars to crowns. They exchanged my Danish kronor there for me." She sat up straight and gave Lena a serious looking over. "But you have to tell me what's really happening later—when you feel safe with me."

They finished their coffee and left the café. By that time, many people crowded the square, and the other cafés across the street were teaming with tourists eating breakfast. They went to the travel office, and Krista strutted inside with money to exchange. The transaction went through easily. Next she purchased writing paper, envelopes, and a ballpoint pen. She returned outside where Lena was anxiously waiting.

The duo reentered the café and ordered more coffee. They sat down at a table so that Lena could write a note to leave at the embassy. She followed the plan that she had worked out the day before. Krista watched her new friend with interest.

Lena wrote the following message in English:

CIA Chief,
My name is Lena Kristoff. I need your help. I worked for your people in Leningrad and am now in Prague. Agents from the KGB and GRU have followed me here after my failure to escape in Berlin. Make contact via a letter to Veronica Vaslova at the travel office. I will check for a response every day. Please help me.

She placed the note inside an envelope she marked "CIA Station Chief" and sealed it. Then she wrote a second note:

URGENT. My name is Lena Kristoff. I have worked for your people in Leningrad. Please give this envelope to your head agent of the CIA immediately.

She placed this note and the first envelope inside a second envelope and sealed it. She printed "Open Immediately" on the outside.

She and Krista walked to within two blocks of the embassy, where she handed the envelope to Krista. She waited there while Krista walked casually to the embassy, through the checkpoint, and delivered the message. When she returned Krista said, "I dropped it off at the front desk and said it should go to someone in charge right away. Now you owe me a big favor."

They spent the rest of the day sightseeing in Old Town. Along the way, Lena bought a hat that she could pull down to cover her face and hair.

***

Every day Krista walked to the travel office to ask if there was a letter for Veronica Vaslova. And every day when there was no response from the embassy, Lena despaired a little more. She tried to stay positive. The days seemed to drag by slowly, deliberately. She knew that Chayka and the StB must be closing in on her, turning over every leaf, scheming every day to find her.

Finally, in the late afternoon on Sunday, April 1, there was an envelope addressed to Veronica Vaslova waiting at the travel office. Krista accepted it and left the building.

She hurried along, clutching the envelope tightly in her hand. There were many people out on the street and in the square today, so she had to maneuver around throngs of tourists and locals enjoying the afternoon weather.

She had just circumnavigated a large group of vacationers on a guided tour when she walked straight into someone. A young man in a tan jacket had just stepped out of the door of a pension, and she ran into him. They were both knocked a little off balance and stopped to see if the other was all right.

On impact, Krista dropped the envelope on the cobblestones. She reached down to pick it up just as the man tried to retrieve it for her. They bumped heads when they both ducked down, and she wobbled on her high heels, so he reached out an arm to steady her. He noticed that she was a very pretty blonde with long legs and green eyes. He handed it to her and grinned.

"You have amazing green eyes," he remarked. "Veronica, is it?"

She smiled at the unexpected compliment. "No. I am not Veronica. Thank you for picking us up. I mean, for picking up the letter. I'm sorry." She looked him over as she backed away. "I must go. I am in a hurry to see my friend."

Krista left the dumbfounded man standing on the street and rushed on. She entered the guesthouse and took the letter straight up to Lena.

Lena opened the envelope and pulled out a single sheet of paper. She quickly perused the page, then read it again more carefully.

"Well?" Krista asked.

"It's from the Americans. They want to meet tomorrow at noon at an outdoor café on the Old Town Square, the Drena Restaurant. They want me to wear a red flower in my coat and have a copy of the day's party newspaper, the *Rudé pravo*, on the table turned to page eight. There is a recognition response listed. It appears to be standard recognition procedure," Lena said absentmindedly. "But it seems too easy, like they were expecting me." She stopped speaking and thought about her circumstance.

"But why would they be expecting you?"

"I suppose they know I am here by now." Lena was thinking out loud.

"How would the Americans know you are here and are coming to them for help?"

Lena realized that she had been caught in an inconsistency in her story and tried to repair the damage by telling Krista yet another white lie. "Oh. I worked for Americans in Leningrad before I left and they knew I was running from my husband."

"Did you work at their embassy there or something?"

"No. I was at the university and worked with visiting scientists who were Americans. They were very kind to me."

"Why would they tell people in the embassy here?"

"They knew I was going to Poland, and when I didn't show up there, that I would probably came here, my second choice."

"But I don't understand. How?"

"Krista, it is better that you do not know some things. I cannot tell you everything, yes? I wish I could, but it might be dangerous for you. Please, don't ask me anymore." She hated misleading Krista, her only friend here in Prague. She hoped she would understand. "I am sorry, but it must be so for now."

Krista acted hurt and rejected. She had been standing beside Lena, reading the message over her shoulder. Now she stepped back and looked down at the floor, her face troubled, her lower lip trembling. "I just want to help you, you know?"

"My dear." Lena put an arm around Krista's shoulders and pulled her against her body. Krista seemed so much like young Katya at that moment. "Someday when this is all over, I will find you in Denmark and tell you everything, but now I must say no more. Trust me in this. The less you know, the better."

Krista put on a brave face and grinned at Lena. "Now let's plan for tomorrow. We should check out the meeting place, right? Isn't that what they always do in the movies?"

Lena laughed out loud.

Chapter 50

Eric passed through the Czech border station easily on his Larson passport stamped with its seemingly valid entry visa to the Czechoslovak state. The border agent was stiff but polite and gave him no trouble, even after a cursory search of his rental car.

The six-hour drive from the border had been nerve racking. The Czech and Slovak drivers who were trying to rush back to the capital after the weekend holiday were a real menace on the road. They apparently expected oncoming traffic to pull over and onto the shoulder so that they could finish passing another vehicle on their side of the road.

Eric drove toward the center of Prague, focusing on the small map of the city streets that he held in his hand. The outskirts of the city were dominated by suburban apartment complexes scattered about with little organization. The dull-gray multistory buildings all looked exactly the same to the casual observer—as if they had been produced by a cookie-cutter mold. But as he approached the center, he began to see signs of the historic city with old brick and stucco buildings along narrow cobblestone streets.

He found the pension where he had a room reserved on a rustic lane near the city center and parked his rental car in a garage two blocks away. There was no parking space available so near the center of town. His accommodation was a clean, second-floor room with a comfortable bed and a window framed by lace curtains that looked out on the street. It was only a few blocks off the Old Town Square, a perfect location for a tourist visiting the city. It would suit him well as he tried to locate Lena amid the crowds of tourists where she was expected to have gone to ground.

Eric decided to reconnoiter the area around his pension and begin searching for Lena right away. He put on a tan-colored jacket to help conceal the handgun he had tucked in a holster in the back of his trousers and stepped out onto the street. He first checked his escape routes from the pension and the path to the garage where the car was parked. Next, he bought a city map at a kiosk and wandered around the central square and surrounding neighborhood. He moved quickly to cover a lot of ground while he had the chance to survey hundreds of people in the square and side streets. Six times he saw women who looked like Lena from afar—all the right height, build, and hair color—before approaching for a closer look.

None of them were her.

He still had trouble accepting the fact that Lena was alive and he hadn't known about it. After so many years thinking she was gone, this required a change in his basic understanding of the world. He was also having trouble adjusting to the photo of Lena with brown hair after knowing her as a blonde throughout their entire relationship.

And then there were the repeating dreams over the years in which she seemed so alive. *Could I have somehow sensed that she was still living? Is that why she came to me at night?*

At 6:30 p.m., he realized that most people were leaving the square to go to restaurants or back to their hotels. He decided to return to his room to get something to read during his solo dinner. He chose to take the city map and a guidebook for reading material.

He closed the door to the pension and stepped out onto the narrow sidewalk. He was immediately run into by a young woman who was obviously in too big a hurry to watch where she was going. He was ready to say something to her about being more careful but then realized what a beauty she was. She was wearing a short skirt and a pair of black high heels and had the most exceptional green eyes. He picked up the envelope she had dropped and then she rushed off. As he walked away, he wished that he had taken the opportunity to talk more. Oh well. Maybe he would see her again.

Eric asked his landlord to recommend a dining place where he could sit outside and watch people. He located the Café Prague he had mentioned on the corner adjacent to the square. It sat across from the Drena Restaurant, a historic Prague landmark. When he arrived at the café, he saw that from there he had a great view of two streets leading onto the square as well as three other cafés with outdoor seating. He picked an outside table discreetly situated where he could sit without being obtrusive or easily observed. He ordered a Pilsner Urquell beer, the original and still the finest pilsner beer in the world, and an appetizer of small sausages and Czech sauerkraut. He planned to take his time over a long dinner, which would provide an excuse to keep this prime viewpoint. As he waited, the sky darkened and the sun sank below the horizon somewhere beyond the buildings surrounding him.

He spent a half hour observing people who passed the restaurant on foot. In so doing, he developed a good feel for the flow of people rounding the street corner. He was able to discern the faces of many passing pedestrians in the dim light radiating from lampposts set up outside several cafés on that portion of the street. He also noticed that a few others were people-watching like he was. After all, people-watching was a favorite pastime for many tourists on vacation.

He noticed two men in particular, each sitting at different cafés, who appeared to be watching the passing humanity rather intently. Both were drinking coffee and seemed out of place. They were wearing suit coats that were anything but stylish. One clearly had a weapon strapped under his armpit. The other made use of a small, black, handheld radio at exactly seven o'clock, obviously reporting to someone. Eric wondered if they were simply undercover cops keeping an eye on things or security agents. He shifted his position slightly to better observe the men and to make himself a little less visible, should they catch him watching them.

A sudden commotion on the square caught his attention. A pickpocket had apparently tried to grab a woman's purse but was apprehended by a bystander. The assailant dropped the purse but made a break for it and managed to escape. Two Good Samaritans ran after him, creating considerable excitement.

Eric looked at the two men he had noticed earlier and saw that, although they both witnessed what had happened, neither lifted a finger to assist in the pursuit of the thief. Now he was convinced that they were undercover policemen by their actions—refusing to give away their position. He watched as the man with the gun turned to look down the street at another café farther away from the square.

Eric tried to follow the man's gaze to see what was so interesting. Then he noticed that a tall, leggy blonde was taking a seat at one of the restaurant's tables. She had her back to him but just then turned to hang her purse over her chair, and he caught a glimpse of her face. She happened to look his way at the same moment and saw him staring at her. She seemed pleased to see him and smiled before turning back to her dining companion. In that moment her green eyes were clearly visible.

It was the same girl he had bumped into earlier on the street. He couldn't believe the coincidence at first but smiled at the thought that perhaps she had recognized him. The man with the gun was staring at her intently. In fact, he appeared more interested than one would normally be in a pretty woman. He looked at her and then down again as if he was comparing her against a photograph he had on the table. This increased Eric's curiosity.

Was the girl wanted for something? Why was he so curious?

Eric watched the second man turn and stare at the girl also. He spoke into his radio just then and paid his bill like he was preparing to leave the restaurant. Eric wondered, *Why are they both interested in her?*

Now Eric returned his gaze to the girl and saw that she had turned in her chair and was looking his way again. She smiled at him, waved, and pointed him out to her tablemate. He hadn't seen who the blonde was sitting with because her friend was behind her. But now her companion leaned to one side to look at him.

***

Lena bent over to see who this good-looking mystery man was who so enthralled Krista, the one she had bumped into earlier in the day. She glanced at the man in the tan jacket.

She stared at him for a moment as her mind tried to fathom why he looked so familiar. Her face quickly changed from recognition to disbelief. *Is it him? Is it possible?*

She was looking at a face that she was sure she knew and yet she wasn't sure at all. It had to be a mistake. He looked exactly like her Eric! But there was no sign of recognition from him, like he didn't know her. He stared back at her as well with his mouth half open. *He looks surprised to see me too,* she thought.

They locked eyes on each other. The hair on the back of her neck stood straight up and a shiver ran through her.

She stood bolt upright at the table, knocking over a water glass.

"No! No! You are dead," she whispered in Russian.

"Elena! What's the matter? You look like you've seen a ghost!" Krista exclaimed, jumping to her feet soon after her friend had done so. Lena had suddenly turned white, and a look of horror appeared on her face.

"That man, he is dead," she said breathlessly. "We must go!" Lena picked up her purse and started to leave the café.

"But we haven't even ordered!" Krista took her jacket and purse and prepared to follow her astonished friend.

Lena looked back at the man and saw that he was also getting up from his table. He started to come their way.

"Elena, wait!" Krista called as Lena turned and jogged away up the street. Krista ran after her, trying to keep up but couldn't in her high heels. She kicked them off, bent down to retrieve them, and ran barefoot along the cobblestones.

Lena looked back one last time and saw that now there were three men following, the man in the tan jacket and two others.

She ran ahead around the corner and along the two or three blocks to the guesthouse. She tried to open the front door, but it was locked. She pushed hard, but it wouldn't yield. Suddenly Krista appeared next to her with the key and nudged past her to open the door. They both squeezed through and bolted it behind them.

They ran up to their room to hide.

***

Eric couldn't believe what he was seeing. When the woman seated behind the pretty blonde leaned sideways, he saw a brunette with a face he knew very well.

It's Lena! Or is it?

She didn't show any sign of recognition. She only stared into his eyes. As she did, her face changed from curiosity to surprise and finally to horror. She must have finally recognized him and couldn't believe what she had seen.

He felt the same. Part of his mind told him that he was looking at a ghost from the past—at someone long thought dead but now alive and afraid.

He rose when she did and reached in his pocket to throw some money on the table to pay his bill. He saw Lena jogging rapidly away, looking over her shoulder in terror, and then the other girl followed. The blonde now had an expression of fear on her face too, as she pulled off her shoes to run faster.

Christ! Lena is afraid of me, he thought.

He left the café and sprinted after the two women. Suddenly someone bumped into him and pushed him aside. It was the large, heavyset man with the gun who was also after Lena. That was when Eric realized that both he and the second man weren't interested in the blonde but in Lena. They were now after her and she was in trouble.

Thinking fast, Eric decided that he could help her if he could waylay the two men who were pursuing her. The heavyset man ran in front of him while the other was just leaving his table and talking on the radio. Eric had a good lead on the second man, but he had to stop the armed man who was just ahead and not running very fast.

Eric rushed forward and passed the gunman before they reached the spot where the women had swept around the street corner to the left. He rounded the corner a few seconds before him. There he had to stop suddenly at the edge of an open trench excavated along the sidewalk where a pipeline repair was underway. In the dark he had almost stepped into it. No one was in the street except for Lena and her friend, disappearing around the next corner to the right. In a split second, he decided that the trench could be an advantage.

The gunman came racing around the corner just then and nearly fell into the excavation. He had just barely stopped at the edge when Eric lunged out of the shadows and pushed him facedown into the trench. When he tried to get up, Eric hit him from behind with a pipe lying nearby.

Eric dropped the pipe and ran up the street, turning right at the corner. He heard footsteps off to the left and veered that way. He entered the side street in time to hear a door slam up ahead.

He stopped where he believed he had heard the door close. He looked up at all the houses. *There!* He saw a curtain move. *They are up there,* he thought.

Loud footsteps came up behind him, so he dashed ahead like a fox pursued by hounds and made it to the next street corner. Someone cried out in Czech, and he could now hear two or three men shouting and following him. He turned left at the next corner just within their sight and continued zig-zagging through the streets for a few blocks out of the square, leading them away. Finally, he ducked into a stairwell and hid as they continued up the street. They hurried to the next corner and apparently heard some noise ahead because they shouted again and ran around the corner.

He climbed out of the stairwell and doubled back on his route.

He walked in the darkness, making sure that he wasn't followed. He arrived at the guesthouse where he had seen the curtain move and knocked on the door. There was no answer, but he persisted, and finally an older woman opened the door. He told her in simple English and using hand gestures that he had to give something to the girls upstairs, Elena and her friend, the blonde one. The old lady stepped back and pointed up the stairs to their door. Then she went back into the small sitting room and reclined in an overstuffed chair to listen to Dvorak's

Fifth Symphony in F major on her small radio with the volume turned way up.

He stepped carefully to the top of the stairs and knocked on the door. There was a pause and he knocked again. The door opened slightly and a green eye peered out at him.

"Oh God! It's him!" She tried to close the door, but Eric pushed hard, and she fell back far enough for him to enter the room and close the door behind him.

"Elena! Look out! It's him!"

Lena stood across the room, backed against the wall, staring at this ghost—this apparition from the past—bewildered. She didn't say anything, just stood there in disbelief. She held a stick in her hand, raised above her head.

"Lena! It's me, Eric," he said as he took two steps toward her.

"Stop, you brute!" cried the blonde.

Then he felt a sharp pain in his left shoulder as something dug into his back. He spun around and found that Ms. Green Eyes had hit him with her high-heeled shoe. She was going to do so again, but he blocked the blow with his forearm.

"Stop it! That hurt!" He twisted the shoe out of her hand and pushed her away toward the bed. He turned to Lena again and started to speak, but he was hit in the head by the other shoe heel.

"Get out, you monster! Get out!" the blonde shouted.

"Jesus! Stop it, woman, will you? Those are like daggers," he pleaded as he blocked the girl again. He stepped closer to Lena.

"Don't you know me? It's Eric! Please, Lena. Tell me you know me."

The green-eyed woman positioned herself between him and Lena and pushed him back. She raised one of the shoes up in her right hand. Eric grabbed her hand before she could strike again.

"Elena!" Krista shouted. "Do something! Hit him with the stick!"

She kicked him in the crotch, and when he doubled over, she hit him in the head with the shoe. He fell to the floor and stopped moving, blood visible on his scalp. After a few seconds, he started to moan and move his head.

"Elena! Do something," the blonde warrior said. "Who is this man? Is he your husband? The one who beats you?"

Krista was panting now and moving around full of adrenaline, like a tiger ready to fight a lot more to protect her friend. She looked at Lena and saw that the fear had gone from her face.

"At first I thought he was a ghost," Lena said breathlessly, as she lowered the stick and dropped it on the floor. "It frightened me to no limit. He is supposed to be dead," she muttered, her fingers over her mouth in surprise.

Still holding the shoe, Krista stared at Lena, ready to strike again.

"I *saw* him die," Lena whispered.

"But what is he doing here?" Krista asked, her face red with exertion, breathing hard and looking afraid. "Why did he run after you? Who is he? Your husband?"

"No. He isn't my husband." A small hint of a smile began to turn the corner of Lena's lips. "He is someone more important than that. I don't know where he has been all these years." She paused and turned her moist eyes toward her friend.

"But, Krista, he is my lost man. My true love! He is my Eric."

***

Lena looked into Eric's pleading eyes then and knew that it was indeed him. Her own eyes began to tear up as joy overtook her.

"Eric? It really is you? Oh, my darling!" She opened her arms and he rose from the floor and rushed toward her, enveloping her in his strong embrace. They hugged each other and swayed together in unison. Both had tears in their eyes now as they pulled away a little to look at each other's face.

Then they kissed, first warmly on the cheeks, then working toward their mouths, they finally pressed their lips together. One deep, long kiss held them until the next kiss began. They smiled and murmured and kissed again.

Krista was bewildered. She dropped her shoe on the floor and sat on the edge of the bed, watching the love pour out between these two people.

"Holy shit, Elena! You really love this guy, don't you?"

Lena began to giggle and broke off a kiss to respond. "Oh yes, Krista! I really love him. Come here." She freed an arm and motioned for Krista to come near. "I will introduce you."

Krista approached tentatively, not sure that she should interrupt the lovefest before her.

"Krista, this is my long lost love, Eric. Eric, this is my newfound friend, Krista." She reached her arm around Krista's slender waist and pulled her to her side in a hug. She turned and kissed Krista on her cheek and then kissed Eric again. She looked between them, smiling, with tears running down her face.

"We must all be best friends. We *will* all be best friends!"

They stood like that for a while, hugging, and then Eric pulled away. "I would love to do this forever, but I'm afraid we don't have the time right now. We need to move or the police will find us."

He said that he had an escape plan, and they set it in motion. The women changed clothes to black pants and jackets so that they could move unseen in the darkness. They packed their bags in under fifteen minutes and wiped down the room to remove fingerprints and other identifying evidence. Krista left enough money to settle her bill with the landlady. She took one last look around the room.

"We had some fun here, didn't we, Elena?"

They quickly descended the stairs, left the key behind, and walked out the door. There was no one on the street just then, so they walked briskly for two blocks, traveling in two groups. Eric scouted ahead, and the women followed when the coast was clear. They did meet a few people walking home or going out to a late dinner, but they looked away so that no one would be able to identify them. They found Eric's pension and quietly went up to his room.

Eric said, "I think we are safe here for now. But we will have to leave at daylight. We must wait until morning because I have a car parked in a garage a short distance away from here and I need to pick up the key to the garage. I didn't keep the key because I didn't expect to be leaving so soon." He glanced at Lena, who seemed concerned. "Bad planning, I know. We'll drive directly to the border station near Brno after we get the car." He looked at the women to gauge their reaction.

"But I need to go to the airport in the morning. I fly to Copenhagen just before ten a.m.," Krista said. "Elena, I thought we could have one last night together before I left."

"We will, Krista. We will." Lena smiled at her.

Eric tried to take in that conversation. He smiled at Lena and then at Krista.

"OK. Here is what we can do. If all goes well, we will drop you off at the airport before Lena and I drive to the border. That actually works better because I can cross the border with only one woman." He turned to Krista. "It would be safer for you, Krista, if you aren't found with us. It would get you in trouble if you were."

They all agreed to his plan and unpacked for the night. There was only one large bed; they would have to compromise. Krista said that she would go down the hall to the bathroom to change into her nightgown and pee one last time. As she walked to the door, Lena caught up with Krista and asked if she could give her and Eric an hour together. Krista looked a little surprised, as if anything could shock her, but she agreed and took a magazine with her, resolved to kill time at her friend's request.

Eric and Lena, now in private, playfully shed their clothes and crawled under the comforter that covered the bed. They began slowly exploring each other's bodies, bodies that they had known so well before. Lena was afraid that her age and childbearing would make her less desirable to Eric now, but he seemed as pleased with her as he had always been. They made love slowly at first and again with great passion.

Then, while Lena and Eric were lying in each other's arms, the door opened and in came Krista, holding her clothes.

"It's me," she said as she tiptoed over and crawled under the covers next to Lena.

"What are you doing?" asked Eric.

"Eric, my dear," Lena said, then giggled at the look on Eric's face. "Krista and I have been sharing a bed for a week now and enjoy snuggling at night. You will have to share too."

Lena lay in the middle of the bed with one arm around Eric on her right and the other around Krista on her left. They spent the night in more or less the same configuration.

Chapter 51

Ivanoff stepped off the Aeroflot flight early Monday afternoon and descended the portable staircase to the tarmac. He was greeted by Chayka's sergeant and Major Cusak of the Czech StB, a man Ivanoff had met once before. They walked to the waiting black Skoda, the Czech version of the Russian Lada—a mediocre automobile on the best of days. The driver took the most direct route into the center of Prague, and they brought Ivanoff up to date on the search for Lena Kristoff, alias Elena Kuzuch, as they drove.

Ivanoff sat back and took in the situation report. He had been surprised indeed to hear from Chayka that they had spotted the woman at all. He credited the agencies involved with good police work and a great deal of luck to have located her after this amount of time. It seemed that after the sighting yesterday evening, one of Chayka's men had been badly mistreated by this woman of unusual talents and who the man claimed was "as skilled in combat as a ninja." No one believed the man, but he had been injured during the chase.

They had followed her and a male accomplice into a neighborhood several blocks from the restaurant where she had originally been seen. The StB men worked an initial two-block area around the point where she had disappeared, and they had now expanded the search perimeter to a five-block radius.

As they were talking, Cusak's radio beeped and he spoke with one of his people. He became animated and called out an address to the driver. He told him, "*Pospěš si!* Hurry up!"

"One of my men has told me that they have now located the guesthouse where Kristoff and another woman, a Krista Johansen, have been staying for a week. We have the place cordoned off and have detained the landlady for questioning. We will go there directly if that meets with your approval, Colonel Ivanoff."

"By all means, proceed," said the senior man.

After several minutes of screeching tires and blaring car horns, they arrived at the guesthouse. There they learned from Chayka himself that Lena Kristoff, using the name Elena Kuzuch, had indeed stayed at that address the whole time she was in Prague except for her first day. It was Johansen who had rented the room for the week. She was from Denmark, a simple tourist who had apparently befriended Lena somehow. They had moved out of the room this morning without even a goodbye and were possibly traveling with a man who had arrived and spoken to the women yesterday.

The landlady thought the Dane had arrived in Prague by air and assumed that she was flying home today. The StB had already contacted security at the airport to see if she was on an outbound flight. The chief of security said that he would call back as soon as they turned up some relevant information. All transportation stations and border crossings near the city had been alerted to keep an eye out for them.

They entered the guest room where police technicians were already combing through every inch for evidence of IDs, papers, and any indication of where the fugitives were going. There was nothing useful left in the room.

As they were discussing what to do next, Chayka's sergeant came up to report that airport security had called back. Unfortunately, one Krista Johansen, a woman fitting the description given them, had boarded a 9:48 a.m. Scandinavia Airlines flight for Copenhagen. The flight had already landed in that city by this time. If they wanted to interrogate her, then they would have to do it through diplomatic channels with the Danish government. It was unfortunate that she wouldn't be available to them now for questioning. As for the main suspects, there were no records of Elena Kuzuch or Lena Kristoff flying out of the airport today.

Cusak commandeered the guesthouse sitting room as a makeshift command post. He, Ivanoff, Chayka, and Chayka's sergeant discussed what they should do next. If the three had left the city early today, then there wasn't much sense continuing the house-to-house search they were conducting. It would consume too many resources to continue that action and carry out large-scale searches at transportation stations at the same time.

A young and energetic patrolman entered the room and excused himself, waiting for a chance to speak.

"Sirs, I have information that might be useful," he said. "A man living a block away saw three people, a man and two women, wheeling small suitcases along the street to a garage near his home this morning. He didn't know where they came from or whose garage it was, but he pointed it out to me. Sir, we followed up, and I believe that we have found the place where the three fugitives spent the night."

The policeman led the four investigators to the pension where the three had stayed. Chayka took the lead in the interrogation of the poor landlord.

"Tell us all you know. These people are fugitives for crimes against the state," Chayka said brusquely.

The first thing the proprietor said was, "I didn't get paid for the entire week for the rental, only for one day. I am out of that income."

"Yes, but tell us about the man you rented the room to."

"He arrived by car yesterday and used the garage for his car overnight." The landlord seemed upset about losing the money, not that he had sheltered three fugitives under his roof. "I didn't see the car itself, so I cannot describe it, and I didn't ask for a license plate number." He looked worried that he would get in trouble for not knowing that. "He had an American passport, and I noticed that he entered Czechoslovakia at the border crossing near Brno because the port of entry was recorded there."

The new revelation led to another round of discussion about how to proceed. The fact that the fugitives were traveling by car was very helpful. In fact, it was possible that they had driven the Danish woman to the airport. If so, it was also possible that the model, license, and registration of the vehicle had been recorded at one of the entry stations.

Cusak got right on it while Ivanoff and Chayka continued their discussion. He called the chief of airport security again and asked if he might have that information. He was told that if the suspects had dropped off their friend inside the airport, the license would surely have been recorded by security cameras. Cusak waited on the phone after giving the chief a probable time frame.

The chief came back on the line after ten minutes. He said that they were in luck because at 8:34 a.m. three occupants had come through in a brown Audi four-door sedan with Austrian license plates. The plate number was MW1096A, the license for a rental car from that nation. The same car exited the airport grounds at 8:51 a.m. with two persons inside. Cusak thanked the chief and hung up.

He reported these findings to the group. They decided that the two fugitives had to be Kristoff and the unknown man. They could have headed anywhere then. There were several border crossings to Germany within a three-hour drive, and they could have left the country by any one of them.

"If I were them, I would cross at the nearest point to Prague. It is faster that way," said Cusak.

Ivanoff agreed that it was logical. "But people are creatures of habit. They might go back to cross near Brno again, even though it is farther away than the other exit points." He looked at Cusak. "How long of a drive is it that way?"

"Five or six hours if traffic is normal," Cusak said, nodding his head as he responded. "There is less chance of a delay there because fewer long-haul trucks cross at that point. Inspections at the Austrian border are slow and very thorough."

Ivanoff was distracted by a subject that the young policeman had forgotten to mention. Cusak asked someone to run the policeman down and bring him back for a few more questions. When he arrived, he looked worried, perhaps afraid that he had done something wrong. Cusak reassured him that they had just thought of a few follow-up questions.

"Did the proprietor give you the renter's name, Officer?" Ivanoff asked.

"Yes, sir. I have it right here." He pulled out his notebook and flipped through several pages. "He is an American citizen with a Swedish resident visa. The man's name is Eric Larson."

Chapter 52

In the morning, Eric, Lena, and Krista took turns trudging down the hall to the bathroom to clean up. When they were all packed, Eric asked the proprietor for the garage key. He told him that he was going to explore the surrounding countryside and visit the Karlštejn Castle for the day and would return by evening. They sneaked out of the guesthouse so that the landlord wouldn't see them leave and walked along the narrow side street to the garage. They met one man on the street and greeted him casually. They entered the garage, loaded their bags in the car, and drove out of the city center.

Eric headed directly to the Prague-Ruzyně Airport, where they dropped Krista off for her flight. It was a tearful farewell during which Lena confirmed that they would be friends forever. Krista gave Lena her telephone number and address in a town near Copenhagen and made her promise to come visit her when everything was over, or at least write about what happened to them at the border. Lena promised. Then after a long hug goodbye, Krista marched away with tears in her eyes.

While the women were saying their farewells, Eric made a call from the pay phone at the airport to Turner's temporary number, letting him know that they were on their way.

He and Lena left the airport and carefully navigated around the city. After several blunders, they merged onto Highway 1, the main route south to Brno. They found a good deal of traffic on the road and had to stop for a full hour near Humpolec while a traffic accident involving two long-haul trucks was cleared from the road. They stopped at a small diner along the road while they were waiting, where they were able to buy hot tea to drink as they drove. Eric did the driving, and Lena helped by reading the simplified map provided by the Austrian car rental agency. It didn't show all the towns along the road but served its purpose.

As they drove through the Czech countryside, they caught up on their years apart. In broad-brush strokes, Eric told Lena about how he had spent the last few years. He had tried to forget Leningrad and move on with his professional life thinking that she was dead. But he felt constrained to leave out the part about his true identity. He couldn't completely level with her, not yet anyway.

He had agreed with Turner that he should maintain the Larson identity until Lena was safely across the border and could be taken to the agency offices for debriefing. Besides, it was enough of a shock for her to suddenly learn that Eric Larson was alive. It might be too much to expect her to accept that Larson was a false identity. She didn't need to know that now, and it could make it harder for her to focus on what must get done at the moment.

He again emphasized that he had no idea that she had survived the incident at Vyborg. He had heard gunshots on the pier, saw her bowl over, hit the pier, and roll into the icy water. He thought she was dead. It wasn't until last Thursday that he had been told otherwise.

"But, Eric," Lena said, "I don't understand why they did not tell each of us that the other was still alive. It makes no sense."

"I was told that it was for security purposes, but I think there is more to it than that. They're holding out on us again," he replied.

An hour from Brno, they drove into a severe thunderstorm accompanied by flashes of lightning and pouring rain. Gusty winds threatened to blow a few of the high-profile trucks off the road. They passed through the storm without incident and continued on toward Czechoslovakia's second largest city.

They reached the outskirts of Brno by 4:00 p.m. and encountered more heavy traffic there. Eric began to worry that the drive was taking too long. They managed to get around the city and onto southbound Highway 2 to Bratislava without getting lost. They made good speed for a while until they turned off the main road and onto the lesser two-lane road to the town of Břeclav. A long-haul truck plodded along the road on its way to the Austrian border. After an hour of frustration spent following the truck without being able to overtake it, they reached the border crossing.

A feeling of dread overcame Eric as he and Lena drove through the last two kilometers on the Czech side of the border. The landscape was devoid of forest or active farms, and the last half kilometer or so of open ground had been devegetated and plowed to create a no-man's-land that was difficult to cross without being seen. He knew, of course, that this was done to deter illegal border crossings. The border itself was defined by a shallow valley with the actual national boundary between Czechoslovakia and Austria located in the vee at the bottom of the valley. The Czech border patrol station was a concrete-and-steel facility on the north ridge overlooking the valley. A long wall and two high steel wire fences ran along the crest, with only the checkpoint and its steel gate providing openings in the barrier. A secondary steel rail gate stretched across the bottom of the slope right on the border. The high fences were separated by several meters of bare ground surveilled by armed soldiers posted in closely spaced guard towers. Attack dogs patrolled between the fences to detect and take down potential escapees. It was clear that any unauthorized person trying to get anywhere close to the border with Austria would be shot.

Eric knew from his border crossing yesterday that on the other side of the valley, the Austrian side, the situation was much different. The Austrian border post was a small wooden house on the far ridge over a kilometer away. There were no attack dogs and no fences, only a modest structure landscaped with decorative rocks, shrubs, and grasses. The border crossing consisted of a simple red-and-white striped wooden gate rail that security guards could raise or lower by hand. Traffic flowed easily into and out of Austrian territory.

The sun was setting when they joined the line of cars and trucks waiting to pass through the checkpoint at the edge of the no-man's-land. They pulled up behind the truck they had been following since Bratislava, plus twelve other cars that were creeping forward to cross the border station.

Eric pulled out their false passports as they waited their turn. He was still impressed that the agency had managed to create the documents so quickly. When he opened Lena's passport, the photo of a pretty, if tired, Elena Larson stared out at him. The fake Czech entry visa issued only a few days ago had other rubber stamps to make the document look legitimate. Lena leaned over to look and commented that everything must go smoothly now that they were officially married.

They advanced to the head of the queue just before dark. They pulled their car up to the vehicle control gate. The gate was massive—made of a steel I beam lying on its side on rails so that it operated like a giant dead bolt to block their path. Both Eric and Lena had to disembark and walk into the control shack. There Eric handed both of their passports over the counter to the security guard—a young but tired-looking man who had perused dozens of passports already that day. The guard carefully examined the passport photos, alternately looking at the pictures and then at their faces. He seemed satisfied and stamped their exit visas into their passports. He also verified the Audi's license plate number and rental papers. Meanwhile, other border patrol agents opened the trunk of the car and conducted a quick search of its interior and their baggage.

The guard said thank you in English and waved to the man operating the gate control, who pressed the button to withdraw the steel I beam that prevented any vehicle from passing through. The beam slowly pulled back on its steel track and began opening all the way.

Then Eric heard a loud thumping as the border patrol agents completed the inspection process. It sounded like a large helicopter was coming in for a landing outside. *That could only mean bad news,* he thought. He quickly picked up their documents and thanked the guard. He hustled Lena out of the control building and told her to get in the car quickly so that they could leave. He looked over and saw a big black police helicopter on the ground and a small group of men running toward the building.

He was right.

Eric closed the car trunk, got in the driver's seat, and started the engine. The guard was now standing in the doorway of the control shack with a mobile radio held to his ear. He was receiving orders from someone and then repeated aloud the name Larson. He looked at Eric, and Eric knew that their time was up. He revved the engine just as the I beam stopped opening and began to reverse course, blocking their path to freedom.

Eric threw the transmission into first, and the car leaped forward through the closing gateway. He had to steer to one side of the gate to avoid hitting the closing I beam. Even so, it just scraped the rear fender as they passed through the barrier and raced down the gravel road that led across the no-man's-land ahead.

Eric increased speed as they drove toward the bottom of the valley and the smaller second gate. It was operated by remote control and was now being lowered into place to prevent their escape. He hoped to have enough momentum to crash through the gate before it could close all the way.

Suddenly a bullet pierced through the rear window, and he realized that the Czech security guards had opened fire using their sidearms. He swerved from side to side on the road to avoid their shots. Several rounds hit the car but did little damage. Soon they would be out of effective range of the semiautomatic pistols. But a few of the guards had AK-47 rifles that would be brought to bear soon enough.

Eric looked over at Lena and could see the terror on her face as more bullets thumped into the car's metal body.

"Oh, Eric! I don't want to die like this!" she blurted out with tears in her eyes.

They were very close to the second gate when rifle bullets began to crash into the car. They whizzed past their heads with frightening speed and lethal intent. Suddenly the windshield was shattered and a pair of rounds buried themselves in the dashboard of the car. Eric swerved again and had just enough time to straighten out before they rammed the steel gate at sixty kilometers an hour and came to an abrupt stop.

Chapter 53

Prague, Czechoslovakia
Monday, April 2, 1979

The helicopter came in for landing nearly one hundred meters from the border crossing administration building. Cusak was beside himself that they had to wait to land. The pilot hovered for nearly a minute while a sergeant of the guard ran out from the building to show him exactly where to put the craft down so as not to hit any obstructions with its rotors. They completed their landing and stepped out of the aircraft.

Cusak had received a report late in the afternoon that the Audi in question had been spotted on the truck bypass road around Brno. It was seen getting onto Highway 2 southbound toward Bratislava. He assumed that this meant their fugitives were headed for the border crossing near Břeclav or they would have taken the road to Pohořelice, which was the most direct crossing. The Břeclav crossing was a much smaller outpost and would let them avoid most of the commercial truck traffic that crossed the border at the larger station.

When he had received the information, Cusak had promptly requisitioned an StB helicopter to fly to the border. Ivanoff, Chayka, his sergeant, and he had all boarded the aircraft and set out on a flight path southeast toward Brno. The pilot had informed them that there was a large thunderstorm just west of Brno that was too dangerous to fly through. He could go around it or they could wait it out. Cusak had chosen to fly around the storm, which took them south and closer to the border with Austria. From there they had flown parallel to the border and headed east to the border station. They made good time, but the longer distance required them to land at a small airport to refuel. That delayed them by another half hour or so. As it was, they had flown dangerously close to the storm and nearly missed a few lightning strikes. They continued to the Břeclav border crossing.

They had radioed ahead to the border station but achieved only a garbled transmission due to the nearby storm. The pilot explained that a static charge had knocked out the radio's antenna and he would have to land to fix it; probably a simple fuse had been overloaded. Cusak had decided that they should fly on to the station rather than lose any more time.

As soon as they landed, Cusak asked the sergeant who had guided their landing to radio the gate control to let no one exit until they arrived. He said they were looking for a man and a woman who might be traveling under the name Larson. They were driving a brown Audi automobile with license plate MW1096A. The guard talked for a few moments on the radio and told Cusak that two people fitting their descriptions, an Eric and Elena Larson, were just passing through the gate toward the Austrian border.

Cusak couldn't believe their bad luck at arriving so late.

"Stop them at all costs!" he raged. "Do you understand me? Stop them! They are spies!"

The sergeant and the others ran toward the gate, arriving in time to see the car speeding away down the gravel road. Cusak saw that a security guard was standing in the building doorway firing his semiautomatic pistol at the car, as were two other guards. But the car was still moving away.

"Use your rifles, you fools! They are getting away." Cusak ran forward and picked up an AK-47 from the rack on the side of the administration building. He charged the rifle and began to fire a series of rapid shots at the receding Audi. The car was far away by then, and it took several shots fired for effect before he found the correct range and began to land a few rounds in the car itself. The guards picked up rifles and began to fire also as the car reached the second gate.

Just then the Audi rammed into and demolished the lowered steel gate at the bottom of the valley. The car rolled into Austrian territory and came to a complete stop. Steam burst into the air from its crushed radiator. The guards ceased fire upon their sergeant's command. There was no motion from the car, only the sound of a racing engine. The sergeant ordered four of his men to walk down the road to investigate the vehicle and to determine whether there were any survivors. The men formed a skirmish line, four abreast, as they advanced at a steady pace down the gravel road.

Then Cusak saw motion. The driver's-side door of the Audi opened and a body fell out onto the ground. Larson was still alive, no doubt stunned by the force of the crash. He crawled around the front of the car toward the passenger door. He yanked it open and pulled the woman, Elena Larson, out onto the ground. She staggered badly but could walk with his support. They stumbled up the road for ten or fifteen meters before they stopped and Larson turned back to the car. He ran to the back seat and extracted a small suitcase. He then returned to assist Elena. They slowly trudged up the road on the Austrian side of the valley to freedom.

Cusak raised his AK to fire at the retreating spies but couldn't get a clean shot by that time because his border guards were so close to the gate. He ordered them to fire on the retreating couple. But the sergeant had now been replaced by the border control captain, who said that they couldn't fire at them once they were on Austrian soil. They had no authorization to do so.

Cusak shouted, "Do it now! I authorize it."

The captain was wary of such reckless behavior and asked to see Cusak's credentials before he would accept such an order. Cusak's StB badge and rank caught him by surprise, but he still insisted that he could not shoot across the border.

At that point, Chayka appeared from the administration building carrying a Dragunov sniper rifle that he had appropriated from the guardroom. He strode directly to the steel pedestal that supported one side of the I beam gate. There he chose a portion of the pedestal that was close to shoulder height and braced the rifle on its surface.

"Did I not tell you, Ivanoff, that I was a sniper in the army when I was a young man?" He looked at the guard near him. "Now, you, sergeant—what is the distance to the second gate?"

The soldier told him that it measured 512 meters from gate to gate and that the targets were now somewhat beyond that. Chayka adjusted the telescopic sights for the range, and in the fading daylight, sighted in on Lena staggering up the road.

Ivanoff suddenly broke his silence. "Chayka, it is unwise to do this."

The colonel fired one shot and watched it kick up soil just behind and to the right of the woman. He made an adjustment to the sight and fired again.

"Don't worry, comrade. I know what I am doing," Chayka called out to Ivanoff.

The second shot must have been a near miss because both fugitives threw themselves on the ground. They got up, however, and continued to struggle up the road, leaving the suitcase behind them.

"Colonel! You cannot fire at the fugitives. They are in Austrian territory now. We aren't authorized to shoot there." The captain of the guard tried to intervene.

"Captain, *you* are not authorized, but *I* have no such limiting orders." Chayka fired again, and this time Lena reacted as if hit in the back by a steel fist. She flew facedown onto the ground and remained motionless.

"My God! You shot her!" exclaimed the captain, now confused about what he should do. "What do we do now?" he asked Cusak, who, although not his direct superior, was at least a Czech security agent.

"Your men are at the car now," Cusak said gravely. "Have them cross over and reclaim the woman's body, the suitcase, and the man if he still remains within reach."

"But that is Austrian soil, Major," the captain whispered.

"The Austrians are too passive to interfere." Cusak turned to the captain and snarled. "Just do it."

The captain did as he was told and radioed to his men. In a short time, his four guards began to walk forward, now stepping on Austrian ground as they followed orders.

Chayka again raised the sniper rifle, sighting in on Larson, who was now picking up his wounded companion and dragging her along the road by the shoulders. Lena was completely limp, her head lolling to one side.

Chayka fired one shot and dirt flew up just uphill from Larson, but he struggled on as fast as he could.

Ivanoff had finally seen enough, and he spoke up. It was clear that Chayka was going too far. "Colonel Chayka, you must desist. You are on the verge of creating an international incident. It is one thing for you to shoot a fleeing Russian citizen but quite another to kill an American spy on Austrian soil. It would be a violation of the Geneva Convention, and more to the point, it could endanger the delicate balance and understanding that exists between our security services and those of the West."

"Thank you, Comrade Ivanoff, for your lecture." Chayka laughed derisively. "But I take full responsibility for this one last shot."

Just then, as Chayka took aim, the advancing Czech border guards were stopped dead in their tracks by the retreating Larson, who had pulled out a handgun and fired several rounds into the ground in front of them. As Larson turned to continue up the road, one of the guards raised his rifle to return fire, aiming directly at him.

Suddenly the guard was thrown violently backward as if he had been kicked by an invisible mule. A few seconds later, the sound of a single rifle shot echoed across the valley. The report came from the crest of the valley near the Austrian border station. The guard fell to the ground, very dead. His fellow guards ducked for cover, then raised their rifles and aimed at Larson. One by one they were all gunned down, each by a single shot of unknown origin.

"Who is shooting?" Cusak asked in shock. "It's from the Austrian side is all I can say." He was now shouting and desperately peering at the darkening scene through binoculars. "Wait! Over there by the car on the ridge!" He pointed at a vehicle parked in front of the Austrian station.

"An American?" Chayka lowered his rifle in response and asked, "Ivanoff, why did you not tell me earlier that American agents were involved?" But he had to take advantage of his last chance to kill the other fugitive. He sighted again on the retreating Larson, who was dragging the injured Lena away.

Then something bewildering happened. Chayka, too, was thrown back from the pedestal with great force, flying onto the ground on his back. He grabbed his left shoulder and lay on the ground screaming. He pulled his hand away and found blood on his fingers. He had been shot.

"My God!" he muttered in surprise. "I'm bleeding." Then he passed out.

Cusak raised his field glasses and looked toward the Austrian border station. He saw a man standing beside a large black sedan, a Mercedes, he thought. He held a long rifle with a telescopic sight mounted on it. He carried it with its butt on his hip and the rifle held out to his side at an angle. Ivanoff couldn't see the man's face in the fading light but could tell from his demeanor and khaki uniform that he was a military man—a high-ranking officer with a gold emblem glistening on his collar.

As Cusak watched helplessly, a truck carrying several Austrian soldiers appeared on the road and descended toward the fallen Czech guardsmen. A medic wearing a jacket bearing a bright-red cross ran forward to assess Elena's wounds. He applied first aid to her and to Larson. He then moved down the road to evaluate the four wounded guards. After a brief inspection, he shook his head and motioned to the Austrian soldiers to pick up the dead bodies. They did so with respect and delivered them to the Czech side of the second gate. They arranged the fallen men with their weapons at their sides and saluted them before withdrawing to the Austrian side of the border. They climbed into the truck and drove up to their border patrol station.

At the same time, the Mercedes sedan rolled downhill and collected Larson, Elena, and the suitcase. It drove away past the Austrian station and into the night.

Cusak stood very still and wondered how all this could have happened. He glanced at Ivanoff to see if he felt the same sense of failure. Ivanoff looked grim and utterly confused by the sudden intensity of the events that had just taken place. Later they would they both wonder why they had shot a Russian citizen who had done little to deserve such a demise.

Chapter 54

Dr. Werner came out of the operating theater with a grim look on his face. He stripped off his surgical gloves as he walked through the door into the hallway. He went directly to Mike Turner and Agent Dunbar. They spoke briefly, the doctor telling them about Lena's injuries.

After a few minutes, Turner shared the results with Eric, who was waiting patiently down the hall.

"Lena is seriously injured, but the doc says that she will probably pull through OK. The bullet entered the back of her shoulder very near the spine."

"But she'll be all right?" Eric asked. "Thank God."

"Yeah, seems so," Turner continued. "It's a severe but clean entry and exit wound. Fortunately, the bullet didn't flatten or fragment too much as it passed through her body. No major blood vessels or nerves were damaged."

"When can I see her, Mike? Is she awake?"

"She's still unconscious from the shock. They say she'll need at least a day to regain consciousness if they don't stimulate her."

"Oh shit," Eric said, sad and still in shock himself.

"The doctor thinks it's best to wait it out and let her heal at her own rate. Not wake her up yet."

"But I've got to see her."

"Look, I know it's tough, but you should wait until they have her cleaned up and in a secure room."

"What do you mean a 'secure room'?"

"There's some concern that the Russians might try to do her harm, even in a Vienna hospital, so the agency plans to move her to a private clinic they use in these cases. That might occur in a couple of days when she's more stable. Right now they want the shock to the vertebrae to improve before they move her. They're going to post a guard outside her room until then." Turner looked at Eric to see how he was reacting to this news. "You'll have to wait, Eric. But she's OK."

Eric looked pale and exhausted. He didn't know what to say.

"Hey. Are you all right? You didn't get hit, did you?" Turner scanned Eric carefully. "Let's get you looked at, OK?"

Turner and a frustrated Eric retreated to the hotel after the doctor gave Eric a quick once-over and a sedative to help him deal with the situation. They could finally grab some well-deserved rest after making it through an exhausting day and a very long night. At the hotel, they both slept like the dead.

***

The next morning, April 3, Turner and Eric were debriefed for hours concerning what was now being unofficially classified as an international incident. They went through the whole story in as much detail as possible. The agency wanted to know why the StB, the Czech border patrol, and probably the KGB and the GRU were all after this Lena Kristoff. The result after hours of questioning was that no one except Lena really knew why at this point. Further follow up with her network in Leningrad would be necessary.

Agent Dunbar told them that the shooting at the border had created outrage in the agencies within the Austrian government. Nothing was said publicly, but relations between Austria and Czechoslovakia had become very tense.

Dunbar explained, "The Czechs are furious that four of their border guards were shot down in pursuit of fugitives. Of course, they'll never admit that their men had actually invaded Austria and fired at persons within this country."

He went on to discuss the gunfire that took place on both sides of the border. It was unusual but not unprecedented for Czech guards to fire upon people trying to escape to Austria. They did sometimes shoot their own citizens to prevent them from being free. Such was the nature of the totalitarian regime that ruled the Czechoslovak nation. However, the

398 • Fred G. Baker

sniper involved was most irregular—very proficient, rating above a marksman level.

"Who was he?" Dunbar asked. "They don't keep that level of sniper tied up at the border stations."

"Maybe he came in on the chopper," Eric said.

Dunbar continued. "The shooting from the Austrian side is being covered up, and the Austrians won't admit that any such shots were fired. Four dead-on heart shots at approximately five hundred meters in low light are difficult, if not unheard of, and because there were no bodies left on Austrian soil—no evidence of these events—the shooting must not have occurred, right? The single long-range shot from over one thousand meters away at twilight that took out the opposing sniper was virtually impossible. So it's unlikely to have come from our side of the border, right?" Dunbar looked at Turner with a smile on his face and then winked. "So your identity is safe with me, Commander."

He continued. "The aftermath of this little operation will be dealt with at diplomatic levels. That's at levels way above our pay grades." Dunbar chuckled. "We're done here. Officially, this never happened."

Late in the afternoon, when Turner and Eric were dismissed, Eric went over to the hospital to check on Lena's condition. He was given her room number, but when he arrived, he found it empty. The bed was completely made up, and the room had been thoroughly cleaned.

Eric asked a passing nurse where patient Larson had been moved to. She said that she didn't know. She looked very nervous and told him she would ask the doctor to come and talk to him.

Eric's radar went up immediately after seeing her face, and he feared that something bad may have happened. Anger began to cloud his emotions as he waited for an explanation.

He recognized the doctor who came to talk to him as the one who had performed the surgery on Lena the day before—Dr. Werner. What he had to say in his clipped Germanic style was very disturbing.

"I am sorry to tell you that the patient, Elena Larson, passed away last night due to unexpected complications resulting from blood clots that migrated to her brain. We could do nothing to clear the clotting before brain death occurred. This sometimes happens in cases of severe shock, especially gunshot wounds near the spine. Once brain death occurred, she also suffered a cardiac event that was fatal."

Eric was too stunned to respond immediately.

"I am sorry. You were her husband, I believe. It was very sudden."

"No," Eric said. "It can't be. She was alive last night."

He couldn't believe what he was hearing. It couldn't be true. Sure, she had been shot. But she was stable. *How can she be dead?* Then his emotions erupted as violently as a volcano venting steam.

"No! She can't be dead. Not again! She can't be gone!" His shouting caused a few nurses to look down the hall from the nursing station to see what was the matter.

"Where is she? I need to see her, even if she has passed away—died." His voice broke with emotion. "I need to talk to her and see her again. I have more to tell her." His eyes began to lose focus as tears formed. "There wasn't time to tell her what was important."

"I'm afraid you are too late for that. You see, the body was cremated a few hours ago. Perhaps you can advise your friend, Mr. Dunbar, that we need to know what to do with the ashes. Again, I am sorry."

The doctor walked down the hall to the elevator and disappeared.

Eric was dumbfounded. *Why was she cremated?* Something didn't seem right here. Now his pain turned into anger. This had all happened very quickly—too quickly—and that made him suspicious.

Where was Turner? What the fuck was he doing?

He rushed back to the agency and tried to locate Turner. He had a feeling that the man was withholding information from him again. Yes, many things needed to be compartmentalized, but this time he had to know more than the upper managers wanted to share.

He was told that Turner had just left for the hotel and that he was in fact looking for Eric.

Eric found Turner in his room at the hotel, sipping Maker's Mark on ice and writing down a few notes on a yellow tablet.

"Eric! Great, you got the message that I wanted to see you," he said cheerfully, still looking down at his tablet. "We didn't have time to talk after the debrief, but there are things you need to know. I couldn't tell you until I was sure that the debriefing was over and we wouldn't be called back for another round of questions. Anyway, the brass all seem content, so we are done with that whole process." Finally he looked up at Eric.

Eric stood just inside the door of the room, his face dark and ominous, clenching his fists in anger. He felt betrayed once more.

Turner looked at Eric and knew what was wrong. "Oh Christ! You didn't go to the hospital, did you?" He jumped to his feet.

Eric marched into the room and swung his fist at Turner, who blocked the blow.

"Wait, man. You've got it wrong. She's not dead." He ducked Eric's second, less direct fist. "Let me explain." He put his hand on Eric's shoulder and pulled him in a boxing clinch to stop another swing. "Eric, you weren't supposed to go there and find out that way." He pushed Eric away and motioned for him to sit down.

Eric stood like a stunned bovine for a moment or two and then took a seat. "Tell me," he whispered.

Turner went to the sideboard and poured Eric a stiff three fingers of the same good bourbon he was drinking and brought it to him. Eric still had blood in his eyes but accepted the drink.

"Don't go all morose on me, and don't hit me again, for Christ's sake. It's not what you think." He looked around the room as if expecting to find small listening devices everywhere.

"Shit! You don't suppose they have these rooms bugged, do you? Our own agency?" He got up and turned on the television and raised the volume. He opened the French doors out onto the balcony.

"Let's go out to get some fresh air, shall we?"

Once they were on the balcony, Turner stepped closer so that he could speak to Eric in a subdued voice.

"You weren't supposed to know this, OK? In order for Lena to be safe, we had to stage her sudden death at the hospital. Dr. Werner arranged quite a show during the early-morning hours. The hospital ran the whole code blue operation, with people wheeling crash carts and everything. After an appropriate show of effort, he declared Lena dead and she was covered over and wheeled down to the morgue." He stopped speaking and grinned sideways at his friend. "I guess this Werner has worked for us before and can be quite helpful."

Eric had been standing next to Turner, trying to contain his anger. Finally he interrupted. "Where is Lena, and how is she doing?"

"Oh, Lena's fine. Well, not 'fine,' but she is recovering normally. She woke up late last night and seemed to have all her senses about her— well, mentally at least."

"Why didn't you tell me?"

"Need to know at the time. You know how it works." Turner faced away from Eric while he spoke. "We had to get her approval for the death ruse, you see. We can't just make one of our own live agents disappear without their consent." He paused and then chuckled.

Eric wasn't amused.

"It happened kind of fast. I know it sounds odd that the agency would be concerned enough to have her give her consent, but stranger things have happened. Anyway, she agreed to play along when we explained that faking her death in a very public and elaborate spectacle was the only way we could ensure that the Russians would stop looking for her and her friends. She was the one they were after, and if she was dead, they would have no interest in her sister and her friends."

Eric thought it all sounded like bullshit, but he held his tongue. He slugged down the bourbon and shuffled into the room to pour himself a refill.

"It all went smoothly," Turner continued when Eric returned. "Werner had her transferred to a clinic in Bavaria that specializes in spinal cases. She will be well cared for there. He said that many of the best specialists in Europe consult there and that there is no better place for her right now." Turner laughed quietly. "Pretty slick, actually."

"Whatever's best for Lena," Eric muttered, but he didn't see the humor in this game.

"In the meantime, he arranged for the cremation to occur, probably a female Jane Doe, and the ashes will be scrubbed to reflect ashes of a Russian citizen with melted steel teeth fillings and all. We will have a clandestine funeral ceremony for her here in the agency office in case the Ruskies have a mole." Turner laughed and slapped Eric on the back. "And then—this is the best part—to sell the story even more, after a while the Austrian security agency will arrange to offer to send her ashes back to Leningrad in a negotiated trade for something they want, maybe a minor prisoner exchange. Isn't that something?"

Eric had heard enough about how clever the agency was. "So how is Lena now? Is she badly hurt? She took a bullet in the back, damn it— but not directly in the spine, right?" He cringed at the thought. "How bad is the injury? Will she walk?"

"They say she will likely recover fully, but she may have a lack of feeling or control in her legs. The swelling has done some damage, but it should be reversible with the right therapy. But the most important thing is she is out of the coma and has no mental impairment at all. It is just a matter of time—several weeks or a few months—before we can know the outcome."

"When can I see her, Mike?" Eric was becoming upset by the whole scenario that he was hearing.

"I'll tell you, but there is something that you need to hear first." Turner stopped, and a serious look came over his face. "Lena was apparently accused of a crime that she didn't commit in Leningrad. Somehow—we don't know the details yet—she had to pull up stakes and go on the run. Being a good field agent, she had prepared for such an eventuality with her handler—a very valuable asset in Russia. She made a deal with him to deliver a digital tape that contained something like the crown jewels of the Russian military design apparatus and a new complete version of the economic model they have been using to direct their economy."

"What do you mean?" Eric asked.

"The nature of the crown jewels is so highly classified that even I can't be read in on it. She is one hell of an agent and a tough bargainer too. She made her handler give his word—again you wonder, 'In this agency?'—but he agreed. He said that if she did these things, he would get her and her friends out of the country to safety and set up a new life for them. And by God, he and the agency are seeing it through!" Turner rolled his eyes in amazement. "It will take a few months to get it all set up, but it will happen. It's marvelous, really." He looked at the forested park across the street from the hotel, a pleased look on his face.

"That's great, Mike." Eric was subdued, processing all this news— good news, bad news. "I would like to think the agency makes good on its promises. Where will she go?"

"Now we come to the hard part of this conversation." Turner looked back to Eric. "What I have just told you and am about to tell you is all highly classified—top secret. I know you won't tell anyone about it because to do so would endanger Lena. Also, I'm not authorized to tell you any of this, so, you know—keep a lid on it." He put his hand on Eric's shoulder.

"Lena needs to spend all her time and energy recovering from her wound. It will be a difficult time for her. Right now she has almost no sensation below her shoulders, except for a little in one leg. She needs to focus on recovery. She is a strong woman and doesn't want to be in her current condition, relying on people for every need. She doesn't want someone who loves her to see her in this way." Turner looked at Eric and raised his eyebrows, waiting for his reaction.

"But I need to see her."

"Eric, I talked to her briefly last night when she woke up, and the situation was explained to her. She is having a hard time accepting the facts. She told me that she doesn't want you to see her like this, weak and unable to respond to you." Turner was quiet for several moments. "She said she wouldn't taint your relationship with pity."

Eric snapped his head around to stare at Turner. "I won't pity her. I love the woman."

Turner looked directly into Eric's eyes to be clear. "Those were her words, not mine. She does not want to be a cripple or appear to be one in front of you. She wants you to stay away until she is well."

"What?" Eric couldn't believe what he was hearing. "That can't be."

"She wants you two to start over again on equal terms," Turner continued, "and pick up your relationship from there. In the meantime, I can give you updates and even pass messages, if you like, when I can. All under the table, you understand?" Turner finished and looked at his beleaguered friend who had just received a hard blow to the gut.

"Now I'll give you some time to think about it." Mike emptied his glass. "It's a raw deal, but she has a point." He turned to go inside. "Here. I'll get you another refill. A stiff one. I know I need one, too, after all this."

Chapter 55

Eric had just finished analyzing the results from his first field experiments when he saw the mailman's white Jeep pull up to his mailbox at the edge of the driveway. He walked out into the warm afternoon air of the Illinois summer, a little cooler now than the last few sweltering weeks had been, with a few fluffy, cotton ball clouds in the sky. He waved at the mailman as he sped away.

Eric opened the mailbox. Inside he found several advertisement pieces that were the staple of the postal service these days. There was also a letter in an airmail envelope postmarked from Copenhagen.

"Finally," he said out loud and smiled. He took the mail and went back inside to the small bedroom that he had converted into his study.

He had been hoping for such a letter for some time. It had been nearly three months since he had last seen Lena on that fateful night in Austria. She had been in rehab for weeks, making good progress by all reports that he had received surreptitiously from Turner. Not that there were many such reports, but Turner did call with short updates two or three times in that interval. He told Eric that Lena had regained feeling in and the use of her arms quickly, but her legs would take more effort. Full recovery was still the prognosis. The last update had been a month ago from Turner by phone. He had learned that she was up and walking with a cane and would soon be released to get settled on her own.

Lena had sent him no notes. Now he hoped that the letter he held in his hand was from the mysterious woman he loved.

He opened the envelope, pulled out the letter, and laughed when he saw the contents. There were three pages of tightly written columns of numbers, each column a set of three closely spaced digits. He laughed and rolled his eyes at the ceiling. Only Lena could have sent such a letter and expected him to be able to read it.

"Oh, Lena! How I've missed you." The smile on his face broadened.

He got up and crossed the room to a shelf that held some of his older books. After rummaging around a bit, he found what he was looking for and came back to the desk. He placed on it his old dog-eared copy of Adam Smith's *The Wealth of Nations*.

He retrieved a beer from the refrigerator, located a ruled yellow tablet, and then began the translation of the long coded message. He worked on it steadily and completed it by 7:00 p.m., needing two beers for the effort. Fortunately, Lena hadn't used the standard substitution algorithm that was often employed to further encode messages back in the day.

The letter read as follows:

My Dear Eric,

I have recovered well since we were last together. I can move all my fingers and toes but still walk with a slight limp. Otherwise I am fine and have needed time to get used to my new life in the West.

There is so much to say, and a letter will not do well to describe how my life has been these many years since we were together in my lovely old hometown of Leningrad. (You see, I am working on my English. Danish too!) Most of that history is best saved when two old friends have time to be together. Which I hope will happen soon.

Let me tell you how I am situated now. My friends at your agency have taken good care of me and my family. I am living now in a rental home in Roskilde, a small city outside of Copenhagen. I live with my dear old friend whom you have met, Nadya. My sister, Katya, and her husband, Misha, are living in Odessa by the Black Sea, but I hope they will come here in a few months. You see, I look after my loved ones as always. We are very happy here and there is much to tell, but it is best done in person.

Oh. I almost forgot to say. My friend Krista and her current flame (Is that correct?) live in a village only a few kilometers away, so I see her often too. She has been a great help to me.

Now to the big thing in my letter. I have had a long time to think about this while recovering and about what to do. It goes back to the night I thought you had died and you thought that I had died. It turned out we were both alive after all, but you and I were also still alive inside me. Yes? You have guessed? I was pregnant. And now I have someone else who is part of my family, my little Eric!

Yes, I named him after you. What else could I name him?

I did not tell you about him in Prague, maybe because I did not think that night was really happening. Or something else. It was too fast. And I did not know if you were ready for children or if you wanted a son.

I did not tell you but I wanted to. And then I was shot and thought I would die again and you would never know you had a son.

So now you see why it has taken me so long to write you. I had to think about what to do. So now I ask you, my darling, would you come see the woman who has loved you all these years and meet a son who does not know his father is still alive? (I told him you were lost at sea. I could not bear to tell him you were dead.)

I will be waiting for your response at my home at the address below.

Forever your true love,

Lena

Chapter 56

The two women, one with long blonde hair, the other a brunette, walked up to the kiosk on the edge of the small park and playground. The blonde approached the vendor named Johan, a pleasant older gentleman who stood behind the counter, to order drinks to take away. A blond teenage boy ran up to join them.

"I would like to buy six orange juice drinks and one Coke, please," said the blonde in Danish, "and two coffees with cream."

"And six hot teas, two with cream, please," added the brunette cheerfully, her Danish a bit more awkward.

"Here, let me give you the cold drinks first," said the vendor as he reached into the upright cooler behind the counter. He set down the drinks for them to take. "Give me a minute to prepare the hot beverages."

The blonde turned to the boy and said in English, "Eric, here is your Coke. Can you take the drinks to the other children for me?"

The boy put the can of Coke in his pocket and collected the orange juice bottles in his arms. "OK, Mum." He started to walk back to the other children as he balanced the bottles carefully.

The blonde gave Johan a credit card, which he ran quickly through his register. She signed the receipt and smiled as she watched her son approach the small merry-go-round where the others were playing.

Johan poured coffee from a Pyrex pot into heavy paper cups and passed them across the counter. "You can add your own cream and sugar here on the side." He pointed to the area where a small pitcher of cream and a basket of sugar packets were arranged. "I have to boil more water for the tea, so please wait one minute." He placed a stainless steel pot on an electric burner and started to heat the water. He set a box filled with different tea choices on the counter for the women to select from.

"I think I have seen you here before, ma'am," he said as they waited for the water to boil. "You seem to be having a good time with the children."

"Oh yes. We enjoy this park immensely," the blonde said as she smiled at him. She watched a tall brown-haired man tossing a baseball to a little girl who missed it and ran to retrieve it on the grass. "That is my husband trying to teach our daughter to play baseball. I told him Krista is too young to catch properly, but he is determined she should learn the game." She paused to watch as young Eric distributed drinks to the children.

"The man pushing the merry-go-round is my husband, Christian. The two dark-haired ones are mine, Lena and little Christian," the brunette said.

"Who are the two who are playing with the small boy on the swing set? The woman looks a little like you," the old man said kindly.

"That is my sister and her husband, Mikhail," the blonde said. "Misha is only one, but he loves the swing. The older blonde girl is theirs, too, little Nadie. She is also my goddaughter."

The teapot boiled, and Johan poured hot water into the paper cups. The women set about adding just the right amount of cream and sugar in various cups. The vendor lent them a tray to carry the tea and coffee across the park.

"And the thin blondeheaded woman?"

"Yes, she is my dear friend. I named my daughter after her because she saved my life once long ago. And the tall woman next to her is her lover. We don't know who the father of little Jens is yet. It is a mystery." The two women laughed out loud at that. They turned to go.

The women walked carefully back toward the park and distributed the hot liquids to their spouses and friends. They stepped aside for a minute to admire the beautiful midsummer afternoon. The sky was clear of clouds, and it held that pure azure color they remembered from their homeland far away.

"We have come a long way, my dear Lena," Nadya said. "And we have a big happy family around us after all."

Lena breathed in the crisp air of freedom and chuckled warmly. "Yes, we are all together again and so happy. I have Eric, my one true love, and all of you with me. Life can't be any better than this."

Who knew what other adventures life would bring? she wondered. At least, for now, her secret war against the state had worked out well for her. How would it all end for her country? Only time would tell.

Epilogue

Omar Kadish was killed in 2001 in Erbil by a bomb placed by a rival Sunni clan who had ties to Al Qaeda. His clan sought revenge for his death for many years afterward.

Leela and Tika went home to Kashmir during the summer of 1972. Due to their father's bad health, Tika had to remain to help his brothers run the family business. He settled down and raised a family in Kashmir, although many of his family members were the victims of a Pakistani terrorist bomb in his hometown in 1977.

Sabrina's parents set her up to meet many potentially good suitors during the summer of 1972 in Catalonia. She eventually found one who wasn't so bad and married him. Six years and four children later, she ran away with the children to Barcelona and began a new life there.

Amad Hussain finished school in Uppsala and pursued further military training. As of 2002, he was a high-ranking member of the Syrian Ba'ath Party.

Gregori Markov continued for many years as a researcher for the Defense Ministry in Moscow. His career suffered from his personality disorder and his volatile temper. He never made any significant discoveries after his working partnership with Minuri Semelov ended.

Minuri Semelov became a professor in the Department of Applied Mathematics at Leningrad Technical Institute. With time she was recognized as the creative force behind the now renamed Semelov-Markov solver and went on to create many unique algorithms. She also crossed over to work on theoretical economics problems with her husband, Dmitri Lachinov, at the university.

Dmitri Lachinov continued to work with the economic modeling team until it was disbanded. Afterward he led a group of researchers on the practical applications of economic theory, eventually becoming department chair and leader of the International Economic Modeling Council.

Major Cusak worked his way up the chain of command in the Czech StB to become chief administrator of border security.

412 • Fred G. Baker

The escapade at the Austrian border that became an international incident left Vasili Chayka's career at a standstill. His masters at the Defense Ministry eventually promoted him into a position where he could do no harm and where few important persons were likely to encounter him again. He did keep up a friendship with Ivan Ivanoff for years after he was shot by the "best sniper in the world," as the legend goes.

Ivan Ivanoff advanced to become head of the Second Chief Directorate at Leningrad until he was replaced by a man named Putin. He later became the chief of all Western European intelligence for the KGB. When the Soviet Union collapsed in 1991, he transferred to the equivalent position in the new Russian Federation. His current position is unknown.

Eric Barrenger completed his postdoctoral research at the University of Illinois in 1981. He then found employment with the US Army Corps of Engineers, working as a principal field engineer for that agency out of its Copenhagen office. His specialty in tunneling and foundation soils engineering kept him busy traveling to areas where new or existing facilities of the State Department or the Department of Defense were under threat from terrorist attack. He settled with his wife, Lena, and their family on a small farm near Roskilde, Denmark.

The information concerning the Russian economics model that Lena had collected and passed on to her handlers was used by US intelligence agencies to undermine the economy of the Soviet Union. During the Reagan administration, a special task force was created to take advantage of the information to bring about the fall of the Soviet economy. The clandestine operation was successfully directed by then newly promoted Rear Admiral Mike Turner. After that, Turner worked at high positions within the CIA and later the NSA, where he was involved in counterterrorism communications. His current rank and position in the agency are classified. He continues to keep in touch with Eric and Lena.

Lena, the person at the center of this story, continued to live a happy life in the Danish countryside with her family and friends. She later became an associate professor at a Danish university and conducted research on the protection of data information systems. She was a popular lecturer but mostly kept a low profile, avoiding photographs and publicity. She was happy to see in 1991 that her efforts to help the Russian people were finally and resoundingly successful in facilitating the collapse of the Soviet government. Her quiet work, her "secret war" to destabilize the Soviet regime, would never really be known except to a small group of friends, intelligence agency operatives, and associates. But she and her friends and family lived in freedom, and they lived happily ever after.

About the Author

Fred G. Baker is a hydrologist, historian, and writer living in Colorado. He is the author of *An Imperfect Crime, Desert Sanctuary, Desert Underworld, Einstein's Raven, Zona: The Forbidden Land, The Black Freighter,* and the *Modern Pirate Series* of short and long stories. He is also the author of nonfiction works such as *Growing Up Wisconsin, The Life and Times of Con James Baker of Des Moines, Chicago, and Wisconsin, The Light from a Thousand Campfires* (with Hannah Pavlik), and others.

***

Request for Reviews.

Thank you for reading my book. If you enjoyed it, please write a review on Amazon.com. Reviews are important to help authors get the word out on their books. I would appreciate your time to write one.

Please look for my other books on Amazon and Kindle Books. Just type in my name to see other titles that may be of interest to you. You can also check out my website at www.othervoicespress.com.

Made in the USA
Columbia, SC
29 February 2024

32457555R00255